CHROMOSOME 6

Also by Robin Cook
in Large Print:

Contagion
Acceptable Risk
Fatal Cure
Terminal
Blindsight
Vital Signs
Harmful Intent
Mutation
Mortal Fear
Outbreak
Mindbend
Sphinx
Coma
The Year of the Intern

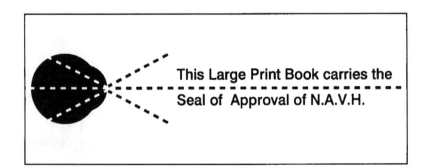

This Large Print Book carries the
Seal of Approval of N.A.V.H.

CHROMOSOME 6

Robin Cook

Thorndike Press • Thorndike, Maine

Published in 1997 by arrangement with G.P. Putnam's Sons, a member of Penguin Putnam Inc.

Thorndike Large Print ® Basic Series.

The tree indicium is a trademark of Thorndike Press.

The text of this Large Print edition is unabridged.
Other aspects of the book may vary from the original edition.

Set in 16 pt. Plantin by Al Chase.

Printed in the United States on permanent paper.

Library of Congress Cataloging in Publication Data

Cook, Robin, 1940–
    Chromosome 6 / Robin Cook.
      p.   cm.
    ISBN 0-7862-1098-2 (lg. print : hc : alk. paper).
    ISBN 0-7862-1099-0 (lg. print : sc : alk. paper)
    1. Large type books. I. Title.
    PS3553.O5545C47 1997b
    813′.54—dc21   97-10885

FOR AUDREY AND BARBARA
Thanks for being wonderful mothers

Acknowledgments

*Matthew J. Bankowski, Ph.D.,
Director of Clinical Virology, Molecular
Medicine, and Research-Development,
DSI Laboratories*

Joe Cox, J.D., L.L.M., tax and corporate law

*John Gilatto, V.M.D., Ph.D., Associate
Professor of Veterinary Pathology, Tufts
University School of Veterinary Medicine*

*Jacki Lee, M.D., Chief Medical Examiner,
Queens, New York*

*Matts Linden, Captain Pilot,
American Airlines*

*Martine Pignede, Director of NIWA Private
Game Reserve, Cameroon*

*Jean Reeds, School Psychologist,
reader, and critic*

*Charles Wetli, M.D., Chief Medical
Examiner, Suffolk County, New York*

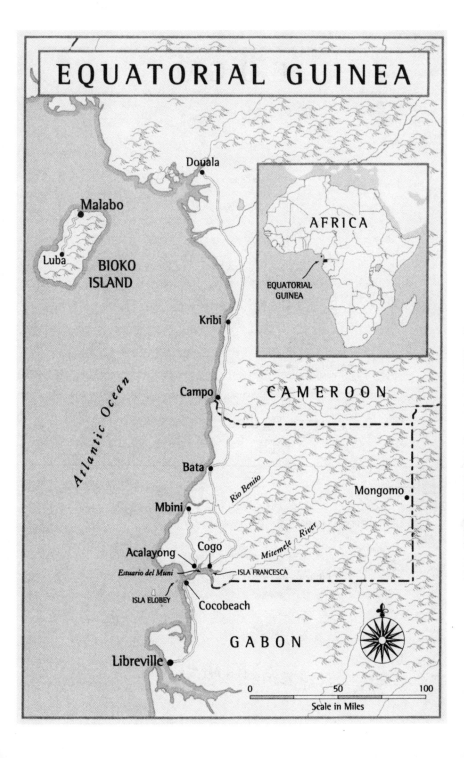

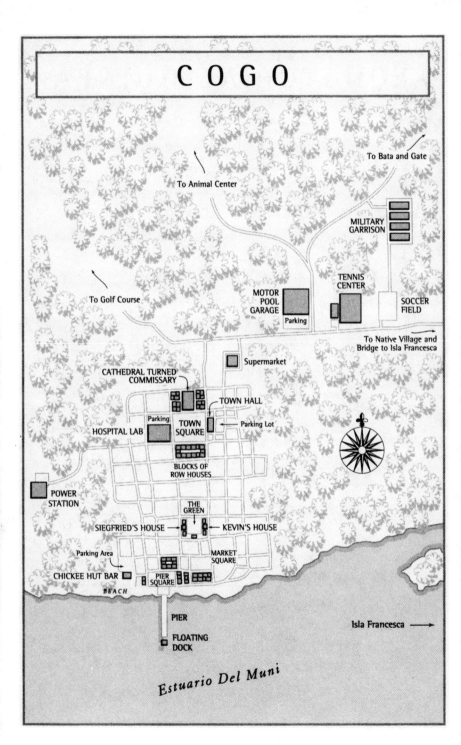

PROLOGUE

Given a Ph.D. in molecular biology from MIT that had been earned in close cooperation with the Massachusetts General Hospital, Kevin Marshall found his squeamishness regarding medical procedures a distinct embarrassment. Although he'd never admitted it to anyone, just having a blood test or a vaccination was an ordeal for him. Needles were his specific bête noire. The sight of them caused his legs to go rubbery and a cold sweat to break out on his broad forehead. Once he'd even fainted in college after getting a measles shot.

At age thirty-four, after many years of postgraduate biomedical research, some of it involving live animals, he'd expected to outgrow his phobia, but it hadn't happened. And it was for that reason he was not in operating room 1A or 1B at the moment. Instead he'd chosen to remain in the intervening scrub room, where he was leaning against the scrub sink, a vantage that allowed him to look through angled windows into both OR's — until he felt the need to avert his eyes.

The two patients had been in their respective rooms for about a quarter hour in preparation for their respective procedures. The two surgical teams were quietly conversing while standing off to the side. They were gowned and gloved and ready to commence.

There'd been little technical conversation in the OR's except between the anesthesiologist and the two anesthetists as the patients were inducted under general anesthesia. The lone anesthesiologist had slipped back and forth between the two rooms to supervise and to be available at any sign of trouble.

But there was no trouble. At least not yet. Nonetheless, Kevin felt anxious. To his surprise he did not experience the same sense of triumph he had enjoyed during three previous comparable procedures when he'd exalted in the power of science and his own creativity.

Instead of jubilation Kevin felt a mushrooming unease. His discomfort had started almost a week previously, but it was now, watching these patients and contemplating their different prognoses, that Kevin felt the disquietude with disturbing poignancy. The effect was similar to his thinking about needles: perspiration appeared on his forehead and his legs trembled. He had to grasp the edge of the scrub sink to steady himself.

The door to operating room 1A opened suddenly, startling Kevin. He was confronted by a figure whose pale blue eyes were framed by a hood and a face mask. Recognition was rapid: It was Candace Brickmann, one of the surgical nurses.

"The IV's are all started, and the patients are asleep," Candace said. "Are you sure you don't want to come in? You'll be able to see much better."

"Thank you, but I'm fine right here," Kevin said.

"Suit yourself," Candace said.

The door swung shut behind Candace as she returned to one of the surgeries. Kevin watched her scurry across the room and say something to the surgeons. Their response was to turn in Kevin's direction and give him a thumbs-up sign. Kevin self-consciously returned the gesture.

The surgeons went back to their conversation, but the effect of the wordless communication with Kevin magnified his sense of complicity. He let go of the scrub sink and took a step backward. His unease was now tinged with fear. What had he done?

Spinning on his heels, Kevin fled from the scrub room and then from the operating suite. A puff of air followed him as he left the mildly positive pressure aseptic OR area and entered his gleaming, futuristic laboratory. He was breathing heavily as if out of breath from exertion.

On any other day, merely walking into his domain would have filled him with anticipation just at the thought of the discoveries awaiting his magic hand. The series of rooms literally bristled with hi-tech equipment the likes of which used to be the focus of his fantasies. Now these sophisticated machines were at his beck and call, day and night. Absently he ran his fingers lightly along the stainless-steel cowlings, casually brushing the analogue dials and digital displays as he headed for his office. He touched the hundred-and-fifty-thousand-dollar DNA sequencer and the five-hundred-thousand-dollar globular NMR machine that sprouted a tangle of wires like a giant sea anemone. He glanced at the PCR's, whose red lights blinked like distant quasars announcing successive DNA-strand doublings. It was an environment that had previously filled Kevin with hope and promise. But now each Eppendorf microcentrifuge tube and each tissue-culture flask stood as mute reminders of the building foreboding he was experiencing.

Advancing to his desk, Kevin looked down at his gene map of the short arm of chromosome 6. His area of principal interest was outlined in red. It was the major histocompatibility complex. The problem was that the MHC was only a small portion of the short arm of chromosome 6. There were large blank areas that represented millions and millions of base pairs, and hence hundreds of other genes. Kevin did not know what they did.

A recent request for information concerning

these genes that he'd put out over the Internet had resulted in some vague replies. Several researchers had responded that the short arm of chromosome 6 contained genes that were involved with muscular-skeletal development. But that was it. There were no details.

Kevin shuddered involuntarily. He raised his eyes to the large picture window above his desk. As usual it was streaked with moisture from the tropical rain that swept across the view in undulating sheets. The droplets slowly descended until enough had fused to reach a critical mass. Then they raced off the surface like sparks from a grinding wheel.

Kevin's eyes focused into the distance. The contrast between the gleaming, air-conditioned interior with the outside world was always a shock. Roiling, gun-metal gray clouds filled the sky despite the fact that the dry season was supposed to have begun three weeks previously. The land was dominated by riotous vegetation that was so dark green as to almost appear black. Along the edge of the town it rose up like a gigantic, threatening tidal wave.

Kevin's office was in the hospital-laboratory complex that was one of the few new structures in the previously decaying and deserted Spanish colonial town of Cogo in the little-known African country of Equatorial Guinea. The building was three stories tall. Kevin's office was on the top floor, facing southeast.

13

From his window he could see a good portion of the town as it sprawled haphazardly toward the Estuario del Muni and its contributory rivers.

Some of the neighboring buildings had been renovated, some were in the process, but most had not been touched. A half dozen previously handsome haciendas were enveloped by vines and roots of vegetation that had gone wild. Over the whole scene hung the perennial mist of super-saturated warm air.

In the immediate foreground Kevin could see beneath the arched arcade of the old town hall. In the shadows were the inevitable handful of Equatoguinean soldiers in combat fatigues with AK-47's haphazardly slung over their shoulders. As usual they were smoking, arguing, and consuming Cameroonean beer.

Finally Kevin let his eyes wander beyond the town. He'd been unconsciously avoiding doing so, but now he focused on the estuary whose rain-lashed surface looked like beaten tin. Directly south he could just make out the forested shoreline of Gabon. Looking to the east he followed the trail of islands that stretched toward the interior of the continent. On the horizon he could see the largest of the islands, Isla Francesca, named by the Portuguese in the fifteenth century. In contrast to the other islands, Isla Francesca had a jungle-covered limestone escarpment that ran down its center like the backbone of a dinosaur.

Kevin's heart skipped a beat. Despite the rain and the mist, he could see what he'd feared he'd see. Just like a week ago there was the unmistakable wisp of smoke lazily undulating toward the leaden sky.

Kevin slumped into his desk chair and cradled his head in his hands. He asked himself what he'd done. Having minored in the Classics as an undergraduate, he knew about Greek myths. Now he questioned if he'd made a Promethean mistake. Smoke meant fire, and he had to wonder if it was the proverbial fire inadvertently stolen from the gods.

6:45 P.M.
BOSTON, MASSACHUSETTS

While a cold March wind rattled the storm windows, Taylor Devonshire Cabot reveled in the security and warmth of his walnut-paneled study in his sprawling Manchester-by-the-Sea home north of Boston, Massachusetts. Harriette Livingston Cabot, Taylor's wife, was in the kitchen supervising the final stages of dinner scheduled to be served at seven-thirty sharp.

On the arm of Taylor's chair balanced a cut-crystal glass of neat, single-malt whiskey. A fire crackled in the fireplace as Wagner played on the stereo, the volume turned low. In addition there were three, built-in televisions tuned respectively to a local news station, CNN, and ESPN.

Taylor was the picture of contentment. He'd spent a busy but productive day at the world headquarters of GenSys, a relatively new biotechnology firm he'd started eight years previously. The company had constructed a new building along the Charles River in Boston to take advantage of the proximity of both Harvard and MIT for recruitment purposes.

The evening commute had been easier than usual, and Taylor hadn't had time to finish his scheduled reading. Knowing his employer's habits, Rodney, his driver, had apologized for getting Taylor home so quickly.

"I'm sure you'll be able to come up with a significant delay tomorrow night to make up," Taylor had quipped.

"I'll do my best," Rodney had responded.

So Taylor wasn't listening to the stereo or watching the TVs. Instead he was carefully reading the financial report scheduled to be released at the GenSys stockholders' meeting scheduled the following week. But that didn't mean he was unaware of what was going on around him. He was very much aware of the sound of the wind, the sputtering of the fire, the music, and alert to the various reporters' banters on the TVs. So when the name Carlo Franconi was mentioned, Taylor's head snapped up.

The first thing Taylor did was lift the remote and turn up the sound of the central television. It was the local news on the CBS affiliate. The anchors were Jack Williams and Liz Walker. Jack Williams had mentioned the name Carlo Franconi, and was going on to say that the station had obtained a videotape of the killing of this known Mafia figure who had some association with Boston crime families.

"This tape is quite graphic," Jack warned. "Parental discretion is recommended. You might remember that a few days ago we reported that the ailing Franconi had disappeared after his indictment, and many had feared he'd jumped bail. But then he'd just reappeared yesterday with the news that he'd struck a deal with the New York City's DA's office to plea-bargain and enter the witness-protection program. However, this evening while emerging from a favorite restaurant, the indicted racketeer was fatally shot."

Taylor was transfixed as he watched an amateur video of an overweight man emerge from a restaurant accompanied by several people who looked like policemen. With a casual wave, the man acknowledged the crowd who'd assembled and then headed to an awaiting limousine. He assiduously ignored questions from any journalists angling to get close to him. Just as he was bending to enter the car, Franconi's body jerked, and he staggered backward with his hand clasping the base of his neck. As he fell to his right, his body jerked again before hitting the ground. The men who'd accompanied him had drawn their guns and were frantically turning in all directions. The pursuing journalists had all hit the deck.

"Whoa!" Jack commented. "What a scene! Sort'a reminds me of the killing of Lee Harvey Oswald. So much for police protection."

"I wonder what effect this will have on future similar witnesses?" Liz asked.

"Not good, I'm sure," Jack said.

Taylor's eyes immediately switched to CNN, which was at that moment about to show the same video. He watched the sequence again. It made him wince. At the end of the tape, CNN went live to a reporter outside the Office of the Chief Medical Examiner for the City of New York.

"The question now is whether there were one or two assailants," the reporter said over the sound of the traffic on First Avenue. "It's our impression that Franconi was shot twice. The police are understandably chagrined over this episode and have refused to speculate or offer any information whatsoever. We do know that an autopsy is scheduled for tomorrow morning, and we assume that ballistics will answer the question."

Taylor turned down the sound on the television, then picked up his drink. Walking to the window, he gazed out at the angry, dark

18

sea. Franconi's death could mean trouble. He looked at his watch. It was almost midnight in West Africa.

Snatching up the phone, Taylor called the operator at GenSys and told him he wanted to speak with Kevin Marshall immediately.

Replacing the receiver, Taylor returned his gaze out the window. He'd never felt completely comfortable about this project although financially it was looking very profitable. He wondered if he should stop it. The phone interrupted his thoughts.

Picking the receiver back up, Taylor was told that Mr. Marshall was available. After some static Kevin's sleepy voice crackled over the line.

"Is this really Taylor Cabot?" Kevin asked.

"Do you remember a Carlo Franconi?" Taylor demanded, ignoring Kevin's question.

"Of course," Kevin said.

"He's been murdered this afternoon," Taylor said. "There's an autopsy scheduled for the morning in New York City. What I want to know is, could that be a problem?"

There was a moment of silence. Taylor was about to question whether the connection had been broken when Kevin spoke up.

"Yes, it could be a problem," Kevin said.

"Someone could figure out everything from an autopsy?"

"It's possible," Kevin said. "I wouldn't say probable, but it is possible."

"I don't like possible," Taylor said. He disconnected from Kevin and called the operator back at GenSys. Taylor said he wanted to speak immediately to Dr. Raymond Lyons. He emphasized that it was an emergency.

NEW YORK CITY

"Excuse me," the waiter whispered. He'd approached Dr. Lyons from the left side, having waited for a break in the conversation the doctor was engaged in with his young, blond assistant and current lover, Darlene Polson. Between his gracefully graying hair and conservative apparel, the good doctor looked like the quintessential, soap-opera physician. He was in his early fifties, tall, tanned, and enviably slender with refined, patrician good looks.

"I'm sorry to intrude," the waiter continued. "But there is an emergency call for you. Can I offer you our cordless phone or would you prefer to use the phone in the hall?"

Raymond's blue eyes darted back and forth between Darlene's affable but bland face and the considerate waiter whose impeccable demeanor reflected Aureole's 26 service rating in Zagat's restaurant guide. Raymond did not look happy.

"Perhaps I should tell them you are not available," the waiter suggested.

"No, I'll take the cordless," Raymond said.

He couldn't imagine who could be calling him on an emergency basis. Raymond had not been practicing medicine since he'd lost his medical license after having been convicted of a major Medicare scam he'd been carrying on for a dozen years.

"Hello?" Raymond said with a degree of trepidation.

"This is Taylor Cabot. There's a problem."

Raymond visibly stiffened and his brow furrowed.

Taylor quickly summarized the Carlo Franconi situation and his call to Kevin Marshall.

"This operation is your baby," Taylor concluded irritably. "And let me warn you: it is small potatoes in the grand scheme of things. If there is trouble, I'll scrap the entire enterprise. I don't want bad publicity, so handle it."

"But what can I do?" Raymond blurted out.

"Frankly, I don't know," Taylor said. "But you'd better think of something, and you'd better do it fast."

"Things couldn't be going any better from my end," Raymond interjected. "Just today I made positive contact with a physician in L.A. who treats a lot of movie stars and wealthy West Coast businessmen. She's interested in setting up a branch in California."

"Maybe you didn't hear me," Taylor said. "There isn't going to be a branch anyplace if this Franconi problem isn't resolved. So you'd better get busy. I'd say you have about twelve hours."

The resounding click of the disconnection made Raymond's head jerk. He looked at the phone as if it had been responsible for the precipitate termination of the conversation. The waiter, who'd retreated to an appropriate distance, stepped forward to retrieve the phone before disappearing.

"Trouble?" Darlene questioned.

"Oh, God!" Raymond voiced. Nervously he chewed the quick of his thumb. It was more than trouble. It was potential disaster. With his attempts at retrieving his medical license tied up in the quagmire of the judicial system, his current work situation was all he had, and things had only recently been clicking. It had taken him five years to get where he was. He couldn't let it all go down the drain.

"What is it?" Darlene asked. She reached out and pulled Raymond's hand away from his mouth.

Raymond quickly explained about the upcoming autopsy on Carlo Franconi and repeated Taylor Cabot's threat to scrap the entire enterprise.

"But it's finally making big money," Darlene said. "He won't scrap it."

Raymond gave a short, mirthless laugh. "It isn't big money to someone like Taylor Cabot and GenSys," he said. "He'd scrap it for certain. Hell, it was difficult to talk him into it in the first place."

"Then you have to tell them not to do the autopsy," Darlene said.

Raymond stared at his companion. He knew she meant well, and he'd never been attracted to her for her brain power. So he resisted lashing out. But his reply was sarcastic: "You think I can just call up the medical examiner's office and tell them not to do an autopsy on such a case? Give me a break!"

"But you know a lot of important people," Darlene persisted. "Ask them to call."

"Please, dear . . ." Raymond said condescendingly, but then he paused. He began to think that unwittingly Darlene had a point. An idea began to germinate.

"What about Dr. Levitz?" Darlene said. "He was Mr. Franconi's doctor. Maybe he could help."

"I was just thinking the same thing," Raymond said. Dr. Daniel Levitz was a Park Avenue physician with a big office, high overhead, and a dwindling patient base, thanks to managed care. He'd been easy to recruit and had been one of the first doctors to join the venture. On top of that, he'd brought in many clients, some of them in the same business as Carlo Franconi.

Raymond stood up, extracted his wallet, and plopped three crisp one-hundred-dollar bills on the table. He knew that was more than enough for the tab and a generous tip.

"Come on," he said. "We've got to make a house call."

"But I haven't finished my entrée," Darlene complained.

Raymond didn't respond. Instead he whisked Darlene's chair out from the table, forcing her to her feet. The more he thought about Dr. Levitz, the more he thought the man could be the savior. As the personal physician of a number of competing New York crime families, Levitz knew people who could do the impossible.

CHAPTER 1

Jack Stapleton bent over and put more muscle into his pedaling as he sprinted the last block heading east along Thirtieth Street. About fifty yards from First Avenue he sat up and coasted no-hands before beginning to brake. The upcoming traffic light was not in his favor, and even Jack wasn't crazy enough to sail out into the mix of cars, buses, and trucks racing uptown.

The weather had warmed considerably and the five inches of slush that had fallen two days previously was gone save for a few dirty piles between parked cars. Jack was pleased the roads were clear since he'd not been able to commute on his bike for several days. The bike was only three weeks old. It was a replacement for one that had been stolen a year previously.

Originally, Jack had planned on replacing the bike immediately. But he'd changed his mind after a terrifyingly close encounter with death made him temporarily conservative about risk. The episode had nothing to do with bike riding in the city, but nonetheless it scared him enough to acknowledge that his riding style had been deliberately reckless.

But time dimmed Jack's fears. The final prod came when he lost his watch and wallet in a subway mugging. A day later, Jack bought himself a new Cannondale mountain bike, and as far as his friends were concerned, he was up to his old tricks. In reality, he was no longer tempting fate by squeezing between speeding delivery vans and parked cars; he no longer slalomed down Second Avenue; and for the most part he stayed out of Central Park after dark.

Jack came to a stop at the corner to wait for the light, and as his foot touched down on the pavement he surveyed the scene. Almost at once he became aware of a bevy of TV vans with extended antennae parked on the east side of First Avenue in front of his destination: the Office of the Chief Medical Examiner for the City of New York, or what some people called simply, the morgue.

Jack was an associate medical examiner, and he'd been in that position for almost a year and a half so he'd seen such journalistic congestion on numerous occasions. Generally it meant that there had been a death of a celebrity, or at least someone made momentarily famous by the media. If it wasn't a single death, then it was a mass disaster like an airplane crash or a train wreck. For reasons both personal and public Jack hoped it was the former.

With a green light, Jack pedaled across First Avenue and entered the morgue through the receiving dock on Thirtieth Street. He parked his bike in his usual location near the Hart Island coffins used for the unclaimed dead and took the elevator up to the first floor.

It was immediately apparent to Jack that the place was in a minor uproar. Several of the day secretaries were busily manning the phones in the communications room: they normally didn't arrive until eight. Their consoles were awash with blinking red lights. Even Sergeant Murphy's cubicle was open and the overhead light was on, and his usual modus operandi was to arrive sometime after nine.

With curiosity mounting, Jack entered the ID room and headed directly for the coffeepot. Vinnie Amendola, one of the mortuary techs, was hiding behind his newspaper as per usual. But that was the only normal circumstance for that time of the morning. Generally Jack was the first pathologist to arrive, but on this particular day the deputy chief, Dr. Calvin Washington, Dr. Laurie Montgomery, and Dr. Chet McGovern were already there. The three were involved in a deep discussion along with Sergeant Murphy and, to Jack's surprise, Detective Lieutenant Lou Soldano from homicide. Lou was a frequent visitor to the morgue, but certainly not at seven-thirty in the morning. On top of that, he looked like he'd never been to bed, or if he had, he'd slept in his clothes.

Jack helped himself to coffee. No one acknowledged his arrival. After adding a dollop of half-and-half as well as a cube of sugar to his cup, Jack wandered to the door to the lobby. He glanced out, and as he'd expected the area was filled to overflowing with media people talking among themselves and drinking take-out coffee. What he didn't expect was that many were also smoking cigarettes. Since smoking was strictly taboo, Jack told Vinnie to go out there and inform them.

"You're closer," Vinnie said, without looking up from his newspaper.

Jack rolled his eyes at Vinnie's lack of respect but had to admit Vinnie was right. So Jack walked over to the locked glass door and opened it. Before he could call out his no smoking pronouncement, he was literally mobbed.

Jack had to push the microphones away that were thrust into his face. The simultaneous questions precluded any real comprehension of what the questions were other than about an anticipated autopsy.

Jack shouted at the top of his lungs that there was no smoking, then had to literally peel hands off his arm before he was able to get the door closed. On the other side the reporters surged forward, pressing colleagues roughly against the glass like tomatoes in a jar of preserves.

Disgusted, Jack returned to the ID room.

"Will someone clue me in to what's going on?" he called out.

Everyone turned in Jack's direction, but Laurie was the first to respond. "You haven't heard?"

"Now, would I be asking if I'd heard?" Jack said.

"It's been all over the TV for crissake," Calvin snapped.

"Jack doesn't own a TV," Laurie said. "His neighborhood won't allow it."

"Where do you live, son?" Sergeant Murphy asked. "I've never heard of neighbors not allowing each other to have a television." The aging, red-faced, Irish policeman had a pronounced paternal streak. He'd been assigned to the medical examiner's office for more years than he was willing to admit and thought of all the employees as family.

"He lives in Harlem," Chet said. "Actually his neighbors would love him to get a set so they could permanently borrow it."

"Enough, you guys," Jack said. "Fill me in on the excitement."

"A Mafia don was gunned down yesterday late afternoon," Calvin's booming voice announced. "It's stirred up a hornet's nest of trouble since he'd agreed to cooperate with the DA's office and was under police protection."

"He was no Mafia don," Lou Soldano said. "He was nothing but a mid-level functionary of the Vaccarro crime family."

"Whatever," Calvin said with a wave of his hand. "The key point is that he was whacked while literally boxed in by a number of New York's finest, which doesn't say much about their ability to protect someone in their charge."

"He was warned not to go to that restaurant," Lou protested. "I know that for a fact. And it's almost impossible to protect someone if the individual refuses to follow suggestions."

"Any chance he could have been killed by the police?" Jack asked. One of the roles of a medical examiner was to think of all angles, especially when situations of custody were concerned.

"He wasn't under arrest," Lou said, guessing what was going through Jack's mind. "He'd been arrested and indicted, but he was out on bail."

"So what's the big deal?" Jack asked.

"The big deal is that the mayor, the district attorney, and the police commissioner are all under a lot of heat," Calvin said.

"Amen," Lou said. "Particularly the police commissioner. That's why I'm here. It's turning into one of those public-relations nightmares that the media loves to blow way out of proportion. We've got to apprehend the perpetrator or perpetrators ASAP, otherwise heads are going to roll."

"And not to discourage future potential witnesses," Jack said.

"Yeah, that too," Lou said.

"I don't know, Laurie," Calvin said, getting back to the discussion they'd been having before Jack's interruption. "I appreciate you coming in early and offering to do this autopsy, but maybe Bingham might want to do it himself."

"But why?" Laurie complained. "Look, it's a straightforward case, and I've recently done a lot of gunshot wounds. Besides, with Dr. Bingham's budget meeting this morning at City Hall, he can't be here until almost noon. By then I can have the autopsy done and whatever information I come up with will be in the hands of the police. With their time constraint, it makes the most sense."

Calvin looked at Lou. "Do you think five or six hours will make a difference with the investigation?"

"It could," Lou admitted. "Hell, the sooner the autopsy is done the better. I mean, just knowing if we're looking for one or two people will be a big help."

Calvin sighed. "I hate this kind of decision." He shifted his massive two-hundred-and-fifty-pound muscular bulk from one foot to the other. "Trouble is, half the time I can't anticipate Bingham's reaction. But what the hell!

Go for it, Laurie. The case is yours."

"Thanks, Calvin," Laurie said gleefully. She snatched up the folder from the table. "Is it okay if Lou observes?"

"By all means," Calvin said.

"Come on, Lou!" Laurie said. She rescued her coat from a chair and started for the door. "Let's head downstairs, do a quick external exam, and have the body X-rayed. In the confusion last night it apparently wasn't done."

"I'm right behind you," Lou said.

Jack hesitated for a moment then hurried after them. He was mystified why Laurie was so interested in doing the autopsy. From his perspective she would have done better to stay clear. Such politically charged cases were always hot potatoes. You couldn't win.

Laurie was moving quickly, and Jack didn't catch up to her and Lou until they were beyond communications. Laurie stopped abruptly to lean into Janice Jaeger's office. Janice was one of the forensic investigators, also called physicians' assistants or PAs. Janice ran the graveyard shift and took her job very seriously. She always stayed late.

"Will you be seeing Bart Arnold before you leave?" Laurie asked Janice. Bart Arnold was the chief of the PAs.

"I usually do," Janice said. She was a tiny, dark-haired woman with prominent circles under her eyes.

"Do me a favor," Laurie said. "Ask him to call CNN and get a copy of the video of Carlo Franconi's assassination. I'd like to have it as soon as possible."

"Will do," Janice said cheerfully.

Laurie and Lou continued on their way.

"Hey, slow down, you two," Jack said. He had to run a couple of steps to catch up to them.

"We've got work to do," Laurie said without breaking stride.

"I've never seen you so eager to do an autopsy," Jack said. He and Lou flanked her as she hurried to the autopsy room. "What's the attraction?"

"A lot of things," Laurie said. She reached the elevator and pressed the button.

"Give me an example," Jack said. "I don't mean to rain on your parade, but this is a politically sensitive case. No matter what you do or say, you'll be irritating someone. I think Calvin was right. This one ought to be done by the chief."

"You're entitled to your opinion," Laurie said. She hit the button again. The back elevator was inordinately slow. "But I feel differently. With the work I've been doing on the forensics of gunshot wounds, I'm fascinated to have a case where there is a video of the event to corroborate my reconstruction of what happened. I was planning on writing a paper on gunshot wounds, and this could be the crowning case."

"Oh, dear," Jack moaned, raising his eyes heavenward. "And her motivations were so noble." Then looking back at Laurie he said: "I think you should reconsider! My intuition tells me you're only going to get yourself into a bureaucratic headache. And there's still time to avoid it. All you have to do is turn around and go back and tell Calvin you've changed your mind. I'm warning you, you're taking a risk."

Laurie laughed. "You are the last person to advise me about risk." She reached out and touched Jack on the end of his nose with her index finger. "Everyone who knows you, me included, pleaded with you not to get that new bike. You're risking your life, not a headache."

The elevator arrived, and Laurie and Lou boarded. Jack hesitated but then squeezed through the doors just before they closed.

"You are not going to talk me out of this," Laurie said. "So save your breath."

"Okay," Jack said, raising his hands in mock surrender. "I promise: no more advice. Now, I'm just interested in watching this story unfold. It's a paper day for me today, so if you don't mind, I'll watch."

"You can do more than that if you want," Laurie said. "You can help."

"I'm sensitive about horning in on Lou." His double entendre was intended.

Lou laughed, Laurie blushed, but the comment went unacknowledged.

"You implied there were other reasons for your interest in this case," Jack said. "If you don't mind my asking, what are they?"

Laurie cast a quick glance at Lou that Jack saw but couldn't interpret.

"Hmmm," Jack said. "I'm getting the feeling there's something going on here that isn't any of my business."

"Nothing like that," Lou volunteered. "It's just an unusual connection. The victim, Carlo Franconi, had taken the place of a midlevel crime hoodlum named Pauli Cerino. Cerino's position had become vacant after Cerino was thrown in the slammer, mostly due to Laurie's persistence and hard work."

"And yours, too," Laurie added as the elevator jerked to a stop and the doors opened.

"Yeah, but mostly yours," Lou said.

The three got off on the basement level and headed in the direction of the mortuary office.

"Did the Cerino case involve that series of overdoses you've made reference to?" Jack asked Laurie.

"I'm afraid so," Laurie said. "It was awful. The experience terrified me, and the problem is some of the characters are still around, including Cerino although he's in jail."

"And not likely to be released for a long time," Lou added.

"Or so I'd like to believe," Laurie said.

"Anyway, I'm hoping that doing the post on Franconi might provide me with some closure. I still have nightmares occasionally."

"They sealed her in a pine coffin to abduct her from here," Lou said. "She was taken away in one of the mortuary vans."

"My god!" Jack said to Laurie. "You never told me about that."

"I try not to think about it," Laurie said. Then without missing a beat she added: "You guys wait out here."

Laurie ducked into the mortuary office to get a copy of the list of refrigerator compartments assigned to the cases that had come in the previous night.

"I can't imagine getting closed in a coffin," Jack said. He shuddered. Heights were his main phobia but tight, confining spaces came a close second.

"Nor can I," Lou agreed. "But she was able to recover remarkably. An hour or so after being released she had the presence of mind to figure out how to save us both. That was particularly humbling since I'd gone there to save her."

"Jeez!" Jack said with a shake of his head. "Up until this minute I thought my getting handcuffed to a sink by a couple of killers who were arguing over who was going to do me in was the worst-case scenario."

Laurie came out of the office waving a sheet of paper. "Compartment one eleven," she said. "And I was right. The body wasn't X-rayed."

Laurie took off like a power walker. Jack and Lou had to hustle to catch up with her. She made a beeline for the proper compartment. Once there she slipped the autopsy folder under her left arm and used her right hand to release the latch. In one, smooth, practiced motion, she swung open the door and slid out the tray on its ball bearings.

Laurie's brow furrowed.

"That's odd!" she remarked. The tray was empty save for a few blood stains and hardened secretions.

Laurie slid the tray back in and closed the door. She rechecked the number. There'd been no mistake. It was compartment one eleven.

After looking at the list once again to make certain she'd not misread the number, she reopened the compartment door, shielded her eyes from the glare of the overhead lights, and peered into the depths of the dark interior. There was no doubt: the compartment did not contain Carlo Franconi's remains.

"What the hell!" Laurie complained. She slammed the insulated door. And just to be sure there wasn't some stupid logistic error, she opened up all the neighboring compartments one after the other. In those which contained bodies, she checked the names and accession numbers. But it soon became obvious: Carlo Franconi was not among them.

"I don't believe this," Laurie said with angry frustration. "The damn body is gone!"

A smile had appeared on Jack's face from the moment compartment one eleven had proved to be empty. Now, facing Laurie's exasperated frown, he couldn't help himself. He laughed heartily. Unfortunately his laughter further piqued Laurie.

"I'm sorry," Jack managed. "My intuition told me this case was going to give you a bureaucratic headache. I was wrong. It's going to give the bureaucracy a headache."

CHAPTER 2

Kevin Marshall put down his pencil and looked out the window above his desk. In contrast to his inner turmoil, the weather outside was rather pleasant with the first patches of blue sky that Kevin had seen for months. The dry season had finally begun. Of course it wasn't dry; it just didn't rain nearly as much as during the wet season. The downside was that the more consistent sun made the temperature soar to ovenlike levels. At the moment it hovered at one hundred and fifteen degrees in the shade.

Kevin had not worked well that morning nor had he slept during the night. The anxiety he'd felt the previous day at the commencement of the surgery had not abated. In fact, it had gotten worse, especially after the unexpected call from the GenSys CEO, Taylor Cabot. Kevin had only spoken with the man on one previous occasion. Most people in the company equated the experience with talking with God.

Adding to Kevin's unease was seeing another wisp of smoke snaking its way up into the sky from Isla Francesca. He'd noticed it when he'd first arrived at the lab that morning. As near as he could tell it was coming from the same location as the day before: the sheer side of the limestone escarpment. The fact that the smoke was no longer apparent failed to comfort him.

Giving up on any attempt at further work, Kevin peeled off his white lab coat and draped it over his chair. He wasn't particularly hungry, but he knew his housekeeper, Esmeralda, would have made lunch, so he felt obliged to make an appearance.

Kevin descended the three flights of stairs in a preoccupied daze. Several co-workers passed him and said hello, but it was as if Kevin did not see them. He was too preoccupied. In the last twenty-four hours he'd come to realize that he would have to take action. The problem wasn't going to pass as he'd hoped it would a week previously when he'd first glimpsed the smoke.

Unfortunately, he had no idea what to do. He knew he was no hero; in fact, over the years he'd come to think of himself as a coward of sorts. He hated confrontation and avoided it. As a boy, he had even shunned competition except for chess. He'd grown up pretty much a loner.

Kevin paused at the glass door to the exterior. Across the square he could see the usual coterie of Equatoguinean soldiers beneath the arches of the old town hall. They were up to their usual sedentary pursuits, aimlessly passing the time of the day. Some were sitting in old rattan furniture playing cards, others were leaning up against the building arguing with each other in strident voices. Almost all of them were smoking. Cigarettes were part of their wages. They were dressed in soiled, jungle-camouflage fatigues with scuffed combat boots and red berets. All of them had automatic assault rifles either slung over their shoulders or within arm's reach.

From the moment of Kevin's arrival at Cogo five years previously, the soldiers had scared him. Cameron McIvers, head of security, who had initially shown Kevin around, told him that GenSys had hired a good portion of the Equatoguinean army for protection. Later Cameron had admitted that the army's so-called employment was in reality an additional payoff to the government as well as to the Minister of Defense and the Minister of Territorial Administration.

From Kevin's perspective the soldiers looked more like a bunch of aimless teenagers than protectors. Their complexions were like burnished ebony. Their blank expressions and arched eyebrows gave them a look of superciliousness that reflected their boredom. Kevin always had the uncomfortable sense they were itching to have an excuse to use their weapons.

Kevin pushed through the door and walked

across the square. He didn't look in the direction of the soldiers, but from past experience he knew at least some of them were watching him, and it made his skin crawl. Kevin didn't know a word of Fang, the major local dialect, so he had no idea what they were saying.

Once out of sight of the central square Kevin relaxed a degree and slowed his pace. The combination of heat and hundred-percent humidity was like a perpetual steam bath. Any activity caused a sweat. After only a few minutes, Kevin could feel his shirt beginning to adhere to his back.

Kevin's house was situated a little more than halfway between the hospital-lab complex and the waterfront, a distance of only three blocks. The town was small but had obviously been charming in its day. The buildings had been constructed primarily of brightly colored stucco with red tile roofs. Now the colors had faded to pale pastels. The shutters were the type that hinged at the top. Most were in a terrible state of disrepair except for the ones on the renovated buildings. The streets had been laid out in an unimaginative grid but had been paved over the years with imported granite that had served as sailing ships' ballast. In Spanish colonial times the town's wealth had come from agriculture, particularly cocoa and coffee production, and it had graciously supported a population of several thousand people.

But the town's history changed dramatically after 1959, the year of Equatorial Guinea's independence. The new president, Macias Nguema, quickly metamorphosed from a popularly elected official to the continent's worst, sadistic dictator whose atrocities managed to out-class even those of Idi Amin of Uganda and Jean-Bedel Bokassa of the Central African Republic. The effect on the country was apocalyptic. After fifty thousand people were murdered, a third of the population of the entire country fled, including all the Spanish settlers. Most of the country's towns were decimated, particularly Cogo which had been completely abandoned. The road connecting Cogo to the rest of the country fell into ruin and quickly became impassable.

For a number of years, the town was fated to be a mere curiosity for the occasional visitor arriving by small motorboat from the coastal town of Acalayong. The jungle had begun to reclaim the land by the time a representative of GenSys had happened upon it seven years previously. This individual recognized Cogo's isolation and its limitless surrounding rain forest as the perfect spot for GenSys's intended primate facility. Returning to Malabo, the capital of Equatorial Guinea, the GenSys official immediately commenced negotiations with the current Equatoguinean government.

Since the country was one of the poorest of Africa and consequently desperate for foreign exchange, the new president was eager and negotiations proceeded apace.

Kevin rounded the last corner and approached his house. It was three stories like most of the other buildings in the town. It had been tastefully renovated by GenSys to give it storybook appeal. In fact it was one of the more desirable houses in the whole town and a source of envy of a number of the other GenSys employees, particularly head of security, Cameron McIvers. Only Siegfried Spallek, manager of the Zone, and Bertram Edwards, chief veterinarian, had accommodations that were equivalent. Kevin had attributed his good luck to intercession on his behalf by Dr. Raymond Lyons, but he didn't know for certain.

The house had been built in the mid-nineteenth century by a successful import/exporter in traditional Spanish style. The first floor was arched and arcaded like the town hall and had originally housed shops and storage facilities. The second floor was the main living floor with three bedrooms, three baths, a large through-and-through living room, a dining room, a kitchen, and a tiny maid's apartment. It was surrounded by a veranda on all four sides. The third floor was an enormous open room with wide-plank flooring illuminated with two huge, cast-iron chandeliers. It was capable of holding a hundred people with ease and had apparently been used for mass meetings.

Kevin entered and climbed a central stairway that led up to a narrow hall. From there he went into the dining room. As he expected, the table had been laid for lunch.

The house was too big for Kevin, especially since he didn't have a family. He'd said as much when he'd first been shown the property, but Siegfried Spallek had told him the decision had been made in Boston and warned Kevin not to complain. So Kevin accepted the assignment, but his co-workers' envy often made him feel uncomfortable.

As if by magic Esmeralda appeared. Kevin wondered how she did it so consistently. It was as if she were always on the lookout for his approaching the house. She was a pleasant woman of indeterminate age with rounded features and sad eyes. She dressed in a shift of brightly colored print fabric with a matching scarf wrapped tightly around her head. Besides her native tongue, she spoke fluent Spanish and passable English that improved on a daily basis.

Esmeralda lived in the maid's quarters Monday through Friday. Over the weekend she stayed with her family in a village that GenSys had constructed to the east along the banks of the estuary to house the many local workers employed in the Zone, as the area occupied by GenSys's Equatoguinean operation was called. She and her family had been moved there from Bata, the main city on the Equatoguinean mainland. The capital of the country, Malabo, was on an island called Bioko.

Kevin had encouraged Esmeralda to go home in the evenings during the week if she so desired, but she declined. When Kevin persisted, she told him she'd been ordered to remain in Cogo.

"There is a phone message for you," Esmeralda said.

"Oh," Kevin said nervously. His pulse quickened. Phone messages were rare, and in his current state he did not need any more unexpected events. The call in the middle of the night from Taylor Cabot had been disturbing enough.

"It was from Dr. Raymond Lyons in New York," Esmeralda said. "He wants you to call him back."

The fact that the call was from overseas did not surprise Kevin. With the satellite communications GenSys had installed in the Zone, it was far easier to call Europe or the U.S. than Bata, a mere sixty miles to the north. Calls to Malabo were almost impossible.

Kevin started for the living room. The phone was on a desk in the corner.

"Will you be eating lunch?" Esmeralda asked.

"Yes," Kevin said. He still wasn't hungry but he didn't want to hurt Esmeralda's feelings.

Kevin sat down at his desk. With his hand on the phone he quickly calculated it was about eight o'clock in the morning in New York. He pondered what Dr. Lyons had called about but guessed it had something to do with his brief conversation with Taylor Cabot. Kevin did not like the idea of an autopsy on Carlo Franconi, and he didn't imagine that Raymond Lyons would either.

Kevin had first met Raymond six years previously. It was during a meeting in New York of the American Association for the Advancement of Science where Kevin presented a paper. Kevin hated giving papers and rarely did, but on this occasion he'd been forced to do so by the chief of his department at Harvard. Dating back to his Ph.D. thesis his interest was the transposition of chromosomes: a process by which chromosomes exchanged bits and pieces to enhance species adaption and hence evolution. This phenomenon happened particularly frequently during the generation of sex cells: a process known as meiosis.

By coincidence, during the same meeting and at the same time Kevin was scheduled to present, James Watson and Francis Crick gave an immensely popular talk on the anniversary of their discovery of the structure of DNA.

Consequently, very few people came to hear Kevin. One of the attendees had been Raymond. It was after this talk that Raymond first approached Kevin. The conversation resulted in Kevin's leaving Harvard and coming to work for GenSys.

With a slightly shaky hand Kevin picked up the receiver and dialed. Raymond answered on the first ring, suggesting he'd been hovering over the phone. The connection was crystal clear as if he were in the next room.

"I've got good news," Raymond said as soon as he knew it was Kevin. "There's to be no autopsy."

Kevin didn't respond. His mind was a jumble.

"Aren't you relieved?" Raymond asked. "I know Cabot called you last night."

"I'm relieved to an extent," Kevin said. "But autopsy or no autopsy, I'm having second thoughts about this whole operation."

Now it was Raymond's turn to be silent. No sooner had he solved one potential problem than another was rearing its unwelcome head.

"Maybe we've made a mistake," Kevin said. "What I mean is, maybe I've made a mistake. My conscience is starting to bother me, and I'm getting a little scared. I'm really a basic science person. This applied science is not my thing."

"Oh, please!" Raymond said irritably.

"Don't complicate things! Not now. I mean, you've got that lab you've always wanted. I've beat my brains out getting you every damn piece of equipment that you've asked for. And on top of that, things are going so well, especially with my recruiting. Hell, with all the stock options you're amassing, you'll be a rich man."

"I've never intended on being rich," Kevin said.

"Worse things could happen," Raymond said. "Come on, Kevin! Don't do this to me."

"And what good is being rich when I have to be out here in the heart of darkness?" Kevin said. Unwittingly his mind conjured up the image of the manager, Siegfried Spallek. Kevin shuddered. He was terrified of the man.

"It's not forever," Raymond said. "You told me yourself, you're almost there, that the system is nearly perfect. When it is and you've trained someone to take your place, you can come back here. With your money you'll be able to build the lab of your dreams."

"I've seen more smoke coming from the island," Kevin said. "Just like last week."

"Forget the smoke!" Raymond said. "You're letting your imagination run wild. Instead of working yourself up into a frenzy over nothing, concentrate on your work so you can finish. If you've got some free time, start fantasizing about the lab you'll be building back here state-side."

Kevin nodded. Raymond had a point. Part of Kevin's concern was that if what he'd been involved with in Africa became common knowledge, he might never be able to go back to academia. No one would hire him much less give him tenure. But if he had his own lab and an independent income, he wouldn't have to worry.

"Listen," Raymond said. "I'll be coming to pick up the last patient when he's ready, which should be soon. We'll talk again then. Meanwhile just remember that we're almost there and money is pouring into our offshore coffers."

"All right," Kevin said reluctantly.

"Just don't do anything rash," Raymond said. "Promise me!"

"All right," Kevin repeated with slightly more enthusiasm.

Kevin hung up the phone. Raymond was a persuasive person, and whenever Kevin spoke to him, Kevin inevitably felt better.

Kevin pushed back from the desk and walked back to the dining room. Following Raymond's advice he tried to think of where he'd build his lab. There were some strong arguments for Cambridge, Massachusetts, because of the associations Kevin had with both Harvard and MIT. But then again maybe it would be better to be out in the countryside like up in New Hampshire.

Lunch was a white fish that Kevin didn't recognize. When he inquired about it, Esmeralda gave him only the name in Fang, which meant nothing to Kevin. He surprised himself by eating more than he'd expected. The conversation with Raymond had had a positive effect on his appetite. The idea of having his own lab still held inordinate appeal.

After eating, Kevin changed his damp shirt for a clean, freshly ironed one. He was eager to get back to work. As he was about to descend the stairs, Esmeralda inquired when he wanted dinner. He told her seven, the usual time.

While Kevin had been lunching a leaden group of gray lavender clouds had rolled in from the ocean. By the time he emerged from his front door, it was pouring, and the street in front of his house was a cascade as the runoff raced down to the waterfront. Looking south over the Estuario del Muni, Kevin could see a line of bright sunshine as well as the arch of a complete rainbow. The weather in Gabon was still clear. Kevin was not surprised. There had been times when it had rained on one side of the street and not the other.

Guessing the rain would continue for at least the next hour, Kevin skirted his house beneath the protection of the arcade and climbed into his black Toyota utility vehicle.

Although it was a ridiculously short drive back to the hospital, Kevin felt it was better to ride than be wet for the rest of the afternoon.

CHAPTER 3

MARCH 4, 1997
8:45 A.M.
NEW YORK CITY

"Well, what do you want to do?" Franco Ponti asked while looking at his boss, Vinnie Dominick, in the rearview mirror. They were in Vinnie's Lincoln Towncar. Vinnie was in the backseat, leaning forward with his right hand holding onto the overhead strap. He was looking out at 126 East 64th Street. It was a brownstone built in a French rococo style with high-arched, multipaned windows. The first-floor windows were heavily barred for protection.

"Looks like pretty posh digs," Vinnie said. "The good doctor is doing okay for himself."

"Should I park?" Franco asked. The car was in the middle of the street, and the taxi behind them was honking insistently.

"Park!" Vinnie said.

Franco drove ahead until he came to a fire hydrant. He pulled to the curb. The taxi went past, the driver frantically giving them the finger. Angelo Facciolo shook his head and made a disparaging comment about expatriate Russian taxi drivers. Angelo was sitting in the front passenger seat.

Vinnie climbed out of the car. Franco and

Angelo quickly followed suit. All three men were impeccably dressed in long, Salvatore Ferragamo overcoats in varying shades of gray.

"You think the car will be okay?" Franco asked.

"I anticipate this will be a short meeting," Vinnie said. "But put the Police Benevolent Association Commendation on the dash. Might as well save fifty bucks."

Vinnie walked back to number 126. Franco and Angelo trailed in their perpetually vigilant style. Vinnie looked at the door intercom. "It's a duplex," Vinnie said. "I guess the doctor isn't doing quite as well as I thought." Vinnie pressed the button for Dr. Raymond Lyons and waited.

"Hello?" a feminine voice inquired.

"I'm here to see the doctor," Vinnie said. "My name is Vinnie Dominick."

There was a pause. Vinnie played with a bottle cap with the tip of his Gucci loafer. Franco and Angelo looked up and down the street.

The intercom crackled back to life. "Hello, this is Dr. Lyons. Can I help you?"

"I believe so," Vinnie said. "I need about fifteen minutes of your time."

"I'm not sure I know you, Mr. Dominick," Raymond said. "Could you tell me what this is in reference to?"

"It's in reference to a favor I did for you

last night," Vinnie said. "The request had come through a mutual acquaintance, Dr. Daniel Levitz."

There was a pause.

"I trust you are still there, Doctor," Vinnie said.

"Yes, of course," Raymond said. A raucous buzzing sounded. Vinnie pushed open the heavy door and entered. His minions followed.

"I don't think the good doctor is terribly excited to see us," Vinnie quipped as they rode up in the small elevator. The three men were pressed together like cigars in a triple pack.

Raymond met his visitors as they exited the lift. He was obviously nervous as he shook hands with all three after the introductions. He gestured for them to enter his apartment and then showed them into a small, mahogany-paneled study.

"Coffee anyone?" Raymond asked.

Franco and Angelo looked at Vinnie.

"I wouldn't turn down an expresso if it's not too much trouble," Vinnie said. Franco and Angelo said they'd have the same.

Raymond used his desk phone to place the order.

Raymond's worst fears had materialized the moment he'd caught sight of his uninvited guests. From his perspective they appeared like stereotypes from a grade-B movie. Vinnie was about five-ten, darkly complected and handsome, with full features and slicked-back hair. He was obviously the boss. The other two men were both over six feet and gaunt. Their noses and lips were thin and their eyes were beady and deeply set. They could have been brothers. The main difference in their appearance was the condition of Angelo's skin. Raymond thought it looked like the far side of the moon.

"Can I take your coats?" Raymond asked.

"We don't intend on staying too long," Vinnie said.

"At least sit down," Raymond said.

Vinnie relaxed into a leather armchair. Franco and Angelo sat stiffly on a velvet-covered settee. Raymond sat behind his desk.

"What can I do for you gentlemen?" Raymond said, trying to assume a confident air.

"The favor we did for you last night was not easy to pull off," Vinnie said. "We thought you'd like to know how it was arranged."

Raymond let out a little, mirthless laugh through a weak smile. He held up his hands as if to ward off something coming his way. "That's not necessary. I'm certain you . . ."

"We insist," Vinnie interrupted. "It makes good business sense. You see, we wouldn't like you to think that we didn't make a significant effort on your behalf."

"I wouldn't think that for a moment," Raymond said.

"Well, just to be sure," Vinnie said. "You see, getting a body out of the morgue is no easy task, since they are open for business twenty-four hours a day, and they have a uniformed security man on duty at all times."

"This isn't necessary," Raymond said. "I'd rather not be privy to the details, but I'm very appreciative of your efforts."

"Be quiet, Dr. Lyons, and listen!" Vinnie said. He paused for a moment to organize his thoughts. "We were lucky because Angelo here knows a kid named Vinnie Amendola, who works in the morgue. This kid was beholden to Pauli Cerino, a guy Angelo used to work for but who is currently in jail. Angelo now works for me, and knowing what he knows, he was able to convince the kid to tell us exactly where Mr. Franconi's remains were stored. The kid was also able to tell us some other information so we'd have some reason to be there in the middle of the night."

At that moment the expressos arrived. They were brought in by Darlene Polson, whom Raymond introduced as his assistant. As soon as the coffees were distributed, Darlene left.

"Good-looking assistant," Vinnie said.

"She's very efficient," Raymond commented. Unconsciously, he wiped his brow.

"I hope we're not making you feel uncomfortable," Vinnie said.

"No, not at all," Raymond said a bit too quickly.

"So we got the body out okay," Vinnie said. "And we disposed of it so it is gone. But as you can understand, it was not a walk in the park. In fact it was one big pain in the ass since we had so little time to plan it."

"Well, if there is ever some favor I can do for you," Raymond commented after an uncomfortable pause in the conversation.

"Thank you, Doctor," Vinnie said. He polished off his expresso like he was drinking a shot. He put the cup and saucer on the corner of the desk. "You've said exactly what I was hoping you'd say, which brings me to why I'm here. Now, you probably know I'm a client just like Franconi was. More important, my eleven-year-old son, Vinnie Junior, is also a client. In fact, he's more apt to need your services than I am. So we're facing two tuitions, as you people call it. What I'd like to propose is that I don't pay anything this year. What do you say?"

Raymond's eyes dropped to his desk surface.

"What we're talking about is a favor for a favor," Vinnie said. "It's only fair."

Raymond cleared his throat. "I'll have to talk to the powers that be," he said.

"Now, that's the first unfriendly thing you've said," Vinnie added. "My information is that *you* are the so-called "powers that be." So I find this foot-dragging insulting. I'll change my offer. I won't pay any tuition this year or next year. I hope you comprehend the direction this conversation is taking."

"I understand," Raymond said. He swallowed with obvious effort. "I'll take care of it."

Vinnie stood up. Franco and Angelo did likewise. "That's the spirit," Vinnie said. "So I'll count on your talking with Dr. Daniel Levitz and let him know about our understanding."

"Of course," Raymond said. He got to his feet.

"Thank you for the coffee," Vinnie said. "It hit the spot. My compliments to your assistant."

Raymond closed the apartment door after the hoodlums had left and leaned against it. His pulse was racing. Darlene appeared in the doorway leading to the kitchen.

"Was it as bad as you feared?" she asked.

"Worse!" Raymond said. "They behaved perfectly in character. Now I've got to deal with petty mobsters demanding a free ride. I tell you, what else can go wrong?"

Raymond pushed off the door and started toward his study. After only two steps he wobbled. Darlene reached out and supported his arm.

"Are you okay?" she demanded.

Raymond waited for a moment before nodding. "Yeah, I'm all right," he said. "Just a bit dizzy. Thanks to this Franconi flap, I didn't sleep a wink last night."

"Maybe you should put off the meeting you've planned with the new prospective doctor," Darlene suggested.

"I think you're right," Raymond said. "In this state, I probably couldn't convince anyone to join our group even if they were on their way to bankruptcy court."

CHAPTER 4

Laurie finished preparing the salad greens, put a paper towel over the bowl, and slipped it into the refrigerator. Then she mixed the dressing, a simple combination of olive oil, fresh garlic, and white vinegar, with just a touch of balsamic. She put that in the refrigerator as well. Turning her attention to the lamb loin, she trimmed off the small amount of fat the butcher had left, put the meat into a marinade she'd made earlier, and then stuck it into the refrigerator with the other makings. The last chore was preparing the artichokes. It took only a moment to cut off the excess base and a few of the large, stringy leaves.

Wiping her hands on the dish towel, Laurie glanced up at the wall clock. Familiar with Jack's schedule, she thought it was exactly the time to call. She used the wall phone next to the sink.

As the connection went through, she could imagine Jack coming up the cluttered stairwell in his dilapidated building. Although she thought she understood why he'd originally rented his apartment, she had trouble comprehending why he stayed. The building was

61

so depressing. On the other hand, as she glanced around at her own flat, she had to admit, there wasn't a lot of difference once Jack got inside his unit except he had almost double the space.

The phone rang at the other end. Laurie counted the rings. When she got to ten she began to doubt her familiarity with his schedule. She was about to hang up when Jack answered.

"Yeah?" he said unceremoniously. He was out of breath.

"Tonight's your lucky night," Laurie said.

"Who is this?" Jack asked. "Is that you, Laurie?"

"You sound out of breath," Laurie said. "Does that mean you lost at basketball?"

"No, it means I ran up four flights of stairs to get the phone," Jack said. "What's happening? Don't tell me you're still at work?"

"Heavens, no," Laurie said. "I've been home for an hour."

"So why is this my lucky night?" Jack asked.

"I stopped by Gristede's on the way home and picked up the makings of your favorite dinner," Laurie said. "It's all ready to go into the broiler. All you have to do is shower and get yourself down here."

"And I thought I owed you an apology for laughing at the vanishing mafioso," Jack said. "If amends are needed it's surely from my side."

"There's no atonement involved," Laurie said. "I would just enjoy your company. But there's one condition."

"Uh-oh," Jack said. "What?"

"No bike tonight," Laurie said. "You have to come by cab or the deal's off."

"Taxis are more dangerous than my bike," Jack complained.

"No argument," Laurie said. "Take it or leave it. If and when you slide under a bus and end up on a slab in the pit, I don't want to feel responsible." Laurie felt her face flush. It was an issue she didn't even like to joke about.

"Okay," Jack said agreeably. "I should be there in thirty-five to forty minutes. Shall I bring some wine?"

"That would be great," Laurie said.

Laurie was pleased. She'd been unsure if Jack would accept the invitation. Over the previous year they had been seeing each other socially, and several months ago, Laurie had admitted to herself that she'd fallen in love with him. But Jack seemed reluctant to allow the relationship to progress to the next level of commitment. When Laurie tried to force the issue, Jack had responded by distancing himself. Feeling rejected, Laurie had responded with anger. For weeks, they only spoke on a professional basis.

Over the last month their relationship had slowly improved. They were seeing each other again casually. This time Laurie realized that she had to bide her time. The problem was that at age thirty-seven it was not easy. Laurie had always wanted to become a mother someday. With forty fast approaching, she felt she was running out of time.

With the dinner essentially prepared, Laurie went around her small one-bedroom apartment straightening up. That meant putting odd books back into their spots on the shelves, stacking medical journals neatly, and emptying Tom's litter box. Tom was her six-and-a-half-year-old tawny tabby who was still as wild as he'd been as a kitten. Laurie straightened the Klimt print that the cat always knocked askew on his daily route from the bookcase to the top of the valence over the window.

Next Laurie took a quick shower, changed into a turtleneck and jeans, and put on a touch of makeup. As she did so she glared at the crow's feet that had been developing at the corners of her eyes. She didn't feel any older than when she'd gotten out of medical school, yet there was no denying the advance of years.

Jack arrived on schedule. When Laurie looked through the peephole, all she could see was a bloated image of his broadly grinning face, which he had positioned a mere inch from the lens. She smiled at his antics as she undid the host of locks that secured her door.

"Get in here, you clown!" Laurie said.

"I wanted to be sure you recognized me,"

Jack said as he stepped past her. "My chipped, upper-left incisor has become my trademark."

Just as Laurie was closing her door she caught a glimpse of her neighbor, Mrs. Engler, who'd cracked her door to see who was visiting Laurie. Laurie glared at her. She was such a busybody.

The dinner was a success. The food was perfect and the wine was okay. Jack's excuse was that the liquor store closest to his apartment specialized in jug wine, not the better stuff.

During the course of the evening, Laurie had to continually bite her tongue to keep the conversation away from sensitive areas. She would have loved to talk about their relationship, but she didn't dare. She sensed that some of Jack's hesitance stemmed from his extraordinary personal tragedy. Six years previously, his wife and two daughters had been tragically killed in a commuter-plane crash. Jack had told Laurie about it after they had been dating for several months, but then refused to talk about it again. Laurie sensed that this loss was the biggest stumbling block to their relationship. In a way, this belief helped her to take Jack's reluctance to commit himself less personally.

Jack had no trouble keeping the conversation light. He'd had a good evening playing pickup basketball at his neighborhood playground and was happy to talk about it. By chance he'd been teamed up with Warren, an all-around impressive African-American, who was the leader of the local gang and by far the best player. Jack and Warren's team didn't lose all evening.

"How is Warren?" Laurie asked. Jack and Laurie had frequently double-dated with Warren and his girlfriend, Natalie Adams. Laurie hadn't seen either of them since before she and Jack had their falling-out.

"Warren's Warren," Jack said. He shrugged. "He's got so much potential. I've tried my best to get him to take some college courses, but he resists. He says my value system isn't his, so I've given up."

"And Natalie?"

"Fine, I guess," Jack said. "I haven't seen her since we all went out."

"We should do it again," Laurie said. "I miss seeing them."

"That's an idea," Jack said evasively.

There was a pause. Laurie could hear Tom's purring. After eating and cleaning up, Jack moved to the couch. Laurie sat across from him in her art-deco club chair she'd purchased in the Village.

Laurie sighed. She felt frustrated. It seemed juvenile that they couldn't talk about emotionally important issues.

Jack checked his watch. "Uh-oh!" he said. He moved himself forward so that he was sitting on the very edge of the couch. "It's quarter to eleven," Jack added. "I've got to be going. It's a school night and bed is beckoning."

"More wine?" Laurie asked. She held up the jug. They'd only drunk a quarter of it.

"I can't," Jack said. "I've got to keep my reflexes sharp for the cab ride home." He stood up and thanked Laurie for the meal.

Laurie put down the wine and got to her feet. "If you don't mind, I'd like to ride with you as far as the morgue."

"What?" Jack questioned. He scrunched up his face in disbelief. "You're not going to work at this hour? I mean, you're not even on call."

"I just want to question the night mortuary tech and security," Laurie said, as she went to the hall closet for their coats.

"What on earth for?" Jack asked.

"I want to figure out how Franconi's body disappeared," Laurie said. She handed Jack his bomber jacket. "I talked to the evening crew when they came on this afternoon."

"And what did they tell you?"

"Not a whole bunch," Laurie said. "The body came in around eight forty-five with an entourage of police and media. Apparently it was a circus. I guess that's why the X ray was overlooked. Identification was made by the mother — a very emotional scene by all reports. By ten forty-five the body was placed in the fridge in compartment one eleven. So

I think it's pretty clear the abduction occurred during the night shift from eleven to seven."

"Why are you worrying yourself about this?" Jack said. "This is the front office's problem."

Laurie pulled on her coat and got her keys. "Let's just say that I've taken a personal interest in the case."

Jack rolled his eyes as they exited into the hall. "Laurie!" he intoned. "You're going to get yourself in trouble over this. Mark my word."

Laurie pushed the elevator button then glared at Mrs. Engler, who'd cracked her door as usual.

"That woman drives me crazy," Laurie said as they boarded the elevator.

"You're not listening to me," Jack said.

"I'm listening," Laurie said. "But I'm still going to look into this. Between this stunt and my run-in with Franconi's predecessor, it irks me that these two-bit mobsters think they can do whatever they please. They think laws are for other people. Pauli Cerino, the man Lou mentioned this morning, had people killed so that he didn't have to wait too long to have corneal transplants. That gives you an idea of their ethics. I don't like the idea that they think they can just come into our morgue and walk off with the body of a man they just killed."

They emerged onto Nineteenth Street and

walked toward First Avenue. Laurie put up her collar. There was a breeze off the East River, and it was only in the twenties.

"What makes you think the mobsters are behind this?" Jack asked.

"You don't have to be a rocket scientist to assume as much," Laurie said. She put up her hand as a cab approached, but it zoomed past without slowing. "Franconi was going to testify as part of a plea bargain. The higher-ups of the Vaccarro organization got angry or scared or both. It's an old story."

"So they killed him," Jack said. "Why take the body?"

Laurie shrugged. "I'm not going to pretend I can put my mind into a mobster's," she said. "I don't know why they wanted the body. Maybe to deny him a proper burial. Maybe they're afraid an autopsy would provide a clue to the killer's identity. Hell, I don't know. But ultimately it doesn't matter why."

"I have a sense the 'why' might be important," Jack said. "I think by getting involved you'll be skating on thin ice."

"Maybe so," Laurie said. She shrugged again. "I get caught up in things like this. I suppose part of the problem is that at the moment my main focus in life is my job."

"Here comes a free cab," Jack said, deliberately avoiding having to respond to Laurie's last comment. He sensed the implications and was reluctant to get drawn into a more personal discussion.

It was a short cab ride down to the corner of First Avenue and Thirtieth Street. Laurie climbed out and was surprised when Jack did the same.

"You don't have to come," Laurie said.

"I know," Jack said. "But I'm coming anyway. In case you haven't guessed, you have me concerned."

Jack leaned back inside the cab and paid the driver.

Laurie was still insisting that Jack's presence was not needed as they walked between the Health and Hospital's mortuary vans. They entered the morgue through the Thirtieth Street entrance. "I thought you told me your bed was beckoning?"

"It can wait," Jack said. "After Lou's story about your getting carted out of here nailed in a coffin, I think I should tag along."

"That was a totally different situation," Laurie said.

"Oh, yeah?" Jack questioned. "It involved mobsters just like now."

Laurie was about to protest further when Jack's comment struck a chord. She had to admit there were parallels.

The first person they came to was the night security man sitting in his cubbyhole office. Carl Novak was an elderly, affable, gray-haired man who appeared to have shrunk inside his uniform that was at least two sizes too big. He was playing solitaire but looked up when Laurie and Jack passed by his window and stopped in his open doorway.

"Can I help you?" Carl asked. Then he recognized Laurie and apologized for not having done so sooner.

Laurie asked him if he'd been informed of Franconi's body's disappearance.

"By all means," Carl said. "I got called at home by Robert Harper, head of security. He was up in arms about it and asked me all sorts of questions."

It didn't take Laurie long to learn that Carl had little light to shed on the mystery. He insisted that nothing out of the ordinary happened. Bodies had come in and bodies had gone out, just the way they did every night of the year. He admitted having left his post twice during his shift to visit the men's room. He emphasized that on both occasions, he'd only been gone for a few minutes and that each time he'd informed the night mortuary tech, Mike Passano.

"What about meals?" Laurie asked.

Carl pulled open a file drawer of his metal desk and lifted out an insulated lunch box. "I eat right here."

Laurie thanked him and moved on. Jack followed.

"The place certainly looks different at night," Jack commented as they passed the wide hall that led down to the refrigerators and the autopsy room.

"It's a bit sinister without the usual daytime hubbub," Laurie admitted.

They looked into the mortuary office and found Mike Passano busy with some receiving forms. A body had recently been brought in that had been fished out of the ocean by the Coast Guard. He looked up when he sensed company.

Mike was in his early thirties, spoke with a strong Long Island accent, and looked decidedly Southern Italian. He was slight of build with sharply defined facial features. He had dark hair, dark skin, and dark eyes. Neither Laurie nor Jack had worked with him although they had met him on multiple occasions.

"Did you docs come in to see the floater?" Mike asked.

"No," Jack said. "Is there a problem?"

"No problem," Mike said. "It's just in bad shape."

"We've come to talk about last night," Laurie said.

"What about it?" Mike asked.

Laurie posed the same questions she'd put to Carl. To her surprise, Mike quickly became irritated. She was about to say as much when Jack tugged on her arm and motioned for her to retreat to the hall.

"Ease off," Jack recommended when they were beyond earshot.

"Ease off from what?" Laurie asked. "I'm not being confrontational."

"I agree," Jack said. "I know I'm the last person to be an expert in office politics or interpersonal relations, but Mike sounds defensive to me. If you want to get any information out of him, I think you have to take that into consideration and tread lightly."

Laurie thought for a minute then nodded. "Maybe you're right."

They returned to the mortuary office, but before Laurie could say anything, Mike said: "In case you didn't know, Dr. Washington telephoned this morning and woke me up about all this. He read me the riot act. But I did my normal job last night, and I certainly didn't have anything to do with that body disappearing."

"I'm sorry if I implied that you did," Laurie said. "All I'm saying is that I believe the body disappeared during your shift. That's not saying you are responsible in any way."

"It sort'a sounds that way," Mike said. "I mean, I'm the only one here besides security and the janitors."

"Did anything happen out of the ordinary?" Laurie asked.

Mike shook his head. "It was a quiet night. We had two bodies come in and two go out."

"What about the bodies that arrived?" Laurie asked. "Did they come in with our people?"

"Yup, with our vans," Mike said. "Jeff Cooper and Peter Molina. Both bodies were from local hospitals."

"What about the two bodies that went out?" Laurie asked.

"What about them?"

"Well, who was it that came to pick them up?"

Mike grabbed the mortuary logbook from the corner of his desk and cracked it open. His index finger traced down the column then stopped. "Spoletto Funeral Home in Ozone Park and Dickson Funeral Home in Summit, New Jersey."

"What were the names of the deceased?" Laurie asked.

Mike consulted the book. "Frank Gleason and Dorothy Kline. Their accession numbers are 100385 and 101455. Anything else?"

"Were you expecting these particular funeral homes to come?" Laurie asked.

"Yeah, of course," Mike said. "They'd called beforehand just like always."

"So you had everything ready for them?"

"Sure," Mike said. "I had the paperwork all done. They just had to sign off."

"And the bodies?" Laurie asked.

"They were in the walk-in cooler as usual," Mike said. "Right in the front on gurneys."

Laurie looked at Jack. "Can you think of anything else to ask?"

Jack shrugged. "I think you've pretty well

74

covered the bases except when Mike was off the floor."

"Good point!" Laurie said. Turning back to Mike she said: "Carl told us that when he left for the men's room twice last night, he contacted you. Do you contact Carl whenever you need to leave your post?"

"Always," Mike said. "We're often the only ones down here. We have to have someone guarding the door."

"Were you away from the office very long last night?" Laurie asked.

"Nope," Mike said. "No more than usual. Couple of times to the head and a half hour for lunch up on the second floor. I'm telling you, it was a normal night."

"What about the janitors?" Laurie asked. "Were they around?"

"Not during my shift," Mike said. "Generally they clean down here evenings. The night shift is upstairs unless there is something out of the ordinary going on."

Laurie tried to think of additional questions but couldn't. "Thanks, Mike," she said.

"No problem," Mike said.

Laurie started for the door but stopped. Turning around she asked: "By any chance did you happen to see Franconi's body?"

Mike hesitated a second before admitting that he had.

"What was the circumstance?" Laurie asked.

"When I get to work Marvin, the evening tech, usually briefs me about what's going on. He was kind of psyched about the Franconi situation because of all the police and the way the family carried on. Anyway, he showed me the body."

"When you saw it, was it in compartment one eleven?"

"Yup."

"Tell me, Mike," Laurie said. "If you had to guess, how do you think the body disappeared?"

"I don't have the foggiest idea," Mike said. "Unless he walked out of here." He laughed, then seemed embarrassed. "I don't mean to joke around. I'm as confused as everybody else. All I know is only two bodies went out of here last night, and they were the two I checked out."

"And you never looked at Franconi again after Marvin showed him to you?"

"Of course not," Mike said. "Why would I?"

"No reason," Laurie said. "Do you happen to know where the van drivers are?"

"Upstairs in the lunchroom," Mike said. "That's where they always are."

Laurie and Jack took the elevator. As they were riding up, Laurie noticed Jack's eyelids were drooping.

"You look tired," Laurie commented.

"No surprise. I am," Jack said.

"Why don't you go home?" Laurie said.

"I've stuck it out this far," Jack said. "I think I'll see it to the bitter end."

The bright fluorescent lighting of the lunchroom made both Laurie and Jack squint. They found Jeff and Pete at a table next to the vending machines, poring over newspapers while snacking on potato chips. They were dressed in rumpled blue coveralls with Health and Hospital Corporation patches on their upper arms. Both had ponytails.

Laurie introduced herself, explained about her interest in the missing body, and asked if there was anything unique about the previous night, particularly about the two bodies they'd brought in.

Jeff and Pete exchanged a look, then Pete responded.

"Mine was a mess," Pete said.

"I don't mean the bodies themselves," Laurie said. "I'm wondering if there was anything unusual about the process. Did you see anyone in the morgue you didn't recognize? Did anything out of the ordinary happen?"

Pete glanced again at Jeff then shook his head. "Nope. It was just like usual."

"Do you remember what compartment you put your body into?" Laurie asked.

Pete scratched the top of his head. "Not really," he said.

"Was it near to one eleven?" Laurie asked.

Pete shook his head. "No, it was around

the other side. Something like fifty-five. I don't remember exactly. But it's written downstairs."

Laurie turned to Jeff.

"My body went into twenty-eight," Jeff said. "I remembered because that's how old I am."

"Did either of you see Franconi's body?" Laurie asked.

The two drivers again exchanged glances. Jeff spoke: "Yeah, we did."

"What time?"

"Around now," Jeff said.

"What was the circumstance?" Laurie said. "You guys don't normally see bodies that you don't transport."

"After Mike told us about it, we wanted to look because of all the excitement. But we didn't touch anything."

"It was only for a second," Pete added. "We just opened the door and looked in."

"Were you with Mike?" Laurie asked.

"No," Pete said. "He just told us which compartment."

"Has Dr. Washington talked to you about last night?" Laurie asked.

"Yeah, and Mr. Harper, too," Jeff said.

"Did you tell Dr. Washington about looking at the body?" Laurie asked.

"No," Jeff said.

"Why not?" Laurie asked.

"He didn't ask," Jeff said. "I guess we know

we're really not supposed to do it. I mean we don't usually. But, as I said, with all the commotion, we were curious."

"Maybe you should tell Dr. Washington," Laurie suggested. "Just so he has all the facts."

Laurie turned around and headed back to the elevator. Jack dutifully followed.

"What do you think?" Laurie asked.

"It's getting harder and harder for me to think the closer it gets to midnight," Jack said. "But I wouldn't make anything of those two peeking at the body."

"But Mike didn't mention it," Laurie said.

"True," Jack said. "But they all know they were bending the rules. It's human nature in such a situation not to be completely forthcoming."

"Maybe so," Laurie said with a sigh.

"Where to now?" Jack asked as they boarded the elevator.

"I'm running out of ideas," Laurie said.

"Thank God," Jack said.

"Don't you think I should ask Mike why he didn't tell us about the van drivers looking at Franconi?" Laurie asked.

"You could, but I think you're just spinning your wheels," Jack said. "Truly, I can't imagine it was anything but harmless curiosity."

"Then let's call it a night," Laurie said. "Bed is sounding good to me, too."

CHAPTER 5

Kevin replaced the tissue culture flasks in the incubator and closed the door. He'd been working since before dawn. His current quest was to find a transponase to handle a minor histocompatability gene on the Y chromosome. It had been eluding him for over a month despite his use of the technique that had resulted in his finding and isolating the transponases associated with the short arm of chromosome 6.

Kevin's usual schedule was to arrive at the lab around eight-thirty, but that morning he'd awakened at four A.M. and had not been able to fall back to sleep. After tossing and turning for three-quarters of an hour, he'd decided he might as well use the time for good purpose. He'd arrived at his lab at five A.M. while it was still pitch dark.

What was troubling Kevin's sleep was his conscience. The nagging notion that he'd made a Promethean mistake resurfaced with a vengeance. Although Dr. Lyons's mention of building his own lab had assuaged him at the time, it didn't last. Lab of his dreams or no, he couldn't deny the horror he feared was evolving on Isla Francesca.

Kevin's feelings had nothing to do with seeing more smoke. He hadn't, but as dawn broke, he'd also consciously avoided looking out the window much less in the direction of the island.

Kevin realized he couldn't go on like this. He decided that the most rational course of action would be to find out if his fears were justified. The best way to do it, he surmised, was to approach someone close to the situation who might be able to shed some light on Kevin's area of concern. But Kevin didn't feel comfortable talking with many people in the Zone. He'd never been very social, especially in Cogo, where he was the sole academician. But there was one working in the Zone with whom he felt slightly more comfortable, mainly because he admired his work: Bertram Edwards, the chief veterinarian.

Impulsively Kevin removed his lab coat, draped it over his chair, and headed out of his office. Descending to the first floor, he exited into the steamy heat of the parking area north of the hospital. The morning weather was clear, with white, puffy cumuli clouds overhead. There were some dark rain clouds looming, but they were out over the ocean in a clump along the western horizon; if they brought rain, it wouldn't be before the afternoon.

Kevin climbed into his Toyota four-wheel

drive and turned right out of the hospital parking lot. Traversing the north side of the town square, he passed the old Catholic church. GenSys had renovated the building to function as the recreational center. On Friday and Saturday nights they showed movies. Monday nights they had bingo. In the basement was a commissary serving American hamburgers.

Bertram Edwards's office was at the veterinary center that was part of the far larger animal unit. The entire complex was bigger than Cogo itself. It was situated north of the town in a dense equatorial rain forest and separated from the town by a stretch of virgin jungle.

Kevin's route took him east as far as the motor-pool facility, where he turned north. The traffic, which was considerable for such a remote spot, reflected the difficult logistics of running an operation the size of the Zone. Everything from toilet paper to centrifuge tubes had to be imported, which necessitated moving a lot of goods. Most supplies came by truck from Bata, where there was a crude deep-water port and an airport capable of handling large jet aircraft. The Estuario del Muni with access to Libreville, Gabon, was only served by motorized canoes.

At the edge of town the granite cobblestone street gave way to newly laid asphalt. Kevin let out a sigh of relief. The sound and the vibration that came up the steering column from the cobblestones was intense.

After fifteen minutes of driving through a canyon of dark green vegetation, Kevin could see the first buildings of the state-of-the-art animal complex. They were constructed of prestressed concrete and cinder block that was stuccoed and painted white. The design had a Spanish flair to complement the Colonial architecture of the town.

The enormous main building looked more like an airport terminal than a primate housing facility. Its front facade was three stories tall and perhaps five hundred feet long. From the back of the structure projected multiple wings that literally disappeared into the canopy of vegetation. Several smaller buildings faced the main one. Kevin wasn't sure of their purpose except for two buildings in the center. One housed the complex's contingent of Equatoguinean soldiers. Just like their comrades in the town square, these soldiers were aimlessly sprawled about with their rifles, cigarettes, and Cameroonean beer. The other building was the headquarters of a group that Kevin found even more disturbing than the teenage soldiers. These were Moroccan mercenaries who were part of the Equatoguinean presidential guard. The local president didn't trust his own army.

These foreign special-forces commandos dressed in inappropriate and ill-fitting dark suits and ties, with obvious bulges from their shoulder holsters. Every one of them had dark skin, piercing eyes, and a heavy mustache. Unlike the soldiers they were rarely seen, but their presence was felt like a sinister evil force.

The sheer size of the GenSys animal center was a tribute to its success. Recognizing the difficulties attached to primate biomedical research, GenSys had sited their facility in Equatorial Africa where the animals were indigenous. This move cleverly sidestepped the industrialized West's inconvenient web of import/export restrictions associated with primates, as well as the disruptive influence of animal-rights zealots. As an added incentive, the foreign exchange-starved local government and its venal leaders were inordinately receptive to all a company like GenSys had to offer. Obstructive laws were conveniently overlooked or abolished. The legislature was so accommodating that it even passed a law making interference with GenSys a capital offense.

The operation proved to be extraordinarily successful so quickly that GenSys expanded it to serve as a convenient spot for other biotechnology companies, especially pharmaceutical giants, to out-source their primate testing. The growth shocked the GenSys economic forecasters. From every point of view, the Zone was an impressive financial success.

Kevin parked next to another four-wheel-drive vehicle. He knew it was Dr. Edwards's from the bumper sticker that said: Man is an Ape. He pushed through the double doors with "Veterinary Center" stenciled on the glass. Dr. Edwards's office and examining rooms were just inside the door.

Martha Blummer greeted him. "Dr. Edwards is in the chimpanzee wing," she said. Martha was the veterinary secretary. Her husband was one of the supervisors at the motor pool.

Kevin set off for the chimpanzee wing. It was one of the few areas in the building he was at all acquainted with. He went through a second pair of double doors and walked the length of the central corridor of the veterinary hospital. The facility looked like a regular hospital, down to its employees who were all dressed in surgical scrubs, many with stethoscopes draped over their necks.

A few people nodded, others smiled, and some said hello to Kevin. He returned the greetings self-consciously. He didn't know any of these people by name.

Another pair of double doors brought him into the main part of the building that housed the primates. The air had a slightly feral odor. Intermittent shrieks and howls reverberated in the corridor. Through doors with windows of wire-embedded glass, Kevin caught glimpses of large cages where monkeys were incarcerated. Outside the cages were men in coveralls and rubber boots, pulling hoses.

The chimpanzee wing was one of the ells that extended from the back of the building into the forest. It, too, was three stories tall. Kevin entered on the first floor. Immediately the sounds changed. Now there was as much hooting as shrieking.

Cracking a door off the central corridor, Kevin got the attention of one of the workers in the coveralls. He asked about Dr. Edwards and was told the vet was in the bonobo unit.

Kevin found a stairwell and climbed to the second floor. He thought it was a coincidence that Dr. Edwards happened to be in the bonobo unit just when Kevin was looking for him. It was through bonobos that Kevin and Dr. Edwards had met.

Six years ago Kevin had never heard of a bonobo. But that changed rapidly when bonobos were selected as the subjects for his GenSys project. He now knew they were exceptional creatures. They were cousins of chimpanzees but had lived in isolation in a twenty-five-thousand-square-mile patch of virginal jungle in central Zaire for one and a half million years. In contrast to chimps, bonobo society was matriarchal with less male aggression. Hence, the bonobos were able to live in larger groups. Some people called them pygmy chimpanzees but the name was a misnomer because some bonobos were actually larger than some chimpanzees, and they were a distinct species.

Kevin found Dr. Edwards in front of a relatively small acclimatization cage. He was reaching through the bars making tentative contact with an adult female bonobo.

Another female bonobo was sitting against the back wall of the cage. Her eyes were nervously darting around her new accommodations. Kevin could sense her terror.

Dr. Edwards was hooting softly in imitation of one of the many bonobo and chimpanzee sounds of communication. He was a relatively tall man, a good three or four inches over Kevin's five foot ten. His hair was a shocking white which contrasted dramatically with his almost black eyebrows and eyelashes. The sharply demarcated eyebrows combined with a habit of wrinkling his forehead gave him a perpetually surprised look.

Kevin watched for a moment. Dr. Edwards's obvious rapport with the animals had been something Kevin had appreciated from their first meeting. Kevin sensed it was an intuitive talent and not something learned, and it always impressed him.

"Excuse me," Kevin said finally.

Dr. Edwards jumped as if he'd been frightened. Even the bonobo shrieked and fled to the back of the cage.

"I'm terribly sorry," Kevin said.

Dr. Edwards smiled and put a hand to his chest. "No need to be sorry. I was just so intent I didn't hear you approach."

"I certainly didn't mean to frighten you, Dr. Edwards," Kevin began, "but I . . ."

"Kevin, please! If I've told you once, I've told you a dozen times: my name is Bertram. I mean, we've known each other for five years. Don't you think first names are more appropriate?"

"Of course," Kevin said.

"It's serendipitous you should come," Bertram said. "Meet our two newest breeding females." Bertram gestured toward the two apes who'd inched away from the back wall. Kevin's arrival had frightened them, but they were now curious.

Kevin gazed in at the dramatically anthropomorphic faces of the two primates. Bonobo's faces were less prognathous than their cousins, the chimpanzees, and hence considerably more human. Kevin always found looking into bonobos' eyes disconcerting.

"Healthy-appearing animals," Kevin commented, not knowing how else to respond.

"They were just trucked in from Zaire this morning," Bertram said. "It's about a thousand miles as the crow flies. But by the circuitous route they had to take to get across the borders of the Congo and Gabon, they probably traveled three times that."

"That's the equivalent of driving across the U.S.," Kevin said.

"In terms of distance," Bertram agreed. "But here they probably didn't see more than short stretches of pavement. It's an arduous trip no matter how you look at it."

"They look like they are in good shape," Kevin said. He wondered how he'd appear if he'd made the journey jammed into wooden boxes and hidden in the back of a truck.

"By this time I've got the drivers pretty well trained," Bertram said. "They treat'em better than they treat their own wives. They know if the apes die, they don't get paid. It's a pretty good incentive."

"With our demand going up they'll be put to good use," Kevin said.

"You'd better believe it," Bertram said. "These two are already spoken for, as you know. If they pass all the tests, which I'm certain they will, we'll be over to your lab in the next couple of days. I want to watch again. I think you are a genius. And Melanie . . . Well, I've never seen such hand-eye coordination, even if you include an eye surgeon I used to know back in the States."

Kevin blushed at the reference to himself. "Melanie is quite talented," he said to deflect the conversation. Melanie Becket was a reproductive technologist. GenSys had recruited her mainly for Kevin's project.

"She's good," Bertram said. "But the few of us lucky enough to be associated with your project know that you are the hero."

Bertram looked up and down the space between the wall of the corridor and the cages to make sure that none of the coverall-clad workers were in earshot.

"You know, when I signed on to come over here I thought my wife and I would do well," Bertram said. "Moneywise I thought it would be as lucrative as going to Saudi Arabia. But we're doing better than I'd ever dreamed. Through your project and the stock options that come along with it, we're going to get rich. Just yesterday I heard from Melanie that we have two more clients from New York City. That will put us over one hundred."

"I hadn't heard about the two additional clients," Kevin said.

"No? Well it's true," Bertram said. "Melanie told me last night when I bumped into her at the rec center. She said she spoke with Raymond Lyons. I'm glad she informed me so I could send the drivers back to Zaire for another shipment. All I can say is that I hope our pygmy colleagues in Lomako can keep up their end of the bargain."

Kevin looked back into the cage at the two females. They returned his stare with pleading expressions that melted Kevin's heart. He wished he could tell them that they had nothing to fear. All that would happen to them was that they would become pregnant within the month. During their pregnancies they'd be kept indoors and would be treated to special, nutritious diets. After their babies were born, they'd be put in the enormous bonobo outdoor enclosure to rear the infants. When the youngsters reached age three the cycle would be repeated.

"They sure are human-looking," Bertram said, interrupting Kevin's musing. "Sometimes you can't help but wonder what they are thinking."

"Or worry what their offspring are capable of thinking," Kevin said.

Bertram glanced at Kevin. His black eyebrows arched more than usual. "I don't follow," he said.

"Listen, Bertram," Kevin said. "I came over here specifically to talk to you about the project."

"How marvelously convenient," Bertram said. "I was going to call you today and have you come over to see the progress we've made. And here you are. Come on!"

Bertram pulled open the nearest door to the corridor, motioned for Kevin to follow, and set out with long strides. Kevin had to hurry to catch up.

"Progress?" Kevin questioned. Although he admired Bertram, the man's tendency toward manic behavior was disconcerting. Under the best of circumstances Kevin would have had trouble discussing what was on his mind. Just broaching the issue was difficult, and Bertram was not helping. In fact, he was making it impossible.

"You bet'cha progress!" Bertram said enthusiastically. "We solved the technical problems with the grid on the island. It's on line now as you'll see. We can locate any individual animal with the push of a button. It's just in time, I might add. With twelve square miles and almost a hundred individuals, it was fast becoming impossible with the handheld trackers. Part of the problem is that we didn't anticipate the creatures would split into two separate sociological groups. We were counting on their being one big happy family."

"Bertram," Kevin said between breaths, marshaling his courage. "I wanted to talk to you because I've been anxious . . ."

"It's no wonder," Bertram said as Kevin paused. "I'd be anxious, too, if I put in the hours that you put in without any form of relaxation or release. Hell, sometimes I see the light in your lab as late as midnight when the wife and I come out of the rec center after a movie. We've even commented on it. We've invited you to dinner at our house on several occasions to draw you out a little. How come you never come?"

Kevin groaned inwardly. This was not the conversation he wanted to get into.

"All right, you don't have to answer," Bertram said. "I don't want to add to your anxiety. We'd enjoy having you over, so if you change your mind, give us a call. But what about the gym or the rec center or even the pool? I've never seen you in any of those places. Being stuck here in this hothouse part of Africa is bad enough, but making yourself a prisoner of your lab or house just makes it worse."

"I'm sure you are right," Kevin said. "But . . ."

"Of course I'm right," Bertram said. "But there is another side to this that I should warn you about. People are talking."

"What do you mean?" Kevin asked. "Talking about what?"

"People are saying that you're aloof because you think you are superior," Bertram said. "You know, the academician with all his fancy degrees from Harvard and MIT. It's easy for people to misinterpret your behavior, especially if they are envious."

"Why would anybody be envious of me?" Kevin asked. He was shocked.

"Very easy," Bertram said. "You obviously get special treatment from the home office. You get a new car every two years, and your quarters are as good as Siegfried Spallek's, the manager for the entire operation. That's bound to raise some eyebrows, particularly from people like Cameron McIvers who was stupid enough to bring his whole damn family out here. Plus you got that NMR machine. The hospital administrator and I have been lobbying for an MRI since day one."

"I tried to talk them out of giving me the house," Kevin said. "I said it was too big."

"Hey, you don't have to defend your perks to me," Bertram said. "I understand because I'm privy to your project. But very few other people are, and some of them aren't happy. Even Spallek doesn't quite understand although he definitely likes participating in the bonus your project has brought those of us who are lucky enough to be associated."

Before Kevin could respond, Bertram was stopped for a series of corridor consultations. He and Bertram had been traversing the veterinary hospital. Kevin used the interruption to ponder Bertram's comments. Kevin had always thought of himself as being rather invisible. The idea that he'd engendered animosities was hard to comprehend.

"Sorry," Bertram offered after the final consult. He pushed through the last of the double doors. Kevin followed.

Passing his secretary, Martha, he picked up a small stack of phone messages. He leafed through them as he waved Kevin into his inner office. He closed his door.

"You're going to love this," Bertram said, tossing the messages aside. He sat down in front of his computer and showed Kevin how to bring up a graphic of Isla Francesca. It was divided into a grid. "Now give me the number of whatever creature you want to locate."

"Mine," Kevin said. "Number one."

"Coming up," Bertram said. He entered the information and clicked. Suddenly a red blinking light appeared on the map of the island. It was north of the limestone escarpment but south of the stream that had been humorously dubbed Rio Diviso. The stream bisected the six-by-two-mile island lengthwise, flowing east to west. In the center of the island was a pond they'd called Lago Hippo for obvious reasons.

"Pretty slick, huh?" Bertram said proudly.

Kevin was captivated. It wasn't so much by the technology, although that interested him. It was more because the red light was blinking exactly where he would have imagined the smoke to have been coming from.

Bertram got up and pulled open a file drawer. It was filled with small handheld electronic devices that looked like miniature notepads with small LCD screens. An extendable antenna protruded from each.

"These work in a similar fashion," Bertram said. He handed one to Kevin. "We call them locators. Of course, they are portable and can be taken into the field. It makes retrieval a snap compared to the struggles we had initially."

Kevin played with the keyboard. With Bertram's help, he soon had the island graphic with the red blinking light displayed. Bertram showed how to go from successive maps with smaller and smaller scales until the entire screen represented a square fifty feet by fifty feet.

"Once you are that close, you use this," Bertram said. He handed Kevin an instrument that looked like a flashlight with a keypad. "On this you type in the same information. What it does is function as a directional beacon. It pings louder the closer it comes to pointing at the animal you're looking for. When there is a clear visual sighting, it emits a continuous sound. Then all you have to do is use the dart gun."

"How does this tracking system operate?" Kevin asked. Having been immersed in the biomolecular aspects of the project, he'd not paid any attention to the logistics. He'd toured the island five years previously at the commencement of the venture, but that had been it. He'd never inquired about the nuts and bolts of everyday operation.

"It's a satellite system," Bertram said. "I don't pretend to know the details. Of course each animal has a small microchip with a long-lasting nickel cadmium battery embedded just under the derma. The afferent signal from the microchip is minuscule, but it's picked up by the grid, magnified, and transmitted by microwave."

Kevin started to give the devices back to Bertram, but Bertram waved them away. "Keep them," he said. "We've got plenty of others."

"But I don't need them," Kevin protested.

"Come on, Kevin," Bertram chided playfully while thumping Kevin on the back. The blow was hard enough to knock Kevin forward. "Loosen up! You're much too serious." Bertram sat at his desk, picked up his phone messages, and absently began to arrange them in order of importance.

Kevin glanced at the electronic devices in his hands and wondered what he'd do with them. They were obviously costly instruments.

"What was it about your project that you wanted to discuss with me?" Bertram asked. He looked up from his phone messages. "People are always complaining I don't allow them to get a word in edgewise. What's on your mind?"

"I'm concerned," Kevin stammered.

"About what?" Bertram asked. "Things couldn't be going any better."

"I've seen the smoke again," Kevin managed.

"What? You mean like that wisp of smoke you mentioned to me last week?" Bertram asked.

"Exactly," Kevin said. "And from the same spot on the island."

"Ah, it's nothing," Bertram declared, with a wave of his hand. "We've been having electrical storms just about every other night. Lightning starts fires; everybody knows that."

"As wet as everything is?" Kevin said. "I thought lightning starts fires in savannas during the dry season, not in dank, equatorial rain forests."

"Lightning can start a fire anyplace," Bertram said. "Think of the heat it generates. Remember, thunder is nothing but expansion of air from the heat. It's unbelievable."

"Well, maybe," Kevin said. He was unconvinced. "But even if it were to start a fire, would it last?"

"You're like a dog with a bone," Bertram commented. "Have you mentioned this crazy idea to anybody else?"

"Only to Raymond Lyons," Kevin said. "He called me yesterday about another problem."

"And what was his response?" Bertram asked.

"He told me not to let my imagination run wild," Kevin said.

"I'd say that was good advice," Bertram said. "I second the motion."

"I don't know," Kevin said. "Maybe we should go out there and check."

"No!" Bertram snapped. For a fleeting moment his mouth formed a hard line and his blue eyes blazed. Then his face relaxed. "I don't want to go to the island except for a retrieval. That was the original plan and by golly we're sticking with it. As well as everything is going, I don't want to take any chances. The animals are to remain isolated and undisturbed. The only person who goes there is the pygmy, Alphonse Kimba, and he goes only to pull supplementary food across to the island."

"Maybe I could go by myself," Kevin suggested. "It wouldn't take me long, and then I can stop worrying."

"Absolutely not!" Bertram said emphatically. "I'm in charge of this part of the project, and I forbid you or anyone else to go on the island."

"I don't see that it would make that much difference," Kevin said. "I wouldn't bother the animals."

"No!" Bertram said. "There are to be no exceptions. We want these to be wild animals. That means minimal contact. Besides, with as small as this enclave is, visits will provoke talk, and we don't want that. And on top of that it could be dangerous."

"Dangerous?" Kevin questioned. "I'd stay away from the hippos and the crocs. The bonobos certainly aren't dangerous."

"One of the pygmy bearers was killed on the last retrieval," Bertram said. "We've kept that very quiet for obvious reasons."

"How was he killed?" Kevin asked.

"By a rock," Bertram said. "One of the bonobos threw a rock."

"Isn't that unusual?" Kevin asked.

Bertram shrugged. "Chimps are known to

throw sticks on occasion when they are stressed or scared. No, I don't think it's unusual. It was probably just a reflex gesture. The rock was there so he threw it."

"But it's also aggressive," Kevin said. "That's unusual for a bonobo, especially one of ours."

"All apes will defend their group when attacked," Bertram said.

"But why should they have felt they were being attacked?" Kevin asked.

"That was the fourth retrieval," Bertram said. He shrugged again. "Maybe they're learning what to expect. But whatever the reason, we don't want anyone going to the island. Spallek and I have discussed this, and he's in full agreement."

Bertram got up from the desk and draped an arm over Kevin's shoulders. Kevin tried to ease himself away, but Bertram held on. "Come on, Kevin! Relax! This kind of wild flight of imagination of yours is exactly what I was talking about earlier. You've got to get out of your lab and do something to divert that overactive mind of yours. You're going stir-crazy and you're obsessing. I mean, this fire crap is ridiculous. The irony is that the project is going splendidly. How about reconsidering that offer for coming over for dinner? Trish and I would be delighted."

"I'll give it serious thought," Kevin said. He felt distinctly uncomfortable with Bertram's arm around his neck.

"Good," Bertram said. He gave Kevin a final pat on his back. "Maybe the three of us could take in a movie as well. There's a terrific double-feature scheduled for this week. I mean, you ought to take advantage of the fact that we get the latest movies. It's a big effort on GenSys's part to fly them in here on a weekly basis. What do you say?"

"I guess," Kevin said evasively.

"Good," Bertram said. "I'll mention it to Trish, she'll give you a call. Okay?"

"Okay," Kevin said. He smiled weakly.

Five minutes later, Kevin climbed back into his vehicle more confused than before he'd come to see Bertram Edwards. He didn't know what to think. Maybe his imagination was working overtime. It was possible, but short of visiting Isla Francesca there was no way of knowing for sure. And on top of that was this new worry that people were feeling resentful towards him.

Braking at the exit of the parking area, Kevin glanced up and down the road in front of the animal complex. He waited for a large truck to rumble by. As he was about to pull out, his eye caught the sight of a man standing motionlessly in the window of the Moroccan headquarters. Kevin couldn't see him well because of the sunlight reflecting off the glass, but he could tell it was one of the mustached guards. He could also tell the man was watching him intently.

Kevin shivered without exactly knowing why.

The ride back to the hospital was uneventful and quick, but the seemingly impenetrable walls of dark green vegetation gave Kevin an uncomfortable claustrophobic feeling. Kevin's response was to press down on the accelerator. He was relieved to reach the edge of town.

Kevin parked in his spot. He opened his door, but hesitated. It was close to noon, and he debated heading home for lunch or going up to his lab for an hour or so. The lab won out. Esmeralda never expected him before one.

Just with the short walk from the car to the hospital, Kevin could appreciate the intensity of the noontime sun. It was like an oppressive blanket that made all movement more difficult, even breathing. Until he'd come to Africa, he'd never experienced true tropical heat. Once inside, enveloped with cool, air-conditioned air, Kevin grasped the edge of his collar and pulled his shirt away from his back.

He started up the stairs, but he didn't get far.

"Dr. Marshall!" a voice called.

Kevin looked behind him. He wasn't accustomed to being accosted in the stairwell.

"Shame on you, Dr. Marshall," a woman said, standing at the base of the stairs. Her voice had a lilting quality that suggested she was being less than serious. She was clad in surgical scrubs and a white coat. The sleeves of the coat were rolled up to her mid-fore-arms.

"Excuse me?" Kevin said. The woman looked familiar, but he couldn't place her.

"You haven't been to see the patient," the woman said. "With other cases you came each day."

"Well, that's true," Kevin said self-consciously. He'd finally recognized the woman. It was the nurse, Candace Brickmann. She was part of the surgical team that flew in with the patient. This was her fourth trip to Cogo. Kevin had met her briefly on all three previous visits.

"You've hurt Mr. Winchester's feelings," Candace said, wagging her finger at Kevin. She was a vivacious gamine in her late twenties. With fine, light-blond hair done up in a French twist. Kevin couldn't remember a time he'd seen her that she wasn't smiling.

"I didn't think he'd notice," Kevin stammered.

Candace threw back her head and laughed. Then she covered her mouth with her hand to suppress further giggles when she saw Kevin's confused expression.

"I'm only teasing," she said. "I'm not even sure Mr. Winchester remembers meeting you on that hectic day of arrival."

"Well, I meant to come and see how he was doing," Kevin said. "I've just been too busy."

"Too busy in this place in the middle of nowhere?" Candace asked.

"Well, I guess it's more that I've been preoccupied," Kevin admitted. "A lot has been happening."

"Like what?" Candace asked, suppressing a smile. She liked this shy, unassuming researcher.

Kevin made some fumbling gestures with his hands while his face flushed. "All sorts of things," he said finally.

"You academic types crack me up," Candace said. "But, teasing aside, I'm happy to report that Mr. Winchester is doing just fine, and I understand from the surgeon that's largely thanks to you."

"I wouldn't go that far," Kevin said.

"Oh, modest, too!" Candace commented. "Smart, cute, and humble. That's a killing combination."

Kevin stuttered but no words came out.

"Would it be out of bounds for me to invite you to join me for lunch?" Candace said. "I thought I'd walk over and get a hamburger. I'm a little tired of the hospital cafeteria food, and it would be nice to get a little air now that the sun is out. What do you say?"

Kevin's mind whirled. The invitation was unexpected, and under normal circumstances he would have found reason to decline for that reason alone. But with Bertram's comments fresh in his mind, he wavered.

"Cat got your tongue?" Candace asked. She lowered her head and flirtatiously peered at him beneath arched eyebrows.

Kevin gestured up toward his lab, then mumbled words to the effect that Esmeralda was expecting him.

"Can't you give her a call?" Candace asked. She had the intuitive feeling Kevin wanted to join her, so she persisted.

"I guess," Kevin said. "I suppose I could call from my lab."

"Fine," Candace said. "Do you want me to wait here or come with you?"

Kevin had never met such a forward female, not that he had a lot of opportunity or experience. His last and only love other than a couple of high school crushes had been a fellow doctorate candidate, Jacqueline Morton. That relationship had taken months to develop out of long hours working together; she'd been as shy as Kevin.

Candace came up the five stairs to stand next to Kevin. She was about five-three in her Nikes. "If you can't decide, and it's all the same to you, why don't I come up."

"Okay," Kevin said.

Kevin's nervousness quickly abated. Usually what bothered him in social circumstances with females was the stress of trying to think of things to talk about. With Candace, he didn't have time to think. She maintained a running conversation. During the ascent of the two flights of stairs she managed to bring up the weather, the town, the hospital, and how the surgery had gone.

"This is my lab," Kevin said, after opening the door.

"Fantastic!" Candace said with sincerity.

Kevin smiled. He could tell she was truly impressed.

"You go ahead and make your call," Candace said. "I'll just look around if it's okay."

"If you'd like," Kevin said.

Although Kevin was concerned about giving Esmeralda so little warning he'd not be there for lunch, she surprised him with her equanimity. Her only response was to ask when Kevin wanted dinner.

"At the usual time," Kevin said. Then after a brief hesitation, he surprised himself by adding: "I might have company. Would that be a problem?"

"Not at all," Esmeralda said. "How many persons?"

"Just one," Kevin said. He hung up the phone and wiped his palms together. They were a little damp.

"Are we on for lunch?" Candace called from across the room.

"Let's go!" Kevin said.

"This is some lab!" she commented. "I

never would have expected to find it here in the heart of tropical Africa. Tell me, what is it that you're doing with all this fantastic equipment?"

"I'm trying to perfect the protocol," Kevin said.

"Can't you be more specific?" Candace asked.

"You really want to know?" Kevin asked.

"Yes," Candace said. "I'm interested."

"At this stage I'm dealing with minor histocompatibility antigens. You know, proteins that define you as a unique, separate individual."

"And what do you do with them?"

"Well, I locate their genes on the proper chromosome," Kevin said. "Then I search for the transponase that's associated with the genes, if there's any, so I can move the genes."

Candace let out a little laugh. "You've lost me already," she admitted. "I haven't the foggiest notion what a transponase is. In fact, I'm afraid a lot of this molecular biology is over my head."

"It really isn't," Kevin said. "The principles aren't that complicated. The critical fact few people realize is that some genes can move around on their chromosome. This happens particularly in B lymphocytes to increase the diversity of antibodies. Other genes are even more mobile and can change places with their twins. You do remember that there are two

107

copies of every gene."

"Yup," Candace said. "Just like there are two copies of each chromosome. Our cells have twenty-three chromosome pairs."

"Exactly," Kevin said. "When genes exchange places on their chromosome pairs it's called homologous transposition. It's a particularly important process in the generation of sex cells, both eggs and sperms. What it does is help increase genetic shuffling, and hence the ability of species to evolve."

"So this homologous transposition plays a role in evolution," Candace said.

"Absolutely," Kevin agreed. "Anyway, the gene segments that move are called transposons, and the enzymes that catalyze their movement are called transponases."

"Okay," Candace said. "I follow you so far."

"Well, right now I'm interested in transposons that contain the genes for minor histocompatibility antigens," Kevin said.

"I see," Candace said, nodding her head. "I'm getting the picture. You're goal is to move the gene for a minor histocompatibility antigen from one chromosome to another."

"Exactly!" Kevin said. "The trick, of course, is finding and isolating the transponase. That's the difficult step. But once I've found the transponase, it's relatively easy to locate its gene. And once I've located and isolated the gene, I can use standard re-

108

combinant DNA technology to produce it."

"Meaning getting bacteria to make it for you," Candace said.

"Bacteria or mammalian tissue culture," Kevin said. "Whatever works best."

"Phew!" Candace commented. "This brain game is reminding me how hungry I am. Let's get some hamburgers before my blood sugar bottoms out."

Kevin smiled. He liked this woman. He was even starting to relax.

Descending the hospital stairs, Kevin felt a little giddy while listening and responding to Candace's entertaining, nonstop questions and chatter. He couldn't believe he was going to lunch with such an attractive, engaging female. It seemed to him that more things had happened in the last couple of days than during the previous five years he'd been in Cogo. He was so preoccupied, he didn't give a thought to the Equatoguinean soldiers as he and Candace crossed the square.

Kevin had not been in the rec center since his initial orientation tour. He'd forgotten its quaintness. He'd also forgotten how blasphemous it was that the church had been recycled to provide worldly diversion. The altar was gone, but the pulpit was still in place off to the left. It was used for lectures and for calling out the numbers on bingo night. In place of the altar was the movie screen: an unintended sign of the times.

The commissary was in the basement and was reached by a stairway in the narthex. Kevin was surprised at how busy it was. A babble of voices echoed off the harsh, concrete ceiling. He and Candace had to stand in a long line before ordering. Then after they'd gotten their food, they had to search in the confusion for a place to sit. The tables were all long and had to be shared. The seats were benches attached like picnic tables.

"There are some seats," Candace called out over the chatter. She pointed toward the rear of the room with her tray. Kevin nodded.

Kevin glanced furtively at the faces in the crowd as he weaved his way after Candace. He felt self-conscious, given Bertram's insight into popular opinion, yet no one paid him the slightest attention.

Kevin followed Candace as she squeezed between two tables. He held his tray high to avoid hitting anyone, then put it down at an empty spot. He had to struggle to get his legs over the seat and under the table. By the time he was situated, Candace had already introduced herself to the two people sitting on the aisle. Kevin nodded to them. He didn't recognize either one.

"Lively place," Candace said. She reached for catsup. "Do you come here often?"

Before Kevin could respond, someone called out his name. He turned and recognized the lone familiar face. It was Melanie

Becket, the reproductive technologist.

"Kevin Marshall!" Melanie exclaimed again. "I'm shocked. What are you doing here?"

Melanie was about the same age as Candace; she'd celebrated her thirtieth birthday the previous month. Where Candace was light, she was dark, with medium-brown hair and coloration that seemed Mediterranean. Her dark brown eyes were nearly black.

Kevin struggled to introduce his lunchmate, and was horrified to realize that for the moment he couldn't remember her name.

"I'm Candace Brickmann," Candace said without missing a beat. She reached out a hand. Melanie introduced herself and asked if she could join them.

"By all means," Candace said.

Candace and Kevin were sitting side by side. Melanie sat opposite.

"Are you responsible for our local genius's presence at the ptomaine palace?" Melanie asked Candace. Melanie was a sharp-witted, playfully irreverent woman who'd grown up in Manhattan.

"I guess," Candace said. "Is this unusual for him?"

"That's the understatement of the year," Melanie said. "What's your secret? I've asked him to come over here so many times to no avail that I finally gave up, and that was several years ago."

"You never asked me specifically," Kevin said in his own defense.

"Oh, really?" Melanie questioned. "What did I have to do — draw you a map? I used to ask if you wanted to grab a burger. Wasn't that specific enough?"

"Well," Candace said, straightening up in her seat. "This must be my lucky day."

Melanie and Candace fell into easy conversation, exchanging job descriptions. Kevin listened but concentrated on his hamburger.

"So we're all three part of the same project," Melanie commented when she heard that Candace was the intensive-care nurse of the surgical team from Pittsburgh. "Three peas in a pod."

"You're being generous," Candace said. "I'm just one of the low men on the therapeutic totem pole. I wouldn't put myself on the same level with you guys. You're the ones that make it all possible. If you don't mind my asking, how on earth do you do it?"

"She's the hero," Kevin said, speaking up for the first time and nodding toward Melanie.

"Come on, Kevin!" Melanie complained. "I didn't develop the techniques I use the way you did. There are lots of people who could have done my job, but only you could have done yours. It was your breakthrough that was key."

"No arguing you two," Candace said. "Just tell me how it's done. I've been curious from day one, but everything has been so hush-hush. Kevin's explained the science to me, but I still don't understand the logistics."

"Kevin gets a bone-marrow sample from a client," Melanie said. "From that, he isolates a cell preparing to divide so that the chromosomes are condensed, preferably a stem cell if I'm correct."

"It's pretty rare to find a stem cell," Kevin said.

"Well, then you tell her what you do," Melanie said to Kevin, with a dismissive wave of her hand. "I'll get it all balled up."

"I work with a transponase that I discovered almost seven years ago," Kevin said. "It catalyzes the homolygous transposition or crossing over of the short arms of chromosome six."

"What's the short arm of chromosome six?" Candace asked.

"Chromosomes have what's called a centromere that divides them into two segments," Melanie explained. "Chromosome six has particularly unequal segments. The little ones are called the short arms."

"Thank you," Candace said.

"So . . ." Kevin said, trying to organize his thoughts. "What I do is add my secret transponase to a client's cell that is preparing to divide. But I don't let the crossing-over go to completion. I halt it with the two short arms detached from their respective chromosomes. Then I extract them."

"Wow!" Candace remarked. "You actually take these tiny, tiny strands out of the nucleus. How on earth can you do that!"

"That's another story," Kevin said. "Actually I use a monoclonal antibody system that recognizes the backside of the transponase."

"This is getting over my head," Candace said.

"Well, forget how he gets the short arms out," Melanie said. "Just accept it."

"Okay," Candace said. "What do you do with these detached short arms?"

Kevin pointed toward Melanie. "I wait for her to work her magic."

"It's not magic," Melanie said. "I'm just a technician. I apply in vitro fertilization techniques to the bonobos, the same techniques that were developed to increase the fertility of captive mountain gorillas. Actually, Kevin and I have to coordinate our efforts because what he wants is a fertilized egg that has yet to divide. Timing is important."

"I want it just ready to divide," Kevin said. "So it's Melanie's schedule that determines mine. I don't start my part until she gives me the green light. When she delivers the zygote, I repeat exactly the same procedure that I'd just done with the client's cell. After removing the bonobo short arms, I inject the client's short arms into the zygote. Thanks to the transponase they hook right up exactly where they are supposed to be."

114

"And that's it?" Candace said.

"Well, no," Kevin admitted. "Actually I introduce four transponases, not one. The short arm of chromosome six is the major segment that we're transferring, but we also transfer a relatively small part of chromosomes nine, twelve, and fourteen. These carry the genes for the ABO blood groups and a few other minor histocompatibility antigens like CD-31 adhesion molecules. But that gets too complicated. Just think about chromosome six. It's the most important part."

"That's because chromosome six contains the genes that make up the major histocompatibility complex," Candace said knowledgeably.

"Exactly," Kevin said. He was impressed and smitten. Not only was Candace socially adept, she was also smart and informed.

"Would this protocol work with other animals?" Candace asked.

"What kind would you have in mind?" Kevin asked.

"Pigs," Candace said. "I know other centers in the U.S. and England have been trying to reduce the destructive effect of complement in transplantation with pig organs by inserting a human gene."

"Compared with what we are doing that's like using leaches," Melanie said. "It's so old-fashioned because it is treating the symptom, not eliminating its cause."

"It's true," Kevin said. "In our protocol there is no immunological reaction to worry about. Histocompatibility-wise we're offering an immunological double, especially if I can incorporate a few more of the minor antigens."

"I don't know why you are agonizing over them," Melanie said. "In our first three transplants the clients haven't had any rejection reaction at all. Zilch!"

"I want it perfect," Kevin said.

"I'm asking about pigs for several reasons," Candace said. "First, I think using bonobos may offend some people. Second, I understand there aren't very many of them."

"That's true," Kevin said. "The total world population of bonobos is only about twenty thousand."

"That's my point," Candace said. "Whereas pigs are slaughtered for bacon by the hundred of thousands."

"I don't think my system would work with pigs," Kevin said. "I don't know for sure, but I doubt it. The reason it works so well in bonobos, or chimps for that matter, is that their genomes and ours are so similar. In fact, they differ by only one and a half percent."

"That's all?" Candace questioned. She was amazed.

"It's kind of humbling, isn't it," Kevin said.

"It's more than humbling," Candace said. "It's indicative of how close bonobos, chimps, and humans are evolutionarily," Melanie said. "It's thought we and our primate cousins have descended from a common ancestor who lived around seven million years ago."

"That underscores the ethical question about using them," Candace said, "and why some people might be offended by their use. They look so human. I mean, doesn't it bother you guys when one of them has to be sacrificed?"

"This liver transplant with Mr. Winchester is only the second that required a sacrifice," Melanie said. "The other two were kidneys, and the animals are fine."

"Well, how did this case make you feel?" Candace asked. "Most of us on the surgical team were more upset this time even though we thought we were prepared, especially since it was the second sacrifice."

Kevin looked at Melanie. His mouth had gone dry. Candace was forcing him to face an issue he'd struggled to avoid. It was part of the reason the smoke coming from Isla Francesca upset him so much.

"Yeah, it bothers me," Melanie said. "But I guess I'm so thrilled with the involved science and what it can do for a patient, that I try not to think about it. Besides, we never expect to have to use many of them. They are more like insurance in case the clients might need them. We don't accept people who already need transplant organs unless they can wait the three plus years it takes for their double to come of age. And we don't have to interact with these creatures. They live off on an island by themselves. That's by design so that no one here has the chance to form emotional bonds of any sort."

Kevin swallowed with difficulty. In his mind's eye he could see the smoke lazily snaking its way into the dull, leaden sky. He could also imagine the stressed bonobo picking up a rock and throwing it with deadly accuracy at the pygmy during the retrieval process.

"What's the term when animals have human genes incorporated into them?" Candace asked.

"Transgenic," Melanie said.

"Right," Candace said. "I just wish we could be using transgenic pigs instead of bonobos. This procedure bothers me. As much as I like the money and the GenSys stock, I'm not so sure I'm going to stick with the program."

"They're not going to like that," Melanie said. "Remember, you signed a contract. I understand they are sticklers about holding people to their original agreements."

Candace shrugged. "I'll give them back all the stock, options included. I can live without it. I'll just have to see how I feel. I'd be much happier if we were using pigs. When we put that last bonobo under anesthesia, I could have sworn he was trying to communicate with us. We had to use a ton of sedative."

"Oh, come on!" Kevin snapped, suddenly furious. His face was flushed.

Melanie's eyes opened wide. "What in heaven's name has gotten into you?"

Kevin instantly regretted his outburst. "Sorry," he said. His heart was still pounding. He hated the fact that he was always so transparent, or felt he was.

Melanie rolled her eyes for Candace's benefit, but Candace didn't catch it. She was watching Kevin.

"I have a feeling you were as bummed out as I was," she said to him.

Kevin breathed out noisily then took a bite of hamburger to avoid saying anything he'd later regret.

"Why don't you want to talk about it?" Candace asked.

Kevin shook his head while he chewed. He guessed his face was still beet-red.

"Don't worry about him," Melanie said. "He'll recover."

Candace faced Melanie. "The bonobos are just so human," she commented, going back to one of her original points, "so I guess we shouldn't be shocked that their genomes differ by only one and a half percent. But something just occurred to me. If you guys are replacing the short arms of chromosome six as well as some other smaller segments of the bonobo genome with human DNA, what percentage do you think you're dealing with?"

Melanie looked at Kevin while she made a mental calculation. She arched her eyebrows. "Hmmm," she said. "That's a curious point. That would be over two percent."

"Yeah, but the one and a half percent is not all on the short arm of chromosome six," Kevin snapped again.

"Hey, calm down, bucko," Melanie said. She put down her soft drink, reached across the table and put her hand on Kevin's shoulder. "You're out of control. All we're doing is having a conversation. You know, it's sort of normal for people to sit and talk. I know you find that weird since you'd rather interact with your centrifuge tubes, but what's wrong?"

Kevin sighed. It went against his nature, but he decided to confide in these two bright, confident women. He admitted he was upset.

"As if we didn't know!" Melanie said with another roll of her eyes. "Can't you be more specific? What's bugging you?"

"Just what Candace is talking about," Kevin said.

"She's said a lot of things," Melanie said.

"Yeah, and they're all making me feel like I've made a monumental mistake."

Melanie took her hand away and stared into the depths of Kevin's topaz-colored eyes. "In what regard?" she questioned.

"By adding so much human DNA," Kevin said. "The short arm of chromosome six has millions of base pairs and hundreds of genes that have nothing to do with the major histocompatibility complex. I should have isolated the complex instead of taking the easy route."

"So the creatures have a few more human proteins," Melanie said. "Big deal!"

"That's exactly how I felt at first," Kevin said. "At least until I put an inquiry out over the Internet, asking if anyone knew what other kinds of genes were on the short arm of chromosome six. Unfortunately, one of the responders informed me there was a large segment of developmental genes. Now I have no idea what I've created."

"Of course you do," Candace said. "You've created a transgenic bonobo."

"I know," Kevin said with his eyes blazing. He was breathing rapidly and perspiration had appeared on his forehead. "And by doing so I'm terrified I've overstepped the bounds."

CHAPTER 6

Bertram pulled his three-year-old Jeep Chero-kee into the parking area behind the town hall and yanked on the brake. The car had been giving him trouble and had spent innumerable days being repaired in the motor pool. But the problem had persisted, and that fact made him particularly irritated when Kevin Marshall pretended not to know how lucky he was to get a new Toyota every two years. Bertram wasn't scheduled for a new car for another year.

Bertram took the stairs that rose up behind the first-floor arcade to reach the veranda that ringed the building. From there he walked into the central office. By Siegfried Spallek's choice, it had not been air-conditioned. A large ceiling fan lazily rotated with a particular wavering hum. The long, flat blades kept the sizable room's warm, moist air on the move.

Bertram had called ahead, so Siegfried's secretary, a broad-faced black man named Aurielo from the island of Bioko, was expect-ing him and waved him into the inner office. Aurielo had been trained in France as a schoolteacher, but had been unemployed until

122

GenSys founded the Zone.

The inner office was larger than the outer and extended the entire width of the building. It had shuttered windows overlooking the parking lot in the back and the town square in the front. The front windows yielded the impressive view of the new hospital/laboratory complex. From where Bertram was standing, he could even see Kevin's laboratory windows.

"Sit down," Siegfried said, without looking up. His voice had a harsh, guttural quality, with a slight Germanic accent. It was commandingly authoritarian. He was signing a stack of correspondence. "I'll be finished in a moment."

Bertram's eyes wandered around the cluttered office. It was a place that never made him feel comfortable. As a veterinarian and moderate environmentalist, he did not appreciate the decor. Covering the walls and every available horizontal surface were glassy-eyed, stuffed heads of animals, many of which were endangered species. There were cats such as lions, leopards, and cheetahs. There was a bewildering variety of antelope, more than Bertram knew existed. Several enormous rhino heads peered blankly down from positions of prominence on the wall behind Spallek. On top of the bookcase were snakes, including a rearing cobra. On the floor was an enormous crocodile with its mouth partially ajar to reveal its fearsome teeth. The table next to Bertram's chair was an elephant's foot topped with a slab of mahogany. In the corners, stood crossed elephant tusks.

Even more bothersome to Bertram than the stuffed animals were the skulls. There were three of them on Siegfried's desk. All three had their tops sawn off. One had an apparent bullet hole through the temple. They were used respectively for paper clips, ashtray, and to hold a large candle. Although the Zone's electric power was the most reliable in the entire country, it did go off on rare occasions because of lightning strikes.

Most people, especially visitors from Gen-Sys, assumed the skulls were from apes. Bertram knew differently. They were human skulls of people executed by the Equatoguinean soldiers. All three of the victims had been convicted of the capital offense of interfering with GenSys operations. In actuality, they had been caught poaching wild chimps on the Zone's designated hundred-square-mile land. Siegfried considered the area his own private hunting reserve.

Years previously, when Bertram had gently questioned the wisdom of displaying the skulls, Siegfried had responded by saying that they kept the native workers on their toes. "It's the kind of communication they comprehend," Siegfried had explained. "They understand such symbols."

Bertram didn't wonder that they got the message. Especially in a country which had suffered the atrocities of a diabolically cruel dictator. Bertram always remembered Kevin's response to the skulls. Kevin had said that they reminded him of the deranged character Kurtz in Joseph Conrad's *Heart of Darkness*.

"There," Siegfried said, pushing the signed papers aside. With his accent it sounded more like "zair." "What's on your mind, Bertram? I hope you don't have a problem with the new bonobos."

"Not at all. The two breeding females are perfect," Bertram said. He eyed the Zone's site boss. His most obvious physical trait was a grotesque scar that ran from beneath his left ear, down across his cheek, and under his nose. Over the years its gradual contraction had pulled up the corner of Siegfried's mouth in a perpetual sneer.

Bertram did not technically report to Siegfried. As the chief vet of the world's largest primate research and breeding facility, Bertram dealt directly with a GenSys senior vice president of operations back in Cambridge, Massachusetts, who had direct access to Taylor Cabot. But on a day-to-day basis, particularly in relation to the bonobo project, it was in Bertram's best interest to maintain a cordial working relationship with the site boss. The problem was, Siegfried was short-tempered and difficult to deal with.

He'd started his African career as a white hunter, who, for a price, could get a client anything he wanted. Such a reputation required a move from East Africa to West Africa, where game laws were less rigidly enforced. Siegfried had built up a large organization, and things went well until some trackers failed him in a crucial situation, resulting in his being mauled by an enormous bull elephant and the client couple being killed.

The episode ended Siegfried's career as a white hunter. It also left him with his facial scar and a paralyzed right arm. The extremity hung limp and useless from its shoulder connection.

Rage over the incident had made him a bitter and vindictive man. Still, GenSys had recognized his bush-based organizational skills, his knowledge of animal behavior, and his heavy-handed but effectual way of dealing with the indigenous African personality. They thought he was the perfect individual to run their multimillion-dollar African operation.

"There's another wrinkle with the bonobo operation," Bertram said.

"Is this new concern in addition to the weird worry of yours that the apes have divided into two groups?" Siegfried asked superciliously.

"Recognizing a change in social organization is a damn, legitimate concern!" Bertram

126

said, his color rising.

"So you said," Siegfried remarked. "But I've been thinking about it, and I can't imagine it matters. What do we care if they hang out in one group or ten? All we want them to do is stay put and stay healthy."

"I disagree," Bertram said. "Splitting up suggests they are not getting along. That would not be typical bonobo behavior, and it could spell trouble down the road."

"I'll let you, the professional, worry about it," Siegfried said. He leaned back in his chair, and it squeaked. "I personally don't care what those apes do as long as nothing threatens this windfall money and stock options. The project is turning into a gold mine."

"The new problem has to do with Kevin Marshall," Bertram said.

"Now what in God's name could that skinny simpleton do to get you to worry?" Siegfried asked. "With your paranoia, it's a good thing you don't have to do my job."

"The nerd has worked himself up because he's seen smoke coming from the island," Bertram said. "He's come to me twice. Once last week and then again this morning."

"What's the big deal about smoke?" Siegfried asked. "Why does he care? He sounds worse than you."

"He thinks the bonobos might be using fire," Bertram said. "He hasn't said so explicitly, but I'm sure that's what is on his mind."

"What do you mean 'using fire'?" Siegfried asked. He leaned forward. "You mean like making a campfire for warmth or cooking?" Siegfried laughed without disturbing his omnipresent sneer. "I don't know about you urban Americans. Out here in the bush you're scared of your own shadow."

"I know it's prepostrous," Bertram said. "Of course no one else has seen it, or if they have, it's probably from a lightning storm. The problem is, he wants to go out there."

"No one goes near the island!" Siegfried growled. "Only during a harvest, and it's only the harvest team! That's a directive from the home office. There are no exceptions save for Kimba, the pygmy, delivering the supplementary food."

"I told him the same thing," Bertram said. "And I don't think he'll do anything on his own. Still, I thought I should tell you about it just the same."

"It's good that you did," Siegfried said irritably. "The little prick. He's a goddamned thorn in my side."

"There is one other thing," Bertram said. "He told Raymond Lyons about the smoke."

Siegfried slapped the surface of his desk with his good hand loud enough to cause Bertram to jump. He stood up and stepped to the shuttered window overlooking the town square. He glared over at the hospital. He'd never liked the epicene bookish researcher from their first meeting. When he'd learned Kevin was to be coddled and accommodated in the second best house in the town, Siegfried had boiled over. He'd wanted to assign the house as a perk to one of his loyal underlings.

Siegfried balled his good hand into a fist and gritted his teeth. "What a meddling pain in the ass," he said.

"His research is almost done," Bertram said. "It would be a shame if he was to muck things up just when everything is going so well."

"What did Lyons say?" Siegfried asked.

"Nothing," Bertram said. "He accused Kevin of letting his imagination run wild."

"I might have to have someone watch Kevin," Siegfried said. "I will not have anyone destroy this program. That's all there is to it. It's too lucrative."

Bertram stood up. "That's your department," he said. He started for the door, confident he'd planted the appropriate seed.

CHAPTER 7

The combination of cheap red wine and little sleep slowed Jack's pace on his morning bicycle commute. His customary time of arrival in the ID room of the medical examiner's office was seven-fifteen. But as he got off the elevator on the first floor of the morgue en route to the ID room, he noticed it was already seven twenty-five, and it bothered him. It wasn't as if he were late, it was just that Jack liked to keep to a schedule. Discipline in relation to his work was one of the ways he'd learned to avoid depression.

His first order of business was to pour himself a cup of coffee from the communal pot. Even the aroma seemed to have a beneficial effect, which Jack attributed to Pavlovian conditioning. He took his first sip. It was a heavenly experience. Though he doubted the caffeine could work quite so quickly, he felt like his mild hangover headache was already on the mend.

He stepped over to Vinnie Amendola, the mortuary tech whose day shift overlapped the night shift. He was ensconced as usual at one of the office's government-issued metal desks.

His feet were parked on the corner, and his face hidden behind his morning newspaper.

Jack pulled the edge of the paper down to expose Vinnie's Italianate features to the world. He was in his late twenties, in sorry physical shape, but handsome. His dark, thick hair was something Jack envied. Jack had been noticing over the previous year a decided thinning of his gray-streaked brown hair on the crown of his head.

"Hey, Einstein, what's the paper say about the Franconi body incident?" Jack asked. Jack and Vinnie worked together on a frequent basis, both appreciating the other's flippancy, quick wit, and black humor.

"I don't know," Vinnie said. He tried to pull his beloved paper from Jack's grasp. He was embroiled in the Knicks stats from the previous night's basketball game.

Jack's forehead furrowed. Vinnie might not have been an academic genius, but about current news items, he was something of a resident authority. He read the newspapers cover to cover every day and had impressive recall.

"There's nothing about it in the paper?" Jack questioned. He was shocked. He'd imagined the media would have had a field day with the embarrassment of the body disappearing from the morgue. Bureaucratic mismanagement was a favorite journalistic theme.

"I didn't notice it," Vinnie said. He yanked harder, freed the paper, and reburied his face.

131

Jack shook his head. He was truly surprised and wondered how Harold Bingham, the chief medical examiner, had managed such a media coverup. Just as Jack was about to turn away, he caught the headlines. It said: MOB THUMBS NOSE AT AUTHORITY. The subhead read: "Vaccarro crime family kills one of its own then steals the body out from under the noses of city officials."

Jack snatched the entire paper from the surprised Vinnie's grasp. Vinnie's legs fell to the floor with a thump. "Hey, come on!" he complained.

Jack folded the paper then held it so that Vinnie was forced to stare at the front page.

"I thought you said the story wasn't in the paper," Jack said.

"I didn't say it wasn't in there," Vinnie said. "I said I didn't see it."

"It's the headlines, for crissake!" Jack said. He pointed at them with his coffee cup for emphasis.

Vinnie lunged out to grab his paper. Jack pulled it away from his grasp.

"Come on!" Vinnie whined. "Get your own freakin' paper."

"You've got me curious," Jack said. "As methodical as you are, you'd have read this front-page story on your subway ride into town. What's up, Vinnie?"

"Nothing!" Vinnie said. "I just went directly to the sports page."

Jack studied Vinnie's face for a moment. Vinnie looked away to avoid eye contact.

"Are you sick?" Jack asked facetiously.

"No!" Vinnie snapped. "Just give me the paper."

Jack slipped out the sports pages and handed them over. Then he went over to the scheduling desk and started the article. It began on the front page and concluded on the third. As Jack anticipated, it was written from a sarcastic, mocking point of view. It cast equal aspersion on the police department and the medical examiner's office. It said the whole sordid affair was just another glowing example of the gross incompetence of both organizations.

Laurie breezed into the room and interrupted Jack. As she removed her coat, she told him that she hoped he felt better than she.

"Probably not," Jack admitted. "It was that cheap wine I brought over. I'm sorry."

"It was also the five hours of sleep," Laurie said. "I had a terrible time hauling myself out of bed." She put her coat down on a chair. "Good morning, Vinnie," she called out.

Vinnie stayed silent behind his sports page.

"He's pouting because I violated his paper," Jack said. Jack got up so Laurie could sit down at the scheduling desk. It was Laurie's week to divvy up the cases for autopsy among the staff. "The headlines and cover story are about the Franconi incident."

"I wouldn't wonder," Laurie said. "It was all over the local news, and I heard it announced that Bingham will be on *Good Morning America* to attempt damage control."

"He's got his hands full," Jack said.

"Have you looked at today's cases?" Laurie asked, as she started glancing through the twenty or so folders.

"I just got here myself," Jack admitted. He continued reading the article.

"Oh, this is good!" Jack commented after a moment's silence. "They're alleging that there is some kind of conspiracy between us and the police department. They suggest we might have deliberately disposed of the body for their benefit. Can you imagine! These media people are so paranoid that they see conspiracy in everything!"

"It's the public who is paranoid," Laurie said. "The media likes to give them what they want. But that kind of wild theory is exactly why I'm going to find out how that body disappeared. The public has to know we are impartial."

"I was hoping you'd have a change of heart and given up on that quest after a night's sleep," Jack mumbled while continuing to read.

"Not a chance," Laurie said.

"This is crazy!" Jack said, slapping the page of newsprint. "First they suggest we here at the ME office were responsible for the body disappearing, and now they say the mob undoubtedly buried the remains in the wilds of Westchester so they will never be found."

"The last part is probably correct," Laurie said. "Unless the body turns up in the spring thaw. With the frost it's hard to dig more than a foot below the surface."

"Gads, what trash!" Jack commented as he finished the article. "Here, you want to read it?" He offered the front pages of the paper to Laurie.

Laurie waved them off. "Thanks, but I already read the version in the *Times*," she said. "It was caustic enough. I don't need the *New York Post*'s point of view."

Jack went back over to Vinnie and quipped that he was willing to return his paper to its virginal state. Vinnie took the pages without comment.

"You are awfully sensitive today," Jack said to the tech.

"Just leave me alone," Vinnie snapped.

"Whoa, watch out, Laurie!" Jack said. "I think Vinnie has pre-mental tension. He's probably planning on doing some thinking and it's got his hormones all out of whack."

"Uh-oh!" Laurie called out. "Here's that floater that Mike Passano mentioned last night. Who should I assign it to? Trouble is I don't think I'm mad at anyone and to forestall guilt I'll probably end up doing it my-self."

"Give it to me," Jack said.

"You don't care?" Laurie asked. She hated floaters, especially those which had been in the water for a long time. Such autopsies were unpleasant and often difficult jobs.

"Nah," Jack said. "Once you get past the smell, you got it licked."

"Please!" Laurie murmured. "That's dis-gusting."

"Seriously," Jack said. "They can be a chal-lenge. I like them better than gunshot wounds."

"This one is both," Laurie commented, as she put Jack down for the floater.

"How delightful!" Jack commented. He walked back to the scheduling desk and looked over Laurie's shoulder.

"There's a presumptive, close range shot-gun blast to the upper-right quadrant," Laurie said.

"It's sounding better and better," Jack said. "What's the victim's name?"

"No name," Laurie said. "In fact, that will be part of your challenge. The head and the hands are missing."

Laurie handed Jack the folder. He leaned on the edge of the desk and slid out the con-tents. There wasn't much information. What there was came from the forensic investigator, Janice Jaeger.

Janice wrote that the body had been discovered in the Atlantic Ocean way out off Coney Island. It had been inadvertently found by a Coast Guard cutter which had been lying in wait under the cover of night for some suspected drug runners. The Coast Guard had acted on an anonymous tip, and, at the time of the discovery, had been essentially dead in the water with their lights out and radar on. The cutter had literally bumped up against the body. The presumption was that it was the remains of the drug runner/informer.

"Not a lot to go on," Jack said.

"All the more challenge," Laurie teased.

Jack slipped off the desk and headed for the communications room en route to the elevator. "Come on, grouchy!" he called to Vinnie. He gave Vinnie's paper a slap and his arm a tug as he passed. "Time's a wasting." But at the door he literally bumped into Lou Soldano. The detective lieutenant had his mind on his goal: the coffee machine.

"Jeez," Jack commented. "You should try out for the New York Giants." Some of his coffee had sloshed out onto the floor.

"Sorry," Lou said. "I'm in sorry need of some java."

Both men went to the coffeepot. Jack used some paper towels to dab at the spill down the front of his corduroy jacket. Lou filled a Styrofoam cup to the brim with a shaky hand, then sipped enough to allow for plenty of cream and sugar.

Lou sighed. "It's been a grueling couple of days."

"Have you been partying all night again?" Jack said.

Lou's face was stubbled with a heavy growth of whiskers. He had on a wrinkled blue shirt with the top button undone and his tie loosened and askew. His Colombo-style trench coat looked like something a homeless person would wear.

"I wish," Lou grunted. "I've seen about three hours of sleep in the last two nights." He walked over, said hello to Laurie, and sat down heavily in a chair next to the scheduling desk.

"Any progress on the Franconi case?" Laurie asked.

"Nothing that pleases the captain, the area commander, or the police commissioner," Lou said dejectedly. "What a mess. The worry is, some heads are going to roll. We in Homicide are starting to worry we might be set up as scapegoats unless we can come up with a break in the case."

"It wasn't your fault Franconi was murdered," Laurie said indignantly.

"Tell that to the commissioner," Lou commented. He took a loud sip from his coffee. "Mind if I smoke?" He looked at Laurie and Jack. "Forget it," he said the moment he saw

138

their expressions. "I don't know why I asked. Must have been a moment of temporary insanity."

"What have you learned?" Laurie asked. Laurie knew that prior to being assigned to Homicide, Lou had been with the Organized Crime unit. With his experience, there was no one more qualified to investigate the case.

"It was definitely a Vaccarro hit," Lou said. "We learned that from our informers. But since Franconi was about to testify, we'd already assumed as much. The only real lead is that we have the murder weapon."

"That should help," Laurie said.

"Not as much as you'd think," Lou said. "It's not so unusual during a mob hit that the weapon is left behind. We found it on a rooftop across from the Positano Restaurant. It was a scoped 30-30 Remington with two rounds missing from its magazine. The two casings were on the roof."

"Fingerprints?" Laurie asked.

"Wiped clean," Lou said, "but the crime boys are still going over it."

"Traceable?" Jack asked.

"Yeah," Lou said with a sigh. "We did that. The rifle belonged to a hunting freak out in Menlo Park. But it was the expected dead end. The guy's place had been robbed the day before. The only thing missing was the rifle."

"So what's next?" Laurie asked.

"We're still following up leads," Lou said. "Plus there are more informers that we've not been able to contact. But mostly we're just keeping our fingers crossed for some sort of break. What about you guys? Any idea how the body walked out of here?"

"Not yet, but I'm looking into it personally," Laurie said.

"Hey, don't encourage her," Jack said. "That's for Bingham and Washington to do."

"He's got a point, Laurie," Lou said.

"Damn straight I got a point," Jack said. "Last time Laurie got involved with the mob she got carried out of here nailed in a coffin. At least that's what you told me."

"That was then and this is now," Laurie said. "I'm not involved in this case the way I was in that one. I think it is important to find out how the body disappeared for the sake of this office, and frankly I'm not convinced either Bingham or Washington will make the effort. From their point of view, it is better to let the episode just fade."

"I can understand that," Lou said. "In fact, if the goddamned media would only let up, the commissioner might even want us to ease up. Who knows?"

"I'm going to find out how it happened," Laurie repeated with conviction.

"Well, knowing the who and the how could help my investigation," Lou said. "It was most likely the same people from the Vaccarro organization. It just stands to reason."

Jack threw up his hands. "I'm getting out of here," he said. "I can tell neither of you will listen to reason." He again tugged on Vinnie's shirt on the way out the door.

Jack poked his head into Janice's office. "Anything I should know about this floater that's not in the folder?" he asked the investigator.

"The little there is, is all there," Janice said. "Except for the coordinates where the Coast Guard picked up the body. They told me that someone would have to call today to make sure it wasn't classified or something. But I can't imagine that information will matter. It's not like anyone could go out there and find the head and the hands."

"I agree," Jack said. "But have someone call anyway. Just for the record."

"I'll leave a note for Bart," Janice said. Bart Arnold was the chief forensic investigator.

"Thanks, Janice," Jack said. "Now get out of here and get some sleep." Janice was so committed to her job that she always worked overtime.

"Wait a second," Janice called out. "There was one other thing that I forgot to note in my report. When the body was picked up, it was naked. Not a stitch of clothing."

Jack nodded. That was a curious piece of information. Undressing a corpse was added

141

effort on the part of the murderer. Jack pondered for a moment, and when he did, he decided it was consistent with the murderer's wish to hide the victim's identity, a fact made obvious by the missing head and hands. Jack waved goodbye to Janice.

"Don't tell me we're doing a floater," Vinnie whined as he and Jack headed for the elevator.

"You sure do tune out when you read the sports page," Jack said. "Laurie and I discussed it for ten minutes."

They boarded the elevator and started down to the autopsy room floor. Vinnie refused to make eye contact with Jack.

"You are in a weird mood," Jack said. "Don't tell me you're taking this Franconi disappearance personally."

"Lay off," Vinnie said.

While Vinnie went off to don his moon suit, lay out all the paraphernalia necessary to do the autopsy, and then get the body into the morgue and onto the table, Jack went through the rest of the folder to make absolutely certain he'd not missed anything. Then he went and found the X rays that had been taken when the body had arrived.

Jack put on his own moon suit, unplugged the power source that had been charging over night, and hooked himself up. He hated the suit in general, but to work on a decomposing floater he hated it less. As he'd teased with Laurie earlier, the smell was the worst part.

At that time in the morning, Jack and Vinnie were the only ones in the autopsy room. To Vinnie's chagrin, Jack invariably insisted on getting a jump on the day. Frequently, Jack was finishing his first case when his colleagues were just starting theirs.

The first order of business was to look at the X rays, and Jack snapped them up on the viewer. With his hands on his hips, Jack took a step back and gazed at the anterioposterior full-body shot. With no head and no hands, the image was decidedly abnormal, like the X ray of some primitive, nonhuman creature. The other abnormality was a bright, dense blob of shotgun pellets in the area of the right upper quadrant. Jack's immediate impression was that there had been multiple shotgun blasts, not just one. There were too many beebee-like pellets.

The pellets were opaque to the X rays and obscured any detail they covered. On the light box they appeared white.

Jack was about to switch his attention to the lateral X ray when something about the opacity caught his attention. At two locations the periphery appeared strange, more lumpy than the usual beebee contour.

Jack looked at the lateral film and saw the same phenomena. His first impression was that the shotgun blasts might have carried some radio-opaque material into the wound. Perhaps it had been some part of the victim's clothing.

"Whenever you're ready, Maestro," Vinnie called out. He had everything prepared.

Jack turned from the X-ray view box and approached the autopsy table. The floater was ghastly pale in the raw fluorescent light. Whoever the victim had been, he'd been relatively obese and had not made any recent trips to the Caribbean.

"To use one of your favorite quotes," Vinnie said. "It doesn't look like he's going to make it to the prom."

Jack smiled at Vinnie's black humor. It was much more in keeping with his personality, suggesting that he had recovered from his early-morning pique.

The body was in sad shape although bobbing around in the water had washed it clean. The good news was that it had obviously been in the water for only a short time. The trauma went far beyond the multiple shotgun blasts to the upper abdomen. Not only were the head and the hands hacked off, but there was a series of wide, deep gashes in the torso and thighs that exposed swaths of greasy adipose tissue. The edges of all the wounds were ragged.

"Looks like the fish have been having a banquet," Jack said.

"Oh, gross!" Vinnie commented.

The shotgun blasts had bared and damaged many of the internal abdominal organs. Some strands of intestines were visible as was one dangling kidney.

Jack picked up one of the arms and looked at the exposed bones. "A hacksaw would be my guess," he said.

"What are all these huge cuts?" Vinnie asked. "Somebody try to slice him up like a holiday turkey?"

"Nah, I'd guess he'd been run over with a boat," Jack said. "They look like propeller injuries."

Jack then began a careful examination of the exterior of the corpse. With so much obvious trauma, he knew it was easy to miss more subtle findings. He worked slowly, frequently stopping to photograph lesions. His meticulousness paid off. At the ragged base of the neck just anterior to the collarbone he found a small circular lesion. He found another similar one on the left side below the rib cage.

"What are they?" Vinnie asked.

"I don't know," Jack said. "Puncture wounds of some sort."

"How many times do you suppose they shot him in the abdomen?" Vinnie asked.

"Hard to say," Jack said.

"Boy, they weren't taking any chances," Vinnie said. "They sure as hell wanted him dead."

A half hour later, when Jack was about to commence the internal part of the autopsy, the door opened and Laurie walked in. She was gowned and held a mask to her face, but she didn't have on her moon suit. Since she was a stickler for rules and since moon suits were now required in the "pit," Jack was immediately suspicious.

"At least your case wasn't in the water for long," Laurie said, looking down at the corpse. "It's not decomposed at all."

"Just a refreshing dip," Jack quipped.

"What a shotgun wound!" Laurie marveled, gazing at the fearsome wound. Then looking at the multiple gashes, she added, "These look like they were done by a propeller."

Jack straightened up. "Laurie, what's on your mind? You didn't come down here just to help us, did you?"

"No," Laurie admitted. Her voice wavered behind her mask. "I guess I wanted a little moral support."

"About what?" Jack questioned.

"Calvin just reamed me out," Laurie said. "Apparently the night tech, Mike Passano, complained that I had been in last night accusing him of being involved in the theft of Franconi's body. Can you imagine? Anyway, Calvin was really angry, and you know how I hate confrontation. I ended up crying, which made me furious at myself."

Jack blew out through pursed lips. He tried

to think of something to say other than "I told you so," but nothing came to mind.

"I'm sorry," Jack said limply.

"Thanks," Laurie said.

"So you shed a few tears," Jack said. "Don't be so hard on yourself."

"But I hate it," Laurie complained. "It's so unprofessional."

"Ah, I wouldn't worry about it," Jack said. "Sometimes I wish I could shed tears. Maybe if we could do some kind of partial trade, we'd both be better off."

"Anytime!" Laurie said with conviction. This was the closest Jack had come to an admission of what Laurie had long suspected: his bottled-up grief was the major stumbling block for his own happiness.

"So, at least now you'll drop your minicrusade," Jack said.

"Heavens, no!" Laurie said. "If anything, it makes me more committed because it suggests just what I feared. Calvin and Bingham are going to try to sweep the episode under the carpet. It's not right."

"Oh, Laurie!" Jack moaned. "Please! This little run-in with Calvin will only be the beginning. You're going to bring yourself nothing but grief."

"It's the principle," Laurie said. "So don't lecture me. I came to you for support."

Jack sighed, fogging up his plastic face mask for a moment. "Okay," he said. "What do you want me to do?"

"Nothing in particular," Laurie said. "Just be there for me."

Fifteen minutes later, Laurie left the autopsy room. Jack had showed her all the external findings on his case, including the two puncture wounds. She'd listened with half an ear, obviously preoccupied with the Franconi business. Jack had had to restrain himself to keep from telling her again how he felt.

"Enough of this external stuff," Jack said to Vinnie. "Let's move on to the internal part of the autopsy."

"It's about time," Vinnie complained. It was now after eight and bodies were coming in along with their assigned techs and medical examiners. Despite the early start, he and Jack were not significantly ahead of the others.

Jack ignored the friendly banter evoked by his hapless corpse. With all the obvious trauma, Jack had to vary the traditional autopsy technique and that took concentration. In contrast to Vinnie, Jack was oblivious to the passage of time. But again his meticulousness paid off. Although the liver had essentially been obliterated by the shotgun blasts, Jack discovered something extraordinary that might have been missed by someone doing a more haphazard, cursory job. He found the tiny remains of surgical sutures in the vena cava and in the ragged end of the hepatic artery. Sutures in such an area were uncommon. The hepatic artery brought blood to the liver, whereas the vena cava was the largest vein in the abdomen. Jack didn't find any sutures in the portal vein, because that vessel was almost entirely obliterated.

"Chet, get over here," Jack called. Chet McGovern was Jack's office mate. He was busy at a neighboring table.

Chet put down his scalpel and stepped over to Jack's table. Vinnie moved to the head to give him space.

"What'cha got?" Chet asked. "Something interesting?" He peered into the hole where Jack was working.

"I sure do," Jack said. "I got a bunch of shotgun pellets, but I also have some vascular sutures."

"Where?" Chet asked. He couldn't make out any anatomical landmarks.

"Here," Jack said. He pointed with the handle of a scalpel.

"Okay, I see them," Chet said with admiration. "Nice pickup. There's not a lot of endothelialization. I'd say they weren't that old."

"That's my thought," Jack said. "Probably within a month or two. Six months at the extreme."

"What do you think it means?"

"I think the chances of me making an iden-

149

tification just went up a thousand percent," Jack said. He straightened up and stretched.

"So the victim had abdominal surgery," Chet said. "Lots of people have had abdominal surgery."

"Not the kind of surgery this guy apparently had," Jack said. "With sutures in the vena cava and the hepatic artery, I'm betting he's in a pretty distinguished group. My guess is that he'd had a liver transplant not too long ago."

CHAPTER 8

Raymond Lyons pulled up his cuff-linked sleeve and glanced at his wafer-thin Piaget watch. It was exactly ten o'clock. He was content. He liked to be punctual especially for business meetings, but he did not like to be early. As far as he was concerned being early reeked of desperation, and Raymond had a penchant for bargaining from a position of strength.

For the previous few minutes he'd been standing on the corner of Park Avenue and Seventy-eighth Street, waiting for the hour to arrive. Now that it had, he straightened his tie, adjusted his fedora, and started walking toward the entrance of 972 Park Avenue.

"I'm looking for Dr. Anderson's office," Raymond announced to the liveried doorman who'd opened the heavy wrought-iron and glass door.

"The doctor's office has its own entrance," the doorman replied. He reopened the door behind Raymond, stepped out onto the sidewalk and pointed south.

Raymond touched the tip of his hat in appreciation before moving down to this private

151

entrance. A sign of engraved brass read: PLEASE RING AND THEN ENTER. Raymond did as he was told.

As the door closed behind him, Raymond was immediately pleased. The office looked and even smelled like money. It was sumptuously appointed with antiques and thick oriental carpets. The walls were covered with nineteenth-century art.

Raymond advanced to an elegant, boullework French desk. A well-dressed, matronly receptionist glanced up at him over her reading glasses. A nameplate sat on the desk facing Raymond. It said: MRS. ARTHUR P. AUCHINCLOSS.

Raymond gave his name, being sure to emphasize the fact that he was a physician. He was well aware that some doctors' receptionists could be uncomfortably imperious if they didn't know a visitor was a member of the trade.

"The doctor is expecting you," Mrs. Auchincloss said. Then she politely asked Raymond to wait in the waiting room.

"It's a beautiful office," Raymond said to make conversation.

"Indeed," Mrs. Auchincloss said.

"Is it a large office?" Raymond asked.

"Yes, of course," Mrs. Auchincloss said. "Dr. Anderson is a very busy man. We have four full examining rooms and an X-ray room."

Raymond smiled. It wasn't difficult for him to guess the astronomical overhead that Dr. Anderson had been duped into assuming by so-called productivity experts during the heyday of "fee-for-service" medicine. From Raymond's point of view, Dr. Anderson was the perfect quarry as a potential partner. Although the doctor undoubtedly still had a small backlog of wealthy patients willing to pay cash to retain their old, comfortable relationship, Dr. Anderson had to have been being squeezed by managed care.

"I suppose that means a large staff," Raymond said.

"We're down to one nurse," Mrs. Auchincloss said. "It's hard to find appropriate help these days."

Yeah, sure, Raymond mused. One nurse for four examining rooms unquestionably meant the doctor was struggling. But Raymond didn't vocalize his thoughts. Instead he let his eyes roam around the carefully wallpapered walls and said: "I've always admired these old-school, Park Avenue offices. They are so civilized and serene. They can't help but impart a feeling of trust."

"I'm sure our patients feel the same way," Mrs. Auchincloss said.

An interior door opened and a bejeweled, Gucci-draped, elderly woman stepped into the reception area. She was painfully thin and had suffered so many face-lifts that her mouth was drawn into a taut, unremitting smirk. Behind her was Dr. Waller Anderson.

Raymond's and Waller's eyes crossed for a fleeting moment as the doctor guided his patient to the receptionist and gave instructions of when he should see her next.

Raymond assessed the doctor. He was tall and had a refined look that Raymond sensed he possessed as well. But Waller wasn't tanned. In fact, his complexion had a grayish cast, and he looked strained with sad eyes and hollow cheeks. As far as Raymond was concerned, hard times were written all over his face.

After warm goodbyes to his patient, Waller motioned Raymond to follow him. He led down a long corridor that gave access to the examining rooms. At the end he preceded Raymond into his private office, then closed the door after them.

Waller introduced himself cordially but with obvious reserve. He took Raymond's hat and coat, which he carefully hung in a small closet.

"Coffee?" Waller asked.

"By all means," Raymond said.

A few minutes later, both with coffee, and with Waller behind his desk and Raymond sitting in a chair in front, Raymond began his pitch.

"These are tough times to be practicing medicine," Raymond said.

Waller made a sound that was akin to a laugh, but it was bereft of humor. Obviously he wasn't amused.

"We can offer you an opportunity to significantly augment your income as well as provide a state-of-the-art service to select patients," Raymond said. For the most part Raymond's presentation was a practiced speech that he'd perfected over the years.

"Is there anything illegal about this?" Waller interjected. His tone was serious, almost irritable. "If there is, I'm not interested."

"Nothing illegal," Raymond assured him. "Just extremely confidential. From our phone call, you said you would be willing to keep this conversation just among you, me, and Dr. Daniel Levitz."

"As long as my silence is not felonious in and of itself," Waller said. "I will not be duped into being an accessory."

"No need to worry," Raymond said. He smiled. "But if you do decide to join our group, you will be asked to sign an affidavit concerning confidentiality. Only then will you be told the specific details."

"I don't have any trouble with signing an affidavit," Waller said. "As long as I'm not breaking any law."

"Well, then," Raymond said. He put his coffee cup on the edge of Waller's desk to free up his hands. He fervently believed that hand gestures were important for impact. He started by telling about his chance meeting seven years previously with Kevin Marshall who'd given a poorly attended presentation at a national meeting that dealt with homologous transposition of chromosome parts between cells.

"Homologous transposition?" Waller questioned. "What the devil is that?" Having been through medical school prior to the revolution in molecular biology, he was unfamiliar with the terms.

Raymond patiently explained and used for his example the short arms of chromosome 6.

"So this Kevin Marshall developed a way to take a piece of chromosome from one cell and exchange it for the same piece in the same location of another cell," Waller said.

"Exactly," Raymond said. "And for me it was like an epiphany. I immediately saw the clinical application. Suddenly it was potentially possible to create an immunological double of an individual. As I'm sure you are aware, the short arm of chromosome six contains the major histocompatibility complex."

"Like an identical twin," Waller said with growing interest.

"Even better than an identical twin," Raymond said. "The immunological double is created in an appropriately sized animal species that can be sacrificed on demand. Few people would be able to have an identical twin sacrificed."

"Why wasn't this published?" Waller asked.

"Dr. Marshall fully intended to publish," Raymond said. "But there were some minor details he wanted to work out before he did so. It was his department head that forced him to present at the meeting. Lucky for us!

"After hearing the talk, I approached him and convinced him to go private. It wasn't easy, but what tipped the scales in our favor was that I promised him the lab of his dreams with no interference from academia. I assured him that he would be given any and every piece of equipment he wanted."

"You had such a lab?" Waller asked.

"Not at the time," Raymond admitted. "Once I had agreement from him, I approached an international biotechnology giant, which will go nameless until you agree to join our group. With some difficulty I sold them on the idea of creatively marketing this phenomenon."

"And how is that done?" Waller asked.

Raymond moved forward in his chair and locked eyes with Waller. "For a price we create an immunological double for a client," he said. "As you can well imagine, it is a significant price but not unreasonable for the peace of mind it affords. But how we really make money is that the client must pay a yearly tuition to maintain his double."

"Sort of like an initiation fee and then dues," Waller said.

"That's another way to look at it," Raymond agreed.

"How do I benefit?" Waller asked.

"Myriad ways," Raymond said. "I've constructed the business like a merchandizing pyramid. For every client you recruit, you get a percentage, not only of the initial price but each year from the tuition. On top of that, we will encourage you to recruit other physicians like yourself with collapsing patient bases but who still have a number of wealthy, health-conscious, cash-paying patients. With every successful physician recruitment, you get percentages from each of his recruitment efforts. For instance, if you choose to join, Dr. Levitz, who recommended you, will receive percentages from all your successes. You don't have to be an accountant to understand that with a little effort you could be earning a substantial income. And as an added incentive, we can offer the payments offshore so they will accrue tax-free."

"Why all the secrecy?" Waller asked.

"For obvious reasons as far as the offshore accounts are concerned," Raymond said. "As for the whole program, there have been ethical issues that have been overlooked. Consequently, the biotechnology company that is making this all possible is paranoid about bad publicity. Frankly, the use of animals for transplantation offends some people, and we certainly do not want to be forced to deal with animal-rights zealots. Besides, this is an expensive operation and can be made available to only a few highly select people. That violates the concept of equality."

"May I ask how many clients have taken advantage of this plan?"

"Laymen or physicians?" Raymond asked.

"Laymen," Waller said.

"Around one hundred," Raymond said.

"Has anybody had to utilize the resource?"

"As a matter of fact, four have," Raymond said. "Two kidneys and two livers have been transplanted. All are doing superbly without medication and without any signs of rejection. And, I might add, there is a substantial additional charge for the harvest and transplantation, and the involved physicians get the same percentages of these fees."

"How many physicians are involved?" Waller asked.

"Fewer than fifty," Raymond said. "We started slowly on recruitment, but it is now speeding up."

"How long has this program been going on?" Waller asked.

"About six years," Raymond said. "It's been a significant outlay of capital and a lot of effort, but it is now beginning to pay off handsomely. I should remind you that you will be getting in at a relatively early date, so the pyramid structure will benefit you greatly."

"It sounds interesting," Waller said. "God knows I could use some additional income with my falling patient base. I've got to do something before I lose this office."

"It would be a pity," Raymond agreed.

"Can I think about it for a day or so?" Waller asked.

Raymond stood up. Experience told him he'd made another score. "By all means," he said graciously. "I'd also invite you to call Dr. Levitz. He'd recommended you highly, and he's extraordinarily satisfied with the arrangements."

Five minutes later Raymond exited onto the sidewalk and turned south down Park Avenue. His walk had an extra bounce to it. With the blue sky, the clear air, and the hint of spring, he felt on top of the world, especially with the pleasurable rush of adrenaline that a successful recruitment always gave him. Even the unpleasantness of the previous couple of days seemed insignificant. The future was bright and full of promise.

But then near disaster came out of nowhere. Distracted by his victory, Raymond almost stepped from the curb into the path of a speeding city bus. Wind from the hurling vehicle blew off his hat while filthy gutter water sprayed the front of his cashmere coat.

Raymond staggered back, dazed from his narrow escape from what might have been a horrible death. New York was a city of sudden extremes.

"You okay, buddy?" a passerby asked. He handed Raymond his dented fedora.

"I'm fine, thank you," Raymond said. He looked down at the front of his coat and felt ill. The episode seemed metaphorical and brought back the anxiety he'd experienced over the unfortunate Franconi business. The muck reminded him of having to deal with Vinnie Dominick.

Feeling chastened, Raymond crossed the street with much more care. Life was full of dangers. As he walked toward Sixty-fourth Street, he began to worry about the other two transplant cases. He'd never considered the problem an autopsy posed to his program until the Franconi dilemma.

All at once, Raymond decided he'd better check the status of the other patients. There was no doubt in his mind that Taylor Cabot's threat had been real. If one of the patients happened to be autopsied sometime in the future for whatever reason, and the media got hold of the results, it could spell disaster. GenSys would probably drop the whole operation.

Raymond quickened his pace. One patient lived in New Jersey, the other in Dallas. He thought he'd better get on the phone and talk with the recruiting doctors.

CHAPTER 9

"Hello!" Candace's voice called out. "Anybody home?"

Kevin's hand flinched at the unexpected noise. The lab techs had long since left for the day, and the laboratory had been silent save for the low hum of the refrigeration units. Kevin had stayed to run another southern blot analysis to separate DNA fragments, but at the sound of Candace's voice, he'd missed one of the wells with the micropipette. The fluid had run out over the surface of the gel. The test was ruined; he'd have to start again.

"Over here!" Kevin yelled. He put down the pipette and stood up. Through the reagent bottles atop the lab bench, he could see Candace across the room, standing in the doorway.

"Am I coming at a bad time?" Candace asked as she approached.

"No, I was just finishing up," Kevin said. He hoped he wasn't being too transparent.

Although he was frustrated about the wasted time he'd spent on the procedure, Kevin was pleased to see Candace. During lunch that day, he'd worked up the courage to invite Candace and Melanie to his house for tea. Both had accepted with alacrity. Melanie had admitted that she'd always been curious to see what the house looked like on the inside.

The afternoon had been a big success. Undoubtedly, the key ingredient for the afternoon's success was the personalities of the two ladies. There was never a pause in the conversation. Another contributing factor had been the wine that they'd all decided upon instead of tea. As a member of the Zone's elite, Kevin was given a regular allotment of French wine which he rarely drank. Consequently, he had an impressive cellar.

The major topic of conversation had been the U.S., a favorite pastime for temporary American expatriates. Each of the three had extolled and argued the virtues of their hometown. Melanie loved New York and contended it was in a class all its own; Candace said that Pittsburgh's quality of life was rated one of the highest; and Kevin praised the intellectual stimulation of Boston. What they had purposefully avoided discussing was Kevin's emotional outburst at the commissary during lunch.

At the time, both Candace and Melanie questioned what he'd meant by being terrified of overstepping the bounds. But they didn't persist when it became clear that Kevin was overly upset and reluctant to explain. Intuitively, the women had decided it best to change the subject, at least for the time.

"I've come to see if I can drag you over to meet Mr. Horace Winchester," Candace said. "I told him about you, and he'd like to thank you in person."

"I don't know if that is a good idea," Kevin said. He could feel himself tense.

"On the contrary," Candace said. "After what you said at lunch, I think you should see the good side of what you have been able to accomplish. I'm sorry that what I said made you feel so terrible."

Candace's remark was the first reference to Kevin's lunch outburst since its occurrence. Kevin's pulse quickened.

"It wasn't your fault," he said. "I'd been upset before your comments."

"Then come meet Horace," Candace said. "His recovery is fantastic. He's doing so well, in fact, that an intensive-care nurse like me is just about unnecessary."

"I wouldn't know what to say," Kevin mumbled.

"Oh, it doesn't matter what you say," Candace said. "The man is so thankful. Just a few days ago, he was so sick he thought he was going to die. Now he feels like he's been given a new lease on life. Come on! It can't help but make you feel good."

Kevin struggled to think up a reason not to

go and then was saved by another voice. It was Melanie.

"Ah, my two favorite drinking buddies," Melanie said coming into the room. She'd caught sight of Candace and Kevin through the open door. She'd been on her way to her own lab down the hall. She was dressed in blue coveralls which had ANIMAL CENTER embroidered on the breast pocket.

"Are either of you guys hungover?" Melanie asked. "I've still got a little buzz. God, we went through two bottles of wine. Can you believe it?"

Neither Candace or Kevin responded.

Melanie looked back and forth between their faces. She sensed something was wrong.

"What is this — a wake?" she asked.

Candace smiled. She loved Melanie's outspoken irreverence. "Hardly," Candace said. "Kevin and I are at a standoff. I was just trying to talk him into going over to the hospital to meet Mr. Winchester. He's already out of bed and feeling chipper. I told him about you guys, and he'd like to meet both of you."

"I hear he owns a string of resort hotels," Melanie said with a wink. "Hey, maybe we can finagle some vouchers for complimentary drinks."

"As appreciative and as wealthy as he is, you could very well do better than that," Candace said. "The problem is that Kevin

165

doesn't want to go."

"How come, sport?" Melanie asked.

"I thought it would be a good idea for him to see the good side of what he's been able to accomplish," Candace added.

Candace caught Melanie's eye. Melanie understood Candace's motivations immediately.

"Yeah," Melanie said. "Let's get some positive feedback from a real, live patient. That should justify all this hard work and give us a boost."

"I think it will make me feel worse," Kevin said. Ever since getting back to the lab, he'd been trying to concentrate on basic research to avoid facing his fears. The ploy had worked to an extent until his curiosity made him call up the Isla Francesca graphic on his computer terminal. Playing with the data had had an effect as bad as the smoke.

Melanie put her hands on her hips. "Why?" she asked. "I don't understand."

"It's hard to explain," Kevin said evasively.

"Try me," Melanie challenged.

"Because seeing him will remind me of things I'm trying not to think about," Kevin said. "Like what happened to the other patient."

"You mean his double, the bonobo?" Melanie asked.

Kevin nodded. His face was now flushed, almost as bad as it had been at the commissary.

"You're taking this animal-rights issue even more seriously than I am," Candace remarked.

"I'm afraid it goes beyond animal rights," Kevin said.

A tense silence intervened. Melanie glanced at Candace. Candace shrugged, suggesting she was at a loss.

"Okay, enough is enough!" Melanie said with sudden resolve. She reached up, placed both hands on Kevin's shoulders, and pushed him down onto his laboratory stool.

"Up until this afternoon I thought we were just colleagues," she said. She leaned over and put her sharp-featured face close to Kevin's. "But now I feel differently. I got to know you a little bit, which I must say I appreciated, and I no longer think of you as an icy, aloof, intellectual snob. In fact I think we are friends. Am I right?"

Kevin nodded. He was forced to look up into Melanie's black, marblelike eyes.

"Friends talk to each other," Melanie said. "They communicate. They don't hide their feelings and make others feel uncomfortable. Do you know what I'm saying?"

"I think so," Kevin said. He'd never considered the idea his behavior was capable of making others uncomfortable.

"Think so?" Melanie chided. "How can I explain it so that you know so!"

Kevin swallowed. "I guess I know so."

167

Melanie rolled her eyes in frustration. "You are so evasive, it drives me bananas. But that's okay; I can deal with it. What I can't deal with is your outburst at lunch. And when I tried to ask you what's wrong, you gave some vague comment about 'overstepping the bounds' and then clammed up, unable to talk about it. You can't let this fester, whatever it is that's bothering you. It will only hurt you and impede your friendships."

Candace nodded agreement with all that Melanie had expressed.

Kevin looked back and forth between the two outspoken and tenacious women. As much as he resisted expressing his fears, at the moment he didn't think he had much choice, especially with Melanie's face inches away from his own. Not knowing how to begin he said: "I've seen smoke coming from Isla Francesca."

"What's Isla Francesca?" Candace asked.

"It's the island where the transgenic bonobos go once they reach age three," Melanie said. "So what's with smoke?"

Kevin stood and motioned for the women to follow him. He walked over to his desk. With his index finger he pointed out the window toward Isla Francesca. "I've seen the smoke three times," he said. "It's always from the same place just to the left of the limestone ridge. It's only a little curl snaking up into the sky, but it persists."

Candace squinted. She was mildly near-sighted, but for vanity reasons didn't wear glasses. "Is it the farthest island?" she asked. She thought she could just make out some brownish smudges on its spine that could have been rock. In the late-afternoon sunlight, the other islands in the chain appeared like homogeneous mounds of dark green moss.

"That's the one," Kevin said.

"So, big deal!" Melanie commented. "A couple of little fires. With all the lightning around here it's no wonder."

"That's what Bertram Edwards suggested," Kevin said. "But it can't be lightning."

"Who's Bertram Edwards?" Candace asked.

"Why can't it be lightning?" Melanie asked ignoring Candace. "Maybe there's some metal ore in that rocky ridge."

"Ever hear the expression lightning never strikes the same place twice?" Kevin questioned. "The fire is not from lightning. Besides, the smoke persisted and has never moved."

"Maybe some native people live out there," Candace said.

"GenSys was very sure that was not the case before choosing the island," Kevin said.

"Maybe some local fishermen visit," Candace suggested.

"All the locals know it is forbidden," Kevin said. "Because of the new Equatoguinean law it would be a capital offense. There's nothing out there that would be worth dying for."

"Then who started the fires?" Candace asked.

"Good God, Kevin!" Melanie exclaimed suddenly. "I'm beginning to get an idea what you're thinking. But let me tell you, it's preposterous."

"What's preposterous?" Candace asked. "Will someone clue me in?"

"Let me show you something else," Kevin said. He turned to his computer terminal and with a few keystrokes called up the graphic of the island. He explained the system to the women, and as a demonstration, brought up the location of Melanie's double. The little red light blinked just north of the escarpment very close to where his own had the day before.

"You have a double?" Candace asked. She was dumbfounded.

"Kevin and I were the guinea pigs," Melanie said. "Our doubles were the first. We had to prove that the technology really works."

"Okay, now that you women know how the locator system operates," Kevin said, "let me show you what I did an hour ago, and we'll see if we get the same disturbing result." Kevin's fingers played over the keyboard. "What I'm doing is instructing the computer to automatically locate all seventy-three of the doubles sequentially. The creatures' numbers will occur in the corner followed by the blinking light on the graphic. Now watch." Kevin clicked to start.

The system worked smoothly with only a short delay between the number appearing and then the red blinking light.

"I thought there were closer to a hundred animals," Candace said.

"There are," Kevin said. "But twenty-two of them are less than three years old. They are in the bonobo enclosure at the animal center."

"Okay," Melanie said after a few minutes of watching the computer function. "It's working just as you said. What's so disturbing?"

"Just hold on," Kevin said.

All at once the number 37 appeared but no blinking red light. After a few moments, a prompt flashed onto the screen. It said: ANIMAL NOT LOCATED: CLICK TO RECOMMENCE.

Melanie looked at Kevin. "Where's number thirty-seven?"

Kevin sighed. "What's left is in the incinerator," he said. "Number thirty-seven was Mr. Winchester's double. But that's not what I wanted to show you." Kevin clicked and the program restarted. Then it stopped again at forty-two.

"Was that Mr. Franconi's double?" Can-

171

dace asked. "The other liver transplant?"

Kevin shook his head. He pressed several keys, asking the computer the identity of forty-two. The name Warren Prescott appeared.

"So where's forty-two?" Melanie asked.

"I don't know for sure, but I know what I fear," Kevin said. Kevin clicked and again the numbers and red lights alternately flashed on the screen.

When the entire program had run its course, it had indicated that seven of the bonobo doubles were unaccounted for, not including Franconi's, which had been sacrificed.

"Is this what you found earlier?" Melanie asked.

Kevin nodded. "But it wasn't seven, it was twelve. And although some of the ones that were missing this morning are still missing, most of them have reappeared."

"I don't understand," Melanie said. "How can that be?"

"When I toured that island way back before all this started," Kevin said, "I remember seeing some caves in that limestone cliff. What I'm thinking is that our creations are going into the caves, maybe even living in them. It's the only way I can think of to explain why the grid would fail to pick them up."

Melanie brought up a hand to cover her

mouth. Her eyes reflected a flicker of horror and dismay.

Candace saw Melanie's reaction. "Hey, come on, guys," she pleaded. "What's wrong? What are you thinking?"

Melanie lowered her hand. Her eyes were locked on Kevin's. "What Kevin was referring to when he said he was terrified he'd overstepped the bounds," she explained in a slow, deliberate voice, "was the fear that he'd created a human."

"You're not serious!" Candace exclaimed, but a glance at Kevin and then at Melanie indicated that she was.

For a full minute no one spoke.

Finally Kevin broke the silence. "I'm not suggesting a real human being in the guise of an ape," Kevin said finally. "I'm suggesting that I've inadvertently created a kind of protohuman. Maybe something akin to our distant ancestral forebears who spontaneously appeared in nature from apelike animals four or five million years ago. Maybe back then the critical mutations responsible for the change occurred in the developmental genes I've subsequently learned are on the short arm of chromosome six."

Candace found herself blankly gazing out the window, while her mind replayed the scene two days previous in the OR when the bonobo was about to be inducted under anesthesia. He'd made curious humanlike sounds and tried desperately to keep his hands free so that he could continue to make the same wild gesture. He'd been constantly opening and closing his fingers and then sweeping his hands away from his body.

"You're talking about some early hominidlike creature, something on the order of Homo erectus," Melanie said. "It's true we noticed the infant transgenic bonobos tended to walk upright more than their mothers. At the time we just thought it was cute."

"Not so early a hominid as not to have used fire," Kevin said. "Only true early man has used fire. And that's what I'm worried I've been seeing on the island: campfires."

"So, to put it bluntly," Candace said, turning away from the window. "We've got a bunch of cavemen out there like back in prehistoric time."

"Something like that," Kevin said. As he'd expected the women were aghast. Strangely, he actually felt a little better now that he'd voiced his anxieties.

"What are we going to do?" Candace demanded. "I'm certainly not going to be involved with sacrificing any more until this is resolved one way or the other. I was having a hard enough time dealing with the situation when I thought the victim was an ape."

"Wait a sec," Melanie said. She spread her hands with fingers apart. Her eyes were blazing anew. "Maybe we're jumping to conclusions here. There's no proof of all this. Everything we've been talking about is circumstantial at best."

"True, but there's more," Kevin said. He turned back to the computer and instructed it to display the locations of all the bonobos on the island simultaneously. Within seconds, two red splotches began pulsating. One was in the location where Melanie's double had been. The other was north of the lake. Kevin looked up at Melanie. "What does this data suggest to you?"

"It suggests there are two groups," she said. "Do you think it is permanent?"

"It was the same earlier," Kevin said. "I think it is a real phenomenon. Even Bertram mentioned it. That's not typical of bonobos. They get along in larger social groups than chimps, plus these are all relatively young animals. They should all be in one group."

Melanie nodded. Over the previous five years she'd learned a lot about bonobo behavior.

"And there is something else more upsetting," Kevin said. "Bertram told me one of the bonobos killed one of the pygmies on the retrieval of Winchester's double. It wasn't an accident. The bonobo aggressively threw a rock. That kind of aggression is more associated with human behavior than with bonobos."

"I'd have to agree," Melanie said. "But it's

still circumstantial. All of it."

"Circumstantial or not," Candace said, "I'm not going to have it on my conscience."

"I feel the same way," Melanie said. "I've spent today getting two new female bonobos started on the egg-collection protocol. I'm not going to proceed until we find out if this wild idea about these possible protohumans is valid or not."

"That's not going to be easy," Kevin said. "To prove it, somebody has to go to the island. The trouble is there are only two people who can authorize a visit: Bertram Edwards or Siegfried Spallek. I already tried to talk with Bertram, and even though I brought up the issue about the smoke, he made it very clear that no one was allowed near the island except for a pygmy who brings supplementary food."

"Did you tell him what you are worried about?" Melanie asked.

"Not in so many words," Kevin said. "But he knew. I'm sure of it. He wasn't interested. The problem is that he and Siegfried have been included in the project bonuses. Consequently, they are going to make damn sure nothing threatens it. I'm afraid they're venal enough not to care what's on the island. And on top of their venality we have to weigh in Siegfried's sociopathy."

"Is he that bad?" Candace asked. "I'd heard rumors."

"Whatever you heard, it's ten times worse," Melanie said. "He's a major sleazeball. To give you an example, he executed some impoverished Equatoguinean men because they'd been caught poaching in the Zone, where he likes to hunt."

"He killed them himself?" Candace questioned with shock and revulsion.

"Not by himself," Melanie said. "He had the men tried in a kangaroo court here in Cogo. Then they were executed by a handful of Equatoguinean soldiers at the soccer field."

"And to add insult to injury," Kevin said, "he uses the skulls as bowls for odds and ends on his desk."

"Sorry I asked," Candace said with a shiver.

"What about Dr. Lyons?" Melanie asked.

Kevin laughed. "Forget it. He's more venal than Bertram. This whole operation is his baby. I tried to talk to him about the smoke, too. He was even less receptive. Claimed it was my imagination. Frankly I don't trust him, although I have to give him credit for being generous with bonuses and stocks. He's cleverly given everyone connected with the project a real stake in the venture, particularly Bertram and Siegfried."

"So, that leaves it all up to us," Melanie said. "Let's find out if it's your imagination or not. What do you say the three of us take a quick trip to Isla Francesca?"

"You're joking," Kevin said. "It's a capital offense without authorization."

"It's a capital offense for locals," Melanie said. "That can't apply to us. In our case, Siegfried has to answer to GenSys."

"Bertram specifically forbade visits," Kevin said. "I offered to go by myself, and he said no."

"Well, big deal," Melanie said. "So he gets mad. What is he going to do, fire us? I've been here long enough so that I don't think that would be half bad. Besides, they can't do without you. That's the reality."

"Do you think it might be dangerous?" Candace asked.

"Bonobos are peaceful creatures," Melanie said. "Much more so than chimps, and chimps aren't dangerous unless you corner them."

"What about the man who was killed?" Candace said.

"That was during a retrieval," Kevin said. "They had to get close enough to shoot a dart gun. Also, it was the fourth retrieval."

"All we want to do is observe," Melanie said.

"Okay, how do we get there?" Candace asked.

"Drive, I guess," Melanie said. "That's how they go when they do a release or a retrieval. There must be some kind of bridge."

"There's a road that goes east along the

coast," Kevin said. "It's paved to the native village then it becomes a track. That's how I went on the visit to the island before we started the program. For a hundred feet or so the island and the mainland are only separated by a channel thirty feet wide. Back then there was a wire suspension bridge stretched between two mahogany trees."

"Maybe we can view the animals without even going across," Candace said. "Let's do it."

"You ladies are fearless," Kevin remarked.

"Hardly," Melanie said. "But I don't see any problem with driving up there and checking the situation out. Once we know what we're dealing with, we can make a better decision about what we want to do."

"When do you want to do this?" Kevin questioned.

"I'd say now," Melanie replied. She glanced at her watch. "There's no better time. Ninety percent of the population of the town is either at the waterfront chickee bar, splashing around in the pool, or sweating buckets at the athletic center."

Kevin sighed, let his arms fall limply to his sides, and capitulated. "Whose car should we take?" he asked.

"Yours," Melanie said without hesitation. "Mine doesn't even have four-wheel drive."

As the trio descended the stairs and made their way across the sweltering blacktop of the parking area, Kevin had the gnawing sense they were making a mistake. But in the face of the women's resolve, he felt reluctant to voice his reservations.

On the east exit of the town, they passed the athletic center's tennis courts, which were chockful of players. Between the humidity and heat, the players looked as drenched as if they'd jumped into a swimming pool with their tennis outfits on.

Kevin drove. Melanie sat in the front passenger seat, while Candace sat in the back. The windows were all open, since the temperature had fallen into the high eighties. The sun was low in the west, directly behind them and peeking in and out of clouds along the horizon.

Just beyond the soccer field the vegetation closed in around the road. Brightly colored birds flitted in and out of the deepening shadows. Large insects annihilated themselves against the windshield like miniature kamikaze pilots.

"The jungle looks dense," Candace said. She'd never traveled east from the town.

"You have no idea," Kevin said. When he'd first arrived he'd tried to take some hikes in the area, but with the profusion of vines and creepers, it was all but impossible without a machete.

"I just had a thought about the aggression issue," Melanie said. "The passivity of bonobo society is generally attributed to its matriarchal character. Because of the skewed demand for male doubles, our program has a population that's mostly male. There has to be a lot of competition for the few females."

"That's a good point," Kevin agreed. He wondered why Bertram hadn't thought of it.

"Sounds like my type of place," Candace joked. "Maybe I should book Isla Francesca instead of Club Med on my next vacation."

Melanie laughed. "Let's go together," she said.

They passed a number of Equatoguineans on their way home from work in Cogo. Most of the women carried jugs and parcels on top of their heads. The men were generally empty-handed.

"It's a strange culture," Melanie commented. "The women do the lion's share of the work: growing the food, carrying the water, raising the kids, cooking the meals, taking care of the house."

"What do the men do?" Candace asked.

"Sit around and discuss metaphysics," Melanie said.

"I just had an idea," Kevin said. "I don't know why I didn't think of it before. Maybe we should talk to the pygmy who takes out the food to the island first and hear what he has to say."

"Sounds like a good idea to me," Melanie said. "Do you know his name?"

"Alphonse Kimba," Kevin said.

When they reached the native village, they pulled to a stop in front of the busy general store and got out. Kevin went inside to inquire after the pygmy.

"This place is almost too charming," Candace said as she looked around the neighborhood. "It looks African but like something you'd see in Disneyland."

GenSys had built the village with the cooperation of the Equatoguinean Minister of the Interior. The homes were circular, white-washed mud brick with thatched roofs. Corrals for domestic animals were made of reed mats lashed to wooden stakes. The structures appeared traditional, but every one of them was new and spotless. They also had electricity and running water. Buried underground were powerlines and modern sewers.

Kevin returned quickly. "No problem," he said. "He lives close by. Come on, we'll walk."

The village was alive with men, women, and children. Traditional cooking fires were in the process of being lit. Everyone acted happy and friendly from having been recently freed from the captivity of the interminable rainy season.

Alphonse Kimba was less than five feet tall with skin as black as onyx. A constant smile dominated his wide, flat face as he welcomed his unexpected visitors. He tried to introduce his wife and child, but they were shy and shrunk back into the shadows.

Alphonse invited his guests to sit on a reed mat. He then got four glasses and poured a dollop of clear fluid into each from an old green bottle that had at one time contained motor oil.

His visitors warily swirled the fluid. They didn't want to seem ungrateful, but they were reluctant to drink.

"Alcohol?" Kevin asked.

"Oh, yes!" Alphonse said. His smile broadened. "It is lotoko from corn. Very good! I bring it from my home in Lomako." He sipped with intense enjoyment. In contrast to the Equatoguineans, Alphonse's English was accented with French, not Spanish. He was a member of the Mongandu people from Zaire. He'd been brought to the Zone with the first shipment of bonobos.

Since the drink contained alcohol, which would presumably kill potential microorganisms, the guests cautiously tasted the brew. All of them made faces in spite of good intentions not to do so. The drink was powerfully pungent.

Kevin explained that they had come to ask about the bonobos on the island. He didn't mention his concern that their number included a strain of protohumans. He asked only if Alphonse thought they were acting like bonobos back in his home province in Zaire.

"They are all very young," Alphonse said. "So they are very unruly and wild."

"Do you go on the island often?" Kevin asked.

"No, I am forbidden," Alphonse said. "Only when we retrieve or release, and only then with Dr. Edwards."

"How do you get the extra food to the island?" Melanie asked.

"There is a small float," Alphonse said. "I pull it across the water with a rope, then pull it back."

"Are the bonobos aggressive with the food or do they share?" Melanie asked.

"Very aggressive," Alphonse said. "They fight like crazy, especially for the fruit. I also saw one kill a monkey."

"Why?" Kevin asked.

"I think to eat," Alphonse said. "He carried it away after the food I brought was all gone."

"That sounds more like a chimp," Melanie said to Kevin.

Kevin nodded. "Where on the island have the retrievals taken place?" he asked.

"All have been on this side of the lake and stream," Alphonse said.

"None have been over by the cliff?" Kevin asked.

"No, never," Alphonse said.

"How do you get to the island for the retrieval?" Kevin asked. "Does everybody use the float?"

Alphonse laughed heartily. He had to dry his eyes with his knuckle. "The float is too small. We'd all be supper for the crocs. We use the bridge."

"Why don't you use the bridge for the food?" Melanie asked.

"Because Dr. Edwards has to make the bridge grow," Alphonse said.

"Grow?" Melanie questioned.

"Yes," Alphonse said.

The three guests exchanged glances. They were confused.

"Have you seen any fire on the island?" Kevin asked, changing the subject.

"No fire," Alphonse said. "But I've seen smoke."

"And what did you think?" Kevin asked.

"Me?" Alphonse questioned. "I didn't think anything."

"Have you ever seen one of the bonobos do this?" Candace asked. She opened and closed her fingers then swept her hand away from her body in imitation of the bonobo in the operating room.

"Yes," Alphonse said. "Many do that when they finish dividing up the food."

"How about noise?" Melanie asked. "Do they make a lot of sounds?"

"A lot," Alphonse said.

"Like the bonobos back in Zaire?" Kevin asked.

"More," Alphonse said. "But back in Zaire I don't see the same bonobos so often as I do here, and I don't feed them. Back home they get their own food in the jungle."

"What kind of noise do they make?" Candace asked. "Can you give us an example."

Alphonse laughed self-consciously. He glanced around at his wife to make sure she wasn't listening. Then he softly vocalized: "Eeee, ba da, loo loo, tad tat." He laughed again. He was embarrassed.

"Do they hoot like chimps?" Melanie asked.

"Some," Alphonse said.

The guests looked at each other. They'd run out of questions for the moment. Kevin got up. The women did the same. They thanked Alphonse for his hospitality and handed back their unfinished drinks. If Alphonse was offended, he didn't show it. His smile didn't falter.

"There's one other thing," Alphonse said just before his guests departed. "The bonobos on the island like to show off. Whenever they come for the food, they make themselves stand up."

"All the time?" Kevin asked.

"Mostly," Alphonse said.

The group walked back through the village to the car. They didn't talk until Kevin had started the motor.

"Well, what do you guys think?" Kevin asked. "Should we continue? The sun's already set."

"I vote yes," Melanie said. "We've come this far."

"I agree," Candace said. "I'm curious to see this bridge that grows."

Melanie laughed. "Me, too. What a charming fellow."

Kevin drove away from the store, which was now busier than earlier. But he wasn't sure of his direction. The road into the village had simply expanded into the parking area for the store, and there was no indication of the track leading further east. To find it, he had to cruise the parking lot's perimeter.

Once on the track, they were impressed with how much easier it had been to travel on the improved road. The track was narrow, bumpy, and muddy. Grass about three feet tall grew down the median strip. Frequently branches stretched from one side to the other, slapping against the windshield and poking through the open windows. To avoid being hit by the snapping branches, they had to raise the windows. Kevin clicked on the air conditioner and the lights. The beams reflected off the surrounding vegetation and gave the impression of driving through a tunnel.

"How far do we have to go on this cow path?" Melanie asked.

"Only three or four miles," Kevin said.

"It's a good thing we have four-wheel drive," Candace remarked. She was holding on tightly to the overhead strap and still bouncing around. The seat belt wasn't helping. "The last thing I'd want to do is get stuck out here." She glanced out the side window at the inky black jungle and shivered. It was eerie. She couldn't see a thing despite patches of luminous sky above. And then there was the noise. Just during their short visit with Alphonse, the night creatures of the jungle had commenced their loud and monotonous chorus.

"What did you make of the things Alphonse said?" Kevin asked finally.

"I'd say the jury is still out," Melanie said. "But they're certainly deliberating."

"I think his comment about the bonobos being bipedal when they come to get the food is very disturbing," Kevin said. "The circumstantial evidence is adding up."

"The suggestion that they are communicating impressed me," Candace said.

"Yeah, but chimps and gorillas have been taught sign language," Melanie said. "And we know bonobos are more bipedal than any other apes. What impressed me was the aggressive behavior, although I stand by my idea that it might be from our mistake not to have produced more females to maintain the balance."

"Can chimps make those sounds that Alphonse imitated?" Candace asked.

"I don't think so," Kevin said. "And that's an important point. It suggests maybe their larynges are different."

"Do chimps really kill monkeys?" Candace asked.

"They do occasionally," Melanie said. "But I've never heard of a bonobo doing so."

"Hang on!" Kevin shouted as he braked.

The car lurched over a log strewn across the track.

"Are you okay?" he asked Candace, while glancing up into the rearview mirror.

"No problem," Candace said, although she'd been severely jolted. Luckily the seat belt had worked, and it had kept her head from hitting the roof.

Kevin slowed considerably for fear of encountering another log. Fifteen minutes later, they entered a clearing which marked the termination of the track. Kevin came to a halt. Directly ahead the headlight beams washed the front of a single-story cinder-block building with an overhead garage door.

"Is this it?" Melanie questioned.

"I guess," Kevin said. "The building is new to me."

Kevin switched off the lights and the engine. With the clearing open to the sky the level of illumination was adequate. For a moment no one moved.

"What's the story?" Kevin asked. "Are we going to check it out or what?"

"Might as well," Melanie said. "We've come this far." She opened her door and got out. Kevin did the same.

"I think I'll stay in the car," Candace said.

Kevin went to the building and tried the door. It was locked. He shrugged. "I can't imagine what's in there." Kevin slapped a mosquito on his forehead.

"How do we get to the island?" Melanie asked.

Kevin pointed to the right. "There's a track over there. It's only about fifty yards to the water's edge."

Melanie glanced up at the sky. It was a pale lavender. "It's going to be dark pretty soon. Do you have a flashlight in the car?"

"I think so," Kevin said. "More important, I have some mosquito spray. We're going to get eaten alive out here unless we use it."

They went back to the car. Just as they arrived, Candace climbed out.

"I can't stay in here by myself," she said. "It's too spooky."

Kevin got the mosquito spray. While the women doused themselves, he searched for the flashlight. He found it in the glove compartment.

After spraying himself, Kevin motioned for the women to follow him. "Stay close," he said. "The crocodiles and the hippos come out of the water at night."

"Is he joking?" Candace asked Melanie.

"I don't think so," Melanie said.

As soon as they entered the path, the illumination fell considerably although it was still light enough to walk without the flashlight. Kevin led while the two women crowded behind. The closer they got to the water the louder the chorus of insects and frogs became.

"How did I get myself into this?" Candace questioned. "I'm no outdoors person. I can't even conceive of a crocodile or a hippo outside of a zoo. Hell, any bug bigger than my thumbnail terrifies me, and spiders, forget it."

All of the sudden, there was a crashing noise off to the left. Candace let out a muffled scream, as she grabbed Melanie who then did likewise. Kevin whimpered and switched on the light. He pointed the beam in the direction of the noise, but it only penetrated a few feet.

"What was that?" Candace demanded when she could find her voice.

"Probably a duiker," Kevin said. "They're a small breed of antelope."

"Antelope or elephant," Candace said. "It scared me."

"It scared me, too," Kevin said. "Maybe we should go back and return in the daytime."

"We've come all this way for crissake," Melanie said. "We're there. I can hear the water."

For a moment no one moved. Sure enough, they could hear water lapping against the shore.

"What happened to all the night creatures?" Candace asked.

"Good question," Kevin said. "The antelope must have scared them as well."

"Turn the light off," Melanie said.

As soon as Kevin did, they all could see the shimmering surface of the water through the vegetation. It looked like liquid silver.

Melanie led the way as the chorus of night creatures recommenced. The path opened up into another clearing at the edge of the river. In the middle of the clearing was a dark object almost the size of the garage back where they'd left the car. Kevin walked up to it. It wasn't hard to figure out what it was: it was the bridge.

"It's a telescoping mechanism," Kevin said. "That's why Alphonse said that it could grow."

About thirty feet across the water was Isla Francesca. In the fading light, its dense vegetation appeared midnight-blue. Directly across from the telescoping bridge was a concrete structure that served as the support for the bridge when it was extended. Beyond that was an expansive clearing that extended to the east.

"Try extending the bridge," Melanie suggested.

Kevin switched on the flashlight. He found the control panel. There were two buttons: one red, the other green. He pushed the red one. When nothing happened, he pushed the green. When there still wasn't a reaction, he noticed a keyhole with the slot aligned with OFF.

"You need a key," he called.

Melanie and Candace had walked over to the water's edge.

"There's a bit of current," Melanie said. Leaves and other debris floated by slowly.

Candace looked up. The top branches of some of the trees that lined either bank almost touched. "Why do the creatures stay on the island?" she asked.

"Apes and monkeys don't go in the water, particularly deep water," Melanie explained. "That's why zoos only need a moat for their primate exhibits."

"What about crossing in the trees?" Candace asked.

Kevin joined the women at the riverbank. "The bonobos are relatively heavy fellows," he explained, "particularly ours. Most of them are already over a hundred pounds, and the branches up there aren't nearly strong enough to support their weight. Back before we put the first animals on the island, there were a couple of questionable places so those trees were cut down. But colobus monkeys still go back and forth."

"What are all those square objects in the field?" Melanie asked.

Kevin shined the flashlight. Its beam wasn't strong enough to make much difference at that distance. He turned it off and squinted in the half light. "They look like transport cages from the animal center," he said.

"I wonder what they are doing out there?" Melanie asked. "There're so many of them."

"No idea," Kevin said.

"How can we get some of the bonobos to appear?" Candace asked.

"By this time they're probably settling down for the night," Kevin said. "I doubt if we can."

"What about the float?" Melanie asked. "The mechanism that pulls it across must be like a clothesline. If it makes noise, they might hear it. It would be like a dinner bell and might bring them around."

"Guess it's worth a try," Kevin said. He glanced up and down the water's edge. "Trouble is, we don't have any idea where the float may be."

"I can't imagine it would be far," Melanie said. "You go east, I'll go west."

Kevin and Melanie walked in opposite directions. Candace stayed were she was, wishing she were back in her room in the hospital quarters.

"Here it is!" Melanie called out. She'd followed a path in the dense foliage for a short distance before coming to a pulley attached to a thick tree. A heavy rope hung around the pulley. One end disappeared into the water. The other end was tied to a four-foot square float nestled against the shore.

Kevin and Candace joined her. Kevin

shined the flashlight across to the island. On the other side a similar pulley was attached to a similar tree.

Kevin handed the flashlight to Melanie and grasped the rope that drooped into the water. When he pulled, he could see the pulley on the other side swing out from the trunk of the tree.

Kevin pulled on the rope hand over hand. The pulleys complained bitterly with high-pitched squeaking noises. The float immediately moved away from the shore on its way to the other side.

"This might work," Kevin said. While he pulled, Melanie swept the other shore with the flashlight beam. When the float was halfway across, there was a loud splash to their right as a large object dropped into the water from the island.

Melanie shined the light in the direction of the splash. Two glowing slits of light reflected back from the surface of the water. Peering at them was a large crocodile.

"Good lord!" Candace said as she stepped back from the water.

"It's okay," Kevin said. He let go of the rope, reached down and picked up a stout stick. He threw the stick at the croc. With another loud splash the crocodile disappeared beneath the water.

"Oh, great!" Candace said. "Now we have no idea where he is."

"He's gone," Kevin said. "They're not dangerous unless you're in the water or they're very hungry."

"Who's to say he's not hungry?" Candace commented.

"There's plenty for them to eat out here," Kevin said as he picked up the rope and recommenced pulling. When the float reached the other side, he switched ropes and started pulling it back.

"Ah, it's too late," he said. "This isn't going to work. The closest nesting area we saw on the computer graphic is over a mile away. We'll have to try this in the daytime."

No sooner had these words escaped from his mouth when the night was shattered by a number of fearsome screams. At the same time, there was wild commotion in the bushes on the island as if a stampeding elephant was about to appear.

Kevin dropped the rope. Both Candace and Melanie fled back along the path a few steps before stopping. With pulses pounding they froze, waiting for another scream. With a shaking hand, Melanie shined the flashlight at the area where the commotion had occurred. Everything was still. Not a leaf moved.

Ten tense seconds passed that seemed more like ten minutes. The group strained their ears to pick up the slightest sound. There was nothing but utter silence. All the night creatures had fallen silent. It was as if the entire jungle was waiting for a catastrophe.

"What in heaven's name was that?" Melanie asked finally.

"I'm not sure I want to find out," Candace said. "Let's get out of here."

"It must have been a couple of the bonobos," Kevin said. He reached out and grabbed the rope. The float was being buffeted in midstream. He quickly hauled it in.

"I think Candace is right," Melanie said. "It's gotten too dark to see much even if they did appear. I'm spooked. Let's go!"

"You'll not get an argument from me," Kevin said as he made his way over to the women. "I don't know what we're doing here at this hour. We'll come back in the daylight."

They hurried along the path to the clearing as best they could. Melanie led with the flashlight. Candace was behind her, holding on to her blouse. Kevin brought up the rear.

"It would be great to get a key for this bridge," Kevin said as they passed the structure.

"And how do you propose to do that?" Melanie asked.

"Borrow Bertram's," Kevin said.

"But you told us he forbid anyone to go to the island," Melanie said. "He's certainly not going to lend the key."

"We'll have to borrow it without his knowledge," Kevin said.

"Oh, yeah, sure," Melanie said sarcastically.

They entered the tunnel-like path leading up to the car. Halfway to the parking area Melanie said: "God, it's dark. Am I holding the light okay for you guys?"

"It's fine," Candace said.

Melanie slowed then stopped.

"What's the matter?" Kevin asked.

"There's something strange," she said. She cocked her head to the side, listening.

"Now don't get me scared," Candace warned.

"The frogs and crickets haven't restarted their racket," Melanie said.

In the next instant all hell broke loose. A loud, repetitive stuttering noise splintered the jungle stillness. Branches, twigs, and leaves rained down on the group. Kevin recognized the noise and reacted by reflex. Extending his arms, he literally tackled the women so that all three fell to the moist insect-infested earth.

The reason Kevin recognized the sound was because he once had inadvertently witnessed the Equatoguinean soldiers practicing. The noise was the sound of a machine gun.

CHAPTER 10

"Excuse me, Laurie," Cheryl Myers said, standing in the doorway to Laurie's office. Cheryl was one of the forensic investigators. "We just received this overnight package, and I thought you might want it right away."

Laurie stood up and took the parcel. She was curious about what it could be. She looked at the label to find out the sender. It was CNN.

"Thanks, Cheryl," Laurie said. She was perplexed. She had no idea for the moment what CNN could have sent her.

"I see Dr. Mehta is not in," Cheryl said. "I brought up a chart for her that came in from University Hospital. Should I put it on her desk?" Dr. Riva Mehta was Laurie's office mate. They'd shared the space since both had started at the medical examiner's office six and a half years previously.

"Sure," Laurie said, preoccupied with her parcel. She got her finger under the flap and pulled it open. Inside was a videotape. Laurie looked at the label. It said: CARLO FRAN-CONI SHOOTING, MARCH 3, 1997.

After having finished her final autopsy that

199

morning, Laurie had been ensconced in her office, trying to complete some of the twenty-odd cases that she had pending. She'd been busy reviewing microscopic slides, laboratory results, hospital records, and police reports, and for several hours had not thought of the Franconi business. The arrival of the tape brought it all back. Unfortunately the video was meaningless without the body.

Laurie tossed the tape into her briefcase and tried to get back to work. But after fifteen minutes of wasted effort, she turned the light off under her microscope. She couldn't concentrate. Her mind kept toying with the baffling question of how the body had disappeared. It was as if it had been an amazing magic trick. One minute the body was safely stored in compartment one eleven and viewed by three employees, then poof, it was gone. There had to be an explanation, but try as she might, Laurie could not fathom it.

Laurie decided to head down to the basement to visit the mortuary office. She'd expected at least one tech to be available, but when she arrived the room was unoccupied. Undaunted, Laurie went over to the large, leather-bound log. Flipping the page, she looked for the entries that Mike Passano had shown her the previous night. She found them without difficulty. Taking a pencil from a collection in a coffee mug and a sheet of scratch paper, Laurie wrote down the names and accession numbers of the two bodies that had come in during the night shift: Dorothy Kline #101455 and Frank Gleason #100385. She also wrote down the names of the two funeral homes: Spoletto in Ozone Park, New York, and the Dickson in Summit, New Jersey.

Laurie was about to leave when her eye caught the large Rolodex on the corner of the desk. She decided to call each home. After identifying herself, she asked to speak to the managers.

What had sparked her interest in telephoning was the outside chance that either one of the pickups could have been bogus. She thought the chances were slim, since the night tech, Mike Passano, had said the homes had called before coming and presumably he was familiar with the people.

As Laurie expected, the pickups indeed were legitimate, both managers attesting to the fact that the bodies had come in to their respective homes and were at that time on view.

Laurie went back to the logbook and looked again at the names of the two arrivals. To be complete, she copied them down along with their accession numbers. The names were familiar to her, since she'd assigned them as autopsies the following morning to Paul Plodgett. But she wasn't as interested in the arrivals as the departures. The arrivals had come in with longtime ME employees, whereas the bodies that had gone out had done so with strangers.

Feeling frustrated, Laurie drummed her pencil on the desk surface. She was sure she had to be missing something. Once again, her eye caught the Rolodex which was open to the Spoletto Funeral Home. In the very back of Laurie's mind, the name made a hazy association. For a moment, she struggled with her memory. Why was that name familiar? Then she remembered. It had been during the Cerino affair. A man had been murdered in the Spoletto Funeral Home on orders from Paul Cerino, Franconi's predecessor.

Laurie pocketed her memo, pushed away from the desk and returned to the fifth floor. She walked directly to Jack's office. The door was ajar. She knocked on the jamb. Both Jack and Chet looked up from their respective labors.

"I had a thought," Laurie said to Jack.

"Just one?" Jack quipped.

Laurie threw her pencil at him, which he easily evaded. She plopped down in the chair to his right and told him about the mob connection with the Spoletto Funeral Home.

"Good grief, Laurie," Jack complained. "Just because there is a mob hit in a funeral home, doesn't mean that it is mob-connected."

"You don't think so?" Laurie asked. Jack didn't have to answer. She could see by his expression. And, now that she thought about her idea, she understood it was a ridiculous notion. She'd been grabbing for straws.

"Besides," Jack said. "Why won't you just leave this alone?"

"I told you," Laurie said. "It's a personal thing."

"Maybe I can channel your efforts into a more positive direction," Jack said. He motioned toward his microscope. "Take a look at a frozen section. Tell me what you think."

Laurie got up from the chair and leaned over the microscope. "What is this, the shotgun entrance wound?" she asked.

"Just as sharp as usual," Jack commented. "You're right on the money."

"Well, it's not a hard call," Laurie said. "I'd say the muzzle was within inches of the skin."

"My opinion exactly," Jack said. "Anything else?"

"My gosh, there's absolutely no extravasation of blood!" Laurie said. "None at all, so this had to have been a postmortem wound." She raised her head and looked at Jack. She was amazed. She'd assumed it had been the mortal wound.

"Ah, the power of modern science," Jack commented. "This floater you foisted on me is turning into a bastard of a case."

"Hey, you volunteered," Laurie said.

"I'm teasing," Jack said. "I'm glad I got the case. The shotgun wounds were definitely postmortem, so was the decapitation and removal of the hands. Of course the propeller injuries were, too."

"What was the cause of death?" Laurie asked.

"Two other gunshot wounds," Jack said. "One through the base of the neck." He pointed to an area just above his right collarbone. "And another in the left side that shattered the tenth rib. The irony was that both slugs ended up in the mass of shotgun pellets in the right upper abdominal area and were difficult to be seen on the X ray."

"Now that's a first," Laurie said. "Bullets hidden by shotgun pellets. Amazing! The beauty of this job is that you see new things every day."

"The best is yet to come," Jack said.

"This is a 'beaut,' " Chet said. He'd been listening to the conversation. "It'll be perfect for one of the forensic pathology dinner seminars."

"I think the shotgun blasts were an attempt to shield the victim's identity as much as the decapitation and removal of the hands," Jack said.

"In what way?" Laurie asked.

"I believe this patient had had a liver transplant," Jack said. "And not that long ago. The killer must have understood that such a procedure put the patient in a relatively small group, and hence jeopardized the chances of hiding the victim's identity."

"Was there much liver left?" Laurie asked.

"Very little," Jack said. "Most of it was destroyed by the shotgun injury."

"And the fish helped," Chet said.

Laurie winced.

"But I was able to find some liver tissue," Jack said. "We'll use that to corroborate the transplant. As we speak, Ted Lynch up in DNA is running a DQ alpha. We'll have the results in an hour or so. But for me the clincher was the sutures in the vena cava and the hepatic artery."

"What's a DQ alpha?" Laurie asked.

Jack laughed. "Makes me feel better that you don't know," he said, "because I had to ask Ted the same question. He told me it is a convenient and rapid DNA marker for differentiating two individuals. It compares the DQ region of the histocompatibility complex on chromosome six."

"What about the portal vein?" Laurie asked. "Were there sutures in it as well?"

"Unfortunately, the portal vein was pretty much gone," Jack said. "Along with a lot of the intestines."

"Well," Laurie said. "This should all make identification rather easy."

"My thought exactly," Jack said. "I've already got Bart Arnold hot on the trail. He's been in contact with the national organ procurement organization UNOS. He's also in the process of calling all the centers actively doing liver transplants, especially here in the city."

"That's a small list," Laurie said. "Good job, Jack."

Jack's face reddened slightly, and Laurie was touched. She thought he was immune to such compliments.

"What about the bullets?" Laurie asked. "Same gun?"

"We've packed them off to the police lab for ballistics," Jack said. "It was hard to say if they came from the same gun or not because of their distortion. One of them made direct contact with the tenth rib and was flattened. Even the second one wasn't in good shape. I think it grazed the vertebral column."

"What calibre?" Laurie asked.

"Couldn't tell from mere observation," Jack said.

"What did Vinnie say?" Laurie asked. "He's become pretty good at guessing."

"Vinnie's worthless today," Jack said. "He's been in the worst mood I've ever seen him in. I asked him what he thought, but he wouldn't say. He told me it was my job, and that he wasn't paid enough to be giving his opinions all the time."

"You know, I had a case similar to this back during that awful Cerino affair," Laurie said. She stared off and for a moment, her eyes glazed over. "The victim was a secretary of the doctor who was involved with the conspiracy. Of course, she'd not had a liver transplant, but the head and the hands were gone, and I did make the indentification because of her surgical history."

"Someday you'll have to tell me that whole grisly story," Jack said. "You keep dropping tantalizing bits and pieces."

Laurie sighed. "I wish I could just forget the whole thing. It still gives me nightmares."

Raymond glanced at his watch as he opened the Fifth Avenue door to Dr. Daniel Levitz's office. It was two forty-five. Raymond had called the doctor three times starting just after eleven A.M., without success. On each occasion, the receptionist had promised Dr. Levitz would phone back, but he hadn't. In his agitated state, Raymond found the discourtesy aggravating. Since Dr. Levitz's office was just around the corner from Raymond's apartment, Raymond thought it was better to walk over than sit by the phone.

"Dr. Raymond Lyons," Raymond said with authority to the receptionist. "I'm here to see Dr. Levitz."

"Yes, Dr. Lyons," the receptionist said. She had the same cultivated, matronly look as Dr. Anderson's receptionist. "I don't have you down on my appointment sheet. Is the doctor expecting you?"

"Not exactly," Raymond said.

"Well, I'll let the doctor know you are here," the receptionist said noncommitally.

Raymond took a seat in the crowded waiting room. He picked up one of the usual doctor waiting-room magazines and flipped the pages without focusing on the images. His agitation was becoming tinged with irritation, and he began to wonder if it had been a bad decision to come to Dr. Levitz's office.

The job of checking on the first of the other two transplant patients had been easy. With one phone call Raymond had spoken with the recruiting doctor in Dallas, Texas. The doctor had assured Raymond that his kidney-transplant patient, a prominent local businessman, was doing superbly and was in no way a possible candidate for an autopsy. Before hanging up the doctor had promised Raymond to inform him if the situation were ever to change.

But with Dr. Levitz's failure to return Raymond's phone call, Raymond had not been able to check on the last case. It was frustrating and anxiety-producing.

Raymond's eyes roamed the room. It was as sumptuously appointed as Dr. Anderson's, with original oils, deep burgundy-colored walls, and oriental carpets. The patients patiently waiting were all obviously well-to-do as evidenced by their clothes, bearing, and jewels.

As the minutes ticked by, Raymond found his irritation mounting. What was adding insult to injury at the moment was Dr. Levitz's obvious success. It reminded Raymond of the absurdity of his own medical license being in legal limbo just because he'd gotten caught padding his Medicare claims. But here was Dr. Levitz working away in all this splendor with at least part of his receipts coming from taking care of a number of crime families. Obviously, it all represented dirty money. And on top of that Raymond was sure Levitz padded his Medicare claims. Hell, everybody did.

A nurse appeared and cleared her throat. Expectantly, Raymond moved to the edge of his seat. But the nurse called out another name. While the summoned patient got up, replaced his magazine, and disappeared into the bowels of the office, Raymond slouched back against the sofa and fumed. Being at the mercy of such people made Raymond long for financial security all the more. With this current "doubles" program he was so close. He couldn't let the whole enterprise crumble for some stupid, unexpected, easily remedied reason.

It was three-fifteen when finally Raymond was ushered into Daniel Levitz's inner sanctum. Levitz was a small, balding man with multiple nervous tics. He had a mustache but it was sparse and decidedly unmanly. Raymond had always wondered what it was about the man that apparently inspired confidence in so many patients.

"It's been one of those days," Daniel said by way of explanation. "I didn't expect you to drop by."

"I hadn't planned on it myself," Raymond said. "But when you didn't return my calls, I didn't think I had a choice."

"Calls?" Daniel questioned. "I didn't get any calls from you. I'll have to have another talk with that receptionist of mine. Good help is so difficult to come by these days."

Raymond was tempted to tell Daniel to cut the bull, but he resisted. After all, he was finally talking to the man, and turning the meeting into a confrontation wouldn't solve anything. Besides, as irritating as Daniel Levitz could be, he was also Raymond's most successful recruit. He had signed up twelve clients for the program as well as four doctors.

"What can I do for you?" Daniel asked. His head twitched several times in its usual and disconcerting way.

"First I want to thank you for helping out the other night," Raymond said. "From the absolute pinnacles of power it was thought to be an emergency. Publicity at this point would have meant an end to the whole enterprise."

"I was glad to be of service," Daniel said. "And pleased that Mr. Vincent Dominick was willing to help out to preserve his investment."

"Speaking of Mr. Dominick," Raymond said. "He paid me an unexpected visit yesterday morning."

"I hope on a cordial note," Daniel said. He was quite familiar with Dominick's career as well as his personality, and surmised that extortion would not be out of the question.

"Yes and no," Raymond admitted. "He insisted on telling me details I didn't want to know. Then he insisted on paying no tuition for two years."

"It could have been worse," Daniel said. "What does that mean to my percentage?"

"The percentage stays the same," Raymond said. "It's just that it becomes a percentage of nothing."

"So, I help and then get penalized!" Daniel complained. "That's hardly fair."

Raymond paused. He'd not thought about Daniel's loss of his cut of Dominick's tuition, yet it was something that had to be faced. At present, Raymond was reluctant to upset the man.

"You have a valid point," Raymond conceded. "Let's say we'll discuss it in the near future. At the moment, I have another concern. What's the status of Cindy Carlson?"

Cindy Carlson was the sixteen-year-old daughter of Albright Carlson, the Wall Street junk-bond mogul. Daniel had recruited Albright and his daughter as clients. As a youngster the daughter had suffered from glomerulonephritis. The malady had worsened during the girl's early teens to the point of kidney failure. Consequently, Daniel not only had the record number of clients, he also had the record number of harvests, two: Carlo Franconi and Cindy Carlson.

"She's been doing fine," Daniel said. "At least healthwise. Why do you ask?"

"This Franconi business has made me realize how vulnerable the enterprise is," Raymond admitted. "I want to be sure there are no other possible loose ends."

"Don't worry about the Carlsons," Daniel said. "They certainly aren't going to cause us any trouble. They couldn't be any more grateful. In fact, just last week Albright was talking about getting his wife out to the Bahamas to give a bone-marrow sample so she can become a client as well."

"That's encouraging," Raymond said. "We can always use more clients. But it's not the demand side of the enterprise that has me worried. Financially we couldn't be doing any better. We're ahead of all projections. It's the unexpected that has me worried, like Franconi."

Daniel nodded and then twitched. "There's always uncertainty," he said philosophically. "That's life!"

"The lower the level of uncertainty, the better I'll feel," Raymond said. "When I asked you about Cindy Carlson's status, you qualified your positive response as healthwise. Why?"

"Because she's a basket case mentally," Daniel said.

"How do you mean?" Raymond asked. Once again his pulse quickened.

"It's hard to imagine a kid not being a bit crazy growing up with a father like Albright Carlson." Daniel said. "Think about it. And then add the burden of a chronic illness. Whether that contributed to her obesity, I don't know. The girl is quite overweight. That's tough enough for anybody but especially so for a teen. The poor kid is understandably depressed."

"How depressed?" Raymond asked.

"Depressed enough to attempt suicide on two occasions," Daniel said. "And they weren't just childish bids for attention. They were bona fide attempts, and the only reason she's still with us is because she was discovered almost immediately and because she'd tried drugs the first time and hanging herself the second. If she'd had a gun she surely would have succeeded."

Raymond groaned out loud.

"What's the matter?" Daniel asked.

"All suicides are medical examiner cases," Raymond said.

"I hadn't thought of that," Daniel said.

"This is the kind of loose end I was referring to," Raymond said. "Damn! Just our luck!"

"Sorry to be the bearer of bad tidings," Daniel said.

"It's not your fault," Raymond said. "The important thing is that we recognize it for what it is, and that we understand we can't sit idly by and wait for catastrophe."

"I don't think we have much choice," Daniel said.

"What about Vincent Dominick?" Raymond said. "He's helped us once and with his own child ill, he has a vested interest in our program's future."

Dr. Daniel Levitz stared at Raymond. "Are you suggesting . . .?"

Raymond didn't reply.

"This is where I draw the line," Daniel said. He stood up. "I'm sorry, but I have a waiting-room full of patients."

"Couldn't you call Mr. Dominick and just ask?" Raymond said. He felt a wave of desperation wash over him.

"Absolutely not," Daniel said. "I might take care of a number of criminally connected individuals, but I certainly don't get involved with their business."

"But you helped with Franconi," Raymond complained.

"Franconi was a corpse on ice at the medical examiner's office," Daniel said.

"Then give me Mr. Dominick's phone number," Raymond said. "I'll call him myself. And I'll need the Carlsons' address."

"Ask my receptionist," Daniel said. "Just tell her you're a personal friend."

"Thank you," Raymond said.

"But just remember," Daniel said. "I deserve and want the percentages that are due to me regardless of what happens between you and Vinnie Dominick."

At first the receptionist was reluctant to give Raymond the phone number and the addresses, but after a quick call to her boss, she relented. Wordlessly, she copied the information onto the back of one of Dr. Daniel Levitz's business cards and handed it to Raymond.

Raymond wasted no time getting back to his apartment on Sixty-fourth Street. As he came through the door, Darlene asked how the meeting with the doctor had gone.

"Don't ask," Raymond said curtly. He went into his paneled study, closed the door, and sat down at his desk. Nervously, he dialed the phone. In his mind's eye, he could see Cindy Carlson either scrounging around in the medicine cabinet for her mother's sleeping pills or hanging out in the local hardware store buying a length of rope.

"Yeah, what is it?" a voice said on the other end of the line.

"I'd like to speak to Mr. Vincent Dominick," Raymond said with as much authority as he could muster. He detested the necessity to deal with the likes of these people, but he had little choice. Seven years of intense labor and commitment were on the line, not to mention his entire future.

"Who's calling?"

"Dr. Raymond Lyons."

There was a pause before the man said: "Hang on!"

To Raymond's surprise he was put on hold with one of Beethoven's sonatas playing in the background. To Raymond it seemed like some sort of oxymoron.

A few minutes later Vinnie Dominick's dulcet voice came over the line. Raymond could picture the man's practiced and deceptive banality as if Vinnie were a well-dressed character actor playing himself.

"How did you get this number, Doctor?" Vinnie asked. His tone was nonchalant, yet somehow more threatening because of it. Raymond's mouth went bone-dry. He had to cough.

"Dr. Levitz gave it to me," Raymond managed.

"What can I do for you, Doctor?" Vinnie asked.

"Another problem has come up," Raymond croaked. He cleared his throat again. "I'd like to see you to discuss it."

There was a pause that went on for longer than Raymond could tolerate. Just when he was about to ask if Vinnie was still there, the mobster responded: "When I got involved with you people I thought it was supposed to

216

give me peace of mind. I didn't think it was supposed to make my life more complicated."

"These are just minor growing pains," Raymond said. "In actuality, the project is going extremely well."

"I'll meet you in the Neopolitan Restaurant on Corona Avenue in Elmhurst in a half hour," Vinnie said. "Think you can find it?"

"I'm certain I can," Raymond said. "I'll take a cab, and I'll leave immediately."

"See you there," Vinnie said before hanging up.

Raymond rummaged hastily through the top drawer of his desk for his New York City map that included all five boroughs. He spread the map out on his desk, and using the index, located Corona Avenue in Elmhurst. He estimated that he could make it easily in half an hour provided the traffic wasn't bad on the Queensborough Bridge. That was a concern because it was almost four o'clock: the beginning of rush hour.

As Raymond came flying out of his study, pulling his coat back on, Darlene asked him where he was going. He told her he didn't have time to explain. He said he'd be back in an hour or so.

Raymond ran to Park Avenue, where he caught a cab. It was a good thing he'd brought his map along because the Afghan taxi driver had no idea even where Elmhurst was, much less Corona Avenue.

The trip was not easy. Just getting across the East Side of Manhattan took almost a quarter of an hour. And then the bridge was stop-and-go. By the time Raymond was supposed to be at the restaurant, his cab had just reached Queens. But from there it was easy going, and Raymond was only fifteen minutes late when he walked into the restaurant and pushed aside a heavy, velvet curtain.

It was immediately apparent the restaurant was not open for business. Most of the chairs were upside down on top of the tables. Vinnie Dominick was sitting by himself in one of the curved, red velvet-upholstered booths that lined the walls. In front of him were a newspaper and a small cup of expresso. A lighted cigarette lay in a glass ashtray.

Four other men were smoking at the bar, sprawled on bar stools. Two of them Raymond recognized from their visit to his apartment. Behind the bar was an overweight bearded man washing glassware. The rest of the restaurant was empty.

Vinnie waved Raymond to his booth.

"Sit down, Doc," Vinnie said. "A coffee?"

Raymond nodded as he slid into the banquette. It took some effort because of the nap of the velvet. The room was chilly, damp, and smelled of the previous night's garlic and the accumulated smoke of five-years' worth of cigarettes. Raymond was happy to keep on his hat and coat.

"Two coffees," Vinnie called out to the man behind the bar. Wordlessly, the man turned to an elaborate Italian expresso machine and began manipulating the controls.

"You surprised me, Doc," Vinnie said. "I truly never expected to hear from you again."

"As I mentioned on the phone there's another problem," Raymond said. He leaned forward and spoke in a low voice just above a whisper.

Vinnie spread his hands. "I'm all ears."

As succinctly as he could, Raymond outlined the situation with Cindy Carlson. He emphasized the fact that all suicides were medical examiner cases and had to be autopsied. There were no exceptions.

The overweight man from behind the bar brought out the coffees. Vinnie didn't respond to Raymond's monologue until the bartender had gone back to his glassware.

"Is this Cindy Carlson the daughter of Albright Carlson?" Vinnie asked. "The Wall Street legend?"

Raymond nodded. "That's partly why this situation is so important," he said. "If she commits suicide it will undoubtedly garner considerable media attention. The medical examiners will be particularly vigilant."

"I get the picture," Vinnie said as he took a sip of his coffee. "What is it exactly that you would want us to do?"

"I wouldn't presume to offer any suggestions," Raymond said nervously. "But you can appreciate that this problem is on a par with the Franconi situation."

"So you want this sixteen-year-old girl to just conveniently disappear," Vinnie said.

"Well, she has tried to kill herself twice," Raymond said limply. "In a way, we'd just be doing her a favor."

Vinnie laughed. He picked up his cigarette, took a drag, and then ran his hand over the top of his head. His hair was slicked back smoothly from his forehead. He regarded Raymond with his dark eyes.

"You're a piece of work, Doc," Vinnie said. "I gotta give you credit for that."

"Perhaps I can offer another year of free tuition," Raymond said.

"That's very generous of you," Vinnie said. "But you know something, Doc, it's not enough. In fact, I'm getting a little fed up with this whole operation. And I'll tell you straight: if it weren't for Vinnie Junior's kidney problems, I'd probably just ask for my money back, and we'd go our separate ways. You see, I'm already looking at potential problems from the first favor I did for you. I got a call from my wife's brother who runs the Spoletto Funeral Home. He's all upset because a Dr. Laurie Montgomery called asking embarrassing questions. Tell me, Doc. Do you know this Dr. Laurie Montgomery?"

"No, I don't," Raymond said. He swallowed loudly.

"Hey, Angelo, come over here!" Vinnie called out.

Angelo slid off his bar stool and came to the table.

"Sit down, Angelo," Vinnie said. "I want you to tell the good doctor here about Laurie Montgomery."

Raymond had to move farther into the booth to give room for Angelo. He felt distinctly uncomfortable being sandwiched between the two men.

"Laurie Montgomery is a smart, persistent individual," Angelo said with his husky voice. "To put it bluntly, she's a pain in the ass."

Raymond avoided looking at Angelo. His face was mostly scar tissue. Since his eyes didn't close properly, they were red and rheumy.

"Angelo had an unfortunate run-in with Laurie Montgomery a few years back," Vinnie explained. "Angelo, tell Raymond what you learned today after we heard from the funeral home."

"I called Vinnie Amendola, our contact in the morgue," Angelo said. "He told me that Laurie Montgomery specifically said that she was going to make it her personal business to find out how Franconi's body disappeared. Needless to say he's very concerned."

"See what I mean," Vinnie said. "We got

a potential problem here just because we did you a favor."

"I'm very sorry," Raymond said lamely. He couldn't think of any other response.

"It brings us back to this tuition issue," Vinnie said. "Under the circumstances I think the tuition should just be waived. In other words, no tuition for me or Vinnie junior forever."

"I do have to answer to the parent corporation," Raymond squeaked. He cleared his throat.

"Fine," Vinnie said. "Doesn't bother me in the slightest. Explain to them it's a valid business expense. Hey, maybe you could even use it as a deduction on your taxes." Vinnie laughed heartily.

Raymond shuddered imperceptibly. He knew he was being unfairly muscled, yet he had little choice. "Okay," he managed.

"Thank you," Vinnie said. "Gosh, I guess this is going to work out after all. We've become sort'a business partners. Now I trust you have Cindy Carlson's address?"

Raymond fumbled in his pocket and produced Dr. Levitz's business card. Vinnie took it, copied down the address from the back, and handed it back. Vinnie gave the address to Angelo.

"Englewood, New Jersey," Angelo said, reading aloud.

"Is that a problem?" Vinnie asked.

Angelo shook his head.

"Then, it's arranged," Vinnie said, looking back at Raymond. "So much for your latest problem. But I advise you not to come up with any more. With our current tuition understanding it seems to me you're out of bargaining chips."

A few minutes later, Raymond was out on the street. He realized he was shaking as he looked at his watch. It was close to five and getting dark. Stepping off the curb, he raised his hand to flag a cab. *What a disaster!* he thought. Somehow he would have to absorb the cost of maintaining Vinnie Dominick's and his son's double for the rest of their lives.

A cab pulled over. Raymond climbed in and gave his home address. As he sped away from the Neopolitan Restaurant, he began to feel better. The actual cost of maintaining the two doubles was minuscule, since the animals lived in isolation on a deserted island. So the situation wasn't that bad, especially since the potential problem with Cindy Carlson was now solved.

By the time Raymond entered his apartment his mood had improved significantly, at least until he got in the door.

"You've had two calls from Africa," Darlene reported.

"Problems?" Raymond asked. There was something about Darlene's voice that set off alarm bells.

"There was good news and bad news," Darlene said. "The good news was from the surgeon. He said that Horace Winchester is doing miraculously and that you should start planning on coming to pick him and the surgical team up."

"What's the bad news?" Raymond asked.

"The other call was from Siegfried Spallek," Darlene said. "He was a little vague. He said there was some trouble with Kevin Marshall."

"What kind of trouble?" Raymond asked.

"He didn't elaborate," Darlene said.

Raymond remembered specifically asking Kevin not to do anything rash. He wondered if the researcher had not heeded his warning. It must have had something to do with that stupid smoke Kevin had seen.

"Did Spallek want me to call back tonight?" Raymond asked.

"It was eleven o'clock his time when he called," Darlene said. "He said he could talk to you tomorrow."

Raymond groaned inwardly. Now he'd have to spend the entire night worrying. He wondered when it was all going to end.

CHAPTER 11

Kevin heard the heavy metal door open at the top of the stone stairs and a crack of light cascaded in. Two seconds later, the string of bare lightbulbs in the ceiling of the corridor went on. Through the bars of his cell, he could see Melanie and Candace in their respective cells. They were squinting as he was in the sudden glare.

Heavy footfalls on the granite stairs preceded Siegfried Spallek's appearance. He was accompanied by Cameron McIvers and Mustapha Aboud, chief of the Moroccan guards.

"It's about time, Mr. Spallek!" Melanie snapped. "I demand to be let out of here this instant, or you'll be in serious trouble."

Kevin winced. It was not the way to talk with Siegfried Spallek on any occasion, much less in their current circumstance.

Kevin, Melanie, and Candace had been huddling in utter blackness in separate cells in the oppressively hot, dank, jail in the basement of the town hall. Each cell had a small, arched window that opened into a window well in the rear arcade of the building. The openings were barred but without glass, so vermin could pass through unimpeded. All three prisoners had been terrified by the sounds of scampering creatures, especially since they'd seen several tarantulas before the lights had been turned out. The only source of comfort had been that they could easily talk to each other.

The first five minutes of the evening's ordeal had been the worst. As soon as the sound of the burst of machine-gun fire died out, Kevin and the women were blinded by large hand-held lights. When their eyes had finally adjusted, they saw that they'd walked into an ambush of sorts. They were surrounded by a jeering group of youthful Equatoguinean soldiers who'd delighted in casually aiming their AK-47's at them. Several had been brazen enough to poke the women with the muzzles of their weapons.

Fearing the worst, Kevin and the others hadn't moved a muscle. They'd been scared witless by the indiscriminate gunfire and terrified it might begin again at the slightest provocation.

Only at the appearance of several of the Moroccan guards did the unruly soldiers back off. Kevin had never imagined the intimidating Arabs as potential saviors, but that's how it had turned out. The guards had assumed custody of Kevin and the women. Then the guards drove them in Kevin's car, first to the Moroccan guard building across from the animal center, where they'd been placed in a windowless room for several hours, and then finally into town, where they'd been incarcerated in the old jail.

"This is outrageous treatment," Melanie persisted.

"On the contrary," Siegfried said. "I have been assured by Mustapha that you have been treated with all due respect."

"Respect!" Melanie sputtered. "To be shot at with machine guns! And kept in this shithole in the dark! That's respect?"

"You were not shot at," Siegfried corrected. "Those were merely a few warning shots directed over your heads. You had, after all, violated an important rule here in the Zone. Isla Francesca is off-limits. Everyone knows that."

Siegfried motioned Cameron toward Candace. Cameron opened her cell with a large, antique key. Candace wasted no time getting out of the cell. She hastily dusted off her clothes to make sure there were no bugs. She was still dressed in her surgical scrubs from the hospital.

"My apologies to you," Siegfried said to Candace. "I imagine you were led astray by our resident researchers. Perhaps you were not even aware of the rule against visiting the island area."

Cameron opened Melanie's cell and then Kevin's.

"As soon as I heard about your detention, I tried to call Dr. Raymond Lyons," Siegfried said. "I wanted to ask his opinion as to the best way to handle this situation. Since he was unavailable, I have to take responsibility myself. I am releasing you all on your own recognizance. I trust that you now know the seriousness of your actions. Under Equatoguinean law it could be considered a capital offense."

"Oh, bull!" Melanie spat.

Kevin cringed. He was afraid Melanie would anger Siegfried enough to order them back into the cells. Benevolence was not a part of Siegfried's character.

Mustapha extended Kevin's car keys to him. "Your vehicle is out back," he said with a heavy French accent.

Kevin took the keys. His hand shook enough to cause them to jingle until he got his hand and the keys into his pocket.

"I'm sure I will be speaking to Dr. Lyons sometime tomorrow," Siegfried said. "I will contact you individually. You may go."

Melanie started to speak again, but Kevin surprised himself by grabbing her arm and propelling her toward the stairs.

"I've had enough manhandling," Melanie sputtered. She tried to pull her arm from Kevin's grasp.

"Let's just get into the car," Kevin whispered harshly through clenched teeth. He forced her to keep moving.

"What a night!" Melanie complained. At the base of the stairs, she managed to yank her arm free. Irritably, she started up.

Kevin waited for Candace to precede him, then followed the women up to the ground floor. They emerged into an office used by the Equatoguinean soldiers that were constantly seen lounging in front of the town hall. There were four of them present.

With the base manager, the head of security, and the chief of the Moroccan guards in the building, the soldiers were a good deal more attentive than usual. All four were standing in their interpretation of attention, with their assault rifles over their shoulders. When Kevin and the women appeared, their expressions suggested they were confused.

Melanie gave them the finger as Kevin herded her and Candace out the door into the parking lot.

"Please, Melanie," Kevin begged. "Don't provoke them!"

Whether the soldiers did not understand the meaning of Melanie's gesture or were bewildered by the anomalous circumstances, Kevin didn't know. One way or the other, they didn't come flying out after them as Kevin feared they might.

They got to the car. Kevin opened the passenger-side door. Candace climbed in eagerly. But not Melanie. She turned to Kevin with her eyes blazing in the dim light.

"Give me the keys," she demanded.

"What?" Kevin asked, even though he'd heard her.

"I said give me the keys," Melanie repeated.

Confused by this unexpected request but not wishing to incite her more than she already was, Kevin handed her the car keys. Melanie immediately went around to the other side of the car and got in behind the wheel. Kevin climbed into the passenger seat. He didn't care who drove as long as they got themselves out of there.

Melanie started the car, spun the tires, and drove out of the parking lot.

"Jeez, Melanie," Kevin said. "Slow down!"

"I'm pissed," Melanie said.

"As if I couldn't tell," Kevin said.

"I'm not going home just yet," Melanie said. "But I'd be happy to take you guys home if you want."

"Where do you want to go?" Kevin asked. "It's almost midnight."

"I'm going out to the animal center," Melanie said. "I'm not going to tolerate being treated like this without finding out what the hell is going on."

"What's at the animal center?" Kevin asked.

"The keys to that goddamned bridge," Melanie said. "I want one, because for me this affair has gone beyond curiosity."

"Maybe we should stop and talk about

this," Kevin suggested.

Melanie jammed on the brakes, bringing them to a lurching stop. Both Kevin and Candace had to push themselves back into their respective seats.

"I'm going to the animal center," Melanie repeated. "You guys can either come along or I'll drop you off. It's your call."

"Why tonight?" Kevin asked.

"One, because I'm really ticked off right now," Melanie said. "And two, because they wouldn't suspect it. Obviously, they intend for us to go home and quake in our beds. That's why we were so mistreated. But you know something, that's not my style."

"That's my style," Kevin said.

"I think Melanie is right," Candace said from the backseat. "They were deliberately trying to scare us."

"And I think they did a damn good job," Kevin said. "Or am I the only sane one in the group?"

"Let's do it," Candace said.

"Oh, no!" Kevin groaned. "I'm outnumbered."

"We'll take you home," Melanie said. "No problem." She started to put the car in reverse.

Kevin reached out and stayed her hand. "How do you propose to get the keys? You don't even know where they'd be."

"I think it's pretty clear they'd be in Bertram's office," Melanie said. "He's the one in charge of logistics for the bonobo program. Hell, you're the one who suggested he had them."

"Okay, they're in Bertram's office," Kevin said. "But what about security? Offices are locked."

Melanie reached into the breast pocket of her animal-center coveralls and pulled out a magnetic card. "You're forgetting that I'm part of the animal-center hierarchy. This is a master card, and not the kind that competes with VISA. This thing gets me in every door of the animal center twenty-four hours a day. Remember, my work with the bonobo project is only a part of the fertility work I do."

Kevin looked over the back of his seat at Candace. Her blond hair was luminous in the half light of the car interior. "If you're game, Candace, I guess I'm game," he said.

"Let's go!" Candace said.

Melanie accelerated and turned north beyond the motor pool. The motor pool was in full operation, with huge mercury-vapor lamps illuminating the entire staging area. The motor pool's night shift was larger than either the day or evening shifts since that's when truck traffic between the Zone and Bata was at its peak.

Melanie zipped past a number of tractor trailers until the turnoff to Bata fell behind. From that point, all the way to the animal center, they didn't see another vehicle.

The animal center worked three shifts just like the motor pool did, although in the animal center the night shift was the smallest. The majority of the night staff worked in the veterinary hospital. Melanie took advantage of this fact by pulling Kevin's Toyota up to one of the animal-hospital doors. There the car had lots of company.

Melanie turned off the ignition and gazed at the animal-center entrance that led directly into the veterinary hospital. She drummed her fingers on the steering wheel.

"Well?" Kevin said. "We're here, what's the plan?"

"I'm thinking," Melanie said. "I can't decide what's best: whether you guys wait here or come with me."

"This place is huge," Candace said. She'd leaned forward and was gazing at the building in front of them. It ran from the street all the way back to where it disappeared into the jungle foliage. "For as many times as I've been to Cogo, I've never been out here at the animal center. I didn't have any idea it was so large. Is this part we're facing the hospital?"

"Yup," Melanie said. "This whole wing."

"I'd be interested to see it," Candace said. "I've never been in a veterinary hospital let alone one that's so palatial."

"It's state-of-the-art," Melanie said. "You

233

should see the ORs."

"Oh my God," Kevin sighed. He rolled his eyes. "I've been ensnared by the insane. We've just had the most harrowing experience in our lives, and you're talking about taking a tour."

"It's not going to be a tour," Melanie said as she alighted from the car. "Come on, Candace. I'm sure I can use your help. Kevin, you can wait here if you'd like."

"Fine by me," Kevin said. But it only took him a few moments of watching the women trudge toward the entrance before he, too, climbed out of the car. He decided that the anxiety of waiting would be worse than the stress of going.

"Wait up," Kevin called out. He had to run a few steps until he'd caught up with the others.

"I don't want to hear any complaining," Melanie told Kevin.

"Don't worry," Kevin said. He felt like a teenager being chastised by his mother.

"I don't anticipate any problems," Melanie said. "Bertram Edwards's office is in the administration part of the building, which at this time will be deserted. But just to be sure we don't arouse any suspicion, once we're inside, we'll head down to the locker room. I want you guys in animal center coveralls. Okay? I mean it's not really the time anyone would expect to encounter visitors."

"Sounds like a good idea to me," Candace said.

"All right," Bertram said into the phone. His eye caught the luminous dial of his bedside clock. It was quarter past midnight. "I'll meet you at your office in five minutes."

Bertram swung his legs over the edge of the bed and parted the mosquito netting.

"Trouble?" Trish, his wife, asked. She'd pushed herself up on one elbow.

"Just a nuisance," Bertram said. "Go back to sleep! I'll be back in a half hour or so."

Bertram closed the door to the bedroom before turning on the dressing-room light. He dressed quickly. Although he'd downplayed the situation to Trish, Bertram was anxious. He had no idea what was going on, but it had to be trouble. Siegfried had never called him in the middle of the night with a request to come to his office.

Outside, it was as bright as daytime with a nearly full moon having risen in the east. The sky was filled with silvery-purple cumulus clouds. The night air was heavy and humid and perfectly still. The sounds of the jungle were an almost constant cacophony of buzzes, chirps, and squawks interrupted with occasional short screams. It was a noise Bertram had grown accustomed to over the years, and it didn't even register in his mind.

Despite the distance to the town hall being

only a few hundred yards, Bertram drove. He knew it would be faster, and every minute that passed raised his curiosity. As he pulled into the parking lot, he could see that the usually lethargic soldiers were strangely agitated, moving around the army post, clutching their rifles. They eyed him nervously as he turned off his headlights and alighted from the car.

Approaching the building on foot, Bertram could see meager light flickering through the slats of the shutters covering Siegfried's second-floor office windows. He went up the stairs, passed through the dark reception area normally occupied by Aurielo, and entered Siegfried's office.

Siegfried was sitting at his desk with his feet propped up on the corner. In the hand of his good arm he held and was gently swirling a brandy snifter. Cameron McIvers, head of security, was sitting in a rattan chair with a similar glass. The only illumination in the room was coming from the candle in the skull. The low level of shimmering light cast dark shadows and gave a lifelike quality to the menagerie of stuffed animals.

"Thanks for coming out at such an ungodly hour," Siegfried said with his usual German accent. "How about a splash of brandy?"

"Do I need it?" Bertram asked, as he pulled a rattan chair over to the desk.

Siegfried laughed. "It can never hurt."

Cameron got the drink from a sideboard. He was a hefty, full-bearded Scotsman with a bulbous, red nose and a strong bias toward alcohol of any sort, although scotch was understandably his favorite. He handed the snifter to Bertram and reclaimed his seat and his own drink.

"Usually when I'm called out in the middle of the night it is a medical emergency with an animal," Bertram said. He took a sip of the brandy and breathed in deeply. "Tonight I have the sense it is something else entirely."

"Indeed," Siegfried said. "First I have to commend you. Your warning this afternoon about Kevin Marshall was well-founded and timely. I asked Cameron to have him watched by the Moroccans, and sure enough this evening he, Melanie Becket, and one of the surgical nurses drove all the way out to the landing area for Isla Francesca."

"Damnation!" Bertram exclaimed. "Did they go on the island?"

"No," Siegfried said. "They merely played with the food float. They'd also stopped to talk with Alphonse Kimba."

"This irritates me to death!" Bertram exclaimed. "I don't like anyone going near that island, and I don't like anyone talking to that pygmy."

"Nor do I," Siegfried agreed.

"Where are they now?" Bertram questioned.

"We let them go home," Siegfried said. "But not before putting the fear of God into them. I don't think they will be doing it again, at least not for a while."

"This is not what I need!" Bertram complained. "I hate to have to worry about this on top of the bonobos splitting into two groups."

"This is worse than the animals living in two groups," Siegfried said.

"They're both bad," Bertram said. "Both have the potential of interrupting the smooth operation of the program and possibly putting an end to it. I think my idea of caging them all and bringing them into the animal center should be reconsidered. I've got the cages out there. It wouldn't be difficult, and it will make retrievals a hell of a lot easier."

From the moment Bertram had determined the bonobos were living in two social groups, he'd thought it best to round up the animals and keep them in separate cages where they could be watched. But he'd been thwarted by Siegfried. Bertram had considered going over Siegfried's head by appealing to his boss in Cambridge, Massachusetts, but had decided against it. Doing so would have alerted the GenSys hierarchy that there was potential trouble with the bonobo program.

"We're not opening that discussion!" Siegfried said emphatically. "We're not giving up on the idea of keeping them isolated on the island. We all decided back when this started that was the best idea. I still think it is. But with this episode with Kevin Marshall, the bridge has me worried."

"Why?" Bertram asked. "It's locked."

"Where are the keys?" Siegfried asked.

"In my office," Bertram said.

"I think they should be here in the main safe," Siegfried said. "Most of your staff has access to your office, including Melanie Becket."

"Perhaps you have a point," Bertram said.

"I'm glad you agree," Siegfried said. "So I'd like you to get them. How many are there?"

"I don't recall exactly," Bertram said. "Four or five. Something like that."

"I want them here," Siegfried said.

"Fine," Bertram said agreeably. "I don't have a problem with that."

"Good," Siegfried said. He let his legs drop from the desk and stood up. "Let's go. I'll come with you."

"You want to go now?" Bertram asked with disbelief.

"Why put off until tomorrow what you can do today?" Siegfried said. "Isn't that an expression you Americans espouse? With the keys in the safe, I know I'll sleep a lot better tonight."

"Would you want me to come along as well?" Cameron asked.

"It's not necessary," Siegfried said. "I'm sure Bertram and I can handle it."

Kevin looked at himself in the full-length mirror at the end of the banks of lockers in the men's room. The trouble with the coveralls was that the small was too small and the medium was a little too big. He had to roll up the sleeves and the pant legs.

"What the hell are you doing in there?" Melanie's voice called out. She'd pushed open the door from the hall.

"I'm coming," Kevin said. He closed the locker where he'd stored his own clothes and hurried out into the hall.

"I thought women were supposed to take a long time dressing," Melanie complained.

"I couldn't decide which size was best," Kevin said.

"Did anybody come in while you were in there?" Melanie asked.

"Not a soul," Kevin said.

"Good," Melanie said. "Same for us in the ladies' room. Let's go!"

Melanie motioned for the others to follow her as she started up the stairs. "To get to the administration area from here, we have to pass through part of the veterinary hospital. I think it's best to avoid the main floor, which has the emergency room and the acute-care unit. There's always a lot of activity there. So let's go up to the second floor and go through the fertility unit. I can even say I'm checking on patients if someone asks."

"Cool," Candace said.

They passed the first floor and climbed to the second. Entering the main corridor, they encountered their first animal-center employee. If the man thought that there was anything abnormal about Kevin and Candace's presence in the middle of the night, he didn't give any evidence. He passed by with merely a nod.

"That was easy," Candace whispered.

"It's the coveralls," Melanie said.

They turned left through a set of double doors and entered a brightly lit, narrow hallway lined with a number of blank doors. Melanie cracked one of them and stuck her head inside. Quietly, she closed the door. "It's one of my patients. She's a low-land gorilla who's almost ready for egg retrieval. They can get a little rambunctious with the hormone level we have to achieve, but she's sleeping soundly."

"Can I see?" Candace asked.

"I suppose," Melanie said. "But be quiet and don't make any sudden movements."

Candace nodded. Melanie opened the door and slipped inside. Candace followed. Kevin stayed by the door, holding it open.

"Shouldn't we be doing what we came here for?" Kevin whispered.

Melanie put her finger to her lips.

There were four large cages in the room, only one of which was occupied. A large gorilla was sleeping on a bed of straw. The illumination came from overhead recessed lighting that was dimmed down to a point of being almost off.

Gently touching the bars of the cage, Candace leaned forward to get a better look. She'd never been so close to a gorilla. If she'd been inclined, she could have touched the huge animal.

With speed that defied belief, the female gorilla awoke and then bounced off the front of the cage. In the next instant, she was pounding the floor with her fists like kettle drums and shrieking.

Candace let out a scream of her own as she leapt back out of harm's way. Melanie grabbed her.

"It's okay," Melanie said.

The gorilla then made another lunge for the front of the cage. She also hurled a handful of fresh feces in the process, which splattered against the far wall.

Melanie directed Candace out the door and Kevin let it shut.

"I'm terribly sorry," Melanie said to Candace. Candace's Nordic complexion was even paler than usual. "Are you all right?"

"I guess," Candace said. She checked the front of her coveralls.

"A little PMS, I'm afraid," Melanie said.

"She didn't hit you with any of her poop, did she?"

"I don't think so," Candace said. She ran a hand through her hair and then examined it.

"Let's get the keys," Kevin said. "We're pushing our luck."

They walked the length of the fertility unit and pushed through a second pair of swinging doors to enter a large room divided into bays. Each bay had several cages, and most of the cages were occupied by youthful primates of different species.

"This is the pediatric unit," Melanie whispered. "Just act natural."

There were four people working in the unit. They were all dressed in surgical scrubs with stethoscopes draped around their necks. Everyone was friendly but busy and preoccupied, and the trio passed through, garnering nothing more than a couple of smiles and nods.

After another set of double doors and a short corridor, they came to a heavy, locked fire door. Melanie had to use her card to open it.

"Here we are!" Melanie whispered, as she let the fire door close quietly behind them. After the bustle they'd just witnessed, the silence and darkness seemed absolute. "This is the administration area. The stairwell is down the hall to the left. So hold on."

There was groping in the dark until Candace got her hand on Melanie's shoulder and Kevin got his on Candace's.

"Come on!" Melanie encouraged. She began to inch her way along the corridor, while running her hand against the wall. The others allowed themselves to be pulled along. Gradually, their eyes adjusted and by the time the group neared the door to the stairwell, they could appreciate the small amount of moonlight that seeped through the cracks.

Inside the stairwell, it was comparatively bright. Large windows on each landing flooded the stairs with moonlight.

The first-floor hall was much easier to walk in than the second-floor hall because of the windows in the main-entrance doors.

Melanie led them to a position just outside Bertram's office.

"Now comes the acid test," Kevin said, as Melanie tried her card in the lock.

There was an immediate, reassuring click. The door opened.

"No problem," Melanie said buoyantly.

The three stepped inside the room and were again thrust into almost complete darkness. The only light was a meager glow that filtered through the open door into the inner office.

"What now?" Kevin questioned. "We're not going to find anything in the dark."

"I agree," Melanie said. She felt along the wall for the switch. As soon as her finger touched it, she switched it on.

For a moment, they blinked at each other. "Whoa, seems awfully bright," Melanie said.

"I hope it doesn't wake up those Moroccan guards across the street," Kevin said.

"Don't even joke about it," Melanie said. She walked into the inner office and turned on the light. Kevin and Candace joined her.

"I think we should be methodical about this," Melanie said. "I'll take the desk. Candace, you take the file cabinet, and, Kevin, why don't you take the outer office and, while you're at it, keep an eye on the hall. Give a yell if anybody appears."

"Now that's a happy thought," Kevin said.

Siegfreid turned left at the motor pool and accelerated his new Toyota LandCruiser toward the animal center. The vehicle had been modified for his disability so that he could shift with his left hand.

"Does Cameron have any idea why we are so concerned about the security of Isla Francesca?" Bertram asked.

"No, not at all," Siegfried said.

"Has he asked?"

"No, he's not that kind of person. He takes orders. He doesn't question them."

"What about telling him and cutting him in on a small percentage?" Bertram suggested. "He could be very helpful."

"I'm not diluting our percentages!" Siegfried said. "Don't even suggest it. Besides,

Cameron is already helpful. He does whatever I tell him to do."

"What worries me the most about this episode with Kevin Marshall is that he must have said something to those women," Bertram said. "The last thing I want is for them to start thinking the bonobos on the island are using fire. If that gets out, it's just a matter of time before we have animal-rights zealots coming out of the woodwork. GenSys will shut the program down faster than you can blink your eye."

"What do you think we should do?" Siegfried asked. "I could arrange to have the three of them just disappear."

Bertram glanced at Siegfried and shivered. He knew the man was not joking.

"No, that could be worse," Bertram said. He looked back out through the windshield. "That might stimulate a major State-side investigation. I'm telling you, I think we should dart the bonobos, put them in the cages I brought out there, and bring them in. Sure as hell, they won't be using fire in the animal center."

"No, goddamn it!" Siegfried snapped. "The animals stay on the island. If they're brought in, you won't be able to keep it a secret. Even if they don't use fire, we know they're cunning little bastards from the problems we've had during retrievals, and maybe they'll start doing something else equally as weird. If they do, handlers will start talking. We'll be in worse shape."

Bertram sighed and ran a nervous hand through his white hair. Reluctantly, he admitted to himself that Siegfried had a point. Still, he thought it best to bring the animals in, mainly to keep them isolated from each other.

"I'll be talking to Raymond Lyons tomorrow," Siegfried said. "I tried to call him earlier. I figured that since Kevin Marshall had already talked to him, we might as well get his opinion about what to do. After all, this whole operation is his creation. He doesn't want trouble any more than we do."

"True," Bertram said.

"Tell me something," Siegfried said. "If the animals are using fire, how do you think they got it? You still think it was lightning?"

"I'm not sure," Bertram said. "It could have been lightning. But, then again, they managed to steal a bunch of tools, rope, and other stuff when we had the crew out there constructing the island side of the bridge mechanism. No one even thought about the possibility of theft. I mean, everything was secured in toolboxes. Anyway, they might have gotten matches. Of course, I have no idea how they could have figured out how to use them."

"You just gave me an idea," Siegfried said. "Why don't we tell Kevin and the women there's been a crew going out to the island over the past week to do some kind of work like cutting trails. We can say that we've just found out that they have been starting the fires."

"Now that's a damn good idea!" Bertram said. "It makes perfect sense. We've even considered putting a bridge over the Rio Diviso."

"Why the hell didn't we think of it earlier?" Siegfried questioned. "It's so obvious."

Ahead the LandCruiser's headlights illuminated the first of the animal-center's buildings.

"Where do you want me to park?" Siegfried asked.

"Pull right up to the front," Bertram said. "You can wait in the car. It will only take me a second."

Siegfried took his foot off the accelerator and began to brake.

"What the hell!" Bertram said.

"What's the matter?"

"There's a light on in my office," Bertram answered.

"This looks promising," Candace called out as she pulled a large folder from the top drawer of the file cabinet. The folder was dark blue and closed with an attached elastic. In the upper right-hand corner it said: ISLA FRANCESCA.

Melanie pushed in the drawer of the desk

she'd been searching and walked over to Candace. Kevin appeared from the outer office and joined them.

Candace snapped off the elastic and opened the folder. She slid the contents out onto a library table. There were wiring diagrams of electronic equipment, computer printouts, and numerous maps. There was also a large and lumpy manila envelope that had the words STEVENSON BRIDGE written across its top.

"Now we're cooking," Candace said. She opened the envelope, reached in, and pulled out a ring with five identical keys.

"Voilà," Melanie said. She took the ring and began to remove one of the keys.

Kevin peeked at the maps and picked up a detailed contour map. He had it partially unfolded when he became aware of a flickering light out of the corner of his eye. Glancing at the window, he saw the reflections of headlight beams dancing along the slats of the half open blinds. Stepping over to the window, he peeked out.

"Uh-oh!" Kevin croaked. "It's Siegfried's car."

"Quick!" Melanie said. "Get this all back into the file cabinet."

Melanie and Candace hastily crammed everything back into the folder, got the folder into the file cabinet, and closed the drawer. No sooner was it closed than they heard the rattle of the front door of the building as it was opened.

"This way!" Melanie whispered frantically. She motioned toward a door behind Bertram's desk. Quickly, the three went through the door. As Kevin closed it, he could hear the door to the outer office being pulled open.

They had entered one of Bertram's examining rooms. It was constructed of white tile and had a central stainless-steel examining table. Like Bertram's inner office it had windows covered with blinds. Enough light filtered in to allow them to rush over to the door to the hall. Unfortunately, en route Kevin kicked a stainless-steel pail standing on the floor next to the examining table.

The pail clanged up against the table leg. In the stillness, it sounded like a gong at an amusement park. Melanie reacted by throwing open the door to the hall and racing toward the stairwell. Candace followed. As Kevin dashed into the hall, he heard the door to Bertram's office slam open. He had no idea if he'd been seen or not.

In the stairwell, Melanie descended as fast as the moonlight would allow. She could hear Candace and Kevin behind her. She slowed at the foot of the stairs to grope for the door to the basement level. She got it open none too soon. Above they heard the first-floor stairwell door open, followed by heavy footfalls on the metal stairs.

The basement was utterly black save for a dim rectangular outline of light in the distance. Holding on to each other, they made their way toward the light. It wasn't until they had reached it that Kevin and Candace realized it was a fire door with light seeping around its periphery. Melanie had it open with her magnetic card once she'd located the slot.

Beyond the fire door was a brightly lit hallway which allowed them to run full tilt. Melanie pulled them to an abrupt halt halfway down the narrow passageway. There she opened a door marked PATHOLOGY.

"Inside," Melanie barked. Wordlessly, everyone complied.

Closing the door, Melanie locked it with a throw bolt.

They were standing in an anteroom for two autopsy theaters. There were scrub sinks, several desks, and a large insulated door leading to a refrigerated room.

"Why did we come in here?" Kevin said with panic in his voice. "We're trapped."

"Not quite," Melanie said breathlessly. "This way." She motioned for them to follow her around the corner. To Kevin's surprise there was an elevator. Melanie pounded the call-button, which brought forth an immediate whine of its machinery. At the same time, the floor indicator illuminated to show the elevator cab was on the third floor.

"Come on!" Melanie pleaded as if her urging could speed up the apparatus. Since it was a freight elevator, it was agonizingly slow. It was just passing the second floor when the door to the hallway rattled on its hinges followed by a muffled expletive.

The three exchanged panicky glances. "They'll be in here in the next few seconds," Kevin said. "Is there another way out?"

Melanie shook her head. "Only the elevator."

"We have to hide," Kevin said.

"What about the refrigerator?" Candace offered.

With no time to argue, the three darted to the refrigerator. Kevin got the door open. A cool mist flowed out to layer itself along the floor. Candace went in first, followed by Melanie and then Kevin. Kevin pulled the door shut. It's hardware clicked soundly.

The room was twenty feet square, with stainless-steel shelving from floor to ceiling that lined the periphery as well as forming a central island. The hulks of a number of dead primates lay on the shelves. The most impressive was the body of a huge silver-back male gorilla on the middle shelf of the central island. The illumination in the room came from bare light bulbs within wire cages attached to the ceiling at intervals along the walkways.

Instinctively, the three rushed around to the back of the central island and squatted down. Their heavy breathing formed fleeting spheres of mist in the frigid temperature. The smell was not pleasant with a hint of ammonia, but it was tolerable.

Surrounded by heavy insulation, Kevin and the others could not hear a sound inside the refrigerator, not even the whine of the elevator. At least not until they heard the unmistakable click of the refrigerator door's latch.

Kevin felt his heart skip a beat as the door was pulled open. Preparing himself to see the sneering face of Siegfried, Kevin slowly raised his head to look over the bulk of the dead gorilla. To his surprise it wasn't Siegfried. It was two men in scrub suits carrying in the body of a chimpanzee.

Wordlessly, the men placed the remains of the dead ape on a shelf to the right just inside the door and then left. Once the door was closed, Kevin looked down at Melanie and sighed. "This has to have been the worst day of my life."

"It's not over yet," Melanie said. "We still have to get out of here. But at least we got what we came for." She opened her fist and held up the key. Light glinted off its chrome-colored surface.

Kevin looked at his own hand. Without realizing it, he was still clutching the detailed contour map of Isla Francesca.

★ ★ ★

Bertram turned on the light in the hallway as he exited the stairwell. He'd gone up to the second floor and had entered the pediatric unit. He'd asked the crew if anybody had just run through. The answer was no.

Entering his examination room, he switched on the light in there as well. Siegfried appeared at the door to Bertram's office.

"Well?" Siegfried questioned.

"I don't know if someone was in here or not," Bertram said. He looked down at the stainless-steel pail that had moved from its normal position under the edge of the examining table.

"Did you see anyone?" Siegfried asked.

"Not really," Bertram said. He shook his head. "Maybe the janitorial crew left the lights on."

"Well, it underlines my concerns about the keys," Siegfried said.

Bertram nodded. He reached out with his foot and pushed the stainless-steel bucket back to its normal position. He turned out the light in the examining room before following Siegfried back into his office.

Bertram opened the top drawer of the file cabinet and pulled out the Isla Francesca folder. He unsnapped the securing elastic and pulled out the contents.

"What's the matter?" Siegfried asked.

Bertram had hesitated. As a compulsively

neat individual he could not imagine having crammed everything into the folder so haphazardly. Fearing the worst, it was with some relief that he lifted the Stevenson Bridge envelope and felt the lump made by the ring of keys.

CHAPTER 12

"This is the damndest thing," Jack said. He was peering into his microscope at one particular slide and had been doing so intently for the previous half hour. Chet had tried to talk with him but had given up. When Jack was concentrating, it was impossible to get his attention.

"I'm glad you are enjoying yourself," Chet said. He'd just stood up in preparation to leave and was about to heft his briefcase.

Jack leaned back and shook his head. "Everything about this case is screwy." He looked up at Chet and was surprised to see he had his coat on. "Oh, are you leaving?"

"Yeah, and I've been trying to say goodbye for the last fifteen minutes."

"Take a look at this before you go," Jack said. He motioned toward his microscope as he pushed away from the desk to give Chet room.

Chet debated. He checked his watch. He was due at his gym for a seven o'clock aerobics class. He'd had his eye on one of the girls who was a regular. In an effort to build up the courage to approach her, he'd been taking

256

the class himself. The problem was that she was in far better shape than he, so that at the end of the class he was always too winded to talk.

"Come on, sport," Jack said. "Give me your golden opinion."

Chet let go of his briefcase, leaned over, and peered into the eyepieces of Jack's microscope. With no explanation from Jack, he first had to figure out what the tissue was. "So, you're still looking at this frozen section of liver," he said.

"It's been entertaining me all afternoon," Jack said.

"Why not wait for the regular fixed sections?" Chet said. "These frozen sections are so limiting."

"I've asked Maureen to get them out as soon as she can," Jack said. "But meanwhile this is all I have. What do you think of the area under the pointer?"

Chet played with the focus. One of the many problems with frozen sections was they were often thick and the cellular architecture appeared fuzzy.

"I'd say it looks like a granuloma," Chet said. A granuloma was the cellular sign of chronic, cell-mediated inflammation.

"That was my thought as well," Jack said. "Now move the field over to the right. It will show a part of the liver surface. What do you see there?"

Chet did as he was told, while worrying that if he was late to the gym, there wouldn't be a spot in the aerobics class. The instructor was one of the most popular.

"I see what looks like a large, scarred cyst," Chet said.

"Does it look at all familiar?" Jack asked.

"Can't say it does," Chet said. "In fact, I'd have to say it looks a little weird."

"Well said," Jack remarked. "Now, let me ask you a question."

Chet raised his head and looked at his office mate. Jack's domed forehead was wrinkled with confusion.

"Does this look like a liver that you'd expect to see in a relatively recent transplant?"

"Hell, no!" Chet said. "I'd expect some acute inflammation but certainly not a granuloma. Especially if the process could be seen grossly as suggested by the collapsed surface cyst."

Jack sighed. "Thank you! I was beginning to question my judgment. It's reassuring to hear you've come to the same conclusion."

"Knock, knock!" a voice called out.

Jack and Chet looked up to see Ted Lynch, the director of the DNA lab, standing in the doorway. He was a big man, almost in Calvin Washington's league. He'd been an all-American tackle for Princeton before going on to graduate school.

"I got some results for you, Jack," Ted said.

"But I'm afraid it's not what you want to hear, so I thought I'd come down and tell you in person. I know you've been thinking you've got a liver transplant here, but the DQ alpha was a perfect match, suggesting it was the patient's own liver."

Jack threw up his hands. "I give up," he said.

"Now there was still a chance it was a transplant," Ted said. "There are twenty-one possible genotypes of the DQ alpha sequence, and the test fails to discriminate about seven percent of the time. But I went ahead and ran the ABO blood groups on chromosome nine, and it was a perfect match as well. Combining the two results, the chances are mighty slim it's not the patient's own liver."

"I'm crushed," Jack said. With his fingers intertwined, he let his hands fall onto the top of his head. "I even called a surgeon friend of mine and asked if there would be any other reason to find sutures in the vena cava, the hepatic artery, and the biliary system. He said no: that it had to be a transplant."

"What can I say?" Ted commented. "Of course, for you I'd be happy to fudge the results." He laughed, and Jack pretended to take a swipe at him with his hand.

Jack's phone jangled insistently. Jack motioned for Ted to stay, while he picked up the receiver. "What?" he said rudely.

"I'm out of here," Chet said. He waved to Jack and pushed past Ted.

Jack listened intently. Slowly, his expression changed from exasperation to interest. He nodded a few times as he glanced up at Ted. For Ted's benefit he held up a finger and mouthed, "One minute."

"Yeah, sure," Jack said into the phone. "If UNOS suggests we try Europe, give it a try." He glanced at his watch. "Of course it's the middle of the night over there, but do what you can!"

Jack hung up the phone. "That was Bart Arnold," he said. "I've had the entire forensics department searching for a missing recent liver transplant."

"What's UNOS?" Ted asked.

"United National Organ Sharing," Jack said.

"Any luck?" Ted asked.

"Nope," Jack said. "It's baffling. Bart's even checked with all the major centers doing liver transplants."

"Maybe it wasn't a transplant," Ted said. "I'm telling you, the probability of my two tests matching by chance is very small indeed."

"I'm convinced it was a transplant," Jack said. "There's no rhyme or reason to take out a person's liver and then put it back."

"You're sure?"

"Of course I'm sure," Jack said.

"You seem committed to this case," Ted commented.

Jack gave a short derisive laugh. "I've decided that I'm going to unravel this mystery come hell or high water," he said. "If I can't, I'll lose respect for myself. There just aren't that many liver transplants. I mean, if I can't solve this one, I might as well hang it up."

"All right," Ted said. "I'll tell you what I can do. I can run a polymarker which compares areas on chromosome four, six, seven, nine, eleven, and nineteen. A chance match will be in the billions to one. And for my own peace of mind, I'll even sequence the DQ alpha on both the liver sample and the patient to try to figure out how they could have matched."

"I'll be appreciative whatever you can do," Jack said.

"I'll even go up and start tonight," Ted said. "That way I can have the results tomorrow."

"What a sport!" Jack said. He put out his hand and Ted slapped it.

After Ted left, Jack switched off the light under his microscope. He felt as if the slide had been mocking him with its puzzling details. He'd been looking at it for so long his eyes hurt.

For a few minutes, Jack sat at his desk and gazed at the clutter of unfinished cases. Folders were stacked in uneven piles. Even his own conservative estimate had the figure somewhere between twenty-five and thirty. That was more than usual. Paperwork had never been Jack's forte, and it got worse when he became enmeshed in a particular case.

Cursing under his breath from frustration at his own ineptitude, Jack pushed back from his desk and grabbed his bomber jacket from the hook on the back of his office door. He'd had as much sitting and thinking as he was capable of. He needed some mindless, hard exercise, and his neighborhood basketball court was beckoning.

The view of the New York City skyline from the George Washington Bridge was breathtaking. Franco Ponti tried to turn his head to appreciate it, but it was difficult because of the rush-hour traffic. Franco was behind the wheel of a stolen Ford sedan on the way to Englewood, New Jersey. Angelo Facciolo was sitting in the front passenger seat, staring out the windshield. Both men were wearing gloves.

"Get a load of the view to the left," Franco said. "Look at all those lights. You can see the whole freakin' island, even the Statue of Liberty."

"Yeah, I've seen it already," Angelo said moodily.

"What's the matter with you?" Franco asked. "You're acting like you're on the rag."

"I don't like this kind of job," Angelo said. "It reminds me of when Cerino went berserk and sent me and Tony Ruggerio all over the goddamn city doing the same kind of shit. We should stick to our usual work, dealing with the usual people."

"Vinnie Dominick is not Pauli Cerino," Franco said. "And what's so bad about picking up some easy extra cash?"

"The cash is fine," Angelo agreed. "It's the risk I don't like."

"What do you mean?" Franco questioned. "There's no risk. We're professionals. We don't take risks."

"There's always the unexpected," Angelo said. "And as far as I'm concerned, the unexpected has already occurred."

Franco glanced over at Angelo's scarred face silhouetted in the half light of the car's interior. He could tell that Angelo was dead serious. "What are you talking about?" he questioned.

"The fact that this Laurie Montgomery is involved," Angelo said. "She gives me nightmares. Tony and I tried to whack her, but we couldn't. It was like God was protecting her."

Franco laughed in spite of Angelo's seriousness. "This Laurie Montgomery would be flattered that someone with your reputation has nightmares about her. That's hilarious."

"I don't find it funny at all," Angelo said.

"Don't get sore at me," Franco said. "Besides, she's hardly involved in what we're doing here."

"It's related," Angelo said. "And she told Vinnie Amendola that she's going to make it her personal business to find out how we managed to get Franconi's body out of the morgue."

"But how is she going to do that?" Franco said. "And worse comes to worse we sent Freddie Capuso and Richie Herns to do the actual dirty work. I think you're jumping to conclusions here."

"Oh yeah?" Angelo questioned. "You don't know this woman. She's one persistent bitch."

"All right!" Franco said with resignation. "You want to be bummed out, fine by me."

As they reached the New Jersey side of the bridge, Franco bore right onto the Palisades Interstate Parkway. With Angelo insisting on sulking, he reached over and turned on the radio. After pushing a few buttons he found a station that played "oldies but goodies." Turning up the volume up he sang "Sweet Caroline" along with Neil Diamond.

By the second refrain, Angelo leaned forward and turned off the radio. "You win," he said. "I'll cheer up if you promise not to sing."

"You don't like that song?" Franco questioned as if he were hurt. "It's got such sweet memories for me." He smacked his lips as if he were tasting. "It reminds me of making out with Maria Provolone."

"I'm not going to touch that one," Angelo said, laughing despite himself. He appreciated working with Franco Ponti. Franco was a professional. He also had a sense of humor, which Angelo knew he himself lacked.

Franco exited the parkway onto Palisades Avenue, passed Route 9W, and headed west down a long hill into Englewood, New Jersey. The environment quickly changed from franchise fast-food restaurants and service stations to upper-class suburban.

"You got the map and the address handy?" Franco asked.

"I got it right here," Angelo said. He reached up and turned on the map light. "We're looking for Overlook Place," he said. "It will be on the left."

Overlook Place was easy to find, and five minutes later, they were cruising along a winding, tree-lined street. The lawns that stretched up to the widely spaced houses were so expansive they looked like fairways on a golf course.

"Can you imagine living in a place like this?" Franco commented, his head swinging from side to side. "Hell, I'd get lost trying to find the street from my front door."

"I don't like this," Angelo said. "It's too peaceful. We're going to stick out like a sore thumb."

"Now don't get yourself all bent out of shape," Franco said. "At this point, all we're doing is reconnoitering. What number are we looking for?"

Angelo consulted the piece of paper in his hand. "Number Eight Overlook Place."

"That means it's going to be on our left," Franco said. They were just passing number twelve.

A few moments later Franco slowed and pulled over to the right side of the road. He and Angelo stared up a serpentine driveway lined with carriage lamps to a massive Tudor-style house set against a backdrop of soaring pine trees. Most of the multipaned windows were aglow with light. The property was the size of a football field.

"Looks like a goddamn castle," Angelo complained.

"I must say, it's not what I was hoping for," Franco said.

"Well, what are we going to do?" Angelo asked. "We can't just sit here. We haven't seen a car since we pulled off the main drag back there."

Franco put the car in gear. He knew Angelo was right. They couldn't wait there. Someone would undoubtedly spot them, become suspicious, and call the police. They'd already passed one of those stupid NEIGHBOR-HOOD WATCH signs with the silhouette of a guy wearing a bandana.

"Let's find out more about this sixteen-year-old chick," Angelo said. "Like, where she goes to school, what she likes to do, and who are her friends. We can't risk going up to the house. No way."

Franco grunted in agreement. Just as he was about to press on the accelerator, he saw a tiny figure come out the front of the house. From such a distance he couldn't tell if it was male or female. "Somebody just came out," he said.

"I noticed," Angelo said.

The two men watched in silence as the figure descended a few stone stairs and then started down the driveway.

"Whoever it is, is kind of fat," Franco said.

"And they got a dog," Angelo said.

"Holy Madonna," Franco said after a few moments. "It's the girl."

"I don't believe this," Angelo said. "Do you think it really is Cindy Carlson? I'm not used to things happening this easy."

Astounded, the two men watched as the girl continued down the driveway as if she were coming directly to greet them. Ahead of her walked a tiny, caramel-colored toy poodle with its little pompom tail sticking straight up.

"What should we do?" Franco questioned. He didn't expect an answer; he was thinking out loud.

"How about the police act?" Angelo suggested. "It always worked for Tony and me."

"Sounds good," Franco said. He turned to Angelo and stuck out his hand. "Let me use your Ozone Park police badge."

Angelo reached into the vest pocket of his Brioni suit and handed over the walletlike badge cover.

"You stay put for the moment," Franco said. "No reason to scare her right off the bat with that face of yours."

"Thanks for the compliment," Angelo said sourly. Angelo cared about his appearance and dressed to the nines in a vain attempt to compensate for his face, which was severely scarred from a combination of chicken pox as a child, severe acne as a teenager, and third-degree burns from an explosion five years previously. Ironically, the explosion had been ignited thanks to Laurie Montgomery.

"Ah, don't be so touchy," Franco teased. He cuffed Angelo on the back of the head. "You know we love you, even though you look like you should be in a horror movie."

Angelo fended off Franco's hand. There were only two people he allowed even to make reference to his facial problem: Franco and his boss, Vinnie Dominick. Still, he didn't appreciate it.

The girl was now nearing the street. She was dressed in a pink down-filled ski parka, which only made her look heavier. Her facial features indented a puffy face with mild acne. Her hair was straight and parted down the middle.

"She look anything like Maria Provolone?"

Angelo questioned, to get in a dig at Franco.

"Very funny," Franco said. He reached for the door handle and got out of the car.

"Excuse me!" Franco called out as sweetly as possible. Having smoked heavily from age eight, he had a voice that normally had a harsh, raspy quality. "Could you, by any chance, be the popular Cindy Carlson?"

"Maybe," the teenager said. "Who wants to know?" She'd stopped at the foot of the driveway. The dog lifted his leg against the gate post.

"We're police officers," Franco said. He held up the badge so that the light from the streetlamp glinted off its polished surface. "We're investigating several of the boys in town and we were told you might be able to help us."

"Really?" Cindy questioned.

"Absolutely," Franco said. "Please come over here so my colleague can talk to you."

Cindy glanced up and down the street, even though not a car had passed in the last five minutes. She crossed the street, pulling her dog who'd been intently sniffing the base of an elm tree.

Franco moved out of the way so that Cindy Carlson could bend over to look into the front seat of the car at Angelo. Before a word was spoken, Franco pushed her into the car headfirst.

Cindy let out a squeal but it was quickly

smothered by Angelo who wrestled her into the car.

Franco swifty yanked the leash out of Cindy's hand and shooed the dog away. Then he squeezed into the front seat, crushing Cindy against Angelo. He put the car in gear and drove away.

Laurie had surprised herself. After the delivery of the Franconi videotape, she'd been able to redirect her attention to her paperwork. She'd worked efficiently and made significant progress. There was now a gratifying stack of completed folders on the corner of her desk.

Taking the remaining tray of histology slides, she started on the final case, which could be completed with the material and reports she had. As she peered into her microscope to examine the first slide, she heard a knock on her open door. It was Lou Soldano.

"What are you doing here so late?" Lou asked. He sat down heavily in the chair next to Laurie's desk. He made no effort to take off his coat or hat, which was tipped way back on his head.

Laurie glanced at her watch. "My gosh!" she remarked. "I had no idea of the time."

"I tried to call you at home as I was coming across the Queensborough Bridge," Lou said. "When I didn't get you, I decided to stop

270

here. I had a sneaking suspicion you'd still be at it. You know, you work too hard!"

"You should talk!" Laurie said with playful sarcasm. "Look at you! When was the last time you got any sleep? And I'm not talking about a catnap at your desk."

"Let's talk about more pleasant things," Lou suggested. "How about grabbing a bite to eat? I've got to run down to headquarters to do about an hour's worth of dictating, then I'd love to go out someplace. The kids are with their aunt, God love her. What do you say to some pasta?"

"Are you sure you're up for going out?" Laurie questioned. The circles under Lou's dark eyes were touching his smile creases. His stubble was more than a five o'clock shadow. Laurie guessed it was at least two days' worth.

"I gotta eat," Lou said. "Are you planning on working much longer?"

"I'm on my last case," Laurie said. "Maybe another half hour."

"You gotta eat, too," Lou said.

"Have you made any progress in the Franconi case?" Laurie asked.

Lou let out an exasperated puff of air. "I wish," he said. "And the trouble is with these mob hits, if you don't score quickly, the trail cools mighty fast. We haven't gotten the break I've been hoping for."

"I'm sorry," Laurie said.

"Thanks," Lou said. "How about you? Any

more of an idea how Franconi's body got out of here?"

"That trail is about equally as cool," Laurie said. "Calvin even gave me a reaming out for interrogating the night mortuary tech. All I did was talk to the man. I'm afraid administration just wants the episode to fade."

"So Jack was right about telling you to lay off," Lou said.

"I suppose," Laurie reluctantly agreed. "But don't tell him that."

"I wish the commissioner would let it fade," Lou said. "Hell, I might get demoted over this thing."

"I did have one thought," Laurie said. "One of the funeral homes that picked up a body the night Franconi disappeared is called Spoletto. It's in Ozone Park. Somehow the name was familiar to me. Then I remembered that one of the more grisly murders of a young mobster took place there back during the Cerino case. Do you think that it's just a coincidence they happened to be making a pickup here the night Franconi disappeared?"

"Yeah," Lou said. "And I'll tell you why. I'm familiar with that funeral home from my years in Queens fighting organized crime. There is a loose and innocent connection by marriage with the Spoletto Funeral Home and the New York crime establishment. But it's with the wrong family. It's with the Lucia people, not with the Vaccarros who killed Franconi."

"Oh, well," Laurie said. "It was just a thought."

"Hey, I'm not knocking your questioning it," Lou said. "Your recall always impresses me. I'm not sure I would have made the association. Anyway, what about some dinner?"

"As tired as you look, how about just coming over to my apartment for some spaghetti?" Laurie suggested. Lou and Laurie had become best of friends over the years. After being thrust together on the Cerino case five years previously, they'd flirted with a romantic relationship. But it hadn't worked out. Becoming friends had been a mutual decision. In the years since, they made it a point to have dinner together every couple of weeks.

"You wouldn't mind?" Lou asked. The idea of kicking back on Laurie's couch sounded like heaven.

"Not at all," Laurie said. "In fact, I'd prefer it. I've got some sauce in the freezer and plenty of salad makings."

"Great!" Lou said. "I'll grab some Chianti on my way downtown. I'll give you a call when I'm leaving headquarters."

"Perfect," Laurie said.

After Lou had left, Laurie went back to her slide. But Lou's visit had broken her concentration by reawakening the Franconi business. Besides, she was tired of looking through the microscope. Leaning back, she rubbed her eyes.

"Damn it all!" she murmured. She sighed and gazed up a at the cobwebbed ceiling. Every time she questioned how Franconi's body could have gotten out of the morgue, she agonized anew. She also felt guilty that she couldn't provide even a modicum of help to Lou.

Laurie got up and got her coat, snapped shut her briefcase, and walked out of her office. But she didn't leave the morgue. Instead, she went down for another visit to the mortuary office. There was a question that was nagging her and which she'd forgotten to ask Marvin Fletcher, the evening mortuary tech, the previous late afternoon.

She found Marvin at his desk busily filling out the required forms for the scheduled pickups for that evening. Marvin was one of Laurie's favorite coworkers. He'd been on the day shift before Bruce Pomowski's tragic murder during the Cerino affair. After that event, Marvin had been switched to evenings. It had been a promotion because the evening mortuary tech had a lot of responsibility.

"Hey, Laurie! What's happening?" Marvin said the moment he caught sight of her. Marvin was a handsome African-American, with the most flawless skin Laurie had ever seen. It seemed to glow as if lit internally.

Laurie chatted with Marvin for a few minutes, catching him up on the intraoffice gossip of the day before getting down to business. "Marvin, I've got to ask you something, but I don't want you to feel defensive." Laurie couldn't help remembering Mike Passano's reaction to her questioning, and she certainly didn't want Marvin complaining to Calvin.

"About what?" Marvin asked.

"Franconi," Laurie said. "I wanted to ask why you didn't X-ray the body."

"What are you talking about?" Marvin questioned.

"Just what I said," Laurie remarked. "There was no X-ray slip in the autopsy folder and there were no films down here with others when I looked prior to finding out that the body had disappeared."

"I took X rays," Marvin said. He acted hurt that Laurie would suggest that he hadn't. "I always take X rays when a body comes in unless one of the doctors tells me otherwise."

"Then where's the slip and where are the films?" Laurie asked.

"Hey, I don't know what happened to the slip," Marvin said. "But the films: They went with Doctor Bingham."

"Bingham took them?" Laurie questioned. Even that was odd, yet she recognized that Bingham probably was planning on doing the post the following morning.

"He told me he was taking them up to his office," Marvin said. "What am I supposed to do, tell the boss he can't take the X rays. No way! Not this dude."

"Right, of course," Laurie said vaguely. She was preoccupied. Here was a new surprise. X rays existed of Franconi's body! Of course, it didn't matter much without the body itself, but she wondered why she'd not been told. Then again she'd not seen Bingham until after it was known that Franconi's body had been stolen.

"Well, I'm glad I spoke to you," Laurie said, coming out of her musing. "And I apologize for suggesting that you'd forgotten to take the films."

"Hey, it's cool," Marvin said.

Laurie was about to leave when she thought about the Spoletto Funeral Home. On a whim, she asked Marvin about it.

Marvin shrugged. "What do you want to know?" he asked. "I don't know much. I've never been there, you know what I'm saying."

"What are the people like who come here from the home?" Laurie asked.

"Normal," Marvin said with another shrug. "I've probably only seen them a couple of times. I mean, I don't know what you want me to say."

Laurie nodded. "It was a silly question. I don't know why I asked."

Laurie left the mortuary office and exited the morgue through the loading area onto Thirtieth Street. It seemed to her that nothing about the Franconi case was routine.

As Laurie commenced walking south along First Avenue another whim hit her. Suddenly, the idea of visiting the Spoletto Funeral Home seemed very appealing. She hesitated for a second while considering the idea and then stepped out into the street to hail a cab.

"Where to, lady?" the driver asked. Laurie could see from his hackney license that his name was Michael Neuman.

"Do you know where Ozone Park is?" Laurie asked.

"Sure, it's over in Queens," Michael said. He was an older man who, Laurie guessed, was in his late sixties. He was sitting on a foam rubber-stuffed pillow with a lot of foam rubber visible. His backrest was constructed of wooden beads.

"How long would it take to get there?" Laurie asked. If it was going to take hours, she wouldn't do it.

Michael made a questioning expression by compressing his lips while thinking. "Not long," he said vaguely. "Traffic's light. In fact, I was just out at Kennedy Airport, and it was a breeze."

"Let's go," Laurie said.

As Michael promised, the trip took only a short time, especially once they got on the Van Wyck Expressway. While they were traveling, Laurie found out that Michael had been driving a cab for over thirty years. He was a loquacious and opinionated man who also exuded a paternal charm.

"Would you know where Gold Road is in Ozone Park?" Laurie asked. She felt privileged to have found an experienced taxi driver. She'd remembered the address of the Spoletto Funeral Home from the Rolodex in the mortuary office. The street name had stuck in her mind as making a metaphorical statement about the undertaking business.

"Gold Road," Michael said. "No problem. It's a continuation of Eighty-ninth Street. You looking for a house or what?"

"I'm looking for the Spoletto Funeral Home," Laurie said.

"I'll have you there in no time," Michael said.

Laurie sat back with a contented feeling, only half listening to Michael's nonstop chatter. For the moment luck seemed to be on her side. The reason she'd decided to visit the Spoletto Funeral Home was because Jack had been wrong about it. The home did have a mob connection, and even though it was with the wrong family according to Lou, the fact that it was associated at all was suspicious to Laurie.

True to his promise, within a surprisingly short time Michael pulled up to a three-storied white clapboard house wedged between several brick tenements. It had Greek-style columns holding up the roof of a wide front porch. A glazed, internally lit sign in the middle of a postage stamp–sized lawn read: "Spoletto Funeral Home, a family business, two generations of caring."

The establishment was in full operation. Lights were on in all the windows. A few cigarette smokers were on the porch. Other people were visible through the ground-floor windows.

Michael was about to terminate the meter when Laurie spoke up: "Would you mind waiting for me?" she asked. "I'm certain I'll only be a few minutes, and I imagine it would be hard catching a cab from here."

"Sure, Lady," Michael said. "No problem."

"Would you mind if I left my briefcase?" Laurie asked. "There's absolutely nothing of value in it."

"It will be safe just the same," Michael said.

Laurie got out and started up the front walk, feeling unnerved. She could remember as if it were yesterday the case Dr. Dick Katzenburg had presented at the Thursday afternoon conference five years earlier. A man in his twenties had been essentially embalmed alive in the Spoletto Funeral Home after having been involved in throwing battery acid in Pauli Cerino's face.

Laurie shuddered but forced herself up the front steps. She was never going to be completely free from the Cerino affair.

The people smoking cigarettes ignored her.

Soft organ music could be heard through the closed front door. Laurie tried the door. It was unlocked, and she walked in.

Save for the music there was little sound. The floors were heavily carpeted. Small groups of people were standing around the entrance hall but they conversed in hushed whispers.

To Laurie's left was a room full of elaborate coffins and urns on display. To the right was a viewing room with people seated in folding chairs. At the far end of the room was a coffin resting on a bed of flowers.

"May I help you?" a soft voice enquired.

A thin man about Laurie's age with an ascetic face and sad features had come up to her. He was dressed in black except for his white shirt. He was obviously part of the staff. To Laurie, he looked like her image of a puritan preacher.

"Are you here to pay respects to Jonathan Dibartolo?" the man asked.

"No," Laurie said. "Frank Gleason."

"Excuse me?" the man enquired.

Laurie repeated the name. There was a pause.

"And your name is?" the man asked.

"Dr. Laurie Montgomery."

"Just one moment if you will," the man said as he literally ducked away.

Laurie looked around at the mourners. This was a side of death that she'd experienced only once. It was when her brother had died from an overdose when he was nineteen and Laurie was fifteen. It had been a traumatic experience for her in all regards, but especially since she'd been the one who had found him.

"Dr. Montgomery," a soft, unctuous voice intoned. "I'm Anthony Spoletto. I understand you are here to pay respects to Mr. Frank Gleason."

"That's correct," Laurie said. She turned to face a man also dressed in a black suit. He was obese and as oily as his voice. His forehead glistened in the soft incandescent light.

"I'm afraid that will be impossible," Mr. Spoletto said.

"I called this afternoon and was told he was on view," Laurie said.

"Yes, of course," Mr. Spoletto said. "But that was this afternoon. At the family's request this afternoon's four P.M. to six P.M. viewing was to be the last."

"I see," Laurie said nonplussed. She'd not had any particular plan in mind concerning her visit and had intended on viewing the body as a kind of jumping-off place. Now that the body was not available, she didn't know what to do.

"Perhaps I could just sign the register book anyway," Laurie said.

"I'm afraid that, too, is impossible," Mr. Spoletto said. "The family has already taken it."

"Well, I guess that's it," Laurie said with a limp gesture of her arms.

"Unfortunately," returned Mr. Spoletto.

"Would you know when the burial is planned?" Laurie asked.

"Not at the moment," Mr. Spoletto said.

"Thank you," Laurie said.

"Not at all," Mr. Spoletto said. He opened the door for Laurie.

Laurie walked out and got into the cab.

"Now where?" Michael asked.

Laurie gave her address on Nineteenth Street and leaned forward to look out at the Spoletto Funeral Home as the taxi pulled away. It had been a wasted trip. Or had it? After she'd been talking with Mr. Spoletto for a moment, she'd realized that his forehead wasn't oily. The man had been perspiring despite the temperature inside the funeral parlor being decidedly on the cool side. Laurie scratched her head, wondering if that meant anything or if it were just another example of her grabbing at straws.

"Was it a friend?" Michael asked.

"Was who a friend?"

"The deceased," Michael said.

Laurie let out a little mirthless laugh. "Hardly," she said.

"I know what you mean," Michael said, looking at Laurie in the rearview mirror. "Relationships today are very complicated. And I'll tell you why it is . . ."

Laurie smiled as she settled back to listen. She loved philosophical taxi drivers, and Michael was a regular Plato of his profession.

When the cab pulled up outside Laurie's building, Laurie saw a familiar figure in the foyer. It was Lou Soldano slouched over against the mailboxes, clutching a bottle of wine in a straw basket. Laurie paid Michael the fare along with a generous tip, then hurried inside.

"I'm sorry," Laurie offered. "I thought you were going to call before you came over."

Lou blinked as if he'd been asleep. "I did," he said, after a brief coughing spree. "I got your answering machine. So I left the message that I was on my way."

Laurie glanced at her watch as she unlocked the inner door. She'd only been gone for a little over an hour, which was what she'd expected.

"I thought you were only going to work for another half hour," Lou said.

"I wasn't working," Laurie said, as she called for the elevator. "I took a trip out to the Spoletto Funeral Home."

Lou frowned.

"Now don't give me extra grief," Laurie said as they boarded the elevator.

"So what did you find? Franconi lying in state?" Lou asked sarcastically.

"I'm not going to tell you a thing if you're going to act that way," Laurie complained.

"Okay, I'm sorry," Lou said.

"I didn't find anything," Laurie admitted. "The body I went to see was no longer on view. The family had cut it off at six P.M."

The elevator opened. While Laurie struggled with her locks, Lou curtsied for Debra Engler, whose door opened against its chain as usual.

"But the director acted a little suspicious," Laurie said. "At least I think he did."

"How so?" Lou asked as they entered Laurie's apartment. Tom came running out of the bedroom to purr and rub against Laurie's leg.

Laurie put her briefcase on the small half moon–shaped hall console table in order to bend down to scratch Tom vigorously behind his ear.

"He was perspiring while I was talking with him," Laurie said.

Lou paused with his coat half off. "Is that all?" he asked. "The man was perspiring?"

"Yes, that's it," Laurie said. She knew what Lou was thinking; it was written all over his face.

"Did he start perspiring after you asked him difficult and incriminating questions about Franconi's body?" Lou asked. "Or was he perspiring before you began talking with him?"

"Before," Laurie admitted.

Lou rolled his eyes. "Whoa! Another Sherlock Holmes incarnate," he said. "Maybe you should take over my job. I don't have your powers of intuition and inductive reasoning!"

"You promised not to give me grief," Laurie said.

"I never promised," Lou said.

"All right, it was a wasted trip," Laurie said. "Let's get some food. I'm starved."

Lou switched the bottle of wine from one hand to the other, allowing him to swing his arm out of his trench coat. When he did, he clumsily knocked Laurie's briefcase to the floor. The impact caused it to spring open and scatter the contents. The crash terrified the cat, who disappeared back into the bedroom after a desperate struggle to gain traction on the highly polished wood floor.

"What a klutz," Lou said. "I'm sorry!" He bent down to retrieve the papers, pens, microscope slides, and other paraphernalia and bumped into Laurie in the process.

"Maybe it's best you just sit down," Laurie suggested with a laugh.

"No, I insist," Lou said.

After they'd gotten most of the contents back into the briefcase, Lou picked up the videotape. "What's this, your favorite X-rated feature?"

"Hardly," Laurie commented.

Lou turned it over to read the label. "The Franconi shooting?" he questioned. "CNN sent you this out-of-the-blue?"

Laurie straightened up. "No, I requested it. I was going to use the tape to corroborate the findings when I did the autopsy. I thought it could make an interesting paper to show how reliable forensics can be."

"Mind if I look at it?" Lou asked.

"Of course not," Laurie said. "Didn't you see it on TV?"

"Along with everyone else," Lou said. "But it would still be interesting to see the tape."

"I'm surprised you don't have a copy at police headquarters," Laurie said.

"Hey, maybe we do," Lou said. "I just haven't seen it."

"Man, this ain't your night," Warren teased Jack. "You must be getting too old."

Jack had decided when he'd gotten to the playground late and had had to wait to get into the game, that he was going to win no matter whom he was teamed up with. But it didn't happen. In fact, Jack lost every game he played in because Warren and Spit had gotten on the same team and neither could miss. Their team had won every game including the last, which had just been capped off with a sweet "give and go" that gave Spit an easy final lay-up.

Jack walked over to the sidelines on rubbery legs. He'd played his heart out and was perspiring profusely. He pulled a towel from where he'd jammed it into the chain-link fence and wiped his face. He could feel his heart pounding in his chest.

"Come on, man!" Warren teased from the edge of the court, where he was dribbling a basketball back and forth between his legs. "One more run. We'll let you win this time."

"Yeah, sure!" Jack called back. "You never let nobody win nothing." Jack made it a point to adapt his syntax for the environment. "I'm out'a here."

Warren sauntered over and hooked one of his fingers through the fence and leaned against it. "What's up with your shortie?" he asked. "Natalie's been driving me up the wall asking questions about her since we haven't seen nothing of you guys, you know what I'm saying?"

Jack looked at Warren's sculpted face. To add insult to injury, as far as Jack was concerned, Warren wasn't even perspiring, nor was he breathing particularly heavily. And to make matters worse, he'd been playing before Jack had arrived. The only evidence of exertion was a tiny triangle of sweat down the front of his cut-off sweatshirt.

"Reassure Natalie that Laurie's fine," Jack said. "She and I were just taking a little vacation from each other. It was mostly my fault. I just wanted to cool things down a bit."

"I hear you," Warren said.

"I was with her last night," Jack added. "And things are looking up. She was asking me about you and Natalie, so you weren't alone."

Warren nodded. "You sure you're finished or do you want to run one more?"

"I'm finished," Jack said.

"Take care, man," Warren said as he pushed off the fence. Then he yelled out to the others: "Let's run, you bad asses."

Jack shook his head in dismay as he watched Warren amble away. He was envious of the man's stamina. Warren truly wasn't tired.

Jack pulled on his sweatshirt and started for home. He'd not won a single game, and although during the play the inability to win had seemed overwhelmingly frustrating, now it didn't matter. The exercise had cleared his mind, and for the hour and a half he'd played, he hadn't thought about work.

But Jack wasn't even all the way across 106th Street when the tantalizing mystery of his floater began troubling him again. As he climbed his refuse-strewn stairs, he wondered if there was a chance that Ted had made a mistake with the DNA analysis. As far as Jack was concerned the victim had had a transplant.

Jack was rounding the third-floor landing when he heard the telltale sound of his phone. He knew it was his because Denise, the single mother of two who lived on his floor, didn't have a phone.

With some effort, Jack encouraged his tired

quadriceps to propel him up the final flight. Clumsily, he fumbled with his keys at his door. The moment he got it open, he heard his answering machine pick up with a voice that Jack refused to believe was his own.

He got to the phone and snatched it up, cutting himself off in mid-sentence.

"Hello," he gasped. After an hour and a half of full-court, all-out basketball, the dash up the final flight of stairs had put him close to collapse.

"Don't tell me you're just coming in from your basketball," Laurie said. "It's going on nine o'clock. That's way off your schedule."

"I didn't get home until after seven-thirty," Jack explained between breaths. He wiped his face to keep his perspiration from dripping on the floor.

"That means you haven't eaten yet," Laurie said.

"You got that right," Jack said.

"Lou is over here, and we were going to have salad and spaghetti," Laurie said. "Why don't you join us?"

"I wouldn't want to break up the party," Jack said jokingly. At the same time he felt a mild stab of jealousy. He knew about Laurie's and Lou's brief romantic involvement and half wondered if the two friends were starting something up.

Jack knew he had no right to such feelings, considering the ambivalence he had about becoming involved with any woman. After the loss of his family, he'd been unsure if he ever wanted to make himself vulnerable to such pain again. At the same time, he'd come to admit both his loneliness and how much he enjoyed Laurie's company.

"You won't be breaking up any party," Laurie assured him. "It's going to be a very, very casual dinner. But we have something we want to show you. Something that is going to surprise you and maybe even make you want to give yourself a boot in the rear end. As you can probably tell, we're pretty excited."

"Oh?" Jack questioned. His mouth had gone dry. Hearing Lou laughing in the background, and putting two and two together, Jack knew what they wanted to show him; it had to be a ring! Lou must have proposed!

"Are you coming?" Laurie asked.

"It's kind of late," Jack said. "I've got to shower."

"Hey, you old sawbones," Lou said. He'd snatched the phone from Laurie. "Get your ass over here. Laurie and I are dying to share this with you."

"Okay," Jack said with resignation. "I'll jump in the shower and be there in forty minutes."

"See ya, dude," Lou said.

Jack hung up the phone. "Dude?" he mumbled. That didn't sound like Lou. Jack mused that the detective must be on cloud nine.

"I wish I knew what I could do to cheer you up," Darlene said. She'd made the effort to put on a slinky silk teddy from Victoria's Secret, but Raymond hadn't even noticed.

Raymond was stretched out on the sofa with an ice pack on his head and his eyes closed.

"Are you sure you don't want anything to eat?" Darlene asked. She was a tall woman over five feet ten, with bleached blond hair and a curvaceous body. She was twenty-six years old, and as she and Raymond joked, halfway to his fifty-two. She'd been a fashion model before Raymond had met her in a cosy East Side bar called the Auction House.

Raymond slowly took his ice pack off and glared at Darlene. Her bubbly vivaciousness was only an irritation.

"My stomach is in a knot," he said deliberately. "I'm not hungry. Is that so difficult to understand?"

"Well, I don't know why you are so upset," Darlene persisted. "You just got a call from the doctor in Los Angeles, and she's decided to come on board. That means we'll soon have some movie stars as clients. I think we should celebrate."

Raymond replaced the ice pack and closed his eyes. "The problems haven't been about the business side. That's all been going like clockwork. It's these unexpected snafus, like

Franconi and now Kevin Marshall." Raymond was loath to explain about Cindy Carlson. In fact, he'd been trying to avoid even thinking about the girl himself.

"Why are you still worried about Franconi?" Darlene asked. "That problem has been taken care of."

"Listen," Raymond said, trying to be patient, "maybe it would be best if you go watch some TV and let me suffer in peace."

"How about some toast or a little cereal?" Darlene asked.

"Leave me alone!" Raymond shouted. He'd sat up suddenly and was clutching his ice pack in his hand. His eyes were bulging and his face was flushed.

"Okay, I can tell when I'm not wanted," Darlene pouted. As she was leaving the room, the phone rang. She looked back at Raymond. "Want me to get it?" she asked.

Raymond nodded and told her to take the call in the study. He also said that if the call was for him, she should be vague about where he was, since he wasn't up to talking with anyone.

Darlene reversed her direction and disappeared into the study. Raymond breathed a sigh of relief and put the ice pack back on his head. Lying back, he tried to relax. He was just getting comfortable when Darlene returned.

"It's the intercom, not the phone," she said.

"There's a man downstairs who wants to see you. His name is Franco Ponti, and he said it was important. I told him that I'd see if you were here. What do you want me to say?"

Raymond sat back up with a new jolt of anxiety. For a moment, he couldn't place the name, but he didn't like the sound of it. Then it hit him. It was one of Vinnie Dominick's men who'd accompanied the mobster to the apartment the previous morning.

"Well?" Darlene questioned.

Raymond swallowed loudly. "I'll talk to him." Raymond reached behind the couch and picked up the telephone extension. He tried to sound authoritative when he said hello.

"Howdy, Doc," Franco said. "I was going to be disappointed if you hadn't been at home."

"I'm about to go to bed," Raymond said. "It's rather late for you to be calling."

"My apologies for the hour," Franco said. "But Angelo Facciolo and I have something we'd like to show you."

"Why don't we do this tomorrow?" Raymond said. "Say between nine and ten."

"It can't wait," Franco said. "Come on, Doc! Don't give us a hard time. It's Vinnie Dominick's express wish that you become intimately acquainted with our services."

Raymond struggled to come up with an excuse to avoid going downstairs. But given

293

his headache, nothing came to mind.

"Two minutes," Franco said. "That's all I'm asking."

"I'm awfully tired," Raymond said. "I'm afraid . . ."

"Hold on, Doc," Franco said. "Listen, I have to insist you come down here or you're going to be very sorry. I hope I'm making myself clear."

"All right," Raymond said, recognizing the inevitable. He was not naive enough to believe that Vinnie Dominick and his people made idle threats. "I'll be right down."

Raymond went to the hall closet and got his coat.

Darlene was amazed. "You're going out?"

"It appears that I don't have a lot of choice," Raymond said. "I suppose I should be happy they're not demanding to come inside."

As Raymond descended in the elevator, he tried to calm himself, but it was difficult since his headache had only gotten worse. This unexpected, unwanted visit was just the kind of turn that was making his life miserable. He had no idea what these people wanted to show him, although he guessed it had something to do with how they were going to deal with Cindy Carlson.

"Good evening, Doc," Franco said as Raymond appeared. "Sorry to trouble you."

"Let's just make this short," Raymond said,

sounding more confident than he felt.

"It will be short and sweet, trust me," Franco said. "If you don't mind." He pointed up the street where the Ford sedan had been pulled to the curb next to a fire hydrant. Angelo was half-sitting, half-leaning against the trunk, smoking a cigarette.

Raymond followed Franco to the car. Angelo responded by straightening up and stepping to the side.

"We just want you to take a quick look in the trunk," Franco said. He reached the car and keyed the luggage compartment. "Come right over here so you can see. The light's not so good."

Raymond stepped between the Ford and the car behind it, literally inches away from the trunk's lid as Franco raised it.

In the next second, Raymond thought his heart had stopped. The instant he glimpsed the ghoulish sight of Cindy Carlson's dead body crammed into the trunk, there was a flash of light.

Raymond staggered back. He felt sick with the image of the obese girl's porcelain face imprinted in his brain and dizzy from the flash of light which he quickly realized was from a Polaroid camera.

Franco closed the trunk and wiped his hands. "How'd the picture come out?" he asked Angelo.

"Gotta wait a minute," Angelo said. He was

holding the edges of the photo as it was developing.

"Just a second longer," Franco said to Raymond.

Raymond involuntarily moaned under his breath, while his eyes scanned the immediate area. He was terrified anybody else had seen the corpse.

"Looks good," Angelo said. He handed the picture to Franco who agreed.

Franco reached out with the photo so Raymond could see it.

"I'd say that's your best side," Franco said.

Raymond swallowed. The picture accurately depicted his shocked terror as well as the awful image of the dead girl.

Franco pocketed the picture. "There, that's it, Doc," he said. "I told you we wouldn't need a lot of your time."

"Why did you do this?" Raymond croaked.

"It was Vinnie's idea," Franco said. "He thought it best to have a record of the favor he'd done for you just in case."

"In case of what?" Raymond asked.

Franco spread his hands. "In case of whatever."

Franco and Angelo got into the car. Raymond stepped up onto the sidewalk. He watched until the Ford had gone to the corner and disappeared.

"Good Lord!" Raymond murmured. He turned and headed back to his door on unsteady legs. Every time he solved one problem another emerged.

The shower had revived Jack. Since Laurie had not included any injunction about riding his bike this time, Jack decided to ride. He cruised south at a good clip. Given the bad experiences he'd had in the park the previous year, he stayed on Central Park West all the way to Columbus Circle.

From Columbus Circle, Jack shot across Fifty-ninth Street to Park Avenue. At that time of the evening, Park Avenue was a dream, and he took it all the way to Laurie's street. He secured his bike with his collection of locks and went to Laurie's door. Before ringing her bell, he took a moment to compose himself, determining how best to act and what to say.

Laurie met him at the door, with a wide grin on her face. Before he could even say a word, she threw her free arm around his neck to give him a hug. In her other hand, she was balancing a glass of wine.

"Uh-oh," she said, stepping back. She eyed the wild state of his close-cropped hair. "I forgot about the bike issue. Don't tell me you rode down here."

Jack shrugged guiltily.

"Well, at least you made it," Laurie said. She unzipped his leather jacket and peeled it off his back.

Jack could see Lou sitting on the sofa, with a grin that rivaled the Cheshire cat's.

Laurie took Jack's arm and pulled him into the living room. "Do you want the surprise first or do you want to eat first?" she asked.

"Let's have the surprise," Jack said.

"Good," Lou said. He bounded off the couch and went to the TV.

Laurie guided Jack to the spot Lou had just vacated. "Do you want a glass of wine?"

Jack nodded. He was confused. He hadn't seen any ring, and Lou was intently studying the VCR remote. Laurie disappeared into the kitchen but was soon back with Jack's wine.

"I don't know how to do this," Lou complained. "At home, my daughter runs the VCR."

Laurie took the remote, then told Lou that he had to turn on the TV first.

Jack took a sip of the wine. It wasn't much better than what he'd brought the previous night.

Laurie and Lou joined Jack on the couch. Jack looked from one to the other, but they were ignoring him. They were intently watching the TV screen.

"What's this surprise?" Jack asked.

"Just watch," Laurie said, pointing toward the electronic snow on the TV.

More confused than ever, Jack looked at the screen. All of a sudden, there was music and the CNN logo followed by the image of a moderately obese man coming out of a Manhattan restaurant Jack recognized as Positano. The man was surrounded by a group of people.

"Should I put on the sound?" Laurie asked.

"Nah, it's not necessary," Lou said.

Jack watched the sequence. When it was over he looked at Laurie and Lou. Both had huge smiles.

"What is going on here?" Jack questioned. "How much wine have you two been drinking?"

"Do you recognize what you've just seen?" Laurie asked.

"I'd say it was somebody getting shot," Jack said.

"It's Carlo Franconi," Laurie said. "After watching it, does it remind you of anything?"

"Sort of reminds me of those old tapes of Lee Harvey Oswald getting shot," Jack said.

"Show it to him again," Lou suggested.

Jack watched the sequence for the second time. He divided his attention between the screen and watching Laurie and Lou. They were captivated.

After the second run-through, Laurie again turned to Jack and said: "Well?"

Jack shrugged. "I don't know what you want me to say."

"Let me run certain sections in slow motion," Laurie said. She used the remote to

299

isolate the sequence to where Franconi was about to climb into the limo. She ran it in slow motion, and then stopped it exactly at the moment he was shot. She walked up to the screen and pointed at the base of the man's neck. "There's the entry point," she said.

Using the remote again, she advanced to the moment of the next impact when the victim was falling to his right.

"Well, I'll be damned!" Jack remarked with astonishment. "My floater might be Carlo Franconi!"

Laurie spun around from facing the TV. Her eyes were blazing. "Exactly!" she said triumphantly. "Obviously, we haven't proved it yet but with the entrance wounds and the paths of the bullets in the floater, I'd be willing to bet five dollars."

"Whoa!" Jack commented. "I'll take you up on a five-dollar wager, but I want to remind you that's a hundred percent higher than any bet you've ever made in my presence."

"I'm that sure," Laurie said.

"Laurie is so fast at making associations," said Lou. "She picked up on the similarities right away. She always makes me feel stupid."

"Get out of here!" Laurie said, giving Lou a friendly shove.

"Is this the surprise you guys wanted to tell me about?" Jack asked cautiously. He didn't want to get his hopes up.

"Yes," Laurie said. "What's the matter? Aren't you as excited as we are?"

Jack laughed with relief. "Oh, I'm just tickled pink!"

"I can never tell when you are serious," Laurie said. She detected a certain amount of Jack's typical sarcasm in his reply.

"It's the best news I've heard in days," Jack added. "Maybe weeks."

"All right, let's not overdo it," Laurie said. She turned off the TV and the VCR. "Enough of the surprise, let's eat."

Over dinner the conversation turned to why no one even considered that the floater might be Franconi.

"For me it was the shotgun wound," Laurie said. "Which I knew Franconi didn't have. Also I was thrown off by the body's being found way out off Coney Island. Now, if it had been fished out of the East River, it might have been a different story."

"I suppose I was thrown off for the same reasons," Jack said. "And then, when I realized the shotgun wound was postmortem, I was already engrossed in the issue about the liver. By the way, Lou, did Franconi have a liver transplant?"

"Not that I know of," Lou said. "He'd been sick for a number of years, but I never knew the diagnosis. I hadn't heard anything about a liver transplant."

"If he didn't have a liver transplant, then

the floater isn't Franconi," Jack said. "Even though the DNA lab is having a hard time confirming it, I'm personally convinced the floater has a donated liver."

"What else can you people do to confirm that the floater and Franconi are the same person?" Lou asked.

"We can request a blood sample from the mother," Laurie said. "Comparing the mitochondrial DNA which all of us inherit only from our mothers, we could tell right away if the floater is Franconi. I'm sure the mother will be agreeable, since she'd been the one to come to identify the body initially."

"Too bad an X ray wasn't taken when Franconi came in," Jack said. "That would have done it."

"But there was an X ray!" Laurie said with excitement. "I just found out this evening. Marvin had taken one."

"Where the hell did it go?" Jack asked.

"Marvin said that Bingham took it," Laurie said. "It must be in his office."

"Then I suggest we make a little foray to the morgue," Jack said. "I'd like to settle this issue."

"Bingham's office will be locked," Laurie said.

"I think this situation calls for some creative action," Jack said.

"Amen," Lou said. "This might be that break I've been hoping for."

As soon as they had finished eating and cleaning up the kitchen, which Jack and Lou had insisted on doing, the three took a cab down to the morgue. They entered through the receiving dock and went directly into the mortuary office.

"My God!" Marvin commented when he saw both Jack and Laurie. It was rare for two medical examiners to show up at the same time during the evening. "Has there been a natural disaster?"

"Where are the janitors?" Jack asked.

"In the pit last time I looked," Marvin asked. "Seriously, what's up?"

"An identity crisis," Jack quipped.

Jack led the others to the autopsy room and cracked the door. Marvin had been right. Both janitors were busy mopping the expansive terrazzo floor.

"I assume you guys have keys to the chief's office," Jack said.

"Yeah, sure," Daryl Foster said. Daryl had been working for the medical examiner's office for almost thirty years. His partner, Jim O'Donnel, was a relatively new employee.

"We've got to get in there," Jack said. "Would you mind opening it?"

Daryl hesitated. "The chief's kind'a sensitive about people being in his office," he said.

"I'll take responsibility," Jack said. "This is an emergency. Besides we have Lieutenant Detective Soldano with us from the police department, who will keep our thievery to a minimum."

"I don't know," Daryl said. He was obviously uncomfortable, as well as unimpressed, with Jack's humor.

"Then give me the key," Jack said. He stuck out his hand. "That way you won't be involved."

With obvious reluctance, Daryl removed two keys from his key chain and handed them to Jack. "One's for the outer office, and one is for Dr. Bingham's inner office."

"I'll have them back for you in five minutes," Jack said.

Daryl didn't respond.

"I think the poor guy was intimidated," Lou commented as the three rose up to the first floor in the elevator.

"Once Jack is on a mission, look out!" Laurie said.

"Bureaucracy irks me," Jack said. "There's no excuse for the X ray to be squirreled away in the chief's office in the first place."

Jack opened the front office's outer door and then Dr. Bingham's inner door. He turned on the lights.

The office was large, with a big desk beneath high windows to the left and a large library table to the right. Teaching paraphernalia, including a blackboard and an X-ray view box, were at the head of the table.

"Where should we look?" Laurie asked.

"I was hoping they'd just be on that view box," Jack said. "But I don't see them. I tell you what, I'll take the desk and the file cabinet, you look around the view box."

"Fine," Laurie said.

"What do you want me to do?" Lou asked.

"You just stand there and make sure we don't steal anything," Jack scoffed.

Jack pulled out several of the file drawers, but closed them quickly. The full-body X rays that were taken by the morgue came in large folders. It wasn't something easily hidden.

"This looks promising," Laurie called out. She'd found a stash of X rays in the cabinet directly under the view box. Lifting the folders out onto the library table, she scanned the names. She found Franconi's and pulled them free of the others.

Returning to the basement level, Jack got the X rays of the floater and took both folders back to the autopsy room. He gave Bingham's office keys to Daryl and thanked him. Daryl merely nodded.

"Okay, everybody!" Jack said walking over to the view box. "The critical moment has arrived." First he slipped up Franconi's X rays and then the headless floater's.

"What do you know," Jack said after only a second's inspection. "I owe Laurie five dollars!"

Laurie gave a cry of triumph, as Jack gave her the money. Lou scratched his head and leaned closer to the light box to stare at the films. "How can you guys tell so quickly?" he asked.

Jack pointed out the lumpy shadows of the bullets almost obscured by the mass of shotgun pellets in the floater's X rays and showed how they corresponded to the bullets on the Franconi films. Then he pointed to identical healed clavicular fractures that appeared on the X rays of the two bodies.

"This is great," Lou said, rubbing his hands together with enthusiasm that almost matched Laurie's. "Now that we have a corpus delicti, we might be able to make some headway in this case."

"And I'll be able to figure out what the hell's going on concerning this guy's liver," Jack said.

"And maybe I'll go on a shopping spree with my money," Laurie said, giving the five-dollar bill a kiss. "But not until I figure out the how and the why this body left here in the first place."

Unable to sleep despite having taken two sleeping pills, Raymond slipped out of bed so as not to disturb Darlene. Not that he was terribly worried. Darlene was such a sound sleeper that the ceiling could fall in without her so much as moving.

Raymond padded into the kitchen and turned on the light. He wasn't hungry but he thought that perhaps a little warm milk might help to settle his roiling stomach. Ever since the shock of having been forced to view the terrible sight in the trunk of the Ford, he'd been suffering with heartburn. He'd tried Maalox, Pepcid AC, and finally Pepto-Bismol. Nothing had helped.

Raymond was not handy in the kitchen, mainly because he didn't know where anything was located. Consequently, it took him some time to heat the milk and find an appropriate glass. When it was ready, he carried it into his study and sat at his desk.

After taking a few sips, he noticed that it was three-fifteen in the morning. Despite the fuzziness in his brain from the sleeping pills, he was able to figure out that at the Zone it was after nine, a good time to call Siegfried Spallek.

The connection was almost instantaneous. At that hour, phone traffic with North America was at a minimum. Aurielo answered promptly and put Raymond through to the director.

"You are up early," Siegfried commented. "I was going to call you in four or five hours."

"I couldn't sleep," Raymond said. "What's going on over there? What's the problem with Kevin Marshall?"

"I believe the problem is over," Siegfried said. Siegfried summarized what had happened and gave credit to Bertram Edwards

307

for alerting him about Kevin so that he could be followed. He said that Kevin and his friends had been given such a scare that they wouldn't dare go near the island again.

"What do you mean 'friends'?" Raymond asked. "Kevin has always been such a loner."

"He was with the reproductive technologist and one of the surgical nurses," Siegfried said. "Frankly, even that surprised us since he's always been such a schlemiel, or what do you Americans call such a socially inept person?"

"A nerd," Raymond said.

"That's it," Siegfried said.

"And presumably the stimulus for this attempted visit to the island was the smoke that's been bothering him?"

"That's what Bertram Edwards says," Siegfried said. "And Bertram had a good idea. We're going to tell Kevin that we've had a work crew out there building a bridge over the stream that divides the island in two."

"But you haven't," Raymond said.

"Of course not," Siegfried said. "The last work crew we had out there was when we built the landing for the extension bridge to the mainland. Of course, Bertram had some people there when he moved those hundred cages out there."

"I don't know anything about cages on the island," Raymond said. "What are you talking about?"

"Bertram has been lobbying lately to give

up on the island isolation idea," Siegfried said. "He thinks that the bonobos should be brought to the animal center and somehow hidden."

"I want them to stay on the island," Raymond said emphatically. "That was the agreement I worked out with GenSys. They could shut the program down if we bring the animals in. They're paranoid about publicity."

"I know," Siegfried said. "That's exactly what I told Bertram. He understands but wants to leave the cages there just in case. I don't see any harm in that. In fact, it is good to be prepared for unexpected contingencies."

Raymond ran a nervous hand through his hair. He didn't want to hear about any "unexpected contingencies."

"I was going to ask you how you wanted us to handle Kevin and the women," Siegfried said. "But with this explanation about the smoke and having given them a good scare, I think the situation is under control."

"They didn't get onto the island, did they?" Raymond asked.

"No, they were only at the staging area," Siegfried said.

"I don't even like people nosing around there," Raymond said.

"I understand," Siegfried said. "I don't think Kevin will go back for the reasons I've given. But just to be on the safe side, I'm leaving a Moroccan guard and a contingent of the Equatoguinean soldiers out there for a few days, provided you think it's a good idea."

"That's fine," Raymond said. "But tell me, what's your feeling about smoke coming out of the island, assuming that Kevin is right about it?"

"Me?" Siegfried questioned. "I couldn't care less what those animals do out there. As long as they stay there and stay healthy. Does it bother you?"

"Not in the slightest," Raymond said.

"Maybe we should send over a bunch of soccer balls," Siegfried said. "That might keep them entertained." He laughed heartily.

"I hardly think this is a laughing matter," Raymond said irritably. Raymond was not fond of Siegfried, although he appreciated his disciplined managerial style. Raymond could picture the director at his desk, surrounded by his stuffed menagerie and those skulls dotting his desk.

"When are you coming for the patient?" Siegfried asked. "I've been told he's doing fantastically well and ready to go."

"So I've heard," Raymond said. "I put in a call to Cambridge, and as soon as the Gen-Sys plane is available, I'll be over. It should be in a day or so."

"Let me know," Siegfried said. "I'll have a car waiting for you in Bata."

Raymond replaced the receiver and breathed a small sigh of relief. He was glad he'd called Africa, since part of his current anxiety had stemmed from Siegfried's disturbing message about there being a problem with Kevin. It was good to know the crisis had been taken care of. In fact, Raymond thought that if he could just get the image of that snapshot of him hovering over Cindy Carlson's body out of his mind, he'd feel almost like himself again.

CHAPTER 13

Kevin was totally unaware of the time when a knock interrupted the intense concentration he'd been directing toward his computer screen for several hours. He opened his laboratory door and was promptly greeted by Melanie as she swooped into the room. She was carrying a large paper bag.

"Where are your techs?" she asked.

"I gave them the day off," Kevin said. "There was no way I was going to get any work done today so I told them to enjoy the sun. It's been a long rainy season, and it will be back before we know it."

"Where's Candace?" Melanie asked. She put down her parcel on the lab bench.

"I don't know," Kevin said. "I haven't seen or talked with her since we dropped her off at the hospital this morning."

It had been a long night. After having hid in the pathology cooler for over an hour, Melanie had talked both Kevin and Candace into sneaking up to the on-call room Melanie had at the animal center. The three had stayed there getting very little sleep, until the early-morning shift change. Blending in with all the

312

employees coming and going, the group had made it back to Cogo without incident.

"Do you know how to get in touch with her?" Melanie asked.

"I guess just call the hospital and have her paged," Kevin suggested. "Unless she's in her room in the Inn, which is what I'd guess since Horace Winchester is doing so well." The Inn was the name given to the temporary quarters for transient hospital personnel. It was physically part of the hospital/laboratory complex.

"Good point!" Melanie said. She picked up the phone and had the operator put her through to Candace's room. Candace answered on the third ring. It was apparent she'd been asleep.

"Kevin and I are going to the island," Melanie said without preamble. "You want to come or hang in here?"

"What are you talking about?" Kevin asked nervously.

Melanie motioned for him to be quiet.

"When?" Candace asked.

"As soon as you get over here," Melanie said. "We're in Kevin's lab."

"It will take me a good half hour," Candace said. "I've got to shower."

"We'll be waiting," Melanie said. She hung up the phone.

"Melanie, are you crazy?" Kevin said. "We've got to let some time go by before we hazard another try at the island."

"This girl doesn't think so," Melanie said, giving herself a poke in the chest. "The sooner we go, the better. If Bertram finds out a key is missing, he could change the lock, and we'll be back to square one. Besides, like I said last night, they expect us to be terrified. Going out there right away will catch them off-guard."

"I don't think I'm up for this," Kevin said.

"Oh really?" Melanie questioned super-ciliously. "Hey, you're the one who's brought up this worry about what we've created. And now I'm really worried. I saw some more circumstantial evidence this morning."

"Like what?" Kevin asked.

"I went into the bonobo enclosure out at the animal center," Melanie said. "I made sure no one saw me go in, so don't get yourself all worked up. It took me over an hour, but I managed to find a mother with one of our infants."

"And?" Kevin questioned. He wasn't sure he wanted to hear the rest.

"The infant walked around on its hindlegs — just like you and I — the whole time I was able to observe," Melanie said. Her dark eyes flashed with emotion akin to anger. "Behavior we used to call cute is definitely bipedal."

Kevin nodded and looked away. He found Melanie's intensity unnerving, and her conversation was underlining all his own fears.

"We have to find out for sure what the status is of these creatures," Melanie said. "And we can do that only by going out there."

Kevin nodded.

"So, I made some sandwiches," Melanie said, pointing toward the paper bag she'd brought in with her. "We'll call it a picnic."

"I came across something disturbing this morning as well," Kevin said. "Let me show you." He grabbed a stool and pushed it over to his computer terminal. He motioned for Melanie to sit down, while he took his own chair. His fingers played over the keyboard. Soon the screen displayed the computer graphic of Isla Francesca.

"I programmed the computer to follow all seventy-three bonobos on the island for several hours of real-time activity," Kevin explained. "Then I had the data condensed so I could watch it in fast-forward. Look what resulted."

Kevin clicked his mouse to start the sequence. The multitude of little red dots rapidly traced out weird geometric designs. It only took a few seconds.

"Looks like a bunch of chicken scratches," Melanie said.

"Except for these two dots," Kevin said. He pointed to two pinpoints.

"They apparently didn't move much," Melanie said.

"Exactly," Kevin said. "Creature number sixty and creature number sixty-seven." Kevin reached over and picked up the detailed contour map he'd inadvertently taken from Bertram's office. "I located creature number sixty to a marshy clearing just south of Lago Hippo. According to the map, there are no trees there."

"What's your explanation?" Melanie asked.

"Hang on," Kevin said. "What I did next was reduce the scale of the grid so that it represented a fifty-by-fifty-foot portion of the island right where creature number sixty was located. Let me show you what happened."

Kevin keyed in the information and then clicked to start the sequence again. Once again the red light for creature number sixty was a pinpoint.

"He didn't move at all," Melanie said.

"I'm afraid not," Kevin said.

"You think he's sleeping?"

"In the middle of the morning?" Kevin asked. "And with such a scale, even turning over in his sleep should result in some movement. The system is that sensitive."

"If he's not sleeping, what is he doing?" Melanie asked.

Kevin shrugged. "I don't know. Maybe he found a way to remove his computer chip."

"I never thought of that," Melanie said. "That's a scary idea."

"The only other thing I could think of is

316

the bonobo died," Kevin said.

"I suppose that's a possibility," Melanie said. "But I don't think it is very probable. Those are young, extraordinarily healthy animals. We've made sure of that. And they are in an environment without natural enemies and have more than enough food."

Kevin sighed. "Whatever it is, it is disturbing, and when we go out there, I think we should check it out."

"I wonder if Bertram knows about this?" Melanie asked. "It doesn't bode well for the program in general."

"I suppose I should tell him," Kevin said.

"Let's wait until we make our visit," Melanie said.

"Obviously," Kevin said.

"Did you come across anything else with this real-time program?"

"Yup," Kevin said. "I pretty much confirmed my earlier suspicion they are using the caves. Watch!"

Kevin changed the coordinates of the displayed grid on the computer screen to correspond to a specific portion of the limestone escarpment. He then asked the computer to trace the activity of his own double, creature number one.

Melanie watched as the red dot traced a geometric shape then disappeared. It then reappeared at the identical spot and traced a second shape. Then a similar sequence repeated itself for a third time.

"I guess I'd have to agree," Melanie said. "It sure looks like your double is going in and out of the rock face."

"When we go out there, I think we should make it a point to see our doubles," Kevin said. "They are the oldest of the creatures, and if any of the transgenic bonobos are acting like protohumans, it should be them."

Melanie nodded. "The idea of facing my double gives me the creeps. But we're not going to have a lot of time out there. And given the twelve-square-mile island it will be extraordinarily difficult for us to find a specific creature."

"You're wrong," Kevin said. "I've got the instruments they use for retrievals." He got up from the computer and went to his desk. When he returned, he was carrying the locator and the directional beacon that Bertram had given to him. He showed the apparatuses to Melanie and explained their use. Melanie was impressed.

"Where is that girl?" Melanie asked as she checked her watch. "I wanted to get this island visit over during lunch hour."

"Did Siegfried talk to you this morning?" Kevin asked.

"No, Bertram did," Melanie said. "He acted really mad and said he was disappointed in me. Can you imagine? I mean, is that suppose to break me up or what?"

"Did he give you any explanation about the smoke I've seen?" Kevin asked.

"Oh, yeah," Melanie said. "He went on at length how he'd just been told that Siegfried had a work crew out there building a bridge and burning trash. He said it was being done without his knowledge."

"I thought so," Kevin said. "Siegfried called me over just after nine. He gave me the same story. He even told me he'd just talked with Dr. Lyons and that Dr. Lyons was disappointed in us as well."

"It's enough to make you cry," Melanie said.

"I don't think he was telling the truth about the work crew," Kevin said.

"Of course he wasn't," Melanie said. "I mean, Bertram makes it a point to know everything that's going on about Isla Francesca. It makes you wonder if they think we were born yesterday."

Kevin stood up, fidgeted, and stared out his window at the distant island.

"What's wrong now?" Melanie questioned.

"Siegfried," Kevin said. He looked back at Melanie. "About his warning to apply Equatoguinean law to us. He reminded us that going to the island could be considered a capital offense. Don't you think we should take that threat seriously?"

"Hell, no!" Melanie said.

"How can you be so sure," Kevin said.

319

"Siegfried scares me."

"He'd scare me, too, if I was an Equatoguinean," Melanie said. "But we're not. We're Americans. While we're here in the Zone, good old American law applies to us. The worst thing that can happen is we get fired. And as I said last night, I'm not sure I wouldn't welcome it. Manhattan is sounding awfully good to me these days."

"I wish I felt as confident as you," Kevin said.

"Has your playing around with the computer this morning confirmed that the bonobos are remaining in two groups?"

Kevin nodded. "The first group is the largest and stays around the caves. It includes most of the older bonobos, including your double and mine. The other group is in a forest area on the north side of the Rio Diviso. It's composed mostly of younger animals, although the third oldest is with them. That's Raymond Lyons's double."

"Very curious," Melanie said.

"Hi, everybody," Candace called out while coming through the door, without knocking. "How'd I do timewise?. I didn't even blow-dry my hair." Instead of her normal French twist, her damp hair was combed back straight off her forehead.

"You did great," Melanie assured her. "And you were the only smart one to get some sleep. I have to admit, I'm exhausted."

"Did Siegfried Spallek get in touch with you?" Kevin asked.

"At about nine-thirty," Candace said. "He woke me up out of a sound sleep. I hope I made sense."

"What did he say?" Kevin asked.

"He was very nice, actually," Candace said. "He even apologized for what happened last night. He also had an explanation about the smoke coming from the island. He said it was from a work crew burning brush."

"We got the same message," Kevin said.

"What's your take on it?" Candace asked.

"We don't buy it," Melanie said. "It's too convenient."

"I sort of assumed as much," Candace said.

Melanie grabbed her paper bag. "Let's get this show on the road."

"Do you have the key?" Kevin questioned. He picked up the locator and the directional beacon.

"Of course I have the key," Melanie said.

As they went out the door Melanie told Candace she'd brought some lunch for them.

"Great!" Candace said. "I'm famished."

"Hold on a second," Kevin said when they reached the stairs. "Something just dawned on me. We must have been followed yesterday. That's the only way I can explain the way they surprised us. Of course, that really means I must have been followed, since I was the one who talked about the smoke situation with Bertram Edwards."

"That's a good point," Melanie said.

The three people stared at each other for a moment.

"What should we do?" Candace asked. "We don't want to be followed."

"The first thing is that we shouldn't use my car," Kevin said. "Where's yours, Melanie? With this dry weather we can manage without four-wheel drive."

"Downstairs in the parking lot," Melanie said. "I just drove in from the animal center."

"Was anybody following you?"

"Who knows?" Melanie said. "I wasn't watching."

"Hmmm," Kevin pondered. "I still think they'll be following me if they follow anybody. So, Melanie, go down and get in your car and head home."

"What will you guys do?"

"There's a tunnel in the basement that goes all the way out to the power station. Wait about five minutes at your house and pick us up at the power station. There's a side door that opens directly onto the parking lot. You know where I mean?"

"I think so," Melanie said.

"All right," Kevin said. "See you there."

They split up at the first floor, with Melanie going out into the noonday heat while Candace and Kevin descended to the basement level.

After walking for fifteen minutes, Candace commented on what a maze the hallways were.

"All the power comes from the same source," Kevin explained. "The tunnels connect all the main buildings except for the animal center, which has its own power station."

"One could get lost down here," Candace said.

"I did," Kevin admitted. "A number of times. But during the middle of the rainy season, I find these tunnels handy. They're both dry and cool."

As they neared the power station they could hear and feel the vibration of the turbines. A flight of metal steps took them up to the side door. As soon as they appeared, Melanie, who'd been parked under a malapa tree, cruised over and picked them up.

Kevin got in the back so Candace could climb into the front. Melanie pulled away immediately. The car's air-conditioning felt good given the heat and hundred-percent humidity.

"See anything suspicious?" Kevin asked.

"Not a thing," Melanie said. "And I drove around for a while pretending I was on errands. There wasn't anyone following me. I'm ninety-nine percent sure."

Kevin looked out the back window of Melanie's Honda and watched the area around the power station as it fell behind, then disappeared as they rounded a corner. No people had appeared, and there were no cars in pursuit.

"I'd say it looks good," Kevin said. He scrunched down on the backseat to be out of sight.

Melanie drove around the north rim of the town. While she did so, Candace broke out the sandwiches.

"Not bad," Candace said, taking a bite of a tuna fish on whole wheat.

"I had them made up at the animal-center commissary," Melanie explained. "There are drinks in the bottom of the bag."

"You want some, Kevin?" Candace called.

"I suppose," Kevin said. He stayed on his side. Candace passed him a sandwich and a soft drink between the front bucket seats.

They were soon on the road that led east out of town toward the native village. From Kevin's perspective, all he could see was the tops of the liana-covered trees that lined the road, plus a strip of hazy blue sky. After so many months of cloud cover and rain, it was good to see the sun.

"Anybody following us?" Kevin asked, after they'd driven for some time.

Melanie glanced in the rearview mirror. "I haven't seen a car," she said. There'd been no vehicular traffic in either direction, although there were plenty of native women carrying various burdens on their heads.

After they passed the parking lot in front of the general store at the native village and entered the track that led to the island staging area, Kevin sat up. He was no longer worried about being seen. Every few minutes, he looked behind to make sure they weren't being followed. Although he didn't admit it to the women, he was a nervous wreck.

"That log we hit last night should be coming up soon," Kevin warned.

"But we didn't go over it when they brought us out," Melanie said. "They must have moved it."

"You're right," Kevin said. He was impressed that Melanie remembered. After the machine-gun fire, the details of the previous night were murky in Kevin's mind.

Guessing they were getting close, Kevin moved forward so he could see out the front windshield between the two front seats. Despite the noontime sun the ability to see into the dense jungle lining the road was hardly any better than it had been the evening before. Little light penetrated the vegetation; it was like moving between two walls.

They drove into the clearing and stopped. The garage stood to their left while to the right they could see the mouth of the track that led down to the water's edge and the bridge.

"Should I drive down to the bridge?" Melanie asked.

Kevin's nervousness increased. Coming into a dead end bothered him. He debated driving down to the water's edge but guessed there wouldn't be enough room to turn around. That would mean they'd have to back out.

"My suggestion would be to park here," Kevin said. "But let's turn the car around first."

Kevin expected an argument, but Melanie put the car in gear without so much as a whimper. They left unspoken the fact that they would now have to walk past the spot where they'd been fired upon.

Melanie completed her three-point turn. "Okay, everybody, here we are," she said airily, as she pulled on the emergency brake. She was trying to buoy everyone's spirits. They were all tense.

"I just had an idea which I don't like," Kevin said.

"Now what?" Melanie asked, looking at him in the rearview mirror.

"Maybe I should quietly walk down to the bridge and make sure no one is around," Kevin said.

"Like who?" Melanie asked, but the thought of unwanted company had occurred to her as well.

Kevin took a deep breath to bolster his sagging courage and climbed out. "Anybody," he said. "Even Alphonse Kimba." He hiked up his pants and started off.

The track down toward the water was so thickly shrouded with vegetation, it was even more like a tunnel than the track in from the road. As soon as Kevin entered it, it twisted to the right. The canopy of trees and vines blocked out much of the light. The center strip of vegetation was so tall that the track was more like two parallel trails.

Kevin rounded the first bend, then stopped. The unmistakable sound of boots running on the damp ground combined with the jingling of metal against metal made his stomach turn. Ahead, the track turned to the left. Kevin held his breath. In the next instant, he saw a group of Equatoguinean soldiers in their camouflage fatigues, rounding the bend and coming in his direction. All were carrying Chinese assault rifles.

Kevin spun on his heels and sprinted back up the trail like he'd never sprinted before. As he reached the clearing, he yelled to Melanie to get the hell out of there. Reaching the car he threw open the rear door and dived in.

Melanie was trying to start the car. "What happened?" she screamed.

"Soldiers!" Kevin croaked. "A bunch of them!"

The car engine caught and roared to life. At the same time, the soldiers spilled into the clearing. One of them yelled as Melanie stomped on the accelerator.

The little car leaped forward, and Melanie fought the wheel. There was a burst of gunfire and the rear window of the Honda shattered into a million cubic shards. Kevin flattened himself against the backseat. Candace screamed as her window was blown out as well.

The track turned left just beyond the clearing. Melanie managed to keep the car in the tracks and then pushed the car to its limit. After they'd gone seventy yards, there was another distant burst of gunfire. A few stray bullets whined over the car as Melanie navigated another slight turn.

"Good God!" Kevin said, as he sat up and brushed the glass from the rear window off his torso.

"Now I'm really mad," Melanie said. "That was hardly a burst over our heads. Look at that rear window!"

"I think I want to retire," Kevin said. "I've always been afraid of those soldiers and now I know why."

"I guess the key to the bridge is not going to do us much good," Candace said. "What a waste after all the effort we went through to get it."

"It's damn irritating," Melanie agreed. "We're just going to have to come up with an alternate plan."

"I'm going to bed," Kevin said. He couldn't

believe these women; they seemed fearless. He put a hand over his heart; it was beating more rapidly than it ever had before.

CHAPTER 14

With a burst of speed, Jack made the green light at the intersection of First Avenue and Thirtieth Street and sailed across without slowing down. Angling the bike up the morgue's driveway, he didn't brake until the last minute. Moments later, he had the bike locked and was on his way to the office of Janice Jaeger, the night forensic investigator.

Jack was keyed up. After near conclusive identification of his floater as Carlo Franconi, Jack had gotten little sleep. He'd been on and off the phone with Janice, finally imploring her to get copies of all of Franconi's records from the Manhattan General Hospital. Her preliminary investigation had determined that Franconi had been hospitalized there.

Jack had also had Janice get the phone numbers of the European human organ distribution organizations from Bart Arnold's desk. Because of the six-hour-time difference, Jack had started calling after three A.M. He was most interested in the organization called Euro Transplant Foundation in the Netherlands. When they had no record of a Carlo Franconi as a recent liver recipient, Jack called

330

all the national organizations whose numbers he had. They included organizations in France, England, Italy, Sweden, Hungary, and Spain. No one had heard of Carlo Franconi. On top of that, most of the people he had spoken with said that it would be rare for a foreign national to get such a transplant because most of the countries had waiting lists comprised of their own citizens.

After only a few hours of sleep, Jack's curiosity had awakened him. Unable to get back to sleep, he'd decided to get into the morgue early to go over the material that Janice had collected.

"My word, you are eager," Janice commented as Jack came into her office.

"This is the kind of case that makes forensics fun," Jack said. "How'd you do at the MGH?"

"I got a lot of material," Janice said. "Mr. Franconi had multiple admissions over the years, mostly for hepatitis and cirrhosis."

"Ah, the plot thickens," Jack said. "When was the last admission?"

"About two months ago," Janice said. "But no transplant. There is mention of it, but if he had one, he didn't have it at the MGH." She handed Jack a large folder.

Jack hefted the package and smiled. "Guess I got a lot of reading to do."

"It looked pretty repetitive to me," Janice said.

"What about his doctor?" Jack asked. "Has he had one in particular or has he been playing the field?"

"One for the most part," Janice said. "Dr. Daniel Levitz on Fifth Avenue between Sixty-fourth and Sixty-fifth Street. His office number is written on the outside of your parcel."

"You are efficient," Jack said.

"I try to do my best," Janice said. "Have any luck with those European organ distribution organizations?"

"A complete strikeout," Jack said. "Have Bart give me a call as soon as he comes in. We have to go back and retry all the transplant centers in this country now that we have a name."

"If Bart's not in by the time I leave, I'll put a note on his desk," Janice said.

Jack whistled as he walked through communications on his way to the ID room. He could taste the coffee already while dreaming of the euphoria that the first cup of the day always gave him. But when he arrived he could see he was too early. Vinnie Amendola was just in the process of making it.

"Hurry up with that coffee," Jack said, as he dropped his heavy package onto the metal desk Vinnie used to read his newspaper. "It's an emergency this morning."

Vinnie didn't answer, which was out of character, and Jack noticed. "Are you still in a bad mood?" he asked.

Vinnie still didn't answer, but Jack's mind was already elsewhere. He'd seen the headlines on Vinnie's paper: Franconi's Body Found. Beneath the headline in slightly smaller print was: "Franconi's corpse languishing in the Medical Examiner's Office for twenty-four hours before identity established."

Jack sat down to read the article. As usual, it was written in a sarcastic bent with the implication that the city's medical examiners were bunglers. Jack thought it was interesting that while the journalist had had enough information to write the article, he didn't appear to know that the body had been headless and handless in a deliberate attempt to conceal its identity. Nor did it mention anything about the shotgun wound to its right upper quadrant.

After finishing with the coffee preparation, Vinnie came over to stand next to the desk while Jack read. Impatiently, he shifted his weight from one foot to the other. When Jack finally looked up Vinnie said irritably: "Do you mind! I'd like to have my paper."

"You see this article?" Jack asked, slapping the front page.

"Yeah, I seen it," Vinnie said.

Jack resisted the temptation to correct his English. Instead he said: "Did it surprise you? I mean, when we did the autopsy yesterday, did it ever cross your mind it might have been the missing Franconi?"

"No, why should it?" Vinnie said.

"I'm not saying it should," Jack said. "I'm just asking if it did."

"No," Vinnie said. "Let me have my paper! Why don't you buy your own? You're always reading mine."

Jack stood up, pushed Vinnie's paper toward him, and lifted the bundle from Janice. "You really are out of sorts lately. Maybe you need a vacation. You're fast becoming a grumpy old man."

"At least I'm not a cheapskate," Vinnie said. He picked up his paper and readjusted the pages that Jack had gotten out of alignment.

Jack went to the coffeemaker and poured himself a brimming cup. He took it over to the scheduling desk. While sipping contentedly, he went through the multitude of Franconi's hospital admissions. On his first perusal of the material, he just wanted the basics, so he read each discharge summary page. As Janice had already told him, the admissions were mostly due to liver problems starting from a bout of hepatitis he contracted in Naples, Italy.

Laurie arrived next. Before she even had her coat off, she asked Jack if he'd seen the paper or heard the morning news. Jack told her he'd seen the *Post*.

"Was it your doing?" Laurie asked, as she folded her coat and put it on a chair.

"What are you talking about?"

"The leak that we tentatively identified Franconi with your floater," Laurie said.

Jack gave a little laugh of disbelief. "I'm surprised you'd even ask. Why would I do such a thing?"

"I don't know, except you were so excited about it last night," Laurie said. "But I didn't mean any offense. I was just surprised to see it in the news so quickly."

"You and me both," Jack said. "Maybe it was Lou."

"I think that would surprise me even more than you," Laurie said.

"Why me?" Jack said. He sounded hurt.

"Last year you leaked the plague story," Laurie said.

"That was a completely different situation," Jack said defensively. "That was to save people."

"Well, don't get mad," Laurie said. To change the subject she asked: "What kind of cases do we have for today?"

"I didn't look," Jack admitted. "But the pile is small and I have a request. If possible, I'd like to have a paper day or really a research day."

Laurie bent over and counted the autopsy folders. "Only ten cases; no problem," she said. "I think I'll only do one myself. Now that Franconi's body is back, I'm even more interested to find out how it left here in the first place. The more I've thought about it, the more I believe it had to have been an inside job in some form or fashion."

There was a splashing sound followed by loud cursing. Both Laurie and Jack looked over at Vinnie, who'd jumped up to a standing position. He'd spilled his coffee all over his desk and even onto his lap.

"Watch out for Vinnie," Jack warned Laurie. "He's again in a foul mood."

"Are you all right, Vinnie?" Laurie called out.

"I'm okay," Vinnie said. He walked stiff-legged over to the coffeepot to get some paper towels.

"I'm a little confused," Jack said to Laurie. "Why does Franconi's return make you more interested in his disappearance?"

"Mainly because of what you found during the autopsy," Laurie said. "At first I thought that whoever stole the body had done it out of pure spite, like the killer wanted to deny the man a proper funeral, something like that. But now it seems that the body was taken to destroy the liver. That's weird. Initially I thought that solving the riddle of how the body disappeared was simply a challenge. Now I think if I can figure out how the body disappeared, we might be able to find out who did it."

"I'm beginning to understand what Lou said about feeling stupid about your ability to make associations," Jack said. "With Franconi's disappearance I always thought the 'why' was more important than the 'how.' You're suggesting they are related."

"Exactly," Laurie said. "The 'how' will lead to the 'who,' and the 'who' will explain the 'why.' "

"And you think someone who works here is involved," Jack said.

"I'm afraid I do," Laurie said. "I don't see how they could have pulled it off without someone on the inside. But I still have no clue how it happened."

After his call to Siegfried, Raymond's brain had finally succumbed to the high levels of hypnotic medication circulating in his bloodstream from the two sleeping pills. He slept soundly through the remaining early hours. The next thing he was aware of was Darlene opening the curtains to let in the daylight. It was almost eight o'clock, the time he'd asked to be awakened.

"Feel better, dear?" Darlene asked. She made Raymond sit forward so she could fluff up his pillow.

"I do," Raymond admitted, although his mind was fuzzy from the sleeping pills.

"I even made you your favorite breakfast," Darlene said. She went over to the bureau and lifted a wicker tray. She carried it over to the bed and placed it across Raymond's lap.

Raymond's eyes traveled around the tray. There was fresh-squeezed orange juice, two strips of bacon, a single-egg omelette, toast, and fresh coffee. In a side pocket was the morning paper.

"How's that?" Darlene asked proudly.

"Perfect," Raymond said. He reached up and gave her a kiss.

"Let me know when you want more coffee," Darlene said. Then she left the room.

With childlike pleasure Raymond buttered his toast and sipped his orange juice. As far as he was concerned, there was nothing quite so wonderful as the smell of coffee and bacon in the morning.

Taking a bite of both bacon and omelette at the same time to savor the combined tastes, Raymond lifted the paper, opened it, and glanced at the headlines.

He gasped, inadvertently inhaling some of his food. He coughed so hard, he bucked the wicker tray off the bed. It crashed upside down on the carpet.

Darlene came running into the room and stood wringing her hands, while Raymond went through series of coughing jags that turned him tomato red.

"Water!" he squeaked between fits.

Darlene dashed into the bathroom and returned with a glass. Raymond clutched it and managed to drink a small amount. The bacon and egg that he'd had in his mouth was now distributed in an arc around the bed.

"Are you all right?" Darlene asked. "Should I call 911?"

"The wrong way down," Raymond croaked. He pointed to his Adam's apple.

It took Raymond five minutes to recover. By that time, his throat was sore and his voice hoarse. Darlene had cleaned up most of the mess he'd caused except for the coffee stain on the white carpet.

"Did you see the paper?" Raymond asked Darlene.

She shook her head, so Raymond spread it out for her.

"Oh, my," she said.

"Oh, my!" Raymond repeated sarcastically. "And you were wondering why I was still worried about Franconi!" Raymond forcibly crumpled the paper.

"What are you going to do?" Darlene asked.

"I suppose I have to go back and see Vinnie Dominick," Raymond said. "He promised me the body was gone. Some job he did!"

The phone rang and Raymond jumped.

"Do you want me to answer it?" Darlene asked.

Raymond nodded. He wondered who could be calling so early.

Darlene picked up the phone and said hello

followed by several yeses. Then she put the phone on hold.

"It's Dr. Waller Anderson," Darlene said with a smile. "He wants to come on board."

Raymond exhaled. Until then he'd not been aware he'd been holding his breath. "Tell him we're pleased, but that I'll have to call him later."

Darlene did as she was told and then hung up the phone. "At least that was good news," she said.

Raymond rubbed his forehead and audibly groaned. "I just wish everything would go as well as the business side."

The phone rang again. Raymond motioned for Darlene to answer it. After saying hello and listening for a moment, her smile quickly faded. She put the phone on hold and told Raymond it was Taylor Cabot.

Raymond swallowed hard. His already irritated throat had gone dry. He took a quick swig of water and took the receiver.

"Hello, sir!" Raymond managed. His voice was still hoarse.

"I'm calling from my car phone," Taylor said. "So I won't be too specific. But I have just been informed of the reemergence of a problem I thought had been taken care of. What I said earlier about this issue still stands. I hope you understand."

"Of course, sir," Raymond squeaked. "I will . . ."

Raymond stopped speaking. He took the phone away from his ear and looked at it. Taylor had cut him off.

"Just what I need," Raymond said, as he handed the phone back to Darlene. "Another threat from Cabot to close down the program."

Raymond put his feet over the side of the bed. As he stood up and slipped on his robe, he could still feel the remnants of yesterday's headache. "I have to go find Vinnie Dominick's number. I need another miracle."

By eight o'clock Laurie and the others were down in the "pit" starting their autopsies. Jack had stayed in the ID room to read through the records of Carlo Franconi's hospital admissions. When he noticed the time, he went back to the forensics area to find out why the chief investigator, Bart Arnold, had not come in that day. Jack was surprised when he found the man in his office.

"Didn't Janice talk to you this morning?" Jack asked. He and Bart were good enough friends so that Jack thought nothing of marching right into Bart's office and plopping himself down.

"I just came in fifteen minutes ago," Bart said. "Janice was already gone."

"Wasn't there a message on your desk?" Jack asked.

Bart started to peek around under the clutter. Bart's desk looked strikingly similar to Jack's. Bart pulled out a note which he read aloud: "Important! Call Jack Stapleton immediately." It was signed "Janice."

"Sorry," Bart said. "I'd have seen it eventually." He smiled weakly, knowing there was no excuse.

"I suppose you've heard that my floater has been just about conclusively identified as Carlo Franconi," Jack said.

"So I've heard," Bart said.

"That means I want you to go back to UNOS and all the centers that do liver transplantation with the name."

"That's a lot easier than asking them to check if any of their recent transplants is missing," Bart said. "With all the phone numbers handy I can do that in a flash."

"I spent most of the night on the phone with the organizations in Europe responsible for organ allocation," Jack said. "I came up with zilch."

"Did you talk to Euro Transplant in the Netherlands?" Bart asked.

"I called them first," Jack said. "They had no record of a Franconi."

"Then it's pretty safe to say that Franconi didn't have his transplant in Europe," Bart said. "Euro Transplant keeps tabs on the whole continent."

"The next thing I want is for someone to go visit Franconi's mother and talk her into giving a blood sample. I want Ted Lynch to run a mitochondrial DNA match with the floater. That will clinch the identity, so it will no longer be presumptive. Also have the investigator ask the woman if her son had a liver transplant. It will be interesting to hear what she has to say."

Bart wrote Jack's requests down. "What else?" Bart asked.

"I think that's it for now," Jack said. "Janice told me Franconi's doctor's name is Daniel Levitz. Is that anyone you have come in contact with?"

"If it's the Levitz on Fifth, then I've come in contact with him."

"What was your take?" Jack asked.

"High-profile practice with wealthy clientele. He's a good internist as far as I could tell. The curious thing is that he takes care of a lot of the crime families, so it's not surprising he was taking care of Carlo Franconi."

"Different families?" Jack questioned. "Even families in competition with each other?"

"Strange, isn't it?" Bart said. "It must be one big headache for the poor receptionist who does the scheduling. Can you imagine having two rival crime figures with their bodyguards in the waiting room at the same time?"

"Life's stranger than fiction," Jack said.

"Do you want me to go to Dr. Levitz and get what I can on Franconi?" Bart asked.

"I think I'll do that myself," Jack said. "I have a sneaking suspicion that when talking with Franconi's doctor what's unsaid is going to be more important than what is said. You concentrate on finding out where Franconi got his transplant. I think that's going to be the key piece of information in this case. Who knows, it might just explain everything."

"There you are!" a robust voice boomed. Both Jack and Bart looked up to see the doorway literally filled with the imposing figure of Dr. Calvin Washington, the deputy chief.

"I've been looking all over for you, Stapleton," Calvin growled. "Come on! The chief wants to see you."

Jack gave Bart a wink before getting to his feet. "Probably just another of the many awards he's given me."

"I wouldn't be so glib if I were you," Calvin snapped, as he made room for Jack to pass. "Once again, you got the old man all riled up."

Jack followed Calvin to the administration area. Just before going into the front office, Jack caught a glimpse of the waiting room. There were more than the usual number of journalists.

"Something going on?" Jack asked.

"As if I have to tell you," Calvin grunted.

Jack didn't understand, but he didn't have a chance to ask more. Calvin was already asking Mrs. Sanford, Bingham's secretary, if they could go into the chief's office.

As it turned out, the timing wasn't good, and Jack was relegated to sitting on the bench that faced Mrs. Sanford's desk. Obviously, she was as upset as her boss and treated Jack to several disapproving looks. Jack felt like a naughty schoolboy waiting to see the principal. Calvin used the time by disappearing into his own office to make a few phone calls.

Having a reasonable idea of what the chief was upset about, Jack tried to come up with an explanation. Unfortunately, none came to mind. After all, he could have waited to get Franconi's X rays until Bingham's arrival that morning.

"You can go in now," Mrs. Sanford said, without looking up from her typing. She'd noticed the light on her extension phone had gone out, meaning the chief was off the phone.

Jack entered the chief's office with a sense of déjà vu. A year ago, during a series of infectious disease cases, Jack had managed to drive the chief to distraction, and there had been several such confrontations.

"Get in here and sit down," Bingham said roughly.

Jack took the seat in front of the man's desk. Bingham had aged in the last few years. He looked considerably older than sixty-three. He glared at Jack through his wire-rimmed glasses. Despite his jowls and sagging flesh,

Jack saw that his eyes were as intense and intelligent as ever.

"I was just beginning to think you were really fitting in around here, and now this," Bingham said.

Jack didn't respond. He felt it best not to say anything until he was asked a question.

"Can I at least ask why?" Bingham said obligingly in his deep, husky voice.

Jack shrugged. "Curiosity," Jack said. "I was excited and I couldn't wait."

"Curiosity!" Bingham roared. "That was the same lame excuse you used last year when you disregarded my orders and went over to the MGH."

"At least I'm consistent," Jack said.

Bingham moaned. "And now here comes the impertinence. You really haven't changed much, have you?"

"My basketball has improved," Jack said.

Jack heard the door open. He turned to see Calvin slip into the room. Calvin folded his massive arms across his chest and stood to the side like an elite harem guard.

"I'm not getting anywhere with him," Bingham complained to Calvin, as if Jack were no longer in the room. "I thought you said his behavior had improved."

"It had, until this episode," Calvin said. He then glared down at Jack. "What irks me," Calvin said, finally addressing Jack, "is that you know damn well that releases from the medical examiner's office are to come from Dr. Bingham or through public relations, period! You examiner grunts are not to take it upon yourselves to divulge information. The reality is that this job is highly politicized, and in the face of our current problems we certainly don't need more bad press."

"Time out," Jack said. "Something's not right here. I'm not sure we're talking the same language."

"You can say that again," Bingham asserted.

"What I mean is," Jack said, "I don't think we are talking about the same issue. When I came in here, I thought I was being called onto the carpet because I bullied the janitor into giving me keys for this office so I could find Franconi's films."

"Hell, no!" Bingham yelled. He pointed his finger at Jack's nose. "It's because you leaked the story about Franconi's body being discovered here at the morgue after it had been stolen. What did you think? This would somehow advance your career?"

"Hold up," Jack said. "First, I'm not all that excited about advancing my career. Second, I was not responsible for this story getting to the media."

"You're not?" Bingham asked.

"Certainly, you're not suggesting that Laurie Montgomery was responsible?" Calvin asked.

"Not at all," Jack said. "But it wasn't me. Look, to tell you the truth, I don't even think it's a story."

"That's not how the media feels," Bingham said. "Nor the mayor for that matter. He's already called me twice this morning, asking what kind of circus we're running around here. This Franconi business continues to make us look bad in the eyes of the entire city — particularly when news about our own office takes us by surprise."

"The real story about Franconi isn't about his body going on an overnight out of the morgue," Jack said. "It's about the fact that the man seemingly had a liver transplant that no one knows about, that's hard to detect by DNA analysis, and that somebody wanted to hide it."

Bingham looked up at Calvin, who raised his hands defensively. "This is the first I've heard about this," he said.

Jack gave a rapid summary of his autopsy findings and then told about Ted Lynch's confusing DNA analysis results.

"This sounds weird," Bingham said. He took off his glasses and wiped his rheumy eyes. "It also sounds bad, considering that I want this whole Franconi business to fade away. If there is something truly screwy going on like Franconi getting an unauthorized liver, then that's not going to happen."

"I'll know more today," Jack said. "I've got

Bart Arnold contacting all the transplant centers around the country, John DeVries up in the lab running assays for immuno suppressants, Maureen O'Conner in histology pushing through the slides, and Ted doing a six polymarker DNA test, which he contends is foolproof. By this afternoon, we'll know for sure whether there'd been a transplant, and, if we're lucky, where it had taken place."

Bingham squinted across his desk at Jack. "And you're sure you didn't leak today's newspaper story to the media?"

"Scout's honor," Jack said, holding up two fingers to form a V.

"All right, I apologize," Bingham said. "But listen, Stapleton, keep this all under your hat. And don't go irritating everyone under the sun, so that I start getting calls complaining about your behavior. You have a knack for getting under people's skin. And finally, promise me that nothing goes to the media unless it goes through me. Understand?"

"As clear as a crystal," Jack said.

Jack could rarely find an excuse to get out on his mountain bike during the day, so that it was with a good deal of pleasure that he pedaled with the traffic up First Avenue on his way to visit Dr. Daniel Levitz. There was no sun, but the temperature was pleasantly in the fifties, heralding the coming spring. For

Jack, spring was the best season in New York City.

With his bike safely secured to a NO PARKING sign, Jack walked up to the sidewalk entrance of Dr. Daniel Levitz's office. Jack had called ahead to make sure the doctor was in, but he'd specifically avoided making an appointment. It was Jack's feeling that a surprise visit might be more fruitful. If Franconi had had a transplant, there was definitely something surreptitious about it.

"Your name please?" the silver-haired matronly receptionist asked.

Jack flashed open his medical examiner badge. Its shiny surface and official appearance confused most people into thinking it was a police badge. In situations like this, Jack didn't explain the difference. The badge never failed to cause a reaction.

"I must see the doctor," Jack said, slipping his badge back inside his pocket. "The sooner the better."

When the receptionist regained her voice, she asked for Jack's name. When he gave it, he left off the title of doctor so as not to clarify the nature of his employ.

The receptionist immediately scraped back her chair and disappeared into the depths of the office.

Jack's eyes roamed the waiting room. It was generous in size and lavishly decorated. It was a far cry from the utilitarian waiting room he'd had when he'd been a practicing ophthalmologist. That had been before the retraining necessitated by the managed-care invasion. To Jack, it seemed like a previous life, and in many ways it was.

There were five well-dressed people in the waiting room. All eyed Jack clandestinely as they continued to peruse their respective magazines. As they noisily flipped the pages, Jack sensed an aura of irritation, as if they knew he was about to upset the schedule and relegate them to additional waiting. Jack hoped none of them were notorious crime figures who might consider such an inconvenience a reason for revenge.

The receptionist reappeared, and with embarrassing subservience, she guided Jack back to the doctor's private study. Once Jack was inside, she closed the door.

Dr. Levitz was not in the room. Jack sat in one of the two chairs facing the desk and surveyed the surroundings. There were the usual framed diplomas and licenses, the family pictures, and even the stacks of unread medical journals. It was all familiar to Jack and gave him a shudder. From his current vantage point, he wondered how he'd lasted as long as he had in a similar, confining environment.

Dr. Daniel Levitz came through a second door. He was dressed in his white coat complete with pocket full of tongue depressors and assorted pens. A stethoscope hung from his neck. Compared with Jack's muscular, thick-shouldered, six-foot frame, Dr. Levitz was rather short and almost fragile in appearance.

Jack immediately noticed the man's nervous tics, which involved slight twists and nods of his head. Dr. Levitz gave no indication he was aware of these movements. He shook hands stiffly with Jack and then retreated behind the vast expanse of his desk.

"I'm very busy," Dr. Levitz said. "But, of course, I always have time for the police."

"I'm not the police," Jack said. "I'm Dr. Jack Stapleton from the Office of the Chief Medical Examiner of New York."

Dr. Levitz's head twitched as did his sparse mustache. He appeared to swallow. "Oh," he commented.

"I wanted to talk to you briefly about one of your patients," Jack said.

"My patients' conditions are confidential," Dr. Levitz said, as if by rote.

"Of course," Jack said. He smiled. "That is, of course, until they have died and become a medical examiner's case. You see, I want to ask you about Mr. Carlo Franconi."

Jack watched as Dr. Levitz went through a number of bizarre motions, making Jack glad the man had not gone into brain surgery.

"I still respect my patients' confidentiality," he said.

"I can understand your position from an ethical point of view," Jack said. "But I should remind you that we medical examiners in the State of New York have subpoena power in such a circumstance. So, why don't we just have a conversation? Who knows, we might be able to clear things up."

"What do you want to know?" Dr. Levitz asked.

"I learned from reading Mr. Franconi's extensive hospital history that he'd had a long bout with liver problems leading to liver failure," Jack said.

Dr. Levitz nodded, which caused his right shoulder to jerk several times. Jack waited until these involuntary movements subsided.

"To come right to the point," Jack said, "the big question is whether or not Mr. Franconi had a liver transplant."

At first Levitz did not speak. He merely twitched. Jack was determined to wait the man out.

"I don't know anything about a liver transplant," Dr. Levitz said finally.

"When did you see him last?" Jack asked.

Dr. Levitz picked up his phone and asked one of his assistants to bring in Mr. Carlo Franconi's record.

"It will just be a moment," Dr. Levitz said.

"In one of Mr. Franconi's hospital admissions about three years ago, you specifically wrote that it was your opinion that a transplant would be necessary. Do you remember writing that?"

"Not specifically," Dr. Levitz said. "But I was aware of a deteriorating condition, as well as Mr. Franconi's failure to stop drinking."

"But you never mentioned it again," Jack said. "I found that surprising when it was easy to see a gradual but relentless deterioration in his liver function tests over the next couple of years."

"A doctor can only do so much to influence his patient's behavior," Dr. Levitz said.

The door opened and the deferential receptionist brought in a fat folder. Wordlessly she placed it on Dr. Levitz's desk and withdrew.

Dr. Levitz picked it up and, after a quick glance, said that he'd seen Carlo Franconi a month previously.

"What did you see him for?"

"An upper respiratory infection," Dr. Levitz said. "I prescribed some antibiotic. Apparently, it worked."

"Did you examine him?"

"Of course!" Dr. Levitz said with indignation. "I always examine my patients."

"Had he had a liver transplant?"

"Well, I didn't do a complete physical," Dr. Levitz explained. "I examined him appropriately in reference to his complaint and his symptoms."

"You didn't even feel his liver, knowing his history?" Jack asked.

"I didn't write it down if I did," Dr. Levitz said.

"Did you do any blood work that would reflect liver function?" Jack asked.

"Only a bilirubin," Dr. Levitz said.

"Why only a bilirubin?"

"He'd been jaundiced in the past," Dr. Levitz said. "He looked better, but I wanted to document it."

"What was the result?" Jack asked.

"It was within normal limits," Dr. Levitz said.

"So, except for his upper respiratory infection, he was doing quite well," Jack said.

"Yes, I suppose you could say that," Dr. Levitz said.

"Almost like a miracle," Jack said. "Especially as you've already mentioned the man was unwilling to curb his alcohol intake."

"Perhaps he finally had stopped," Dr. Levitz said. "After all, people can change."

"Would you mind if I looked at his record?" Jack asked.

"Yes, I would mind," Dr. Levitz said. "I've already stated my ethical position about confidentiality. If you want these records, you will have to subpoena them. I'm sorry. I don't mean to be obstructive."

"That's quite all right," Jack said agreeably. He stood up. "I'll let the state's attorney's office know how you feel. Meanwhile, thanks for your time, and if you don't mind, I'll

355

probably be talking with you in the near future. There's something very strange about this case, and I intend to get to the bottom of it."

Jack smiled to himself, as he undid the locks on his bike. It was so obvious that Dr. Levitz knew more than he was willing to say. How much more, Jack didn't know, but certainly it added to the intrigue. Jack had an intuitive sense that not only was this the most interesting case he'd had so far in his forensics career, it might be the most interesting case he'd ever have.

Returning to the morgue, he stashed his bike in the usual location, went up to his office to drop off his coat, then went directly to the DNA lab. But Ted wasn't ready for him.

"I need a couple more hours," Ted said. "And I'll call you! You don't have to come up here."

Disappointed but undeterred, Jack descended a floor to histology and checked on the progress of his permanent microscopic sections on what was now labeled the Franconi case.

"My god!" Maureen complained. "What do you expect, miracles? I'm rushing your slides through ahead of everybody else, but still you'll be lucky to get them today."

Still trying to keep his spirits up and his curiosity at bay, Jack rode the elevator down to the second floor and sought out John

DeVries in the lab.

"The assays for cyclosporin A and FK506 are not easy," John snapped. "Besides, we're backed up as it is. You can't expect instant service with the budget I have to work with."

"Okay!" Jack said agreeably, as he backed out of the lab. He knew that John was an irascible individual, and if aroused, he could be passive aggressive. If that happened, it might be weeks before Jack got the test results.

Descending yet another floor, Jack went into Bart Arnold's office and implored the man to give him something since he'd struck out every place else.

"I've made a lot of calls," Bart said. "But you know the situation with voice mail. You almost never get anyone on the phone anymore. So, I got a lot of messages out there, waiting for callbacks."

"Jeez," Jack complained. "I feel like a teenage girl with a new dress, waiting to get asked to the prom."

"Sorry," Bart said. "If it's any consolation, we did manage to get a blood sample from Franconi's mother. It's already up in the DNA lab."

"Was the mother asked whether her son had a liver transplant?"

"Absolutely," Bard said. "Mrs. Franconi assured the investigator that she didn't know anything about a transplant. But she did admit that her son had been much healthier lately."

"To what did she attribute his sudden health?" Jack asked.

"She says he went away to a spa someplace and came back a new man."

"Did she happen to say where?" Jack questioned.

"She didn't know," Bart said. "At least that's what she told the investigator, and the investigator told me that she thought she was telling the truth."

Jack nodded as he got to his feet. "Figures," he said. "Getting a bona fide tip from the mother would have been much too easy."

"I'll keep you informed as soon as I start getting callbacks," Bart said.

"Thanks," Jack said.

Feeling frustrated, Jack walked through communications to the ID room. He thought maybe some coffee would cheer him up. He was surprised to find Lieutenant Detective Lou Soldano busily helping himself to a cup.

"Uh-oh," Lou said. "Caught red-handed."

Jack eyed the homicide detective. He looked better than he had in days. Not only was the top button of his shirt buttoned, but his tie was cinched up in place. On top of that, he was close shaven and his hair was combed.

"You look almost human today," Jack said.

"I feel that way," Lou said. "I got my first decent night's sleep in days. Where's Laurie?"

"In the pit, I presume," Jack said.

"I gotta pat her on the back again for making that association with your floater after watching the video," Lou said. "All of us down at headquarters think it might lead to a break in this case. Already we've gotten a couple of good tips from our informers because it's stimulated a lot of talk in the streets, especially over in Queens."

"Laurie and I were surprised to see it in the papers this morning," Jack commented. "That was a lot faster than we expected. Do you have any idea who was the source?"

"I was," Lou said innocently. "But I was careful not to give any details other than the fact that the body had been identified. Why, is there a problem?"

"Only that Bingham went mildly ballistic," Jack said. "And I was hauled in as the culprit."

"Gosh, I'm sorry," Lou said. "It didn't dawn on me it could cause a problem here. I guess I should have run it by you. Well, I owe you."

"Forget it," Jack said. "It's already patched up." He poured himself some coffee, shoveled in some sugar, and added a dollop of cream.

"At least it had the desired effect on the street," Lou said. "And we learned something important already. The people who killed him were definitely not the same people who took his body and mauled it."

"Doesn't surprise me," Jack said.

"No?" Lou questioned. "I thought that was the general consensus around here. At least that's what Laurie said."

"She now thinks the people that took the body did it because they didn't want anyone to know he'd had a liver transplant," Jack said. "I still favor the idea it was done to conceal the individual's identity."

"Really," Lou said pensively, sipping his coffee. "That doesn't make any sense to me. You see we're reasonably sure the body was taken on orders from the Lucia crime family, the direct competitors of the Vaccarros, who we understand had Franconi killed."

"Good grief!" Jack exclaimed. "Are you sure about that?"

"Reasonably," Lou said. "The informer who divulged it is usually reliable. Of course, we don't have any names. That's the frustrating part."

"Just the idea that organized crime is involved is appalling," Jack said. "It means that the Lucia people are somehow involved in organ transplants. If that doesn't make you lose sleep, nothing will."

"Calm down!" Raymond yelled into the phone. The moment he'd been about to leave the apartment, the phone had rung. When he heard it was Dr. Daniel Levitz on the line, he'd taken the call.

"Don't tell me to calm down!" Daniel

360

shouted back. "You've seen the papers. They have Franconi's body! And already a medical examiner by the name of Dr. Jack Stapleton has been in my office asking for Franconi's records."

"You didn't give them, did you?" Raymond asked.

"Of course not!" Daniel snapped. "But he condescendingly reminded me that he could subpoena them. I'm telling you, this guy was very direct and very aggressive, and he vowed to get to the bottom of the case. He suspects Franconi had a transplant. He asked me directly."

"Do your records have any information at all about his transplant or our program?" Raymond asked.

"No, I followed your suggestions in that regard to the letter," Daniel said. "But it's going to look very strange if anybody looks at my records. After all, I'd been documenting Franconi's deteriorating status for years. Then all of a sudden, his liver function studies are normal without any explanation, nothing! Not even a comment. I'm telling you there'll be questions, and I don't know whether I can handle them. I'm very upset. I wish I'd never gotten involved in all this."

"Now let's not get carried away," Raymond said with a calmness that he himself did not feel. "There's no way Stapleton could get to the bottom of the case. Our concern about an autopsy was purely hypothetical and based on an infinitesimally small chance someone with the IQ of Einstein could figure out the source of the transplant. It's not going to happen. But I appreciate your calling me about Dr. Stapleton's visit. As it turns out, I'm on my way this very minute to have a meeting with Vinnie Dominick. With his resources, I'm sure he'll be able to take care of everything. After all, to a large measure, he's responsible for the present situation."

As soon as he could, Raymond got off the phone. Appeasing Dr. Daniel Levitz wasn't doing anything for his own anxiety. After advising Darlene what to say in the unlikely chance Taylor Cabot called back, he left the apartment. Catching a taxi at the corner of Madison and Sixty-fourth, he instructed the cabbie how to get to Corona Avenue in Elmhurst.

The scene at the Neopolitan Restaurant was exactly the same as it had been the day before, with the addition of the stale smell of a couple of hundred more cigarettes. Vinnie Dominick was sitting in the same booth and his minions were lounging on the same bar stools. The obese bearded man was again busily washing glassware.

Raymond lost no time. After coming through the heavy red velvet drape at the door, he made a beeline for Vinnie's booth and slid in without invitation. He pushed forward the crumpled newspaper, which he'd painstakingly smoothed out, across the table.

Vinnie gazed down at the headlines nonchalantly.

"As you can see, there's a problem," Raymond said. "You promised me the body was gone. Obviously, you screwed up."

Vinnie picked up his cigarette, took a long drag, then blew the smoke at the ceiling.

"Doc," Vinnie said. "You never fail but to amaze me. You either have a lot of nerve or you're crazy. I don't tolerate this kind of disrespect even from my trusted lieutenants. Either you reword what you just said to me or get up and get yourself lost before I get really pissed."

Raymond swallowed hard while he got a finger between his neck and his shirt and adjusted his collar. Remembering to whom he was speaking gave him a chill. A mere nod from Vinnie Dominick could find him bobbing around in the East River.

"I'm sorry," Raymond said meekly. "I'm not myself. I'm very upset. After I saw the headlines, I got a call from the CEO of Gen-Sys, threatening the whole program. I also got a call from Franconi's doctor, who told me he'd been approached by one of the medical examiners. An ME named Jack Stapleton dropped by his office wanting to see Franconi's records."

"Angelo!" Vinnie called out. "Come over here!"

Angelo ambled over to the booth. Vinnie asked him if he knew a Dr. Jack Stapleton at the morgue. Angelo shook his head.

"I've never seen him," Angelo said. "But Vinnie Amendola mentioned him when he called this morning. He said Stapleton was all fired up about Franconi because Franconi is his case."

"You see, I've gotten a few calls myself," Vinnie said. "Not only did I get a call from Vinnie Amendola who's still sweating it because we leaned on him to help us get Franconi out of the morgue. I also got another call from my wife's brother who runs the funeral home that took the body out. Seems that Dr. Laurie Montgomery paid a visit and was asking about a body that doesn't exist."

"I'm sorry that this has all gone so badly," Raymond said.

"You and me both," Vinnie said. "To tell you the truth, I can't understand how they got the body back. We went to some effort knowing the ground was too hard to bury it out in Westchester. So we took it way the hell out off Coney Island and dumped it into the ocean."

"Obviously, something went wrong," Raymond said. "With all due respect, what can be done at this point?"

"As far as the body is concerned, we can't

364

do anything. Vinnie Amendola told Angelo that the autopsy was already done. So that's that."

Raymond moaned and cradled his head. His headache had intensified.

"Just a second, Doc," Vinnie said. "I want to reassure you about something. Since I knew the reason why an autopsy might cause problems for your program, I had Angelo and Carlo destroy Franconi's liver."

Raymond raised his head. A ray of hope had appeared on the horizon. "How did you do that?" he asked.

"With a shotgun," Vinnie said. "They blasted the hell out of the liver. They totally destroyed this whole portion of the abdomen." Vinnie made a circling motion with his hand over his right upper quadrant. "Right, Angelo?"

Angelo nodded. "The entire magazine of a pump action Remington. The guy's gut looked like hamburger."

"So I don't think you have as much to worry about as you think," Vinnie said to Raymond.

"If Franconi's liver was totally destroyed, why is Jack Stapleton asking whether Franconi had a transplant?" Raymond asked.

"Is he?" Vinnie asked.

"He asked Dr. Levitz directly," Raymond said.

Vinnie shrugged. "He must have gotten a clue some other way. At any rate, the problem now seems to be focused on these two characters: Dr. Jack Stapleton and Dr. Laurie Montgomery."

Raymond raised his eyebrows expectantly.

"As I already told you, Doc," Vinnie continued. "If it weren't for Vinnie Junior and his bum kidneys, I wouldn't have gotten involved in all this. The fact that I've since gotten my wife's brother into this situation compounds my problem. Now that I got him involved I can't leave him dangling, you see what I'm saying? So, here's what I'm thinking. I'll have Angelo and Franco pay a visit to these two doctors and take care of things. Would you mind that, Angelo?"

Raymond looked hopefully at Angelo, and for the first time since Raymond had seen Angelo, Angelo smiled. It wasn't much of a smile because all the scar tissue precluded most facial movement, but it was a smile nonetheless.

"I've been looking forward to meeting Laurie Montgomery for five years," Angelo said.

"I suspected as much," Vinnie said. "Can you get their addresses from Vinnie Amendola?"

"I'm sure he'll be happy to give us Dr. Stapleton's," Angelo said. "He wants this messy situation cleared up as much as anybody. As far as Laurie Montgomery is concerned, I already know her address."

Vinnie stubbed out his cigarette and raised his own eyebrows. "So, Doc, what do you think of the idea of Angelo and Franco visiting the two pesky medical examiners and convincing them to see things our way? They have to be convinced that they are causing us considerable inconvenience, if you know what I mean." A wry smile appeared on his face, and he winked.

Raymond let out a little laugh of relief. "I can't think of a better solution." He worked his way along the curved, velvet banquette seat and stood up. "Thank you, Mr. Dominick. I'm much obliged, and apologize again for my thoughtless outburst when I first arrived."

"Hold on, Doc," Vinnie said. "We haven't discussed compensation yet."

"I thought this would be covered under the rubric of our prior agreement," Raymond said, trying to sound businesslike without offending Vinnie. "After all, Franconi's body was not supposed to reappear."

"That's not the way I see it," Vinnie said. "This is an extra. Since you've already bargained away the tuition issue, I'm afraid we're now talking about recouping some of my initiation fee. What about twenty thousand? That sounds like a nice round figure."

Raymond was outraged, but he managed to stifle a response. He also remembered what happened the last time he tried to bargain with Vinnie Dominick: the cost doubled.

"It might take me a little time to get that kind of money together," Raymond said.

"That's fine, Doc," Vinnie said. "Just as long as we have an agreement. From my end, I'll get Angelo and Franco right on it."

"Wonderful," Raymond managed to say before leaving.

"Are you serious about this?" Angelo asked Vinnie.

"I'm afraid so," Vinnie said. "I guess it wasn't such a smart idea to get my brother-in-law involved in all this, although at the time we didn't have much choice. One way or the other, I got to clean it up otherwise my wife will have my balls. The only good part is that I was able to get the good doc to pay for what I'd have to do anyway."

"When do you want us to take care of those two?" Angelo asked.

"The sooner the better," Vinnie said. "In fact, you'd better do it tonight!"

CHAPTER 15

"At what time did you expect your guests?" Esmeralda asked Kevin. Her body and head were wrapped in a handsome bright orange-and-green fabric.

"Seven o'clock," Kevin said, happy for the distraction. He'd been sitting at his desk, trying to fool himself into believing he was reading one of his molecular biology journals. In reality, he was tortured by repeatedly running through the harrowing events of that afternoon.

He could still see the soldiers in their red berets and jungle camouflage fatigues seemingly coming out of nowhere. He could hear their boots pounding against the moist earth and the jangle of their equipment as they ran. Worse yet, he could feel the same sickening terror that he'd felt when he'd turned to flee, expecting at any instant to hear the sound of machine-gun fire.

The dash across the clearing to the car and the wild ride had been somehow anti-climactic to that initial fright. The windows being shot out had an almost surreal quality that somehow couldn't compare to his first

369

glimpse of those soldiers.

Melanie had once again responded to the event completely differently than Kevin. It made Kevin wonder if growing up in Manhattan had somehow toughened her for such experiences. Rather than expressing fear, Melanie was more angry than afraid. She was furious at the soldiers' wanton destruction of what she considered her property, even though the car technically belonged to Gen-Sys.

"The dinner is prepared," Esmeralda said. "I shall keep it warm."

Kevin thanked his attentive housekeeper, and she disappeared back into the kitchen. Tossing aside his journal, Kevin got up from his desk and walked out onto the veranda. Night had fallen, and he was beginning to worry about where Melanie and Candace could be.

Kevin's house fronted a small grassy square illuminated by old-fashioned street lamps. Directly across the square was Siegfried Spallek's house. It was similar to Kevin's with an arcaded first floor, a veranda around the second, and dormers in its steeply pitched roof. At present, there were lights only in the kitchen end of the house. Apparently, the manager had not yet come home.

Hearing laughter to his left, Kevin turned in the direction of the waterfront. There had been a tropical downpour for an hour that had just ended fifteen minutes previously. The cobblestones were steaming since they'd still been hot from the sun. Into this lighted mist walked the two women, arm in arm, laughing merrily.

"Hey, Kevin!" Melanie shouted, spying Kevin on his balcony. "How come you didn't send a carriage?"

The women walked to a point directly beneath Kevin who was embarrassed by their revelry.

"What are you talking about?" Kevin asked.

"Well, you didn't expect us to get soaked, did you?" Melanie joked. Candace giggled.

"Come on up," Kevin encouraged. His eyes roamed around the small square, hoping that his neighbors weren't being disturbed.

The women came up the stairs with great commotion. Kevin met them in the hall. Melanie insisted on giving Kevin a kiss on both cheeks. Candace did likewise.

"Sorry we're late," Melanie said. "But the rain forced us to take shelter at the Chickee Bar."

"And a friendly group of men from the motor pool insisted on buying us piña coladas," Candace said gaily.

"It's okay," Kevin said. "But dinner is ready."

"Fantastic," Candace said. "I'm famished."

"Me too," Melanie said. She reached down and slipped off her shoes. "I hope you don't mind my going barefoot. My shoes got a little wet on the way up here."

"Me too," Candace said as she followed suit.

Kevin motioned toward the dining room and trailed the women in. Esmeralda had laid the table at one end since it was large enough for twelve. There was a small tablecloth just covering the area under the dishes. There were also candles burning in glass holders.

"How romantic," Candace commented.

"I hope we're having wine," Melanie said as she took the seat closest to her.

Candace went around and sat opposite Melanie, leaving the head of the table for Kevin.

"White or red?" Kevin asked.

"Any color," Melanie said. Then she laughed.

"What are we eating?" Candace asked.

"It's a local fish," Kevin said.

"A fish! How appropriate," Melanie said, which caused both women to laugh to the point of tears.

"I don't get it," Kevin said. He had the distinct feeling that when he was around these two women, he wasn't in control of anything and understood less than half the conversation.

"We'll explain later," Melanie managed. "Get the wine. That's more important."

"Let's have white," Candace said.

Kevin went into the kitchen and got the wine that he had earlier put into the refrigerator. He avoided looking at Esmeralda, worried what she must be thinking with these tipsy women as guests. Kevin didn't know what to think himself.

As he opened the wine, he could hear them carrying on with lively conversation and laughter. The good side, he reminded himself, was that with Melanie and Candace there were never any uncomfortable silences.

"What kind of wine are we having?" Melanie asked when Kevin reappeared. Kevin showed her the bottle. "Oh, my," she said with feigned condescension. "Montrachet! Aren't we lucky tonight."

Kevin had had no idea what he'd picked from his collection of wine bottles, but he was pleased Melanie was impressed. He poured the wine as Esmeralda appeared with the first course.

The dinner was an unqualified success. Even Kevin began to relax after attempting to keep up with the women as far as the wine was concerned. About halfway through the meal he was forced to return to the kitchen for another bottle.

"You can't guess who else was at the Chickee Hut," Melanie said as the entrée dishes were being cleared. "Our fearless leader Siegfried."

Kevin choked on his wine. He wiped his

face with his napkin. "You didn't talk to him, did you?"

"It would have been hard not to," Melanie said. "He graciously asked if he could join us and even bought a round, not only for us but also for the guys from the motor pool."

"He was actually quite charming," Candace said.

Kevin felt a chill descend down his spine. The second ordeal of the afternoon which scared him almost as much as the first was a visit to Siegfried's office. No sooner had they evaded the Equatoguinean soldiers then Melanie had insisted on driving there. It made no difference what Kevin said in an attempt to talk her out of it.

"I'm not going to stand for this kind of treatment," Melanie had said as they mounted the stairs. She didn't even bother to speak with Aurielo. She just sailed into Siegfried's office and demanded that he personally see to it that her car was repaired.

Candace had gone in with Melanie, but Kevin had held back, watching from just beyond Aurielo's desk.

"Last night I lost my sunglasses," Melanie had said. "So we go out there just to see if we can find them, and we get shot at again!"

Kevin had expected Siegfried to explode. But he didn't. Instead, he was immediately apologetic, said that the soldiers were only out there to keep people away from the island,

and that they shouldn't have fired their guns. He agreed not only to fix Melanie's car but to make sure she got a loaner in the interim. He also offered to have the soldiers scour the area for the lost sunglasses.

Esmeralda appeared with the dessert. The women were pleased. It was made with locally grown cocoa.

"Did Siegfried mention anything about what happened today?" Kevin asked.

"He apologized again," Candace said. "He said he spoke with the Moroccan guard and assured us that there won't be any more shooting. He said that if anybody wanders out there by the bridge, they will just be spoken to and told that the area is off-limits."

"Likely story," Kevin said. "As trigger-happy as those kids they call soldiers are, it's not going to happen."

Melanie laughed. "Talk about the soldiers, Siegfried said that they spent hours searching for the nonexistent sunglasses. Serves them right!"

"He did ask us if we wanted to talk with some of the workers who'd been on the island and who'd been burning underbrush," Candace said. "Can you believe it?"

"And how did you respond?" Kevin asked.

"We told him it wasn't necessary," Candace said. "I mean, we don't want him to think we're still concerned about the smoke, and we definitely don't want him to think we're planning on visiting the island."

"But we're not," Kevin said. He eyed the women while they smiled at each other conspiratorially. "Are we?" As far as Kevin was concerned, getting shot at twice had been more than enough to convince him that visiting the island was out of the question.

"You wondered why we laughed when you told us we were having fish for dinner," Melanie said. "Remember?"

"Yeah," Kevin said with concern. He had the distinct feeling he wasn't going to like what Melanie was about to say.

"We laughed because we spent a good deal of the late afternoon talking to fishermen who come to Cogo a couple of times a week," Melanie said. "Probably the ones who caught the fish we just ate. They come from a town called Acalayong about ten to twelve miles east of here."

"I know the town," Kevin said. It was the jumping-off place for people going from Equatorial Guinea to Cocobeach, Gabon. The route was served by motorized canoes called pirogues.

"We rented one of their boats for two or three days," Melanie said proudly. "So we don't have to even go near the bridge. We can visit Isla Francesca by water."

"Not me," Kevin said emphatically. "I've had it. Frankly, I think we're lucky to be alive. If you guys want to go, go! I know that nothing I could ever say would influence what you do."

"Oh, that's great!" Melanie said derisively. "You're giving up already! If that's the case, how do you intend to find out whether you and I have created a race of protohumans? I mean, you're the one who's raised this issue and got us all upset."

Melanie and Candace stared at Kevin across the table. For a few minutes, no one said a word. The night sounds of the jungle drifted in, which until then no one had heard.

After feeling progressively uncomfortable, Kevin finally broke the silence. "I don't know what I'm going to do yet," he said. "I'll think of something."

"Like hell you will," Melanie said. "You already said the only way to find out what those animals are doing is to visit the island. Those were your words. Have you forgotten?"

"No, I haven't forgotten," Kevin said. "It's just that . . . well . . ."

"That's okay," Melanie said condescendingly. "If you're too chicken to go and find out what you might have done with your genetic tinkering, fine. We were counting on you coming to help run the motor in the pirogue, but that's okay. Candace and I can manage. Right, Candace?"

"Right," Candace said.

"You see we've planned this out pretty carefully," Melanie said. "Not only did we rent the large, motorized canoe, but we had them bring back a smaller, paddle version as well. We plan to tow the paddle boat. Once we get to the island, we'll paddle up the Rio Diviso. Maybe we won't even have to go on land at all. All we want to do is observe the animals for a while."

Kevin nodded. He looked back and forth between the two women who were relentlessly staring at him. Acutely uncomfortable, he scraped back his chair and started from the room.

"Where are you going?" Melanie asked.

"To get more wine," Kevin said.

With strange emotion akin to anger, Kevin got a third bottle of white Burgundy, opened it, and brought it back into the dining room. He gestured with it toward Melanie and she nodded. Kevin filled her glass. He did the same to Candace. Then he filled his own.

After taking his seat, Kevin took a healthy swig of wine. He coughed a little after swallowing, and then asked when they planned on going on their great expedition.

"Tomorrow, bright and early," Melanie said. "We figure it will take a little over an hour to get to the island, and we'd like to be back before the sun gets really strong."

"We already got food and drink from the commissary," Candace said. "And I got a portable cooler from the hospital to pack it in."

"We'll stay far away from the bridge and the staging area," Melanie said. "So that won't be a problem."

"I think it's going to be kind of fun," Candace said. "I'd love to see a hippopotamus."

Kevin took another gulp of wine.

"I suppose you don't mind if we take those electronic gizmos to locate the animals," Melanie said. "And we could use the contour map. Of course, we'll be careful with them."

Kevin sighed and sagged in his chair. "All right, I give up. What time is this mission scheduled?"

"Oh goody," Candace said, clapping her hands together. "I knew you'd come."

"The sun comes up after six," Melanie said. "I'd like to be in the boat and on our way by then. My plan is to head west, then swing way out into the estuary before going east. That way we won't evoke any suspicions here in town if anyone sees us getting into the boat. I'd like them to think we were going off to Acalayong."

"What about work?" Kevin asked. "Won't you be missed?"

"Nope," Melanie said. "I told the people in the lab I'd be unreachable at the animal center. Whereas the people in the animal center I told . . ."

"I get the picture," Kevin interjected. "What about you, Candace?"

"No problem," Candace said. "As long as

379

Mr. Winchester keeps doing as well as he's doing, I'm essentially unemployed. The surgeons are golfing and playing tennis all day. I can do what I like."

"I'll call my head tech," Kevin said. "I'll tell him I'm under the weather with an acute attack of insanity."

"Wait a second," Candace said suddenly. "I just thought of a problem."

Kevin sat bolt upright. "What?" he asked.

"I don't have any sunblock," Candace said. "I didn't bring any because on my three previous visits I never saw the sun."

CHAPTER 16

With all the tests on Franconi pending, Jack had forced himself to go to his office and try to concentrate on some of his other outstanding cases. To his surprise, he'd made reasonable headway until the phone rang at two-thirty.

"Is this Dr. Stapleton?" a female voice with an Italian accent asked.

"It is indeed," Jack said. "Is this Mrs. Franconi?"

"Imogene Franconi. I got a message to call you."

"I appreciate it, Mrs. Franconi," Jack said. "First let me extend my sympathies to you in regards to your son."

"Thank you," Imogene said. "Carlo was a good boy. He didn't do any of those things they said in the newspapers. He worked for the American Fresh Fruit Company here in Queens. I don't know where all that talk about organized crime came from. The newspapers just make stuff up."

"It's terrible what they'll do to sell papers," Jack said.

"The man that came this morning said that

381

you got his body back," Imogene said.

"We believe so," Jack said. "That's why we needed some blood from you to confirm it. Thank you for being cooperative."

"I asked him why he didn't want me to come down there and identify it like I did last time," Imogene said. "But he told me he didn't know."

Jack tried to think of a graceful way of explaining the identity problem, but he couldn't think of any. "Some parts of the body are still missing," he said vaguely, hoping that Mrs. Franconi would be satisfied.

"Oh?" Imogene commented.

"Let me tell you why I called," Jack said quickly. He was afraid that if Mrs. Franconi became offended, she might not be receptive to his question. "You told the investigator that your son's health had improved after a trip. Do you remember saying that?"

"Of course," Imogene said.

"I was told you don't know where he went," Jack said. "Is there any way you could find out?"

"I don't think so," Imogene said. "He told me it had nothing to do with his work and that it was very private."

"Do you remember when it was?" Jack asked.

"Not exactly," Imogene said. "Maybe five or six weeks ago."

"Was it in this country?" Jack asked.

"I don't know," Imogene said. "All he said was that it was very private."

"If you find out where it was, would you give me a call back?" Jack asked.

"I suppose," Imogene said.

"Thank you," Jack said.

"Wait," Imogene said. "I just remembered he did say something strange just before he left. He said that if he didn't come back that he loved me very much."

"Did that surprise you?" Jack asked.

"Well, yes," Imogene said. "I thought that was a fine thing to say to your mother."

Jack thanked Mrs. Franconi again and hung up the phone. Hardly had he had his hand off the receiver when it rang again. It was Ted Lynch.

"I think you'd better come up here," Ted said.

"I'm on my way," Jack said.

Jack found Ted sitting at his desk, literally scratching his head.

"If I didn't know better I'd think you were trying to put one over on me," Ted spat. "Sit down!"

Jack sat. Ted was holding a ream of computer-generated paper plus a number of sheets of developed film with hundreds of small dark bands. Ted reached over and dropped the mass into Jack's lap.

"What the hell's this?" Jack questioned. He picked up several of the celluloid sheets and held them up to the light.

Ted leaned over and with the eraser end of an old-fashioned wooden pencil pointed to the films. "These are the results of the DNA polymarker test." He fingered the computer printout. "And this mass of data compares the nucleotide sequences of the DQ alpha regions of the MHC."

"Come on, Ted!" Jack urged. "Talk English to me, would you please? You know I'm a babe in the woods when it comes to this stuff."

"Fine," Ted exclaimed as if vexed. "The polymarker test shows that Franconi's DNA and the DNA of the liver tissue you found inside him could not be any more different."

"Hey, that's good news," Jack said. "Then, it was a transplant."

"I guess," Ted said without conviction. "But the sequence with the DQ alpha is identical, right down to the last nucleotide."

"What does that mean?" Jack asked.

Ted spread his hands like a supplicant and wrinkled his forehead. "I don't know. I can't explain it. Mathematically, it couldn't happen. I mean the chances are so infinitesimally small, it's beyond belief. We're talking about an identical match of thousands upon thousands of base pairs even in areas of long repeats. Absolutely identical. That's why we got the results that we did with the DQ alpha screen."

"Well, the bottom line is that it was a transplant," Jack said. "That's the issue here."

"If pressed, I'd have to agree it was a transplant," Ted said. "But how they found a donor with the identical DQ alpha is beyond me. It's the kind of coincidence that smacks of the supernatural."

"What about the test with the mitochondrial DNA to confirm the floater is Franconi?" Jack asked.

"Jeez, you give a guy an inch and he wants a mile," Ted complained. "We just got the blood, for chrissake. You'll have to wait on the results. After all, we turned the lab upside down to get what you got so quickly. Besides I'm more interested in this DQ alpha situation compared to the polymarker results. Something doesn't jibe."

"Well, don't lose any sleep over it," Jack said. He stood up and gave Ted back all the material Ted had dumped in his lap. "I appreciate what you've done. Thanks! It's the information I needed. And when the mitochondrial results are back, give me a call."

Jack was elated by Ted's results, and he wasn't worried about the mitochondrial study. With the correlation of the X rays, he was already confident the floater and Franconi were one and the same.

Jack got on the elevator. Now that he'd documented that it had been a transplant, he was counting on Bart Arnold to come up with

385

the answers to solve the rest of the mystery. As he descended, Jack found himself wondering about Ted's emotional reaction to the DQ alpha results. Jack was aware that Ted didn't get excited about too many things. Consequently, it had to be significant. Unfortunately, Jack didn't know enough about the test to have much of an opinion. He vowed that when he had the chance he'd read up on it.

Jack's elation was short-lived; it faded the moment he walked into Bart's office. The forensic investigator was on the phone, but he shook his head the moment he caught sight of Jack. Jack interpreted the gesture as bad news. He sat down to wait.

"No luck?" Jack asked as soon as Bart disconnected.

"I'm afraid not," Bart said. "I really expected UNOS to come through, and when they said that they had not provided a liver for Carlo Franconi and that he'd not even been on their waiting list, I knew the chances of tracing where he'd gotten the liver fell precipitously. Just now I was on the phone with Columbia-Presbyterian, and it wasn't done there. So I've heard from just about every center doing liver transplants, and no one takes credit for Carlo Franconi."

"This is crazy," Jack said. He told Bart that Ted's findings confirmed that Franconi had had a transplant.

"I don't know what to say," Bart commented.

"If someone didn't get their transplant in North America or Europe, where could it have taken place?" Jack asked.

Bart shrugged. "There are a few other possibilities. Australia, South Africa, even a couple of places in South America, but having talked to my contact at UNOS, I don't think any of them are likely."

"No kidding?" Jack said. He was not hearing what he wanted to hear.

"It's a mystery," Bart commented.

"Nothing about this case is easy," Jack complained as he got to his feet.

"I'll keep at it," Bart offered.

"I'd appreciate it," Jack said.

Jack wandered out of the forensic area, feeling mildly depressed. He had the uncomfortable sensation that he was missing some major fact, but he had no idea what it could be or how to go about finding out what it was.

In the ID room he got himself another cup of coffee, which was more like sludge than a beverage by that time of the day. With cup in hand, he climbed the stairs to the lab.

"I ran your samples," John DeVries said. "They were negative for both cyclosporin A and FK506."

Jack was astounded. All he could do was stare at the pale, gaunt face of the laboratory director. Jack didn't know what was more surprising: the fact that John had already run the samples or that the results were negative.

"You must be joking," Jack managed to say.

"Hardly," John said. "It's not my style."

"But the patient had to be on immunosuppressants," Jack said. "He'd had a recent liver transplant. Is it possible you got a false negative?"

"We run controls as standard procedure," John said.

"I expected one or the other drug to be present," Jack said.

"I'm sorry that we don't gear our results to your expectations," John said sourly. "If you'll excuse me, I have work to do."

Jack watched the laboratory director walk over to an instrument and make some adjustments. Then Jack turned and made his way out of the lab. Now he was more depressed. Ted Lynch's DNA results and John DeVries's drug assays were contradictory. If there'd been a transplant, Franconi had to be on either cyclosporin A or FK506. That was standard medical procedure.

Getting off the elevator on the fifth floor, he walked down to histology while trying to come up with some rational explanation for the facts he'd been given. Nothing came to mind.

"Well, if it isn't the good doctor yet again," Maureen O'Conner said in her Irish brogue. "What is it? You only have one case? Is that why you are dogging us so?"

"I only have one that is driving me bananas," Jack said. "What's the story with the slides?"

"There's a few that are ready," Maureen said. "Do you want to take them or wait for the whole batch?"

"I'll take what I can get," Jack said.

Maureen's nimble fingers picked out a sampling of the sections that were dry and placed them in a microscopic slide holder. She handed the tray to Jack.

"Are there liver sections among these?" Jack asked hopefully.

"I believe so," Maureen said. "One or two. The rest you'll have later."

Jack nodded and walked out. A few doors down the hall, he entered his office. Chet looked up from his work and smiled.

"Hey, sport, how's it going?" Chet said.

"Not so good," Jack said. He sat down and turned on his microscope light.

"Problems with the Franconi case?" Chet asked.

Jack nodded. He began to hunt through the slides for liver sections.

He only found one. "Everything about it is like squeezing water from a rock."

"Listen, I'm glad you came back," Chet said. "I'm expecting a call from a doctor in North Carolina. I just want to find out if a patient had heart trouble. I have to duck out to get passport photos taken for my upcoming trip to India. Would you take the call for me?"

"Sure," Jack said. "What's the patient's name?"

"Clarence Potemkin," Chet said. "The folder is right here on my desk."

"Fine," Jack said, while slipping the sole liver section onto his microscope's stage. He ignored Chet as Chet got his coat from behind the door and left. Jack ran the microscopic objective down to the slide and was about to peer into the eyepieces, when he paused. Chet's errand had started him thinking about international travel. If Franconi had gotten his transplant out of the country, which seemed increasingly probable, there might be a way to find out where he'd been.

Jack picked up his phone and called police headquarters. He asked for Lieutenant Detective Lou Soldano. He expected to have to leave a message and was pleasantly surprised to get the man himself.

"Hey, I'm glad you called," Lou said. "Remember what I told you this morning about the tip it was the Lucia people who stole Franconi's remains from the morgue? We just got confirmation from another source. I thought you might like to know."

"Interesting," Jack said. "Now I have a question for you."

"Shoot," Lou said.

Jack outlined the reasons for his belief that Carlo Franconi might have traveled abroad for his liver transplant. He added that according to the man's mother, he'd taken a trip to a supposed spa four to six weeks previously.

"What I want to know is, is there a way to find out by talking to Customs if Franconi left the country recently, and if so, where did he go?"

"Either Customs or the Immigration and Naturalization," Lou said. "Your best bet would be Immigration unless, of course, he brought back so much stuff he had to pay duty. Besides, I have a friend in Immigration. That way I can get the information much faster than going through the usual bureaucratic channels. Want me to check?"

"I'd love it," Jack said. "This case is bugging the hell out of me."

"My pleasure," Lou said. "As I said this morning, I owe you."

Jack hung up the phone with a tiny glimmer of hope that he'd thought of a new angle. Feeling a bit more optimistic, he leaned forward, looked into his microscope, and began to focus.

Laurie's day had not gone anything like she'd anticipated. She'd planned on doing only one autopsy but ended up doing two. And then George Fontworth ran into trouble with his multiple gunshot wound case, and Laurie volunteered to help him. Even with no lunch, Laurie didn't get out of the pit until three.

After changing into her street clothes, Laurie was on her way up to her office when she caught sight of Marvin in the mortuary office. He'd just come on duty and was busy putting the office in order after the tumult of a normal day. Laurie made a detour and stuck her head in the door.

"We found Franconi's X rays," she said. "And it turned out that floater that came in the other night was our missing man."

"I saw it in the paper," Marvin said. "Far out."

"The X rays made the identification," Laurie said. "So I'm extra glad you took them."

"It's my job," Marvin said.

"I wanted to apologize again for suggesting you didn't take them," Laurie said.

"No problem," Marvin said.

Laurie got about four steps away, when she turned around and returned to the mortuary office. This time she entered and closed the door behind her.

Marvin looked at her questioningly.

"Would you mind if I asked you a question just between you and me?" Laurie asked.

"I guess not," Marvin said warily.

"Obviously, I've been interested in how

Franconi's body was stolen from here," Laurie said. "That's why I talked to you the afternoon before last. Remember?"

"Of course," Marvin said.

"I also came in that night and talked with Mike Passano," Laurie said.

"So I heard," Marvin said.

"I bet you did," Laurie said. "But believe me I wasn't accusing Mike of anything."

"I hear you," Marvin said. "He can be sensitive now and then."

"I can't figure out how the body was stolen," Laurie said. "Between Mike and security, there was always someone here."

Marvin shrugged. "I don't know, either," he said. "Believe me."

"I understand," Laurie said. "I'm sure you would have said something to me if you had any suspicions. But that's not what I wanted to ask. My feeling at this point is that there had to be some help from inside. Is there any employee here at the morgue that you think might have been involved in this somehow? That's my question."

Marvin thought for a minute and then shook his head. "I don't think so."

"It had to have happened on Mike's shift," Laurie said. "The two drivers, Pete and Jeff, do you know them very well?"

"Nope," Marvin said. "I mean, I've seen them around and even talked with them a few times, but since we're on different shifts, we don't have a lot of contact."

"But you don't have any reason to suspect them?"

"Nope, no more than anybody else," Marvin said.

"Thanks," Laurie said. "I hope my question didn't make you feel uncomfortable."

"No problem," Marvin said.

Laurie thought for a minute, while she absently chewed on her lower lip. She knew she was missing something. "I have an idea," she said suddenly. "Maybe you should describe to me the exact sequence you go through when a body leaves here."

"You mean everything that happens?" Marvin said.

"Please," Laurie said. "I mean, I have a general idea, but I don't know the specifics."

"Where do you want me to start?" Marvin asked.

"Right from the beginning," Laurie said. "Right from the moment you get the call from the funeral home."

"Okay," Marvin said. "The call comes in, and they say they're from so-and-so funeral home and they want to do a pickup. So they give me the name and the accession number."

"That's it?" Laurie asked. "Then you hang up."

"No," Marvin said. "I put them on hold while I enter the accession number into the computer. I gotta make sure the body has been released by you guys and also find out where it is."

"So then you go back to the phone and say what?"

"I say it's okay," Marvin said. "I tell them I'll have the body ready. I guess I usually ask when they think they'll be here. I mean, no sense rushing around if they're not going to be here for two hours or something."

"Then what?" Laurie said.

"I get the body and check the accession number," Marvin said. "Then I put it in the front of the walk-in cooler. We always put them in the same place. In fact, we line them up in the order we expect them to go out. It makes it easier for the drivers."

"And then what happens?" Laurie asked.

"Then they come," Marvin said with another shrug.

"And what happens when they arrive?" Laurie asked.

"They come in here and we fill out a receipt," Marvin said. "It's all got to be documented. I mean they have to sign to indicate they have accepted custody."

"Okay," Laurie said. "And then you go back and get the body?"

"Yeah, or one of them gets it," Marvin said. "All of them have been in and out of here a million times."

"Is there any final check?" Laurie asked.

"You bet," Marvin said. "We always check the accession number one more time before they wheel the body out of here. We have to indicate that being done on the documents. It would be embarrassing if the drivers got back to the home and realized they had the wrong corpse."

"Sounds like a good system," Laurie said, and she meant it. With so many checks it would be hard to subvert such a procedure.

"It's been working for decades without a screwup," Marvin said. "Of course, the computer helps. Before that, all they had was the logbook."

"Thanks, Marvin," Laurie said.

"Hey, no problem, Doc," Marvin said.

Laurie left the mortuary office. Before going up to her own she stopped off on the second floor to get a snack out of the vending machines in the lunch room. Reasonably fortified, she went up to the fifth floor. Seeing Jack's office door ajar, she walked over and peeked in. Jack was at his microscope.

"Something interesting?" she asked.

Jack looked up and smiled. "Very," he said. "Want to take a look?"

Laurie glanced into the eyepieces as Jack leaned to the side. "It looks like a tiny granuloma in a liver," she said.

"That's right," Jack said. "It's from one of those tiny pieces I was able to find of Franconi's liver."

"Hmmm," Laurie commented, continuing to look into the microscope. "That's weird they would have used an infected liver for a transplant. You'd think they would have screened the donor better. Are there a lot of these tiny granulomas?"

"Maureen has only given me one slide of the liver so far," Jack said. "And that's the only granuloma I found, so my guess would be that there aren't a lot. But I did see one on the frozen section. Also on the frozen section were tiny collapsed cysts on the surface of the liver which would have been visible to the naked eye. The transplant team must have known and didn't care."

"At least there's no general inflammation," Laurie said. "So the transplant was being tolerated pretty well."

"Extremely well," Jack said. "Too well, but that's another issue. What do you think that is under the pointer?"

Laurie played with the focus so that she could visually move up and down in the section. There were a few curious flecks of basophilic material. "I don't know. I can't even be sure it's not artifact."

"Don't know, either," Jack said. "Unless it's what stimulated the granuloma."

"That's a thought," Laurie said. She straightened up. "What did you mean by the liver being tolerated too well?"

"The lab reported that Franconi had not

been taking any immunosuppressant drugs," Jack said. "That seems highly improbable since there is no general inflammation."

"Are we sure it was a transplant?" Laurie asked.

"Absolutely," Jack said. He summarized what Ted Lynch had reported to him.

Laurie was as puzzled as Jack. "Except for identical twins I can't imagine two people's DQ alpha sequences being exactly the same," she said.

"It sounds like you know more about it than I do," Jack said. "Until a couple of days ago, I'd never even heard of DQ alpha."

"Have you made any headway as to where Franconi could have had this transplant?" Laurie asked.

"I wish," Jack said. He then told Laurie about Bart's vain efforts. Jack explained that he himself had spent a good portion of the previous night calling centers all over Europe.

"Good Lord!" Laurie remarked.

"I've even enlisted Lou's help," Jack said. "I found out from Franconi's mother that he'd gone off to what she thought was a spa and came home a new man. I'm thinking that's when he might have gotten the transplant. Unfortunately, she has no idea where he went. Lou's checking Immigration to see if he'd gone out of the country."

"If anyone can find out, Lou can," Laurie said.

"By the way," Jack said assuming a teasingly superior air. "Lou 'fessed up that he was the source of the leak about Franconi to the newspapers."

"I don't believe it," Laurie said.

"I got it from the horse's mouth," Jack said. "So I expect an abject apology."

"You've got it," Laurie said. "I'm amazed. Did he give any reason?"

"He said they wanted to release the information right away to see if it would smoke out any more tips from informers. He said it worked to an extent. They got a tip which was later confirmed that Franconi's body had been taken under orders from the Lucia crime family."

"Good grief!" Laurie said and shuddered. "This case is starting to remind me too much of the Cerino affair."

"I know what you mean," Jack said. "Instead of eyes, it's livers."

"You don't suppose there's a private hospital here in the United States that's doing undercover liver transplants, do you?" Laurie asked.

"I can't imagine," Jack said. "No doubt there could be big money involved, but there is the issue of supply. I mean, there's seven thousand plus people in this country waiting for livers as it is. Few of these people have the money to make it worthwhile."

"I wish I were as confident as you," Laurie

said. "The profit motive has taken over American medicine by storm."

"But the big money in medicine is in volume," Jack said. "There are too few wealthy people who need livers. The investment in the physical plant and the requisite secrecy wouldn't pay off, especially without a supply of organs. You'd have to postulate some modern version of Burk and Hare, and although such a scenario might work in a B movie, in reality it would be too risky and uncertain. No businessman in his right mind would go for it, no matter how venal."

"Maybe you have a point," Laurie said.

"I'm convinced there's something else involved here," Jack said. "There are just too many unexplained facts from the DQ alpha nonsense to the fact that Franconi wasn't taking any immunosuppressant drugs. We're missing something: something key, something unexpected."

"What an effort!" Laurie exclaimed. "One thing is for sure, I'm glad I foisted this case onto you."

"Thanks for nothing," Jack quipped. "It's certainly a frustrating case. On a happier note, last night at basketball, Warren told me that Natalie has been asking about you. What do you say that we all get together this weekend for dinner and maybe a movie, provided they don't have any plans?"

"I'd enjoy that very much," Laurie said. "I

400

hope you told Warren that I was asking about them as well."

"I did," Jack admitted. "Not to change the subject, but how was your day? Did you make any headway in figuring out how Franconi managed to go on his overnight? I mean, Lou telling us that a crime family was responsible isn't telling us a whole bunch. We need specifics."

"Unfortunately, no," Laurie admitted. "I was caught in the pit until just a little while ago. I've gotten nothing done that I'd planned."

"Too bad," Jack said with a smile. "With my lack of progress, I might have to rely on you providing the breakthrough."

After promises to talk with each other by phone that evening, specifically about the weekend plans, Laurie headed to her own office. With good intentions she sat down at her desk and started to go through the lab reports and other correspondence that had come in that day involving her uncompleted cases. But she found it difficult to concentrate.

Jack's generosity in crediting her with providing the breakthrough in the Franconi case only made her feel guilty for not coming up with a working hypothesis about how Franconi's body was taken. Seeing the effort Jack was expending on the case made her want to redouble her efforts.

Pulling out a fresh sheet of paper, Laurie began to write down everything Marvin had related. Her intuition told her that Franconi's mysterious abduction had to involve the two bodies that went out the same night. And now that Lou had said the Lucia crime family was implicated, she was more convinced than ever that the Spoletto Funeral Home was somehow involved.

Raymond replaced the phone and raised his eyes to Darlene who'd come into his study.

"Well?" Darlene asked. She had her blond hair pulled back into a ponytail. She'd been working out on an exercise bike in the other room and was clothed in sexy workout gear.

Raymond leaned back in his desk chair and sighed. He even smiled. "Things seem to be working out," he said. "That was the GenSys operational officer up in Cambridge, Mass. The plane will be available tomorrow evening so I'll be on my way to Africa. Of course, we'll stop to refuel, but I don't know where yet."

"Can I come?" Darlene asked hopefully.

"I'm afraid not, dear," Raymond said. He reached out and took her by the hand. He knew he'd been difficult over the previous couple of days and felt badly. He guided her around the desk and urged her to sit on his lap. As soon as she did, he was sorry. She was, after all, a big woman.

"With the patient and the surgical team, there'll be too many people on the plane on the return trip," he managed, even though his face was becoming red.

Darlene sighed and pouted. "I never get to go anywhere."

"Next time," Raymond croaked. He patted her on her back and eased her up into a standing position. "It's just a short trip. There and back. It's not going to be fun."

With a sudden burst of tears Darlene fled from the room. Raymond considered following her to console her, but a glance at his desk clock changed his mind. It was after three and therefore after nine in Cogo. If he wanted to talk to Siegfried, he felt he'd better try now.

Raymond called the manager's home. The housekeeper put Siegfried on the line.

"Things still going okay?" Raymond asked expectantly.

"Perfectly," Siegfried said. "My last update on the patient's condition was fine. He couldn't be doing any better."

"That's reassuring," Raymond said.

"I suppose that means our harvest bonuses will be forthcoming," Siegfried said.

"Of course," Raymond said, although he knew there would be a delay. With the necessity of raising twenty thousand cash for Vinnie Dominick, bonuses would have to wait until the next initiation fee came in.

"What about the situation with Kevin Mar-

403

shall?" Raymond asked.

"Everything is back to normal," Siegfried said. "Except for one incident when they went back to the staging area around lunch time."

"That hardly sounds normal," Raymond complained.

"Calm down," Siegfried said. "They only went back to look for Melanie Becket's sunglasses. Nevertheless, they ended up getting fired at again by the soldiers I'd posted out there." Siegfried laughed heartily.

Raymond waited until Siegfried had calmed down.

"What's so funny?" Raymond asked.

"Those numbskull soldiers shot out Melanie's rear window," Siegfried said. "It made her very angry, but it had the desired effect. Now I'm really sure they won't be going out there again."

"I should hope not," Raymond said.

"Besides, I had an opportunity to have a drink with the two women this afternoon," Siegfried said. "I have a feeling our nerdy researcher has something risqué going on."

"What are you talking about?" Raymond asked.

"I don't believe he'll be having the time or the energy to worry about smoke from Isla Francesca," Siegfried said. "I think he's got himself involved in a ménage à trois."

"Seriously?" Raymond asked. Such an idea seemed preposterous for the Kevin Marshall

Raymond knew. In all of Raymond's dealing with Kevin Marshall he'd never expressed the slightest interest in the opposite sex. The idea he'd have the inclination and stamina for one woman let alone two seemed ludicrous.

"That was the implication I got," Siegfried said. "You should have heard the two women carrying on about their cute researcher. That's what they called him. And they were on their way to Kevin's for a dinner party. That's the first dinner party he's ever had as far as I know, and I live right across from him."

"I suppose we should be thankful," Raymond said.

"Envious is a better word," Siegfried said, with another burst of laughter that grated on Raymond's nerves.

"I've called to say that I'll be leaving here tomorrow evening," Raymond said. "I can't say when I'll arrive in Bata because I don't know where we'll refuel. I'll have to call from the refueling stop or have the pilots radio ahead."

"Anyone else coming with you?" Siegfried asked.

"Not that I know of," Raymond said. "I doubt it because we'll be almost full on the way back."

"We'll be waiting for you," Siegfried said.

"See you soon," Raymond said.

"Maybe you could bring our bonuses with you," Siegfried suggested.

"I'll see if it can be arranged," Raymond said.

He hung up the phone and smiled. He shook his head in amazement concerning Kevin Marshall's behavior. "You never know!" Raymond commented out loud as he got up and started from the room. He wanted to find Darlene and cheer her up. He thought that maybe as a consolation they should go out to dinner at her favorite restaurant.

Jack had scoured the single liver section Maureen had given him from one end to the other. He'd even used his oil-immersion lens to stare vainly at the basophilic specks in the heart of the tiny granuloma. He still had no idea whether they were a true finding, and if they were, what they were.

Having exhausted his histological and pathological knowledge with respect to the slide, he was about to take it over to the pathology department at New York University Hospital when his phone rang. It was Chet's call from North Carolina, so Jack asked the appropriate question and wrote down the response. Hanging up the phone, Jack got his jacket from the file cabinet. With the jacket on, he picked up the microscopic slide only to have the phone ring again. This time it was Lou Soldano.

"Bingo!" Lou said cheerfully. "I got some good news for you."

"I'm all ears," Jack said. He slipped out of his bomber jacket and sat down.

"I put in a call to my friend in Immigration, and he just phoned me back," Lou said. "When I asked him your question, he told me to hang on the line. I could even hear him entering the name into the computer. Two seconds later, he had the info. Carlo Franconi entered the country exactly thirty-seven days ago on January twenty-ninth at Teterboro in New Jersey."

"I've never heard of Teterboro," Jack said.

"It's a private airport," Lou said. "It's for general aviation, but there's lot's of fancy corporate jets out there because of the field's proximity to the city."

"Was Carlo Franconi on a corporate jet?" Jack asked.

"I don't know," Lou said. "All I got is the plane's call letters or numbers or whatever they call it. You know, the numbers and letters on the airplane's tail. Let's see, I got it right here. It was N69SU."

"Was there any indication where the plane had come from?" Jack asked as he wrote down the alphanumeric characters and the date.

"Oh yeah," Lou said. "That's gotta be filed. The plane came from Lyon, France."

"Nah, it couldn't have," Jack said.

"That's what's in the computer," Lou said. "Why don't you think it's correct?"

"Because I talked with the French organ

allocation organization early this morning," Jack said. "They had no record of an American with the name of Franconi, and they categorically denied they'd be transplanting an American since they have a long waiting list for French citizens."

"The information that Immigration has must correlate with the flight plan filed with both the FAA and the European equivalent," Lou said. "At least that's how I understand it."

"Do you think your friend in Immigration has a contact in France?" Jack asked.

"It wouldn't surprise me," Lou said. "Those upper-echelon guys have to cooperate with each other. I can ask him. Why would you like to know?"

"If Franconi was in France I'd like to find out the day he arrived," Jack said. "And I'd like to know any other information the French might have on where he went in the country. They keep close tabs on most non-European foreigners through their hotels."

"Okay, let me see what I can do," Lou said. "Let me call him, and I'll call you back."

"One other thing," Jack said. "How can we find out who owns N69SU?"

"That's easy," Lou said. "All you have to do is call the FAA Control Aviation Center in Oklahoma City. Anybody can do it, but I've got a friend there, too."

"Jeez, you have friends in all the convenient

places," Jack remarked.

"It comes with the territory," Lou said. "We do favors for each other all the time. If you have to wait for everything to go through channels, nothing gets done."

"It's certainly convenient for me to take advantage of your web of contacts," Jack said.

"So you want me to call my friend at the FAA?" Lou asked.

"I'll be much obliged," Jack said.

"Hey, it's my pleasure," Lou said. "I have a feeling that the more I help you the more I'm helping myself. I'd like nothing better than to have this case solved. It might save my job."

"I'm leaving my office to run over to the University Hospital," Jack said. "What if I call you back in a half hour or so?"

"Perfect," Lou said before disconnecting.

Jack shook his head. Like everything else with this case, the information he'd gotten from Lou was both surprising and confusing. France probably was the last country Jack suspected Franconi to have visited.

After donning his coat for the second time, Jack left his office. Given the proximity of the University Hospital, he didn't bother with his bike. It only took ten minutes by foot.

Inside the busy medical center, Jack took the elevator up to the pathology department. He was hoping that Dr. Malovar would be available. Peter Malovar was a giant in the field, and even at the age of eighty-two he was one of the sharpest pathologists Jack had ever met. Jack made it a point to go to seminars Dr. Malovar offered once a month. So when Jack had a question about pathology, he didn't go to Bingham because Bingham's strong point was forensics, not general pathology. Instead, Jack went to Dr. Malovar.

"The professor's in his lab as usual," the harried pathology department secretary said. "You know where it is?"

Jack nodded and walked down to the aged, frosted-glass door which led to what was known as "Malovar's lair." Jack knocked. When there was no response, he tried the door. It was unlocked. Inside, he found Dr. Malovar bent over his beloved microscope. The elderly man looked a little like Einstein with wild gray hair and a full mustache. He also had kyphotic posture as if his body had been specifically designed to bend over and peer into a microscope. Of his five senses only his hearing had deteriorated over the years.

The professor greeted Jack cursorily while hungrily eyeing the slide in his hand. He loved people to bring him problematic cases, a fact that Jack had taken advantage of on many occasion.

Jack tried to give a little history of the case as he passed the slide to the professor, but

Dr. Malovar lifted his hand to quiet him. Dr. Malovar was a true detective who didn't want anyone else's impressions to influence his own. The aged professor replaced the slide he'd been studying with Jack's. Without a word, he scanned it for all of one minute.

Raising his head, Dr. Malovar put a drop of oil on the slide and switched to his oil-immersion lens for higher magnification. Once again, he examined the slide for only a matter of seconds.

Dr. Malovar looked up at Jack. "Interesting!" he said, which was a high compliment coming from him. Because of his hearing problem, he spoke loudly. "There's a small granuloma of the liver as well as the cicatrix of another. Looking at the granuloma, I think I might be seeing some merozoites, but I can't be sure."

Jack nodded. He assumed that Dr. Malovar was referring to the tiny basophilic flecks Jack had seen in the core of the granuloma.

Dr. Malovar reached for his phone. He called a colleague and asked him to come over for a moment. Within minutes, a tall, thin, overly serious, African-American man in a long white coat appeared. Dr. Malovar introduced him as Dr. Colin Osgood, chief of parasitology.

"What's your opinion, Colin?" Dr. Malovar asked as he gestured toward his microscope.

Dr. Osgood looked at the slide for a few

seconds longer than Dr. Malovar had before responding. "Definitely parasitic," he intoned with his eyes still glued to the eye pieces. "Those are merozoites, but I don't recognize them. It's either a new species or a parasite not seen in humans. I recommend that Dr. Lander Hammersmith view it and render his opinion."

"Good idea," Dr. Malovar said. He looked at Jack. "Would you mind leaving this overnight? I'll have Dr. Hammersmith view it in the morning."

"Who is Dr. Hammersmith?" Jack asked.

"He's a veterinary pathologist," Dr. Osgood said.

"Fine by me," Jack said agreeably. Having the slide reviewed by a veterinary pathologist was something he'd not thought of.

After thanking both men, Jack went back out to the secretary and asked if he could use a phone. The secretary directed him to an empty desk and told him to push nine for an outside line. Jack called Lou at police headquarters.

"Hey, glad you called," Lou said. "I think I'm getting some interesting stuff here. First of all, the plane is quite a plane. It's a G4. Does that mean anything to you?"

"I don't think so," Jack said. From Lou's tone it sounded as if it should have.

"It stands for Gulfstream 4," Lou explained. "It's what you would call the Rolls

Royce of the corporate jet. It's like twenty million bucks."

"I'm impressed," Jack said.

"You should be," Lou said. "Okay, let's see what else I learned. Ah, here it is: The plane is owned by Alpha Aviation out of Reno, Nevada. Ever hear of them?"

"Nope," Jack said. "Have you?"

"Not me," Lou said. "Must be a leasing organization. Let's see, what else? Oh, yeah! This might be the most interesting. My friend from Immigration called his counterpart in France at his home, if you can believe it, and asked about Carlo Franconi's recent French holiday. Apparently, this French bureaucrat can access the Immigration mainframe from his own PC, because guess what?"

"I'm on pins and needles," Jack said.

"Franconi never visited France!" Lou said. "Not unless he had a fake passport and fake name. There's no record of his entering or departing."

"So what's this about the plane incontrovertibly coming from Lyon, France?" Jack demanded.

"Hey, don't get testy," Lou said.

"I'm not," Jack said. "I was only responding to your point that the flight plan and the Immigration information had to correlate."

"They do!" Lou said. "Saying the plane came from Lyon, France, doesn't mean anybody or everybody got out. It could have refueled for all I know."

"Good point," Jack said. "I didn't think of that. How can we find out?"

"I suppose I can call my friend back at the FAA," Lou said.

"Great," Jack said. "I'm heading back to my office at the morgue. You want me to call you or you call me?"

"I'll call you," Lou said.

After Laurie had written down all that she could remember from her conversation with Marvin concerning how bodies were picked up by funeral homes, she'd put the paper aside and ignored it while she did some other busywork. A half hour later, she picked it back up.

With her mind clear, she tried to read it with fresh eyes. On the second read-through, something jumped out at her: namely, how many times the term "accession number" appeared. Of course, she wasn't surprised. After all, the accession number was to a body what a Social Security number was to a living individual. It was a form of identi-fication that allowed the morgue to keep track of the thousands of bodies and con-sequent paperwork that passed through its portals. Whenever a body arrived at the medi-cal examiner's office, the first thing that hap-pened was that it was given an accession number. The second thing that happened was that a tag with the number was tied around the big toe.

Looking at the word "accession," Laurie realized to her surprise that if asked she wouldn't have been able to define it. It was a word she'd just accepted and used on a daily basis. Every laboratory slip and report, every X-ray film, every investigator's report, every document intramurally had the accession number. In many ways, it was more important than the victim's name.

Taking her American Heritage dictionary from its shelf, Laurie looked up the word "accession." As she began reading the definitions, none of them made any sense in the context of the word's use at the morgue, until the next to last entry. There it was defined as "admittance." In other words, the accession number was just another way of saying admittance number.

Laurie searched for the accession numbers and names of the bodies that had been picked up during the night shift of March fourth when Franconi's body disappeared. She found the piece of scratch paper beneath a slide tray. On it was written: Dorothy Kline #101455 and Frank Gleason #100385.

Thanks to her musing about accession numbers, Laurie noticed something she'd not paid any attention to before. The fact that the accession numbers differed by over a thousand! That was strange because the numbers were given out sequentially. Knowing the approximate volume of bodies processed through the morgue, Laurie estimated that there must have been several weeks separation between the arrivals of these two individuals.

The time differential was strange since bodies rarely stayed at the morgue more than a couple of days, so Laurie keyed Frank Gleason's accession number into her computer terminal. His was the body picked up by the Spoletto Funeral Home.

What popped up on the screen surprised her.

"Good grief!" Laurie exclaimed.

Lou was having a great time. Contrary to the general public's romantic image of detective work, actual gumshoeing was an exhausting, thankless task. What Lou was doing now, namely sitting in the comfort of his office and making productive telephone calls, was both entertaining and fulfilling. It was also nice to say hello to old acquaintances.

"My word, Soldano!" Mark Servert commented. Mark was Lou's contact at the FAA in Oklahoma City. "I don't hear from you for a year and then twice in the same day. This must be some case."

"It's a corker," Lou said. "And I have a follow-up question. We found out that the G4 plane I called you about earlier had flown from Lyon, France, to Teterboro, New Jersey, on January twenty-ninth. However, the guy we're interested in didn't pass through French Immigration. So, we're wondering if it's possible to find out where N69SU came from before it landed in Lyon."

"Now that's a tricky question," Mark said. "I know the ICAO . . ."

"Wait a second," Lou interrupted. "Keep the acronyms to a minimum. What's the ICAO?"

"International Civil Aviation Organization," Mark said. "I know they file all flight plans in and out of Europe."

"Perfect," Lou said. "Anybody there you can call?"

"There's someone I can call," Mark said. "But it wouldn't do you much good. The ICAO shreds all their files after fifteen days. It's not stored."

"Wonderful," Lou commented sarcastically.

"The same goes for the European Air Traffic Control Center in Brussels," Mark said. "There's just too much material, considering all the commercial flights."

"So, there's no way," Lou remarked.

"I'm thinking," Mark said.

"You want to call me back?" Lou said. "I'll be here for another hour or so."

"Yeah, let me do that," Mark said.

Lou was about to hang up when he heard

Mark yell his name.

"I just thought of something else," Mark said. "There's an organization called Central Flow Management with offices in both Paris and Brussels. They're the ones who provide the slot times for takeoffs and landings. They handle all of Europe except for Austria and Slovenia. Who knows why those countries aren't involved? So, if N69SU came from anyplace other than Austria or Slovenia, their flight plan should be on file."

"Do you know anybody in that organization?" Lou asked.

"No, but I know somebody who does," Mark said. "Let me see if I can find out for you."

"Hey, I appreciate it," Lou said.

"No problem," Mark said.

Lou hung up the phone and then drummed his pencil on the surface of his scarred and battle-worn gray-metal desk. There were innumerable burn marks where he'd left smoldering cigarette butts. He was thinking about Alpha Aviation and wondering how to run down the organization.

First, he tried telephone information in Reno. There was no listing for Alpha Aviation. Lou wasn't surprised. Next, he called the Reno police department. He explained who he was and asked to be connected to his equivalent, the head of Homicide. His name was Paul Hersey.

After a few minutes of friendly banter, Lou gave Paul a thumbnail sketch of the Franconi case. Then he asked about Alpha Aviation.

"Never heard of them," Paul said.

"The FAA said it was out of Reno, Nevada," Lou said.

"That's because Nevada's an easy state to incorporate in," Paul explained. "And here in Reno we've got a slew of high-priced law firms who spend their time doing nothing else."

"What's your suggestion about getting the lowdown on the organization?" Lou asked.

"Call the Office of the Nevada Secretary of State in Carson City," Paul said. "If Alpha Aviation is incorporated in Nevada, it will be on public record. Want us to call for you?"

"I'll call," Lou said. "At this point, I'm not even sure what I want to know."

"We can at least give you the number," Paul said. He went off the line for a moment, and Lou could hear him bark an order to an underling. A moment later, he was back and gave Lou the telephone number. Then he added: "They should be helpful, but if you have any trouble, call me back. And if you need any assistance in Carson City for whatever reason call Todd Arronson. He's head of Homicide down there, and he's a good guy."

A few minutes later Lou was on the line with the Office of the Nevada Secretary of State. An operator connected him to a clerk,

419

who couldn't have been nicer or more cooperative. Her name was Brenda Whitehall.

Lou explained that he was interested to find out all he could about Alpha Aviation out of Reno, Nevada.

"Just a moment, please," Brenda said. Lou could hear the woman typing the name onto a keyboard. "Okay, here it is," she added. "Hang on and let me pull the folder."

Lou lifted his feet up onto his desk and leaned back in his chair. He felt an almost irresistable urge to light up, but he fought it.

"I'm back," Brenda said. Lou could hear the rustle of papers. "Now what is it that you want to know?"

"What do you have?" Lou asked.

"I have the Articles of Incorporation," Brenda said. There was a short period of silence while she read, then she added: "It's a limited partnership and the general partner is Alpha Management."

"What does that mean in plain English?" Lou asked. "I'm not a lawyer or a businessman."

"It simply means that Alpha Management is the corporation that runs the limited partnership," Brenda said patiently.

"Does it have any people's names?" Lou asked.

"Of course," Brenda said. "The Articles of Incorporation have to have the names and addresses of the directors, the registered agent for service of process, and the officers of the corporation."

"That sounds encouraging," Lou said. "Could you give them to me?"

Lou could hear the sound of rustling papers.

"Hmmmm," Brenda commented. "Actually, in this instance there's only one name and address."

"One person is wearing all those hats?"

"According to this document," Brenda said.

"What's the name and address?" Lou asked. He reached for a piece of paper.

"It's Samuel Hartman of the firm, Wheeler, Hartman, Gottlieb, and Sawyer. Their address is Eight Rodeo Drive, Reno."

"That sounds like a law firm," Lou said.

"It is," Brenda said. "I recognize the name."

"That's no help!" Lou said. He knew that the chances of getting any information out of a law firm were unlikely.

"A lot of Nevada corporations are set up like this," Brenda explained. "But let's see if there are any amendments."

Lou was already thinking of calling Paul back to get the rundown on Samuel Hartman, when Brenda made a murmur of discovery.

"There are amendments," she said. "At the first board meeting of Alpha Management, Mr. Hartman resigned as president and secretary. In his place Frederick Rouse was appointed."

"Is there an address for Mr. Rouse?" Lou asked.

"There is," Brenda said. "His title is Chief Financial Officer of the GenSys Corporation. The address is 150 Kendall Square, Cambridge, Massachusetts."

Lou got all the information written down and thanked Brenda. He was particularly appreciative because he couldn't imagine getting the same service from his own Secretary of State's Office in Albany.

Lou was about to call Jack to give him the information about the ownership of the plane, when the phone literally rang under his hand. It was Mark Servert calling back already.

"You are in luck," Mark said. "The fellow I'm acquainted with who knows people in the Central Flow Management organization in Europe happened to be on the job when I called him. In fact, he's in your neck of the woods. He's out at Kennedy Airport, helping direct air traffic across the north Atlantic. He talks to these Central Flow Management people all the time, so he slipped in a query about N69SU on January twenty-ninth. Apparently, it popped right up on the screen. N69SU flew into Lyon from Bata, Equatorial Guinea."

"Whoa!" Lou said. "Where's that?"

"Beats me," Mark said. "Without looking at a map, I'd guess West Africa."

"Curious," Lou said.

"It's also curious that as soon as the plane touched down in Lyon, France, it radioed to obtain a slot time to depart for Teterboro, New Jersey," Mark said. "Near as I can figure, it just sat on the runway until it got clearance."

"Maybe it refueled," Lou offered.

"Could be," Mark said. "Even so, I would have expected them to have filed a through-flight plan with a stop in Lyon, rather than two separate flight plans. I mean, they could have gotten hung up in Lyon for hours. It was taking a chance."

"Maybe they just changed their minds," Lou said.

"It's possible," Mark agreed.

"Or maybe they didn't want anyone knowing they were coming from Equatorial Guinea," Lou suggested.

"Now, that's an idea that wouldn't have crossed my mind," Mark admitted. "I suppose that's why you're an engaging detective, and I'm a boring FAA bureaucrat."

Lou laughed. "Engaging I'm not. On the contrary, I'm afraid this job has made me cynical and suspicious."

"It's better than being boring," Mark said.

Lou thanked his friend for his help, and after they exchanged the usual well-meaning promises to get together, they hung up.

For a few minutes, Lou sat and marveled

at why a twenty-million-dollar airplane was carrying a midlevel crime boss from Queens, New York, from some African country Lou had never heard of. Such a third-world backwater certainly wasn't a medical mecca where a person would go to have sophisticated surgery like a liver transplant.

After entering Frank Gleason's accession number into the computer, Laurie sat pondering the apparent discrepancy for some time. She'd tried to imagine what the information meant in terms of the Franconi body disappearance. Slowly, an idea took root.

Suddenly pushing back from her desk, Laurie headed to the morgue level to look for Marvin. He wasn't in the mortuary office. She found him by stepping into the walk-in cooler. He was busy moving the gurneys around to prepare for body pickups.

The moment Laurie entered the cooler, she flashed on the horrid experience she'd had during the Cerino affair inside the walk-in unit. The memory made her distinctly uncomfortable, and she decided against attempting to have a conversation with Marvin while inside. Instead, she asked him to meet her back in the mortuary office when he was finished.

Five minutes later, Marvin appeared. He plopped a sheaf of papers on the desk and then went to a sink in the corner to wash his hands.

"Everything in order?" Laurie asked, just to make conversation.

"I think so," Marvin said. He came to the desk and sat down. He began arranging the documents in the order that the bodies were to be picked up.

"After talking with you earlier, I learned something quite surprising," Laurie said, getting to the point of her visit.

"Like what?" Marvin said. He finished arranging the papers and sat back.

"I entered Frank Gleason's accession number into the computer," Laurie said. "And I found out that his body had come into the morgue over two weeks ago. There was no name associated with it. It was an unidentified corpse!"

"No shit!" Marvin exclaimed. Then realizing what he'd said, he added: "I mean, I'm surprised."

"So was I," Laurie said. "I tried to call Dr. Besserman, who'd done the original autopsy. I wanted to ask if the body had been recently identified as Frank Gleason, but he's out of the office. Do you think it was surprising that Mike Passano didn't know the body was still labeled in the computer as an unidentified corpse?"

"Not really," Marvin said. "I'm not sure I would have, either. I mean, you enter the accession number just to find out if the body is released. You don't really worry too much about the name."

"That was the impression you gave me earlier," Laurie said. "There was also something else you said that I've been mulling over. You said that sometimes you don't get the body yourself but rather one of the funeral home people does."

"Sometimes," Marvin said. "But it only happens if two people come and if they've been here lots of times so they know the process. It's just a way of speeding things up. One of them goes to the cooler to get the body while me and the other guy finish the documents."

"How well do you know Mike Passano?" Laurie asked.

"As well as I know most of the other techs," Marvin said.

"You and I have known each other for six years," Laurie said. "I think of us as friends."

"Yeah, I suppose," Marvin said warily.

"I'd like you to do something for me as a friend," Laurie said. "But only if it doesn't make you feel uncomfortable."

"Like what?" Marvin said.

"I'd like you to call Mike Passano and tell him that I found out that one of the bodies that he sent out the night Franconi disappeared was an unidentified corpse."

"That's strange, man!" Marvin said. "Why would I be calling him rather than just waiting for him to come on duty?"

"You can act like you just heard it, which is the case," Laurie said. "And you can say that you thought he should know right away since he was on duty that night."

"I don't know, man," Marvin said unconvinced.

"The key thing is that coming from you, it won't be confrontational," Laurie said. "If I call, he'll think I'm accusing him, and I'm interested to hear his reaction without his feeling defensive. But more important, I'd like you to ask him if there were two people from Spoletto Funeral Home that night, and if there were two, whether he can remember who actually went to get the body."

"That's like setting him up, man," Marvin complained.

"I don't see it that way," Laurie said. "If anything, it gives him a chance to clear himself. You see, I think the Spoletto people took Franconi."

"I don't feel comfortable calling him," Marvin said. "He's going to know something is up. Why don't you call him yourself, you know what I'm saying?"

"I already told you, I think he'll be too defensive," Laurie said. "Last time he was defensive when I asked him purely vague questions. But okay, if you feel uncomfortable, I don't want you to do it. Instead, I want you to go on a little hunt with me."

"Now what?" Marvin asked. His patience was wearing thin.

"Can you produce a list of all the refrigerator compartments that are occupied at the moment?" Laurie asked.

"Sure, that's easy," Marvin said.

"Please," Laurie said, while gesturing towards Marvin's computer terminal. "While you're at it, make two copies."

Marvin shrugged and sat down. Using a relatively rapid hunt-and-peck style, he directed the computer to produce the list Laurie wanted. He handed the two sheets to her the moment they came out of the printer.

"Excellent," Laurie said, glancing at the sheets. "Come on!" As she left the mortuary office, she waved over her shoulder. Marvin followed at her heels.

They walked down the stained cement corridor to the giant island that dominated the morgue. On opposite sides were the banks of refrigerated compartments used to store the bodies before autopsy.

Laurie handed one of the lists to Marvin.

"I want to search every compartment that is not occupied," Laurie said. "You take this side and I'll take the other."

Marvin rolled his eyes but took the list. He started opening the compartments, peering inside, then slamming the doors. Laurie went around to the other side of the island and did the same.

"Uh-oh!" Marvin intoned after five minutes.

Laurie paused. "What is it?"

"You'd better come over here," Marvin said.

Laurie walked around the island. Marvin was standing at the far end of the island, scratching his head while staring at his list. In front of him was an open refrigerated compartment.

"This one is supposed to be empty," Marvin said.

Laurie glanced within and felt her pulse race. Inside, was a naked male corpse with no tag on its big toe. The number of the compartment was ninety-four. It wasn't too far away from number one eleven, where Franconi was supposed to have been.

Marvin slid out the tray. It rattled on its ball bearings in the stillness of the deserted morgue. The body was a middle-aged male with signs of extensive trauma to the legs and torso.

"Well, this explains it," Laurie said. Her voice reflected an improbable mixture of triumph, anger, and fear. "It's the unidentified corpse. He'd been a hit-and-run accident on the FDR Drive."

Jack stepped off the elevator and could hear

a phone ringing insistently. As he proceeded down the hall he became progressively aware it had to be his phone, especially since his office was the only one with an open door.

Jack picked up speed and then almost missed his door as he slid on the vinyl flooring. He snapped the phone off the hook just in time. It was Lou.

"Where the hell have you been?" Lou complained.

"I got stuck over at the University Hospital," Jack said. After Jack had last talked with Lou, Dr. Malovar had appeared and had him look at some forensic slides for him. So soon on the heels of his consulting Malovar, Jack didn't feel he could refuse.

"I've been calling every fifteen minutes," Lou remarked.

"Sorry," Jack said.

"I've got some surprising information that I've been dying to give you," Lou said. "This is one weird case."

"That's not telling me anything I didn't already know," Jack said. "What did you learn?"

Movement out of the corner of Jack's eye attracted his attention. Turning his head, he saw Laurie standing in the doorway. She did not look normal. Her eyes were blazing, her mouth was set in an angry grimace, and her skin was the color of ivory.

"Wait a sec!" Jack said, interrupting Lou.

"Laurie, what the hell is the matter?"

"I have to talk with you," Laurie sputtered.

"Sure," Jack said. "But could it wait for two minutes?" He pointed at the phone to indicate that he was talking with someone.

"Now!" Laurie barked.

"Okay, okay," Jack repeated. It was clear to him she was as tense as a piano wire about to snap.

"Listen, Lou," Jack said into the phone. "Laurie just came in, and she's upset. Let me call you right back."

"Hold on!" Laurie snapped. "Is that Lou Soldano you're talking with?"

"Yeah," Jack said hesitantly. For an irrational instant, he thought that Laurie was overwrought because he was talking with Lou.

"Where is he?" Laurie demanded.

Jack shrugged. "I guess he's in his office."

"Ask him," Laurie snapped.

Jack posed the question, and Lou answered in the affirmative. Jack nodded to Laurie. "He's there," he said.

"Tell him we're coming down to see him," Laurie said.

Jack hesitated. He was confused.

"Tell him!" Laurie repeated. "Tell him we're leaving right away."

"Did you hear that?" Jack asked Lou. Laurie then disappeared down the corridor toward her office.

"I did," Lou said. "What's going on?"

"Damned if I know," Jack said. "She just barreled in. Unless I call you right back, we'll be there."

"Fine," Lou said. "I'll wait."

Jack hung up the phone and rushed out into the hall. Laurie was already on her way back and was struggling into her coat. She eyed him as she brushed past on her way to the elevators. Jack hustled to catch up with her.

"What's happened?" Jack asked hesitantly. He was afraid to upset her any more than she already was.

"I'm about ninety-nine percent sure how Franconi's body was taken from here," Laurie said angrily. "And two things are becoming clear. First, the Spoletto Funeral Home was involved and second, the abduction was surely abetted by someone who works here. And to tell you the truth, I'm not sure which of these two things bothers me more."

"Jeez, look at that traffic," Franco Ponti said to Angelo Facciolo. "I'm sure as hell glad we're going into Manhattan instead of going out."

Franco and Angelo were in Franco's black Cadillac, heading west on the Queensboro Bridge. It was five-thirty, the height of rush hour. Both men were dressed as if they were going to a ritzy dinner.

432

"What order do you want to do this in?" Franco asked.

Angelo shrugged. "Maybe the girl first," he said. His face twisted into a slight smile.

"You're looking forward to this, aren't you?" Franco commented.

Angelo raised his eyebrows as much as his facial scar tissue would allow. "Five years I've been dreaming about seeing this broad professionally," he said. "I guess I never thought I would get my chance."

"I know I don't have to remind you that we follow orders," Franco said. "To the letter."

"Cerino was never so specific," Angelo said. "He'd just tell us to do a job. He didn't tell us how to do it."

"That's why Cerino is in jail and Vinnie is running the show," Franco said.

"I'll tell you what," Angelo said. "Why don't we do a drive by Jack Stapleton's place. I've already been inside Laurie Montgomery's apartment, so I know what we're getting ourselves into. But I'm a little surprised by this other address. West One Hundred-sixth Street isn't where I'd expect a doctor to be living."

"I think a drive-by sounds smart," Franco said.

When they reached Manhattan, Franco continued west on Fifty-ninth Street. He rounded the southern end of Central Park and headed north on Central Park West.

Angelo thought back to the fateful day on the pier of the American Fresh Fruit Company when Laurie caused the explosion. Angelo had had skin problems from chicken pox and acne, but it had been the the burns he suffered because of Laurie Montgomery that had turned him into what he called a "freak."

Franco posed a question, but Angelo hadn't heard him because of his angry musings. He had to ask him to repeat it.

"I bet you'd like to stick it to that Laurie Montgomery," Franco said. "If it had been me, I sure would."

Angelo let out a sarcastic laugh. Unconsciously, he moved his left arm so that he could feel the reassuring mass of his Walther TPH auto pistol snuggled into its shoulder holster.

Franco turned left onto One Hundred-sixth Street. They passed a playground on the right that was in full use, particularly the basketball court. There were lots of people standing on the sidelines.

"It must be on the left," Franco said.

Angelo consulted the piece of paper he was holding with Jack's address. "It's coming up," he said. "It's the building with the fancy top."

Franco slowed and then stopped to double-park a few buildings short of Jack's on the opposite side of the street. A car behind beeped. Franco lowered his window and motioned for the car to pass. There was cursing as the car did so. Franco shook his head. "You hear that guy? Nobody in this city has any manners."

"Why would a doctor live there?" Angelo said. He was eyeing Jack's building through the front windshield.

Franco shook his head. "Doesn't make any sense to me. The building looks like a dump."

"Amendola said he was a little strange," Angelo said. "Apparently, he rides a bike from here all the way down to the morgue at First Avenue and Thirtieth Street every day."

"No way!" Franco commented.

"That's what Amendola said," Angelo said.

Franco's eyes scanned the area. "The whole neighborhood is a dump. Maybe he's into drugs."

Angelo opened the car door and got out.

"Where are you going?" Franco asked.

"I want to check to make sure he lives here," Angelo said. "Amendola said his apartment is the fourth floor rear. I'll be right back."

Angelo rounded the car and waited for a break in the traffic. He crossed the street and climbed to the stoop in front of Jack's building. Calmly, he pushed open the outer door and glanced at the mailboxes. Many were broken. None had locks that worked.

Quickly, Angelo sorted through the mail. As soon as he came across a catalogue addressed to Jack Stapleton, he put it all back. Next, he tried the inner door. It opened with ease.

Stepping into the front hall, Angelo took a breath. There was an unpleasant musty odor. He eyed the trash on the stairs, the peeling paint, and the broken light bulbs in the once-elegant chandelier. Up on the second floor, he could hear the sounds of a domestic fight with muffled screaming. Angelo smiled. Dealing with Jack Stapleton was going to be easy. The tenement looked like a crack house.

Returning to the front of the house, Angelo took a step away to determine which underground passageway belonged to Jack's building. Each house had a sunken corridor reached by a half dozen steps. These corridors led to the backyards.

After deciding which was the appropriate one, Angelo gingerly walked its length. There were puddles and refuse which threatened his Bruno Magli shoes.

The backyard was a tumult of decaying and collapsed fencing, rotting mattresses, abandoned tires, and other trash. After carefully picking his way a few feet from the building, Angelo turned to look at the fire escape. On the fourth floor two windows had access. The windows were dark. The doctor wasn't at home.

Angelo returned and climbed back into the car.

"Well?" Franco asked.

"He lives there all right," Angelo said. "The building is worse on the inside if you can believe it. It's not locked. I could hear a couple fighting on the second floor and someone else's TV on full blast. The place is not pretty but for our purposes it's perfect. It'll be easy."

"That's what I like to hear," Franco said. "Should we still do the woman first?"

Angelo smiled as best he could. "Why deny myself?"

Franco put the car in gear. They headed south on Columbus Avenue to Broadway then cut across town to Second Avenue. Soon they were on Nineteenth Street. Angelo didn't need the address. He pointed out Laurie's building without difficulty. Franco found a convenient no-parking zone and parked.

"So, you think we should go up the back way?" Franco said, while eyeing the building.

"For several reasons," Angelo said. "She's on the fifth floor, but her windows face the back. To tell if she's there, we have to go back there anyway. Also she's got a nosy neighbor who lives in the front, and you can see her lights are on. This woman opened her door to gawk at me the two times I was up at Montgomery's front door. Besides, Montgomery's apartment has access to the back stairs, and the back stairs dump directly into the backyard. I know because we chased her out that way."

"I'm convinced," Franco said. "Let's do it."

Franco and Angelo got out of the car. Angelo opened up the backseat and lifted out his bag of lock-picking tools along with a Halligan bar, a tool firefighters use to get through doors in cases of emergency.

The two men headed for the passageway to the backyard.

"I heard she got away from you and Tony Ruggerio," Franco said. "At least for a while. She must be quite a number."

"Don't remind me," Angelo said. "Of course, working with Tony was like carrying around a bucket of sand."

Emerging into the backyard, which was a dark warren of neglected gardens, Franco and Angelo carefully moved away from the building far enough to see up to the fifth floor. The windows were all dark.

"Looks like we have time to prepare a nice homecoming," Franco said.

Angelo didn't answer. Instead, he took his lock-picking tools over to the metal fire door that led to the back stairs. He slipped on a tight-fitting pair of leather gloves, while Franco readied the flashlight.

At first Angelo's hands shook from sheer anticipatory excitement of coming face-to-face with Laurie Montgomery after five years of smoldering resentment. When the lock resisted Angelo's efforts, he made a point to control himself and concentrate. The lock responded, and the door opened.

Five floors up, Angelo didn't bother with the lock-picking tools. He knew that Laurie had several dead bolts. He used the Halligan bar. With a quiet splintering sound, it made short work of the door. Within twenty seconds, they were inside.

For a few minutes, the two men stood motionless in the darkness of Laurie's pantry so that they could listen. They wanted to be certain there were no sounds suggestive that their forced entry had been noticed by any of the other tenants.

"Jesus Christ!" Franco forcibly whispered. "Something just touched my leg!"

"What is it?" Angelo demanded. He'd not expected such an outburst, and it caused his heart to flutter.

"Oh, it's only a goddamn cat!" Franco said with relief. All at once, both men could hear the animal purring in the darkness.

"Aren't we lucky," Angelo said. "That will be a nice touch. Bring it along."

Slowly, the men made their way from the pantry through the dark kitchen and into the living room. There they could see significantly better with the city night light coming through the windows.

"So far so good," Angelo said.

"Now we just have to wait," Franco said. "Maybe I'll see if there's any beer or wine in the refrigerator. Are you interested?"

"A beer would be nice," Angelo said.

At police headquarters, Laurie and Jack had to get ID badges and go through a metal detector before they were allowed to go up to Lou's floor. Lou was at the elevator to welcome them.

The first thing he did was take Laurie by the shoulders, look her in the eye, and ask what had happened.

"She's okay," Jack said, patting Lou reassuringly on the back. "She's back to her old, rational, calm self."

"Really?" Lou questioned, still giving Laurie a close inspection.

Laurie couldn't help but smile under Lou's intense scrutiny. "Jack's right," she said. "I'm fine. In fact, I'm embarrassed I made us rush down here."

Lou breathed a sigh of relief. "Well, I'm happy to see both of you. Come on back to my palace." He led the way to his office.

"I can offer you coffee, but I strongly advise against it," Lou said. "At this time of day the janitorial staff considers it strong enough to clean out sink drains."

"We're fine," Laurie said. She took a chair.

Jack did likewise. He glanced around the spartan quarters with an unpleasant shiver. The last time he'd been there about a year ago, it had been after he'd narrowly escaped an attempt on his life.

"I think I figured out how Franconi's body was taken from the morgue," Laurie began. "You teased me about suspecting the Spoletto Funeral Home, but now I think you're going to have to take that back. In fact, I think it's time that you took over."

Laurie then outlined what she thought had happened. She told Lou that she suspected that someone from the medical examiner's office had given the Spoletto people the accession number of a relatively recent, unidentified body as well as the location of Franconi's remains.

"Often when two drivers come to pick up a body for a funeral home, one of them goes in the walk-in cooler while the other handles the paperwork with the mortuary tech," Laurie explained. "In these instances, the mortuary tech prepares the body for pickup by covering it with a sheet and positioning its gurney in a convenient location just inside the cooler door. In the Franconi situation, I believe the driver took the body whose accession number he had, removed its tag, stashed the body in one of the many unoccupied refrigerator compartments, replaced Franconi's tag with that one, and then calmly appeared outside the mortuary office with Franconi's remains. All the tech did at that point was check the accession number."

"That's quite a scenario," Lou said. "Can

I ask if you have any proof of this or is it all conjecture?"

"I found the body whose accession number Spoletto called in," Laurie said. "It was in a compartment which was supposed to be vacant. The name Frank Gleason was bogus."

"Ahhhh!" Lou said, becoming much more interested. He leaned forward on his desk. "I'm beginning to like this very much, especially considering the matrimonial association between the Spoletto and the Lucia people. This could be something important. It kind'a reminds me of getting Al Capone on tax evasion. I mean, it would be fantastic if we could get some of the Lucia people on body theft!"

"Of course, it also raises the specter of an organized crime connection to illicit liver transplantation," Jack said. "This could be a frightening association."

"Dangerous as well," Lou said. "So I must insist on no more amateur sleuthing on your part. We take over from here. Do I have your word on that?"

"I'm happy to let you take over," Laurie said. "But there is also the issue of a mole in the medical examiner's office."

"I think it's best I deal with that, too," Lou said. "With the involvement of organized crime, I'd expect some element of extortion or criminal coercion. But I'll deal directly with Bingham. I shouldn't have to warn you that these people are dangerous."

"I learned that lesson all too well," Laurie said.

"I'm too preoccupied with my end of the mystery to interfere," Jack said. "What did you learn for me?"

"Plenty," Lou said. He reached over to the corner of his desk and hefted a large book the size of a coffee-table art book. With a grunt, he handed it to Jack.

With a look of confusion, Jack cracked the book. "What the hell!" he commented. "What's an atlas for?"

"Because you're going to need it," Lou said. "I can't tell you how long it took me to scrounge one up here at police headquarters."

"I don't get it," Jack said.

"My contact at the FAA was able to call someone who knew someone who works in a European organization that doles out landing and takeoff times all over Europe," Lou explained. "They also get the flight plans and store them for over sixty days. Franconi's G4 came to France from Equatorial Guinea."

"Where?" Jack questioned as his eyebrows collided in an expression of total confusion. "I never even heard of Equatorial Guinea. Is it a country?"

"Check out page one hundred fifty-two!" Lou said.

"What's this about a Franconi and a G4?" Laurie asked.

"A G4 is a private jet," Lou explained. "I was able to find out for Jack that Franconi had been out of the country. We thought he'd been in France until I got this new information."

Jack got to page 152 in the atlas. It was a map labeled "the Western Congo Basin," covering a huge portion of western Africa.

"All right, give me a hint," Jack said.

Lou pointed over Jack's shoulder. "It's this little tiny country between Cameroon and Gabon. The city that the plane flew out of is Bata, on the coast." He pointed to the appropriate dot. The atlas depicted the country as mostly uninterrupted green.

Laurie got up from her chair and looked over Jack's other shoulder. "I think I remember hearing about that country one time. I think that's where the writer Frederick Forsyth went to write *Dogs of War.*"

Lou slapped the top of his head in utter amazement. "How do you remember stuff like that? I can't remember where I had lunch last Tuesday."

Laurie shrugged. "I read a lot of novels," she said. "Writers interest me."

"This doesn't make any sense whatsoever," Jack complained. "This is an undeveloped part of Africa. This country must be covered with nothing but jungle. In fact, this whole part of Africa is nothing but jungle. Franconi couldn't have gotten a liver transplant there."

"That was my reaction, too," Lou said. "But the other information makes a little more sense. I tracked Alpha Aviation through its Nevada management corporation to its real owner. It's GenSys Corp in Cambridge, Massachusetts."

"I've heard of GenSys," Laurie said. "It's a biotech firm that's big in vaccines and lymphokines. I remember because a girlfriend of mine who's a broker in Chicago recommended the stock. She's forever giving me tips, thinking I've got tons of money to invest."

"A biotech company!" Jack mused. "Hmmm. That's a new twist. It must be significant, although I don't quite know how. Nor do I know what a biotech firm would be doing in Equatorial Guinea."

"What's the meaning of this indirect corporate trail in Nevada?" Laurie asked. "Is GenSys trying to hide the fact that they own an aircraft?"

"I doubt it," Lou said. "I was able to learn the connection too easily. If GenSys was trying to conceal ownership, the lawyers in Nevada would have continued to be the directors and officers of record for Alpha Aviation. Instead, at the first board meeting the chief financial officer of GenSys assumed the duties of president and secretary."

"Then why Nevada for an airplane owned by a Massachusetts-based company?" Laurie asked.

"I'm no lawyer," Lou admitted. "But I'm sure it has something to do with taxes and limitation of liability. Massachusetts is a terrible state to get sued in. I imagine GenSys leases its plane out for the percentage of the time it doesn't use it, and insurance for a Nevada-based company would be a lot less."

"How well do you know this broker friend of yours?" Jack asked Laurie.

"Really well," Laurie said. "We went to Wesleyan University together."

"How about giving her a call and asking her if she knows of any connection between GenSys and Equatorial Guinea," Jack said. "If she recommended the stock, she'd probably thoroughly researched the company."

"Without a doubt," Laurie said. "Jean Corwin was one of the most compulsive students I knew. She made us premeds seem casual by comparison."

"Is it all right if Laurie uses your phone?" Jack asked Lou.

"No problem," Lou said.

"You want me to call this minute?" Laurie asked with surprise.

"Catch her while she's still at work," Jack said. "Chances are if she has any file, it would be there."

"You're probably right," Laurie admitted. She sat down at Lou's desk and called Chicago information.

While Laurie was on the phone, Jack

quizzed Lou in detail about how he was able to find out what he had. He was particularly interested and impressed with the way Lou had come up with Equatorial Guinea. Together, they looked more closely at the map, noticing the country's proximity to the equator. They even noticed that its major city, presumably its capital, wasn't on the mainland but rather on an island called Bioko.

"I just can't imagine what it's like in a place like that," Lou said.

"I can," Jack said. "It's hot, buggy, rainy, and wet."

"Sounds delightful," Lou quipped.

"Not the place someone would choose to vacation," Jack said. "On the other hand, it's off the beaten track."

Laurie hung up the phone and twisted around in Lou's desk chair to face the others. "Jean was as organized as I expected," she said. "She was able to put her finger on her GenSys material in a flash. Of course, she had to ask me how much of the stock I'd bought and was crushed when I admitted I hadn't bought any. Apparently, the stock tripled and then split."

"Is that good?" Lou asked facetiously.

"So good I might have missed my opportunity to retire," Laurie said. "She said this is the second successful biotech company started by its CEO, Taylor Cabot."

"Did she have anything to say about Equatorial Guinea?" Jack asked.

"For sure," Laurie said. "She said that one of the main reasons the company has been doing so well is that it established a huge primate farm. Initially, the farm was to do in-house research for GenSys. Then someone hit on the idea of creating an opportunity for other biotech companies and pharmaceutical firms to out-source their primate research to GenSys. Apparently, the demand for this service has trampled even the most optimistic forecasts."

"And this primate farm is in Equatorial Guinea?" Jack asked.

"That's right," Laurie said.

"Did she suggest any reason why?" Jack asked.

"A memorandum she had from an analyst said that GenSys chose Equatorial Guinea because of the favorable reception they received from the government, which even passed laws to aid their operation. Apparently, GenSys has become the government's major source of much-needed foreign currency."

"Can you imagine the amount of graft that must be involved in that kind of scenario?" Jack asked Lou.

Lou merely whistled.

"The memorandum also pointed out that most of the primates they use are indigenous to Equatorial Guinea," Laurie added. "It allows them to circumvent all the international restrictions in exportation and importation of endangered species like chimpanzees."

"A primate farm," Jack repeated while shaking his head. "This is raising even more bizarre possibilities. Could we be dealing with a xenograft?"

"Don't start that doctor jargon on me," Lou complained. "What in God's name is a xenograft?"

"Impossible," Laurie said. "Xenografts cause hyper-acute rejections. There was no evidence of inflammation in the liver section you showed me, neither humoral nor cell-mediated."

"True," Jack said. "And he wasn't even on any immunosuppressant drugs."

"Come on, you guys," Lou pleaded. "Don't make me beg. What the hell is a xenograft?"

"It's when a transplant organ is taken from an animal of a different species," Laurie said.

"You mean like that Baby Fae baboon heart fiasco ten or twelve years ago?" Lou asked.

"Exactly," Laurie said.

"The new immunosuppressant drugs have brought xenografts back into the picture," Jack explained. "And with considerable more success than with Baby Fae."

"Especially with pig heart valves," Laurie said.

"Of course, it poses a lot of ethical questions," Jack said. "And it drives animal-rights people berserk."

"Especially now that they are experimenting with inserting human genes into the pigs to ameliorate some of the rejection reaction," Laurie added.

"Could Franconi have gotten a primate liver while he was in Africa?" Lou asked.

"I can't imagine," Jack said. "Laurie's point is well taken. There was no evidence of any rejection. That's unheard of even with a good human match short of identical twins."

"But Franconi was apparently in Africa," Lou said.

"True, and his mother said he came home a new man," Jack said. He threw up his hands and stood up. "I don't know what to make of it. It's the damnedest mystery. Especially with this organized crime aspect thrown in."

Laurie stood up as well.

"Are you guys leaving?" Lou asked.

Jack nodded. "I'm confused and exhausted," he said. "I didn't sleep much last night. After we made the identification of Franconi's remains, I was on the phone for hours. I called every European organ allocation organization whose phone number I could get."

"How about we all head over to Little Italy for a quick dinner?" Lou suggested. "It's right around the corner."

"Not me," Jack said. "I've got a bike ride ahead of me. At this point, a meal would do me in."

"Nor I," Laurie said. "I'm looking forward to getting home and taking a shower. It's been two late nights for me in a row, and I'm frazzled."

Lou admitted to having another half hour of work to do, so Laurie and Jack said good-bye and descended to the first floor. They returned their temporary-visitor badges and left police headquarters. In the shadow of City Hall, they caught a cab.

"Feel better?" Jack asked Laurie, as they headed north up the Bowery. A kaleidoscope of light played across their faces.

"Much," Laurie admitted. "I can't tell you how relieved I am to dump it all in Lou's capable lap. I'm sorry I got myself so worked up."

"No need to apologize," Jack said. "It's unsettling, to say the least, there's a potential spy in our midst and that organized crime has an interest in liver transplants."

"And how are you bearing up?" Laurie asked. "You're getting a lot of bizarre input on the Franconi case."

"It's bizarre, but it's also intriguing," Jack said. "Especially this association with a biotech giant like GenSys. The scary part about these corporations is that their research is all behind closed doors. Cold-war style secrecy is their modus operandi. No one knows what they are doing in their quest for return on investment. It's a big difference from ten or twenty years ago when the NIH funded most biomedical research in a kind of open forum. In those days, there was oversight in the form of peer review, but not today."

"Too bad there's no one like Lou that you can turn the case over to," Laurie said with a chuckle.

"Wouldn't that be nice," Jack said.

"What's your next step?" Laurie asked.

Jack sighed. "I'm running out of options. The only thing that's scheduled is for a veterinary pathologist to review the liver section."

"So, you already thought about a xenograft?" Laurie asked with surprise.

"No, I didn't," Jack admitted. "The suggestion to have a veterinary pathologist look at the slide wasn't my idea. It came from a parasitologist over at the hospital who thought the granuloma was due to a parasite, but one he didn't recognize."

"Maybe you should mention the possibility of a xenograft to Ted Lynch," Laurie suggested. "As a DNA expert he might have something in his bag of tricks that could say yes or no definitively."

"Excellent idea!" Jack said with admiration. "How can you come up with such a great suggestion when you're so beat? You amaze me! My mind has already shut down for the night."

"Compliments are always welcome," Laurie

teased. "Especially in the dark, so you can't see me blush."

"I'm starting to think that the only option that might be open to me if I really want to solve this case is a quick trip to Equatorial Guinea."

Laurie twisted around in the seat so she could look directly into Jack's broad face. In the half light, it was impossible to see his eyes. "You're not serious. I mean you're joking, right?"

"Well, there's no way I could phone GenSys or even go up to Cambridge and walk into their home office and say: 'Hi folks, what's going on in Equatorial Guinea?' "

"But we're talking about Africa," Laurie said. "That's crazy. It's halfway around the world. Besides, if you don't think you'd learn anything going up to Cambridge, what makes you think you'd learn anything going to Africa?"

"Maybe because they wouldn't expect it," Jack said. "I don't suppose they get many visitors."

"Oh, this is insane," Laurie said, flapping her hands into the air and rolling her eyes.

"Hey, calm down," Jack said. "I didn't say I was going. I just said it was something I was beginning to think about."

"Well, stop thinking about it," Laurie said. "I've got enough to worry about."

Jack smiled at her. "You really are concerned. I'm touched."

"Oh, sure!" Laurie remarked cynically. "You're never touched by my pleas not to ride your mountain bike around the city."

The taxi pulled up in front of Laurie's apartment building and came to a halt. Laurie started to get some money out. Jack put a hand on her arm. "My treat."

"All right, I'll get it next time," Laurie said. She started to climb out of the cab, then stopped. "If you were to promise to take a cab home, I think we could rustle up something to eat in my apartment."

"Thanks, but not tonight," Jack said. "I've got to get the bike home. I'd probably fall asleep on a full stomach."

"Worse things could happen," Laurie said.

"Let me take a rain check," Jack said.

Laurie climbed out of the cab and then leaned back in. "Just promise me one thing: you won't leave for Africa tonight."

Jack took a playful swipe at her, but she easily evaded his hand.

"Good night, Jack," Laurie said with a warm smile.

"Good night, Laurie," Jack said. "I'll call you later after I talk with Warren."

"Oh, that's right," Laurie said. "With everything that's happened, I'd forgotten. I'll be waiting for your call."

Laurie closed the taxi door and watched the cab until it disappeared around the corner on

First Avenue. She turned toward her door, musing that Jack was a charming but complicated man.

As she rode up in her elevator, Laurie began to anticipate her shower and the warmth of her terry-cloth robe. She vowed she'd turn in early.

Laurie treated Debra Engler to an acid smile before keying her multiple locks. She slammed her door behind her to give Mrs. Engler an extra message. Moving her mail from one hand to the other, she removed her coat. In the darkness of the closet, she groped for a hanger.

It wasn't until Laurie entered the living room that she flipped the wall switch that turned on a floor lamp. She got two steps toward the kitchen when she let out a muffled scream and dropped her mail on the floor. There were two men in the living room. One was in her art-deco chair, the other sitting on the couch. The one on the couch was petting Tom, who was asleep on his lap.

The other thing Laurie noticed was a large handgun with an attached silencer on the arm of the art-deco chair.

"Welcome home, Dr. Montgomery," Franco said. "Thank you for the wine and beer."

Laurie's eyes went to the coffee table. There was an empty beer bottle and wineglass.

"Please come over and sit down," Franco

said. He pointed to a side chair they'd put in the middle of the room.

Laurie didn't move. She was incapable of it. She thought vaguely about running into the kitchen for the phone but immediately dismissed the idea as ridiculous. She even thought about fleeing back to her front door, but with all the locks, she knew it would be a futile gesture.

"Please!" Franco repeated with a false politeness that only augmented Laurie's terror.

Angelo moved the cat to the side and stood up. He took a step toward Laurie and, without warning, backhanded her viciously across the face. The blow propelled Laurie back against the wall, where her legs gave way. She slumped to her hands and knees. A few drops of bright red blood dropped from her split upper lip, splattering on the hardwood floor.

Angelo grabbed her by the upper arm and roughly hoisted her to her feet. Then he powered her over to the chair and pushed her into a sitting position. Laurie's terror made her incapable of resisting.

"That's better," Franco said.

Angelo leaned over and stuck his face in Laurie's. "Recognize me?"

Laurie forced herself to look up into the man's horribly scarred face. He looked like a character in a horror movie. She swallowed; her throat had gone dry. Incapable of speech, all she could do was shake her head.

"No?" Franco questioned. "Doctor, I'm afraid you are going to hurt Angelo's feelings and, under the circumstances, that's a dangerous thing to do."

"I'm sorry," Laurie squeaked. But no sooner had the words come out, then Laurie associated the name with the fact that the man standing in front of her had been burned. It was Angelo Facciolo, Cerino's main hit man, now obviously out of jail.

"I've been waiting five years," Angelo snarled. Then he struck Laurie again, half knocking her off the chair. She ended up with her head down. There was more blood. This time it came from her nose and soaked into the carpet.

"Okay, Angelo!" Franco said. "Remember! We've got to talk with her."

Angelo trembled for a moment over Laurie, as if struggling to restrain himself. Abruptly, he went back to the couch and sat down. He picked the cat back up and began roughly petting it. Tom didn't mind and began to purr.

Laurie managed to right herself. With her hand, she felt both her lip and her nose. Her lip was already beginning to swell. She pinched her nose to halt the bleeding.

"Listen, Doctor Montgomery," Franco said. "As you might imagine, it was very easy for us to come in here. I say this so you will comprehend how vulnerable you are. You see,

457

we have a problem that you can help us with. We're here to ask you nicely to leave the Franconi thing alone. Am I making myself clear?"

Laurie nodded. She was afraid not to.

"Good," Franco said. "Now, we are very reasonable people. We'll consider this a favor on your part, and we're willing to do a favor in return. We happen to know who killed Mr. Franconi, and we're willing to pass that information on to you. You see, Mr. Franconi wasn't a nice man, so he was killed. End of story. Are you still with me?"

Laurie nodded again. She glanced at Angelo but quickly averted her eyes.

"The killer's name is Vido Delbario," Franco continued. "He's not a nice person, either, although he did do the world a favor in getting rid of Franconi. I've even taken the trouble to write the name down." Franco leaned forward and put a piece of paper on the coffee table. "So, a favor for a favor."

Franco paused and looked expectantly at Laurie.

"You do understand what I'm saying, don't you?" Franco asked after a moment of silence.

Laurie nodded for the third time.

"I mean, we're not asking much," Franco said. "To be blunt, Franconi was a bad guy. He killed a bunch of people and deserved to die himself. Now, as far as you are concerned, I hope you will be sensible because in a city this size there's no way to protect yourself, and Angelo here would like no better than have his way with you. Lucky for you, our boss is not heavy-handed. He's a negotiator. Do you understand?"

Franco paused again. Laurie felt compelled to respond. With difficulty, she managed to say she understood.

"Wonderful!" Franco said. He slapped his knees and stood up. "When I heard how intelligent and resourceful you are, Doc, I was confident we could see eye to eye."

Franco slipped his handgun into his shoulder holster and put on his Ferragamo coat. "Come on, Angelo," he said. "I'm sure the doctor wants to shower and have her dinner. She looks kind'a tired to me."

Angelo got up, took a step in Laurie's direction, and then viciously wrenched the cat's neck. There was a sickening snap, and Tom went limp without a sound. Angelo dumped the dead cat in Laurie's lap, and followed Franco out the front door.

"Oh, no!" Laurie whimpered as she cradled her pet of six years. She knew its neck had been cruelly broken. She stood up on rubbery legs. Out in the hall, she heard the elevator arrive and then descend.

With sudden panic she rushed to the front door and relocked all the locks while still clutching Tom's body. Then, realizing the intruders had to have come in the back door, she raced there only to find it wide open and splintered. She forced it closed as best she could.

Back in the kitchen she took the phone off the hook with trembling hands. Her first response was to call the police, but then she hesitated, hearing Franco's voice in the back of her mind warning her how vulnerable she was. She also could see Angelo's horrid face and the intensity of his eyes.

Recognizing she was in shock and fighting tears, Laurie replaced the receiver. She thought she'd call Jack, but she knew he wouldn't be home yet. So, instead of calling anyone for the moment, she tenderly packed her pet in a Styrofoam box with several trays of ice cubes. Then she went into the bathroom to check out her own wounds.

Jack's bike ride from the morgue home was not the ordeal he expected. In fact, once he got under way, he felt better than he had for most of the day. He even allowed himself to cut through Central Park. It had been the first time he'd been in the park after dark for a year. Although he was uneasy, it was also exhilarating to sprint along the dark, winding paths.

For most of the trip, he'd pondered about GenSys and Equatorial Guinea. He wondered what it was really like in that part of Africa. He'd joked earlier with Lou that it was buggy, hot, and wet, but he didn't know for sure.

He also thought about Ted Lynch and wondered what Ted would be able to do the following day. Before Jack had left the morgue, he'd called him at home to outline the unlikely possibility of a xenograft. Ted said that he thought he'd be able to tell by checking an area on the DNA that specified ribosomal proteins. He'd explained that the area differed considerably from species to species and that the information to make a species identification was available on a CD-ROM.

Jack turned onto his street with the idea of going to the local bookstore to see if there was any material on Equatorial Guinea. But as he approached the playground with its daily late afternoon and evening game of basketball under way, he had another idea. It occurred to him that there might be expatriate Equatoguineans in New York. After all, the city harbored people from every country in the world.

Turning his bike into the playground, Jack dismounted and leaned it up against the chain-link fence. He didn't bother to lock it, though most people would have thought the neighborhood a risky place to leave a thousand-dollar bike. In reality, the playground was the only place in New York Jack felt he didn't have to lock up.

Jack walked over to the sidelines and nodded to Spit and Flash, who were part of the crowd waiting to play. The game in progress swept up and down the court as the ball changed hands or baskets were made. As usual, Warren was dominating the play. Before each of his shots he'd say "money," which was aggravating to the opponents because ninety percent of the time, the ball would sail through the basket.

A quarter hour later the game was decided by one of Warren's "money" shots, and the losers slunk off the court. Warren caught sight of Jack and strutted over.

"Hey, man, you going to run or what?" Warren asked.

"I'm thinking about it," Jack said. "But I've got a couple of questions. First of all, how about you and Natalie getting together with Laurie and me this weekend?"

"Hell, yes," Warren said. "Anything to shut my shortie up. She's been ragging on me fierce about you and Laurie."

"Secondly, do you know any brothers from a tiny African country called Equatorial Guinea?"

"Man, I never know what's going to come out of your mouth," Warren complained. "Let me think."

"It's on the west coast of Africa," Jack said. "Between Cameroon and Gabon."

"I know where it is," Warren said indignantly. "It was supposedly discovered by the Portuguese and colonized by the Spanish. Actually, it was discovered a long time earlier by black people."

"I'm impressed you know of it," Jack said. "I'd never heard of the country."

"I'm not surprised," Warren said. "I'm sure you didn't take any black history courses. But to answer your question, yes, I do know a couple of people from there, and one family in particular. Their name is Ndeme. They live two doors down from you, toward the park."

Jack looked over at the building, then back at Warren. "Do you know them well enough to introduce me?" Jack asked. "I've developed a sudden interest in Equatorial Guinea."

"Yeah, sure," Warren said. "The father's name is Esteban. He owns the Mercado market over on Columbus. That's his son over there with the orange kicks."

Jack followed Warren's pointing finger until he spotted the orange sneakers. He recognized the boy as one of the basketball regulars. He was a quiet kid and an intense player.

"Why don't you come down and run a few games?" Warren suggested. "Then I'll take you over and introduce you to Esteban. He's a friendly dude."

"Fair enough," Jack said. After being revived by the bicycle ride, he was looking for an excuse to play basketball. The events of the day had him in knots.

Jack went back and got his bike. Hurrying over to his building, he carried the bicycle up the stairs. He unlocked his door without even taking it off his shoulder. Once inside, he made a beeline for his bedroom and his basketball gear.

Within five minutes, Jack was already on his way out when his phone rang. For a moment, he debated answering it, but thinking it might be Ted calling back with a bit of arcane DNA trivia, Jack picked it up. It was Laurie, and she was beside herself.

Jack crammed enough bills through the Plexiglas partition in the taxi to more than cover the fare and jumped out. He was in front of Laurie's apartment building, where he'd been less than an hour earlier. Dressed in his basketball gear he raced to the front door and was buzzed in. Laurie met him in the elevator foyer on her floor.

"My god!" Jack wailed. "Look at your lip."

"That will heal," Laurie said stoically. Then she caught Debra Engler's eye peering through the crack in her door. Laurie lunged at the woman and shouted for her to mind her own business. The door snapped shut.

Jack put his arm around Laurie to calm her and led her into her apartment.

"All right," Jack said, after getting Laurie seated on the couch. "Tell me what happened."

"They killed Tom," Laurie whimpered. After the initial shock, Laurie had cried for her pet, but her tears had dried until Jack's question.

"Who?" Jack demanded.

Laurie waited until she had her emotions under control. "There were two of them, but I only knew one," she said. "And he's the one who struck me and killed Tom. His name is Angelo. He's the person I've had nightmares about. I had a terrible run-in with him during the Cerino affair. I thought he was still in prison. I can't imagine how or why he is out. He's horrid to look at. His face is terribly scarred from burns, and I'm sure he blames me."

"So this visit was for revenge?" Jack asked.

"No," Laurie said. "This was a warning for me. In their words I'm to 'leave the Franconi thing alone.' "

"I don't believe this," Jack said. "I'm the one investigating the case, not you."

"You warned me. I've obviously irritated the wrong people by trying to find out how Franconi's body was lifted from the morgue," Laurie said. "For all I know it was my visit to the Spoletto Funeral Home that set them off."

"I'm not going to take any credit for foreseeing this," Jack said. "I thought you would get in trouble with Bingham, not mobsters."

"Angelo's warning was presented in the guise of a favor for a favor," Laurie said. "His favor was to tell me who killed Franconi. In fact, he wrote the name down." Laurie lifted the piece of paper from the coffee table and handed it to Jack.

"Vido Delbario," Jack read. He looked back at Laurie's battered face. Both her nose and lip were swollen, and she was developing a black eye. "This case has been bizarre from the start, now it's getting out of hand. I think you'd better tell me everything that happened."

Laurie related to Jack the details from the moment she'd walked in the door until she'd called him on the phone. She even told him why she'd hesitated calling 911.

Jack nodded. "I understand," he said. "There's little the local precinct could do at this point."

"What am I going to do?" Laurie asked rhetorically. She didn't expect an answer.

"Let me look at the back door," Jack said.

Laurie led him through the kitchen and into the pantry.

"Whoa!" Jack said. Because of the multiple dead bolts the entire edge split when the door had been forced. "I'll tell you one thing, you're not staying here tonight."

"I suppose I could go home to my parents," Laurie said.

"You're coming home with me," Jack said. "I'll sleep on the couch."

Laurie looked into the depths of Jack's eyes. She couldn't help but wonder if there were more to this sudden invitation than the issue of her safety.

"Get your things," Jack said. "And pack for a few days. It will take that long to replace this door."

"I hate to bring this up," Laurie said. "But I have to do something with poor Tom."

Jack scratched the back of his head. "Do you have access to a shovel?"

"I have a gardening trowel," Laurie said. "What are you thinking?"

"We could bury him in the backyard," Jack said.

Laurie smiled. "You are a softie, aren't you?"

"I just know what it's like to lose things you love," Jack said. His voice caught. For a painful moment he recalled the phone call that had informed him of his wife and daughter's death in a commuter plane crash.

While Laurie packed her things, Jack paced her bedroom. He forced his mind to concentrate on current concerns. "We're going to have to tell Lou about this," Jack said, "and give him Vido Delbario's name."

"I was thinking the same thing," Laurie said from the depths of her walk-in closet. "Do you think we should do it tonight?"

"I think we should," Jack said. "Then he can decide when he wants to act on it. We'll call from my house. Do you have his home number?"

"I do," Laurie said.

"You know, this episode is disturbing for more reasons than just your safety," Jack said. "It adds to my worry that organized crime is somehow involved in liver transplantation. Maybe there is some kind of black-market operation going on."

Laurie came out of her closet with a hangup bag. "But how can it be transplantation when Franconi wasn't on immunosuppressant drugs? And don't forget the strange results Ted got with his DNA testing."

Jack sighed. "You're right," he admitted. "It doesn't fit together."

"Maybe Lou can make sense of it all," Laurie said.

"Wouldn't that be nice," Jack said. "Meanwhile, this episode makes the idea of going to Africa a lot more appealing."

Laurie stopped short on her way into the bathroom. "What on earth are you talking about?" she demanded.

"I haven't had any personal experience with organized crime," Jack said. "But I have with street gangs, and I believe there's a similarity that I learned the hard way. If either of these groups gets it in their mind to get rid of you, the police can't protect you unless they are committed to guarding you twenty-four hours a day. The problem is, they don't have the manpower. Maybe it would be good for both of us to get out of town for a while. It could give Lou a chance to sort this out."

"I'd go, too?" Laurie asked. Suddenly the idea of going to Africa had a very different connotation. She'd never been to Africa, and it could be interesting. In fact, it might even be fun.

"We'd consider it a forced vacation," Jack said. "Of course, Equatorial Guinea might not be a prime destination, but it would be . . . different. And perhaps, in the process, we'll be able to figure out exactly what GenSys is doing there and why Franconi made the trip."

"Hmmm," Laurie said. "I'm starting to warm to the idea."

After Laurie had her things ready, she and Jack took Tom's Styrofoam casket into the backyard. In the far corner of the garden where there was loose loam, they dug a deep hole. The chance discovery of a rusted spade made the job easy, and Tom was put to rest.

"My word!" Jack complained as he hauled Laurie's suitcase out the front door. "What did you put in here?"

"You told me to pack for several days," Laurie said defensively.

"But you didn't have to bring your bowling ball," Jack quipped.

"It's the cosmetics," Laurie said. "They are not travel size."

They caught a cab on First Avenue. En route to Jack's they stopped at a bookstore on Fifth Avenue. While Jack waited in the taxi,

Laurie dashed inside to get a book on Equatorial Guinea. Unfortunately, there weren't any, and she had to settle for a guidebook for all of Central Africa.

"The clerk laughed at me when I asked for a book on Equatorial Guinea," Laurie said, when she got back in the cab.

"That's one more hint it's not a top vacation destination," Jack said.

Laurie laughed. She reached over and gave Jack's arm a squeeze. "I haven't thanked you yet for coming over," she said. "I really appreciated it, and I'm feeling much better."

"I'm glad," Jack said.

Once in Jack's building, Jack had to struggle with Laurie's suitcase up the cluttered stairs. After a series of exaggerated grunts and groans, Laurie asked him if he wanted her to carry it. Jack told her that her punishment for packing such a heavy bag was to listen to him complain.

Eventually, he got it outside his door. He fumbled for his key, got it into the cylinder and turned. He heard the dead bolt snap back.

"Hmmm," he commented. "I don't remember double-locking the door." He turned the key again to release the latch bolt and pushed open the door. Because of the darkness, he preceded Laurie into the apartment to flip on the light. Laurie followed and collided with him because he'd stopped suddenly.

"Go ahead, turn it on," a voice said.

Jack complied. The silhouettes he'd glimpsed a moment before were now men dressed in long, dark coats. They were seated on Jack's sofa, facing into the room.

"Oh my god!" Laurie said. "It's them!"

Franco and Angelo had made themselves at home, just as they had at Laurie's. They'd even helped themselves to beers. The half-empty bottles were on the coffee table, along with a handgun and its attached silencer. A straight-backed chair had been brought into the center of the room to face the couch.

"I assume you are Dr. Jack Stapleton," Franco said.

Jack nodded, as his mind began to go over ways of handling the situation. He knew the front door behind him was still ajar. He berated himself for not being more suspicious to have found it double-locked. The problem was he'd gone out so quickly, he couldn't remember which locks he'd secured.

"Don't do anything foolish," Franco admonished as if reading Jack's mind. "We won't be staying long. And if we'd known that Dr. Montgomery was going to be here, we could have saved ourselves a trip to her place, not to mention the effort of going over the same message twice."

"What is it you people are afraid we might learn that makes you want to come and threaten us?" Jack asked.

Franco smiled and looked at Angelo. "Can you believe this guy? He thinks we made all this effort to get in here to answer questions."

"No respect," Angelo said.

"Doc, how about getting another chair for the lady," Franco said to Jack. "Then we can have our little talk, and we'll be on our way."

Jack didn't move. He was thinking about the gun on the coffee table and wondering which of the men was still armed. As he tried to gauge their strength, he noticed that both were on the thin side. He figured they were most likely out of shape.

"Excuse me, Doc," Franco said. "Are you with us or what?"

Before Jack could answer, there was commotion behind him and someone roughly bumped him to the side. Another person shouted: "Nobody move!"

Jack recovered from his momentary confusion to comprehend that three African-Americans had leaped into the room, each armed with machine pistols. The guns were trained unwaveringly on Franco and Angelo. These newcomers were all dressed in basketball gear, and Jack quickly recognized them. It was Flash, David, and Spit, all of whom were still sweating from activity on the playground.

Franco and Angelo were taken completely unawares. They simply sat there, eyes wide. Since they were accustomed to being on the other side of lethal weapons, they knew enough not to move.

For a moment there was frozen silence. Then Warren strutted in. "Man, Doc, keeping you alive has become a full-time job, you know what I'm saying? And I'm going to have to tell you, you're dragging down the neighborhood, bringing in this kind of white trash."

Warren took the machine pistol away from Spit and told Spit to frisk the visitors. Wordlessly, Spit relieved Angelo of his Walther auto pistol. After frisking Franco, he collected the gun from the coffee table.

Jack noisily let out a breath of air. "Warren, old sport, I don't know how you manage to drop in on such a timely basis in my life, but it's appreciated."

"These scumbags were seen casing this place earlier tonight," Warren explained. "It's as if they think they're invisible, despite their expensive threads and that big, black, shiny Cadillac. It's kind of a joke."

Jack rubbed his hands together in appreciation of the sudden change of power. He asked Angelo and Franco their names but got cold stares in return.

"That one is Angelo Facciolo," Laurie said, while pointing toward her nemesis.

"Spit, get their wallets," Warren ordered.

Spit complied and read out their names and addresses. "Uh-oh, what's this?" he questioned when he opened the wallet containing the Ozone Park police badge. He held it up for Warren to see.

"They're not police officers," Warren said with a wave of dismissal. "Don't worry."

"Laurie," Jack said. "I think it's time to give Lou a call. I'm sure he'd like nothing better than to talk with these gentlemen. And tell him to bring the paddy wagon in case he'd like to invite them to stay the night at the city's expense."

Laurie disappeared into the kitchen.

Jack walked over to Angelo and towered above him.

"Stand up," Jack said.

Angelo got to his feet and glowered insolently at Jack. To everyone's surprise, especially Angelo, Jack sucker punched him as hard as he could in the face. There was a crunching sound as Angelo was knocked backward over the sofa to land in a heap on the floor.

Jack winced, cursed, and grabbed his hand. Then he shook it up and down. "Jeez," he complained. "I've never hit anybody like that. It hurts!"

"Hold up," Warren warned Jack. "I don't like beatin' on these dog turds. It's not my style."

"I'm all done," Jack said, still shaking his injured hand. "You see, that dog turd on the other side of the couch beat up on Laurie earlier this evening after they broke into her apartment. I'm sure you noticed her face."

Angelo pushed himself up to a sitting position. His nose angled to the right. Jack invited him to come back around the couch and sit down. Angelo moved slowly, while cupping his hand beneath his nose to catch the dripping blood.

"Now, before the police get here," Jack said to the two men, "I'd like to ask you guys again about what you're afraid Laurie and I might learn. What is going on with this Franconi nonsense?"

Angelo and Franco stared at Jack as if he weren't there. Jack persisted and asked what they knew about Franconi's liver, but the men remained stone silent.

Laurie returned from the kitchen. "I got Lou," she reported. "He's on his way, and I have to say he's excited, especially about the Vido Delbario tip."

An hour later, Jack found himself comfortably ensconced in Esteban Ndeme's apartment along with Laurie and Warren.

"Sure, I'll have another beer," Jack said in response to Esteban's offer. Jack was feeling a pleasant buzz from his first beer and progressively euphoric that the evening had worked out so auspiciously after such a bad start.

Lou had arrived at Jack's with several patrolmen less than twenty minutes after

Laurie's call. He'd been ecstatic to take Angelo and Franco downtown to book them on breaking and entering, possession of unauthorized firearms, assault and battery, extortion, and impersonation of a police officer. His hope was to hold them long enough to get some real information out of them about New York City organized crime, particularly the Lucia organization.

Lou had been disturbed by the threats Laurie and Jack had received, so when Jack mentioned that he and Laurie were thinking of going out of town for a week or so, Lou was all for it. Lou was concerned enough that in the interim, he'd assigned a guard for Laurie and Jack. To make the job easier, Jack and Laurie agreed to stay together.

At Jack's urging, Warren had taken him and Laurie to the Mercado Market and to meet Esteban Ndeme. As Warren had intimated, Esteban was an amiable and gracious man. He was close to Jack's age of forty-two, but his body type was the opposite of Jack's. Where Jack was stocky, Esteban was slender. Even his facial features seemed delicate. His skin was a deep, rich brown, many shades darker than Warren's. But his most noticeable physical trait was his high-domed forehead. He'd lost his hair in the front so that his hairline ran from ear to ear over the top of his head.

As soon as he'd learned Jack was considering a trip to Equatorial Guinea, he'd invited Jack, Laurie, and Warren back to his apartment.

Teodora Ndeme had turned out to be as congenial as her husband. After the group had been in the apartment for only a short time, she'd insisted everyone stay for dinner.

With savory aromas drifting from the kitchen, Jack sat back contentedly with a second beer. "What brought you and Teodora to New York City?" he asked Esteban.

"We had to flee our country," Esteban said. He went on to describe the the reign of terror of the ruthless dictator Nguema that forced a third of the population, including all of Spanish descent, to leave. "Fifty thousand people were murdered," Esteban said. "It was terrible. We were lucky to get out. I was a schoolteacher trained in Spain and therefore suspect."

"Things have changed, I hope," Jack said.

"Oh, yes," Esteban said. "A coup in 1979 has changed a lot. But it is a poor country, although there is some talk of offshore oil, as was discovered off Gabon. Gabon is now the wealthiest country in the region."

"Have you been back?" Jack asked.

"Several times," Esteban said. "The last time, a few years ago," Esteban said. "Teodora and I still have family there. Teodora's brother even has a small hotel on the mainland in a town called Bata."

"I've heard of Bata," Jack said. "I understand it has an airport."

"The only one on the mainland," Esteban said. "It was built in the eighties for a Central African Congress. Of course, the country couldn't afford it, but that is another story."

"Have you heard of a company called Gen-Sys?" Jack asked.

"Most definitely," Esteban said. "It is the major source of foreign currency for the government, especially since cocoa and coffee prices have fallen."

"So I've heard," Jack said. "I've also heard GenSys has a primate farm. Do you know if that is in Bata?"

"No, it is in the south," Esteban said. "They built it in the jungle near an old deserted Spanish town called Cogo. They have rebuilt much of the town for their people from America and Europe, and they have built a new town for local people who work for them. They employ many Equatoguinean people."

"Do you know if GenSys built a hospital?" Jack asked.

"Yes, they did," Esteban said. "They built a hospital and laboratory on the old town square facing the town hall."

"How do you know so much about it?" Jack asked.

"Because my cousin used to work there," Esteban said. "But he quit when the soldiers executed one of his friends for hunting. A lot of people like GenSys because they pay well, but others don't like GenSys because they have too much power with the government."

"Because of money," Jack said.

"Yes, of course," Esteban said. "They pay a lot of money to the ministers. They even pay part of the army."

"That's cozy," Laurie commented.

"If we were to go to Bata, would we be able to visit Cogo?" Jack asked.

"I suppose," Esteban said. "After the Spanish left twenty-five years ago, the road to Cogo was abandoned and became impassable, but GenSys has rebuilt it so the trucks can go back and forth. But you'd have to hire a car."

"Is that possible?" Jack asked.

"If you have money, anything is possible in Equatorial Guinea," Esteban said. "When are you planning to go? Because it's best to go in the dry season."

"When's that?" Jack asked.

"February and March," Esteban said.

"That's convenient," Jack said. "Because Laurie and I are thinking of going tomorrow night."

"What?" Warren spoke for the first time since they'd arrived at Esteban's apartment. He'd not been privy to Jack and Lou's conversation. "I thought me and Natalie were going out on the town with you guys this weekend. I've already told Natalie."

"Ohhhh!" Jack commented. "I forgot about that."

"Hey, man, you gotta wait 'til after Saturday night, otherwise I'm in deep shit, you know what I'm saying. I told you how much she's been ragging on me to see you guys."

In his euphoric mood Jack had another suggestion. "I have a better idea. Why don't you and Natalie come along with Laurie and me to Equatorial Guinea? It will be our treat."

Laurie blinked. She wasn't sure she'd heard correctly.

"Man, what are you talking about?" Warren said. "You're out'a your friggin' mind. You're talking about Africa."

"Yeah, Africa," Jack said. "If Laurie and I have to go, we might as well make it as fun as possible. In fact, Esteban, why don't you and your wife come, too? We'll make it a party."

"Are you serious?" Esteban asked.

Laurie's expression was equally as incredulous.

"Sure, I'm serious," Jack said. "The best way to visit a country is to go with someone who used to live there. That's no secret. But tell me, do we all need visas?"

"Yes, but the Equatorial Guinean Embassy is here in New York," Esteban said. "Two pictures, twenty-five dollars, and a letter from a bank saying you're not poor gets you a visa."

"How do you get to Equatorial Guinea?" Jack asked.

"For Bata the easiest is through Paris," Esteban said. "From Paris there is daily service to Douala, Cameroon. From Douala there's daily service to Bata. You can go through Madrid, too, but that's only twice a week to Malabo on Bioko."

"Sounds like Paris wins out," Jack said gaily.

"Teodora!" Esteban called out to his wife in the kitchen. "You'd better come in here."

"You're crazy, man," Warren said to Jack. "I knew it the first day you walked out on that basketball court. But, you know something, I'm beginning to like it."

CHAPTER 17

Kevin's alarm went off at six-fifteen. It was still completely dark outside. Emerging from his mosquito net, he turned on the light to find his robe and slippers. A cottony feeling in his mouth and a mild bitemporal headache reminded him of the wine he'd drunk the night before. With a shaky hand he took a long drink of the water he had at his bedside. Thus fortified, he set out on shaky legs to knock on his guest rooms' doors.

The previous night, he and the women had decided that it made sense for Melanie and Candace to spend the night. Kevin had plenty of room, and they all agreed being together would make the departure in the morning far easier and probably elicit less attention. Consequently, at about eleven P.M., amid lots of laughter and gaiety, Kevin had driven the women to their respective quarters to collect their overnight necessities, a change of clothes, and the food they'd gotten from the commissary.

While the women had been packing, Kevin had made a quick detour to his lab to get the locator, the directional beacon, a flashlight, and the contour map.

On each guest room door, Kevin had to knock twice. Once quite softly, and when there was no response, he rapped more vigorously until he heard a response. He sensed the women were hungover, especially after it took them significantly longer than they planned to show up in the kitchen. Both of them poured themselves a mug of coffee and drank the first cup without conversation.

After breakfast they all revived significantly. In fact, as they emerged from Kevin's house they felt exhilarated, as if they were setting off on a holiday. The weather was as good as could be expected in that part of the world. Dawn was breaking and the pink and silver sky was generally clear overhead. To the south, there was a line of small puffy clouds. On the horizon to the west, there were ominous purple storm clouds, but they were way out over the ocean and would most likely stay there for the day.

As they walked toward the waterfront, they were enthralled by the profusion of bird life. There were blue turacos, parrots, weaverbirds, African fish eagles, and a kind of African blackbird. The air was filled with their color and shrieks.

The town seemed deserted. There were no pedestrians or vehicles, and the homes were still shuttered against the night. The only person they saw was a local mopping the floor in the Chickee Hut Bar.

They walked out on the impressive pier GenSys had built. It was twenty feet wide and six feet high. The rough-hewn planks were wet from the humid night air. At the end of the pier, there was a wooden ramp that led down to a floating dock. The dock seemed to be mysteriously suspended; the surface of the perfectly calm water was hidden by a layer of mist that extended as far as the eye could see.

As the women had promised, there was a motorized thirty-foot-long pirogue languidly moored to the end of the dock. Long ago, it had been painted red with a white interior, but the paint had faded or had been scraped off in large areas. A thatched roof supported by wooden poles extended over three-quarters of the boat's length. Under the shelter were benches. The motor was an antique Evinrude outboard. Tethered to the stern was a small canoe with four narrow benches extending from gunwale to gunwale.

"Not bad, eh?" Melanie said, as she grabbed the mooring line and pulled the boat to the dock.

"It's bigger than I expected," Kevin said. "As long as the motor keeps going, we should be fine. I wouldn't want to paddle it very far."

"Worst-case scenario we float back," Melanie said undaunted. "After all, we are going upriver."

They got the gear and food aboard. While

Melanie continued to stand on the pier, Kevin made his way to the stern to examine the motor. It was self-explanatory with instructions written in English. He put the throttle on start and pulled the cord. To his utter surprise, the engine started. He motioned for Melanie to hop in, shifted the motor into forward, and they were off.

As they pulled away from the pier, they all looked back at Cogo to see if anyone took note of their departure. The only person they saw was the lone man cleaning the Chickee Hut, and he didn't bother to look in their direction.

As they had planned, they motored west as if they were going to Acalayong. Kevin advanced the throttle to half-open and was pleased at the speed. The pirogue was large and heavy but it had very little draw. He checked the canoe they had in tow; it was riding easily in the water.

The sound of the motor made conversation difficult so they were content to enjoy the scenery. The sun had yet to come up, but the sky was brighter and the eastern ends of the cumulus clouds over Gabon were edged in gold. To their right, the shoreline of Equatorial Guinea appeared as a solid mass of vegetation that abruptly dumped into the water. Dotted about the wide estuary were other pirogues moving ghostlike through the mist that still layered the surface of the water.

When Cogo had fallen significantly astern, Melanie tapped Kevin on the shoulder. Once she had his attention, she made a wide sweeping motion with her hand. Kevin nodded and began to steer the boat to the south.

After traveling south for ten minutes, Kevin began a slow turn to the west. They were now at least a mile offshore, and when they passed Cogo, it was difficult to make out specific buildings.

When the sun did finally make its appearance, it was a huge ball of reddish gold. At first, the equatorial mists were so dense that the sun could be examined directly without the need to shield one's eyes. But the heat of the sun began to evaporate the mist which, in turn, rapidly made the sun's rays stronger. Melanie was the first to slip on her sunglasses, but Candace and Kevin quickly did the same. A few minutes later, everyone began to peel off layers of clothing they'd donned against the comparative morning chill.

To their left was the string of islands that hugged the Equatoguinean coast. Kevin had been steering north to complete the wide circle around Cogo. Now he pushed over the helm to point the bow directly toward Isla Francesca, which loomed in the distance.

Once the mists had dissipated from the sun's glare, a welcome breeze stirred the water, and waves began to mar the hitherto glassy surface. Pushing into a mounting headwind the pirogue began to slap against the crests, occasionally sprinkling its passengers with spray.

Isla Francesca looked different than her sister islands, and the closer they got, the more apparent it became. Besides being considerably larger, Isla Francesca's limestone escarpment gave it a much more substantial appearance. There were even bits of cloudlike mist that clung to its summits.

An hour and fifteen minutes after they had left the pier in Cogo, Kevin cut back on the throttle and the pirogue slowed. A hundred feet ahead was the dense shoreline of the southwestern tip of Isla Francesca.

"From this vantage point it looks sort of forbidding," Melanie yelled over the sound of the engine.

Kevin nodded. There was nothing about the island that was inviting. There was no beach. The entire shoreline appeared to be covered with dense mangroves.

"We've got to find Rio Diviso's outlet," Kevin yelled back. After approaching the mangroves as close as he thought prudent, he pushed the helm to starboard and headed along the western shore. In the lee of the island, the waves disappeared. Kevin stood up in hopes of seeing possible underwater obstructions. But he couldn't. The water was an impenetrable muddy color.

"What about where all those bulrushes

are?" Candace called out from the bow. She pointed ahead to an expansive marsh that had appeared.

Kevin nodded and cut back on the throttle even farther. He nosed the boat toward the six-foot reeds.

"Can you see any obstructions underwater?" he called out to Candace.

Candace shook her head. "It's too murky," she said.

Kevin turned the boat so that they were again moving parallel with the island shoreline. The reeds were dense, and the marsh now extended inland for a hundred yards.

"This must be the river outlet," Kevin said. "I hope there is a channel or we're out of luck. There's no way we could get the canoe through those reeds."

Ten minutes later, without having found a break in the reeds, Kevin turned the boat around. He was careful not to foul the towline for the small canoe.

"I don't want to go any further in this direction," Kevin said. "The width of the marsh is decreasing. I don't think we're going to find a channel. Besides, I'm afraid of getting too close to the staging area where the bridge is."

"I agree," Melanie said. "What about going to the other end of the island where Rio Diviso has its inlet?"

"That was exactly my thought," Kevin said.
Melanie raised her hand.

"What are you doing?" Kevin asked.

"It's called a high five, you jerk," Melanie teased.

Kevin slapped her hand with his and laughed.

They motored back the way they'd come and rounded the island to head east along its length. Kevin opened up the throttle to about half speed. The route gave them a good view of the southern aspect of the island's mountainous backbone. From that angle, no limestone was visible. The island appeared to be an uninterrupted mountain of virgin jungle.

"All I see are birds," Melanie yelled over the sound of the engine.

Kevin nodded. He'd seen lots of ibises and shrikes.

The sun had now risen enough so that the thatched shelter was useful. They all crowded into the stern to take advantage of the shade. Candace put on some sunblock that Kevin had found in his medicine cabinet.

"Do you think the bonobos on the island are going to be as skittish as bonobos normally are?" Melanie yelled.

Kevin shrugged. "I wish I knew," he yelled back. "If they are, it might be difficult for us to see any of them, and all this effort will have been in vain."

"They did have diminishing contact with humans until they were there in the bonobo enclosure at the animal center," Melanie yelled. "I think we have a good chance as long as we don't try to get too close."

"Are bonobos timid in the wild?" Candace asked Melanie.

"Very much so," Melanie said. "As much or more than chimpanzees. Chimps unexposed to humans are almost impossible to see in the wild. They're inordinately timid, and their sense of hearing and smell is so much more acute than ours that people cannot get near them."

"Are there still truly wild areas left in Africa?" Candace asked.

"Oh, my Lord, yes!" Melanie said. "Essentially, from this coastal part of Equatorial Guinea and extending west northwest there are huge tracts that are still essentially unexplored virginal rain forest. We're talking about as much as a million square miles."

"How long is that going to last?" Candace questioned.

"That's another story," Melanie said.

"How about handing me a cold drink," Kevin yelled.

"Coming up," Candace said. She moved over to the Styrofoam chest and lifted the lid.

Twenty minutes later, Kevin again throttled back on the motor and turned north around the eastern end of Isla Francesca. The sun was higher in the sky and it was significantly hotter. Candace pushed the Styrofoam chest over to the port side of the pirogue to keep it in the shade.

"There's another marsh coming up," Candace said.

"I see it," Kevin said.

Kevin again guided the boat in close to the shore. In terms of size, the marsh appeared to be similar to the one on the western end of the island. Once again, the jungle dropped back to approximately a hundred yards from the edge of the water.

Just when Kevin was about to announce that they had again been foiled, an opening appeared in the otherwise unremitting wall of reeds.

Kevin turned the canoe toward the opening and throttled back even more. The boat slowed. About thirty feet away, Kevin put the motor into neutral and then turned it off.

As the sound of the engine died off, they were thrust into a heavy stillness.

"God, my ears are ringing," Melanie complained.

"Does it look like a channel?" Kevin asked Candace, who'd again gone up to the bow.

"It's hard to tell," Candace said.

Kevin grabbed the back of the motor and tilted it up out of the water. He didn't want to foul the propeller in underwater vegetation.

The pirogue entered among the reeds. It scraped against the stems, then glided to a halt. Kevin reached behind the boat to keep the towed canoe from banging into the pirogue's stern.

"It looks like it goes forward in a meandering fashion," Candace said. She was standing on the gunwale and holding onto the thatched roof of the shelter so she could see over the top of the reeds.

Kevin snapped off a stem and broke it into small pieces. He tossed them into the water next to the boat and watched them. They drifted slowly but inexorably in the direction they were pointing.

"There seems to be some current," Kevin said. "I think that's a good sign. Let's give it a try with the canoe." Kevin moved the smaller boat alongside the larger.

With difficulty because of the canoe's unsteadiness, they managed to get themselves into the smaller boat along with their gear and the food chest. Kevin sat in the stern while Candace took the bow. Melanie sat in the middle but not on one of the seats. Canoes made her nervous; she preferred to sit on the bottom.

By a combination of paddling, pulling on reeds, and pulling on the pirogue, they managed to get ahead of the larger boat. Once in what they hoped was the channel, the going was considerably easier.

With Kevin paddling in the rear and Candace in the front they were able to move at the pace of a slow walk. The narrow six-foot-wide passage twisted and turned as it worked its way across the marsh. The sun was now evidencing its equatorial power even though it was only eight o'clock in the morning. The reeds blocked the breeze, effectively raising the temperature even higher.

"There're not many trails on this island," Melanie commented. She'd unfolded the contour map and was studying it.

"The main one is from the staging area to Lago Hippo." Kevin said.

"There are a few more," Melanie said. "All leading away from Lago Hippo. I suppose they'd been made to facilitate retrievals."

"That would be my guess," Kevin said.

Kevin looked into the dark water. He could see strands of plant life trailing in the direction they were paddling, suggesting there was current. He was encouraged.

"Why don't you try the locator?" Kevin said. "See if bonobo number sixty has moved since we last checked."

Melanie entered the information and clicked.

"He doesn't appear to have moved," she said. She reduced the scale until it was equivalent to the scale on the contour map, then located the red dot. "He's still in the same spot in the marshy clearing."

"At least we can solve that mystery, even if we don't see any of the others," Kevin said.

Ahead, they approached the hundred-foot-high wall of jungle. As they rounded the final bend in the marsh, they could see the channel disappear into the riot of vegetation.

"We'll be in shade in a moment," Candace said. "That should make it a lot cooler."

"Don't count on it," Kevin said.

Pushing branches to the side, they silently slid into the perpetual darkness of the forest. Contrary to Candace's hopes it was like a muggy, claustrophobic hot house. There was not a breath of air, and everything dripped moisture. Although the thick canopy of tree limbs, twisted vines, and hanging mosses completely blocked the sunlight, it also held in the heat like a heavy woolen blanket. Some of the leaves were up to a foot in diameter. Everyone was shocked by how dark it was in the tunnel of vegetation until their eyes began to adjust. Slowly details appeared out of the dank gloom until the scene resembled late twilight just before night fall.

Almost from the moment the first branches snapped in place behind them, they were assaulted by swarms of insects: mosquitoes, deer flies, and trigona bees. Melanie frantically located the insect repellant. After dousing herself, she passed it to the others.

"It smells like a damn swamp," Melanie complained.

"This is scary," Candace commented from her position in the bow. "I just saw a snake, and I hate snakes."

"As long as we stay in the boat, we'll be fine," Kevin said.

"So, let's not tip over," Melanie said.

"Don't even suggest it!" Candace moaned. "You guys have to remember I'm a newcomer. You've been in this part of the world for years."

"All we have to worry about are the crocs and hippos," Kevin said. "When you see one, let me know."

"Oh, great!" Candace complained nervously. "And just what do we do when we see one?"

"I didn't mean to worry you," Kevin said. "I don't think we'll see any until we come to the lake."

"And what then?" Candace questioned. "Maybe I should have asked about the dangers of this trip before I signed on."

"They won't bother us," Kevin said. "At least that's what I've been told. As long as they are in the water, all we have to do is stay a reasonable distance away. It's when they're caught on land that they can be unpredictably aggressive, and both crocs and hippos can run faster than you'd think."

"All of a sudden, I'm not enjoying this at all," Candace admitted. "I thought it was going to be fun."

"It wasn't supposed to be a picnic," Melanie said. "We're not sightseeing. We're here for a reason."

"Let's just hope we're successful," Kevin said. He could appreciate Candace's state of mind. Kevin marveled that he'd been talked into coming himself.

Besides the insects, the dominant wildlife were the birds. They ceaselessly flitted among the branches, filling the air with melodies.

On either side of the channel the forest was impenetrably dense. Only occasionally could Kevin or the others see for more than twenty feet in any direction. Even the shoreline was invisible, hidden behind a tangle of water plants and roots.

As he paddled Kevin looked down into the inky water that was covered with a plethora of darting water spiders. The disturbance he caused with each stroke made fetid bubbles rise to the surface.

The channel soon became straighter than it had been in the marsh, making the paddling considerably easier. By observing the rate at which they floated by the passing tree trunks, Kevin estimated that they were moving at about the speed of a fast walk. At this rate, he figured they'd arrive at the Lago Hippo in ten to fifteen minutes.

"How about putting the locator on scan?" Kevin suggested to Melanie. "If you narrow the graphic to this area, we'll know if there are any bonobos in the neighborhood."

Melanie was huddled over the compact computer, when there was a sudden commotion in the branches to their left. A moment later, deeper into the forest, they heard twigs snapping.

Candace had a hand clasped to her chest. "Oh my," she said. "What the hell was that?"

"I'd guess another one of those duikers," Kevin said. "Those little antelopes are common even on these islands."

Melanie redirected her attention to the locator. Soon she was able to report that there were no bonobos in the area.

"Of course not," Kevin said. "That would have been too easy."

Twenty minutes later, Candace reported that she could see a lattice of sunlight coming through the branches directly ahead.

"That must be the lake," Kevin said.

After a few more paddle strokes, the canoe glided out into the open water of Lago Hippo. The trio blinked in the bright sunlight, then scrambled for their sunglasses.

The lake was not large. In fact, it was more like an elongated pond dotted with several lushly thicketed islands chock-a-block with white ibises. The shore was lined with dense reeds. Here and there on the surface of the lake were pure white water lilies. Patches of free-floating vegetation thick enough to allow small birds to walk across them turned lazily in slow circles, pushed by the gentle breezes.

The wall of surrounding forest dropped away on both sides to form grassy fields, some as big as an acre. A few of these fields were peppered with pockets of palm trees. To the left, above the line of the forest rim, the very top of the limestone escarpment was clearly discernable against the hazy morning sky.

"It's actually quite beautiful," Melanie said.

"It reminds me of paintings of prehistoric times," Kevin said. "I could almost imagine a couple of brontosauruses in the fore-ground."

"Oh my god, I see hippos over to the left!" Candace called out with alarm. She pointed with her paddle.

Kevin looked in the direction she was indicating. Sure enough, the heads and small ears of a dozen of these huge mammals were just visible in the water. Standing on their crowns were a number of white birds preening.

"They're okay," Kevin assured Candace. "See how they are slowly moving away from us. They won't be any trouble."

"I've never been much of a nature lover," Candace admitted.

"You don't have to explain," Kevin said. He could remember clearly his unease about wildlife during his first year in Cogo.

"According to the map, there should be a trail not too far away from the left bank," Melanie said, while studying the contour map.

"If I remember correctly, there's a trail that goes around the whole eastern end of the lake," Kevin said. "It originates at the bridge."

"That's true, but it comes closest to our left," Melanie said.

Kevin angled the canoe toward the left shore and began looking for an opening in the reeds. Unfortunately, there wasn't one.

"I think we'll just have to try to paddle right through the vegetation," Kevin said.

"I'm certainly not getting out of this boat until there's dry land," Melanie announced.

Kevin told Candace not to paddle as he aimed the canoe at the six-foot-high wall of reeds and took a number of forceful strokes. To everyone's surprise, the boat skimmed through the vegetation with no trouble at all, despite the scraping noise of the reeds on the hull. Sooner than they expected, they bumped against dry land.

"That was easy," Kevin said. He looked behind at the path they'd created to the lake, but already the reeds were springing back to their original position.

"Am I supposed to get out?" Candace said. "I can't see the ground. What if there are bugs and snakes?"

"Make yourself a clearing with your paddle," Kevin suggested.

As soon as Candace climbed out of the bow, Kevin paddled against the vegetation and succeeded to force the canoe still further onto the shore. Melanie got out easily.

"What about the food?" Kevin asked as he moved forward.

"Let's leave it here," Melanie said. "Just bring the bag with the directional beacon and flashlight. I've got the locator and the contour map."

The women waited for Kevin to get out of the boat, then motioned for him to go ahead of them. With the gear bag over his shoulder, he pushed aside the reeds and began moving inland. The ground was marshy and the muck sucked at his shoes. But within ten feet, he emerged onto the grassy field.

"This looks like a field, but it's actually a swamp," Melanie complained as she looked down at her tennis shoes. They were already black with mud and completely soaked.

Kevin struggled with the contour map to get his bearings, then pointed off to the right. "The transmitting chip from bonobo number sixty should be no more than a hundred feet from here in the direction of that cul de sac of trees," he said.

"Let's get this over with," Melanie said. With her new tennis shoes ruined, even she was beginning to question if they should have come. In Africa, nothing was easy.

Kevin struck off with the women following. At first, walking was difficult because of the unstable footing. Although the grass appeared generally uniform, it grew in small, lumpy hummocks surrounded by muddy water. But the going became easier about fifty feet from the pond, where the ground rose and became comparatively drier. A moment later, they came across a trail.

They were surprised to discover that the trail looked well-used. It ran parallel with the shoreline of the lake.

"Siegfried must send work crews out here more than we thought," Melanie said. "This trail has been maintained."

"I'd have to agree," Kevin said. "I suppose they'd need to keep them up for retrievals. The jungle is so thick and grows so fast out here. Lucky for us, they'll certainly help us get around as well. As I recall, this one heads up to the limestone cliff."

"If they come out here to maintain trails, maybe there is something to Siegfried's story about workmen making the fires," Melanie said.

"Wouldn't that be nice," Kevin said.

"I smell something bad," Candace said, while sniffing the air. "In fact, it smells putrid."

Hesitantly, the others sniffed and agreed.

"That's not a good sign," Melanie said.

Kevin nodded and moved off in the direction of the cul de sac. A few minutes later, with their fingers pinching their nostrils shut, the three stared down at a disgusting sight: It was the remains of bonobo number sixty. The carcass was in the process of being devoured by insects. Larger scavengers had also taken a toll.

Far more gruesome than the state of the corpse was the evidence of how the animal had died. A wedge-shaped piece of limestone had struck the poor creature between the eyes effectively splitting his head in two. The rock was still in place. Exposed soft eyeballs stared off in opposite directions.

"Ugh!" Melanie said. "It's what we didn't want to see. This suggests that not only the bonobos have split into two groups, but they're killing each other. I wonder if number sixty-seven is dead, too."

Kevin kicked the rock out of the decomposing head. All three stared at it.

"That's also what we didn't want to see," Kevin said.

"What are you talking about?" Candace asked.

"That rock was shaped artificially," Kevin said. With the toe of his shoe, he pointed to an area along the side of the rock where there appeared to be freshly made gouges. "That suggests tool-making."

"More circumstantial evidence I'm afraid," Melanie said.

"Let's move upwind," Kevin managed. "Before I get sick. I can't stand this smell."

Kevin got three steps away in an easterly direction when someone grabbed his arm and yanked him to a stop. He turned to see Melanie with her index finger pressed against her lips. Then she pointed to the south.

Kevin turned his gaze in that direction, then caught his breath. About fifty yards away in the shadows of the very back of the cul de sac was one of the bonobos! The animal was standing ramrod straight and absolutely motionless, as if he were a military honor guard. He appeared to be staring back at Kevin and the others just as they were staring at him.

Kevin was surprised at the creature's size. The animal was well over five feet tall. It also seemed oversized in terms of weight. Given its enormously muscular torso, Kevin guessed the bonobo weighed between one hundred twenty-five and one hundred fifty pounds.

"He's taller than the bonobos that have been brought in for transplant surgery," Candace said. "At least I think he is. Of course, the bonobos for the transplants were already sedated and strapped to a gurney by the time they got to me."

"Shhhhhh," Melanie admonished. "Let's not scare him. This might be our only chance to see one."

Being careful not to move too quickly, Kevin pulled the gear bag off his shoulder and got out the directional beacon. He turned it on to scan. It began to quietly beep until he pointed it toward the bonobo; then it let out a continuous note. Kevin looked at the LCD screen and gasped.

"What's the matter?" Melanie whispered.

She had seen Kevin's expression change.

"It's number one!" Kevin whispered back. "It's my double."

"Oh my god!" Melanie whispered. "I'm jealous. I'd like to see mine, too."

"I wish we could see better," Candace said. "Do we dare try to get closer?"

Kevin was struck by two things. First was the coincidence that the first live bonobo they'd come across would happen to be his double. Secondly, if he had inadvertently created a race of protohumans, then he was in some metamorphic way meeting himself six million years earlier. "This is too much," Kevin couldn't help but whisper aloud.

"What are you talking about?" Melanie asked.

"In some ways that's me standing over there," Kevin answered.

"Now let's not jump the gun," Melanie said.

"He's certainly standing like a human," Candace remarked. "But he's hairier than any human I've ever been out with."

"Very funny," Melanie said without laughing.

"Melanie, use the locator to scan the area," Kevin said. "Bonobos usually travel together. Maybe there are more around that we can't see. They could be hiding in the bushes."

Melanie played with the instrument.

"I can't believe how still he is," Candace said.

"He's probably scared stiff," Kevin said. "I'm sure he doesn't know what to make of us. Or if Melanie is right about there not being enough females out here, maybe he's smitten with you two."

"That I don't find funny at all," Melanie said, without looking up from the keyboard of the locator.

"Sorry," Kevin said.

"What's he got around his waist?" Candace asked.

"I was wondering that, too," Kevin said. "I can't make it out, unless it's just a vine that got caught on him when he came through the bushes."

"Look at this," Melanie said with excitement. She held up the instrument so the others could see. "Kevin, you were right. There's a whole group of bonobos in the trees behind your double."

"Why would he venture out on his own?" Candace asked.

"Maybe he's like an alpha male in chimp society," Melanie said. "Since there are so few females, it stands to reason these bonobos might act more like chimps. If that's the case, he might be proving himself to be courageous."

Several minutes passed. The bonobo did not move.

"This is like a Mexican standoff," Candace complained. "Come on! Let's see how close we can get. What do we have to lose? Even if he runs off, I'd say this little episode is encouraging that we'll see more."

"All right," Kevin said. "But no sudden movement. I don't want to scare him. That would only ruin our chances for seeing the others."

"You guys first," Candace said.

The three advanced carefully, moving forward step by step. Kevin was in the lead followed immediately by Melanie. Candace brought up the rear. When they reached the midway mark, between them and the bonobo, they stopped. Now they could see the bonobo much better. He had prominent eyebrows and a sloped forehead like a chimp, but the lower half of his face was significantly less prognathous than even a normal bonobo. His nose was flat, his nostrils flared. His ears were smaller than those of either chimps or bonobos and flush against the side of his head.

"Are you guys thinking what I'm thinking?" Melanie whispered.

Candace nodded. "He reminds me of the pictures I saw in the third grade. Of very early cavemen."

"Uh, oh, can you guys see his hands?" Kevin whispered.

"I think so," Candace said softly. "What's wrong with them?"

"It's the thumb," Kevin whispered. "It's

not like a chimp's. His thumb juts out from the palm."

"You're right," Melanie whispered. "And that means he might be able to oppose his thumb with his fingers."

"Good god! The circumstantial evidence keeps mounting," Kevin whispered. "I suppose if the developmental genes responsible for the anatomical changes necessary for bipedalism are on the short arm of chromosome six, then it's entirely possible that the ones for the opposable thumb are, too."

"It is a vine around his waist," Candace commented. "Now I can see it clearly."

"Let's try moving closer," Melanie suggested.

"I don't know," Kevin said. "I think we're pushing our luck. Frankly, I'm surprised he hasn't bolted already. Maybe we should just sit down right here."

"It's hotter than blazes here in the sun," Melanie said. "And it's not even nine o'clock, so it'll only get worse. When we decide to sit and observe, I vote we do it in the shade. I'd also like to have the food chest."

"I agree," Candace said.

"Of course, you agree," Kevin said mockingly. "I'd be surprised if you didn't." Kevin was becoming tired of Melanie making a suggestion only to have Candace eagerly support it. It had already gotten him into trouble.

"That's not very nice," Candace said indignantly.

"I'm sorry," Kevin said. He'd not meant to hurt her feelings.

"Well, I'm going closer," Melanie announced. "Jane Goodall was able to get right up next to her chimps."

"True," Kevin said. "But that was after months of acclimatization."

"I'm still going to try," Melanie said.

Kevin and Candace let Melanie get ten feet in front of them before they looked at each other, shrugged, and joined her.

"You don't have to do this for me," Melanie whispered.

"Actually, I want to to get close enough to see if my double has any facial expression," Kevin whispered. "And I want to look into his eyes."

With no more talk and by moving slowly and deliberately, the three were able to come within twenty feet of the bonobo. Then they stopped again.

"This is incredible," Melanie whispered without taking her eyes from the animal's face. The only way it was apparent the bonobo was alive was an occasional blink, movements of his eyes, and a flaring of his nostrils with each respiration.

"Look at those pectorals," Candace said. "It looks like he's spent most of his life in a gym."

"How do you think he got that scar?" Melanie asked.

The bonobo had a thick scar that ran down the left side of his face almost to his mouth.

Kevin leaned forward and stared into the animal's eyes. They were brown just like his own. Since the sun was in the bonobo's face, his pupils were pinpoint. Kevin strained to detect intelligence, but it was difficult to tell.

Without the slightest warning the bonobo suddenly clapped his hands with such force that an echo reverberated between the leafy walls of the cul de sac. At the same time he yelled: "Atah!"

Kevin, Melanie, and Candace leaped from fright. Having worried from the start that the bonobo was about to flee at any moment, they'd not considered the possibility of him acting aggressively. The violent clap and yell panicked them, and made them fear the animal was about to attack. But he didn't. He reverted back to his stonelike state.

After a moment's confusion they recovered a semblance of their previous poise. They eyed the bonobo nervously.

"What was that all about?" Melanie asked.

"I don't think he's as scared of us as we'd thought," Candace said. "Maybe we should just back away."

"I agree," Kevin said uneasily. "But let's go slowly. Don't panic." Following his own advice, he took a few careful steps backward and motioned for the women to do likewise.

The bonobo responded by reaching around behind his back and grabbing a tool he had suspended by the vine around his waist. He held the tool aloft over his head and cried "Atah" again.

The three froze, wide-eyed with terror.

"What can 'Atah' mean?" Melanie whined after a few moments when nothing happened. "Can it be a word? Could he be talking?"

"I don't have any idea," Kevin sputtered. "But at least he hasn't come toward us."

"What is he holding?" Candace asked apprehensively. "It looks like a hammer."

"It is," Kevin managed. "It's a regular carpenter's clawhammer. It must be one of the tools the bonobos stole when the bridge was being built."

"Look at the way he is grasping it. Just the way you or I would," Melanie said. "There's no question he has an opposable thumb."

"We got to get away from here!" Candace half cried. "You two promised me these creatures were timid. This guy is anything but!"

"Don't run!" Kevin said, keeping his eyes glued to the bonobo's.

"You can stay if you want, but I'm going back to the boat," Candace said desperately.

"We'll all go, but slowly," Kevin said.

Despite warnings not to do so, Candace turned on her heels and started to run. But she only went a few steps before she froze and let out a scream.

Kevin and Melanie turned in her direction. Both of them caught their breaths when they saw what had shocked her: Twenty more bonobos had silently emerged from the surrounding forest and had arrayed themselves in an arc, effectively blocking the exit from the cul de sac.

Candace slowly backed up until she bumped against Melanie.

For a full minute no one spoke or moved, not even any of the bonobos. Then bonobo number one repeated his cry: "Atah!" Instantly, the animals began to circle around the humans.

Candace moaned as she, Kevin, and Melanie backed into each other, forming a tight triangle. The ring the animals formed around them began to close like a noose. The bonobos came closer a step at a time. The humans could now distinctly smell them. Their odor was strong and feral. The animals' faces were expressionless but intent. Their eyes flashed.

The animals stopped advancing when they were an arm's length from the three friends. Their eyes ran up and down the humans' bodies. Some of them were holding stone wedges similar to the one that had killed bonobo number sixty.

Kevin, Melanie, and Candace did not move. They were paralyzed with fear. All the animals looked as powerful as bonobo number one.

Bonobo number one remained outside the tight ring. He was still clutching the clawhammer but no longer had it raised over his head. He advanced and made a full circuit of the group, staring at the humans between the heads of his compatriots. Then he let out a string of sounds accompanied by hand gestures.

Several of the other animals answered him. Then one of them reached out his hand toward Candace. Candace moaned.

"Don't move," Kevin managed to say. "I think the fact that they haven't harmed us is a good sign."

Candace swallowed with difficulty as the bonobo's hand caressed her hair. He seemed enthralled by its blond color. It took all the resolve she could muster not to scream or duck away.

Another animal began to speak and gesture. He then pointed to his side. Kevin saw a long healing surgical scar. "It's the animal whose kidney went to the Dallas businessman," Kevin said fearfully. "See how he's pointing at us. I think he's connecting us to the retrieval process."

"That can't be good," Melanie whispered.

Another animal reached out tentatively and touched Kevin's comparatively hairless forearm. Then he touched the directional beacon

Kevin was holding in his hand. Kevin was surprised when he didn't try to take it away from him.

The bonobo standing directly in front of Melanie reached out and pinched the fabric of her blouse between his thumb and forefinger as if feeling its texture. Then he gently touched the locator she was holding with just the tip of his index finger.

"They seem mystified by us," Kevin said hesitantly. "And strangely respectful. I don't think they are going to hurt us. Maybe they think we are gods."

"How can we encourage that belief?" Melanie asked.

"I'll try to give them something," Kevin said. Kevin considered the objects he had on his person and immediately settled on his wristwatch. Moving slowly, he put the directional beacon under his arm and slipped the watch from his wrist. Holding it by its bracelet, he extended it toward the animal in front of him.

The animal tilted his head, eyeing the watch, then reached for it. No sooner had he had it in his hand than bonobo number one vocalized the sound: "Ot." The animal with the watch responded by quickly giving it up. Bonobo number one examined the watch, then slipped it onto his forearm.

"My god!" Kevin voiced. "My double is wearing my watch. This is a nightmare."

Bonobo number one appeared to admire the watch for a moment. Then he brought his thumbs and forefinger together to form a circle while saying: "Randa."

One of the bonobos immediately ran off and disappeared for a moment into the forest. When he reappeared, he was carrying a length of rope.

"Rope?" Kevin said with trepidation. "Now what?"

"Where did they get rope?" Melanie asked.

"They probably stole it with the tools," Kevin said.

"What are they going to do?" Candace asked nervously.

The bonobo went directly to Kevin and looped the rope around his waist. Kevin watched with a mixture of fear and admiration as the animal tied a crude knot and then cinched it tight against Kevin's abdomen.

Kevin looked up at the women. "Don't struggle," he said. "I think everything is going to be okay as long as we don't anger them or scare them."

"But I don't want to be tied up," Candace cried.

"As long as we're not hurt it's okay," Melanie said, hoping to calm Candace.

The bonobo roped Melanie and then Candace in a similar fashion. When he was finished, he stepped back, still holding the long end of the rope.

"Obviously, they want us to stay for a while," Kevin said, trying to make light of the situation.

"Don't be mad if I don't laugh," Melanie said.

"At least they don't mind our talking," Kevin said.

"Strangely enough, they seem to find it interesting," Melanie said. Each time one of them spoke the nearest bonobo would cock its head as if listening.

Bonobo number one suddenly opened and closed his fingers while sweeping his hands away from his chest. At the same time he said: "Arak."

Immediately, the group started moving, including the animal holding the rope. Kevin, Melanie, and Candace were forced forward.

"That gesture was the same as the bonobo did in the operating room," Candace said.

"Then it must mean 'go' or 'move' or 'away,' " Kevin said. "It's incredible. They're speaking!"

They left the cul de sac and moved across the field until they came to the trail. At that point they were led right. While they walked, the bonobos remained silent but vigilant.

"I suspect that it isn't Siegfried who maintains these trails," Melanie said. "I think it's the bonobos."

The trail curved to the south and soon entered the jungle. Even in the forest it was well cleared and the ground underfoot was packed smooth.

"Where are they taking us?" Candace asked nervously.

"I guess toward the caves," Kevin said.

"This is ridiculous," Melanie said. "We're being taken for a walk like dogs on a leash. If they're so impressed with us, maybe we should resist."

"I don't think so," Kevin said. "I think we should make every effort not to get them riled up."

"Candace?" Melanie asked. "What are you thinking?"

"I'm too scared to think," Candace said. "I just want to get back to the canoe."

The bonobo leading with the rope turned and gave the rope a yank. The tug almost knocked all three people down. The bonobo repeatedly waved his hand palm down while whispering: "Hana."

"My god, is he strong or what?" Melanie commented as she regained her footing.

"What do you think he means?" Candace asked.

"If I had to guess, I'd say he's telling us to be quiet," Kevin said.

All at once, the entire group stopped. There were some hand signals among the bonobos. Several pointed up toward the trees to the right. A small group of bonobos slipped silently into the vegetation. Those remaining formed a wide circle, except for three who climbed directly up into the canopy of the forest with an ease that defied gravity.

"What's happening?" Candace whispered.

"Something important," Kevin said. "They all seem to be tense."

Several minutes went by. None of the bonobos on the ground moved or made the slightest noise. Then suddenly, there was a tremendous commotion to the right, accompanied by high-pitched shrieks. At once, the trees were alive with desperately fleeing colobus monkeys on a course bringing them directly toward the bonobos who'd climbed up into the trees.

The terrified monkeys tried to change direction, but in their haste several of them lost their hold on the branches and fell to the ground. Before they could recover they were set upon by waiting bonobos on the ground who killed them instantly with stone wedges.

Candace winced in horror, then turned away.

"I'd say that was a good example of coordinated hunting," Melanie whispered. "That requires a high level of cooperation." Despite the circumstances, she couldn't help but be impressed.

"Don't rub it in," Kevin whispered. "I'm afraid the jury is in, and the verdict is bad. We've only been on the island for an hour, but the question that brought us here has already been answered. Besides collective hunting, we've seen totally upright posture, opposable thumbs, toolmaking, and even rudimentary speech. I sense they can vocalize just like you and I."

"It's extraordinary," Melanie whispered. "These animals have gone through four or five million years of human evolution in the few years they've been out here."

"Oh, shut up!" Candace cried. "We're prisoners of these beasts and you two are having a scientific discussion."

"It's more than a scientific discussion," Kevin said. "We're acknowledging a terrible mistake, and I'm responsible. The reality is worse than I feared when I saw the smoke coming from this island. These animals are protohumans."

"I have to share some of the blame," Melanie said.

"I disagree," Kevin said. "I'm the one who created the chimeras by adding the human chromosome segments. That wasn't your doing."

"What are they doing now?" Candace asked.

Kevin and Melanie turned to see bonobo number one coming toward them, carrying the bloodied corpse of one of the colobus monkeys. He was still wearing the wristwatch, which only underlined the beast's odd position between man and ape.

Bonobo number one brought the dead monkey directly to Candace and held it out toward her in both his hands and said: "Sta."

Candace moaned and turned her head. She looked like she was about to get sick.

"He's offering it to you," Melanie told Candace. "Try to respond."

"I can't look at it," Candace said.

"Try!" Melanie pleaded.

Candace slowly turned. Her face reflected her disgust. The monkey's head had been crushed.

"Just bow or do something," Melanie encouraged.

Candace smiled weakly and bowed her head.

Bonobo number one bowed and then withdrew.

"Incredible," Melanie said, watching the animal leave. "Although he's obviously the alpha male, there must still be remnants of the typical matriarchal bonobo society."

"Candace, you did great," Kevin said.

"I'm a wreck," Candace said.

"I knew I should have been a blond," Melanie said with her own attempt at humor.

The bonobo holding the rope gave a tug significantly less forceful than the previous one. The group was on the move again and Kevin, Melanie, and Candace were forced to follow.

"I don't want to go any farther," Candace said tearfully.

"Pull yourself together," Melanie said. "Everything is going to be okay. I'm starting to think Kevin's suggestion was right. They think of us like gods, especially you with that blond hair. They could have killed us instantly if they'd been inclined, just like they killed the monkeys."

"Why did they kill the monkeys?" Candace asked.

"I assume for food," Melanie said. "It is a little surprising since bonobos are not carnivorous, but chimps can be."

"I was afraid they were human enough for the killing to be for sport," Candace said.

The group passed through a marshy area, then began a climb. Fifteen minutes later, they emerged from the forest twilight onto a rocky but grassy area at the foot of the limestone escarpment.

Halfway up the rock face was the opening of a cave that appeared to be accessible only by a series of extremely steeply tiered ledges. At the lip of the cave were a dozen more bonobos. Most were female. They were striking their chests with the flat of their hands and yelling "bada" over and over again.

The bonobos with Kevin, Melanie, and Candace did the same and then held up the dead colobus monkeys. That resulted in hooting from the females that Melanie said reminded her of chimps.

Then the group of bonobos at the base of the cliff parted. Kevin, Melanie, and Candace were pulled forward. At the sight of them, the females above fell silent.

"Why do I have the feeling the females aren't so happy to see us?" Melanie whispered.

"I'd rather think they were just confused," Kevin whispered back. "They hadn't expected company."

Finally bonobo number one said "zit" and pointed up with his thumb. The group surged forward pulling Kevin, Melanie, and Candace along.

CHAPTER 18

Jack's lids blinked open, and he was instantly awake. He sat up and rubbed his gritty eyes. He was still tired from the poor night's sleep the night before last and from having stayed up later than he planned the previous evening, but he was too keyed up to fall back asleep.

Getting up off the couch, Jack wrapped himself in his blanket against the morning chill and went to the bedroom door. He listened for a moment. Convinced that Laurie was still sound asleep, he cracked the door. As he'd expected, Laurie was on her side under a mound of covers, breathing deeply.

As quietly as possible, Jack tiptoed across the bedroom and entered the bathroom. Once the door was closed, he quickly shaved and showered. When he reappeared, he was pleased to see that Laurie had not budged.

Getting fresh clothes from his closet and bureau, Jack carried them out into the living room and got dressed. A few minutes later, he emerged from his building into the pre-dawn light. It was raw and cold with a few snowflakes dancing in the gusts of wind.

Across the street was a squad car with two

uniformed policemen drinking coffee and reading the morning papers with the help of the interior light. They recognized Jack and waved. Jack waved back. Lou had kept his word.

Jack jogged down the street to the local deli on Columbus Avenue. One of the policemen dutifully followed. Jack thought about buying him a donut but decided against it; he didn't want the cop to take it the wrong way.

With an armload of juice, coffee, fruit, and fresh bagels, he returned to the apartment. Laurie was up and was in the shower. Jack knocked on the door to announce that breakfast was served whenever she was ready.

Laurie appeared a few minutes later clad in Jack's robe. Her hair was still wet. The sequelae from the previous night's run-in with Angelo did not look bad. All that was apparent was a mild black eye.

"Now that you've had a night's sleep to think about this trip, do you still feel the same?" Laurie asked.

"Absolutely," Jack said. "I'm psyched."

"Are you really going to pay for everyone's ticket?" she asked. "This could get expensive."

"What else do I have to spend my money on?" Jack said. He glanced around his apartment. "Certainly not my lifestyle, and the bike is all paid for."

"Seriously," Laurie said. "I can understand

Esteban to some extent, but Warren and Natalie?"

The previous night when the proposal had been presented to Teodora, she had reminded her husband that one of them had to stay in the city to mind the market and be there for their teenage son. The decision that Esteban would go instead of Teodora had been decided by the flip of a coin.

"I was serious about making it fun," Jack said. "Even if we don't learn anything, which is a possibility, it will at least be a great trip. I could see in Warren's eyes his interest to visit that part of Africa. And on the way back, we'll spend a night or two in Paris."

"You don't have to convince me," Laurie said. "I was against your going at first, but now I'm excited myself."

"Now all we have to do is convince Bingham," Jack said.

"I don't think that will be a problem," Laurie said. "Neither of us has taken the vacation time they've wanted us to. And Lou said he'd put in his two cents about the threats. He'd like to get us out of town."

"I never trust bureaucracy," Jack said. "But I'll be optimistic. And assuming we're going, let's divvy up the errands. I'll go ahead and get the tickets while you, Warren, and Natalie take care of the visa situation. Also, we've got to arrange for some shots and start malaria prophylaxis. We really should have more time for immunizations, but we'll do the best we can, and we'll take a lot of insect repellant."

"Sounds good," Laurie said.

Because of Laurie, Jack left his beloved mountain bike in his apartment. Together, they cabbed down to the medical examiner's office. When they walked into the ID room Vinnie lowered his newspaper and looked at them as if they were ghosts.

"What are you guys doing here?" he asked with a voice that broke. He cleared his throat.

"What kind of question is that?" Jack asked. "We work here, Vinnie. Have you forgotten?"

"I just didn't think you two were on call," Vinnie said. He hastily took a drink from his coffee cup before coughing again.

Jack and Laurie went to the coffee urn. "He's been in a weird mood for the last couple of days," Jack whispered.

Laurie glanced back at Vinnie over her shoulder. Vinnie had gone back behind his newspaper.

"That was a strange reaction," she agreed. "I noticed he was nervous around me yesterday."

Jack and Laurie's eyes met. They regarded each other for a moment.

"Are you thinking what I'm thinking?" Laurie asked.

"Maybe," Jack said. "It kind of fits. He certainly has access."

"I think we should say something to Lou,"

Laurie said. "I'd hate it to be Vinnie, but we have to find out who's been giving out confidential information around here."

Conveniently for Laurie, her week-long rotation as the day chief was over, and Paul Plodgett's was starting. Paul was already at the desk, going over the cases that had come in the previous night. Laurie and Jack told him they were planning on taking vacation time and wanted to skip doing any autopsies that day unless there was a glut. Paul assured them that the case load was light.

Laurie was more politically minded than Jack, and it was her opinion that they should approach Calvin about their vacation plans before they talked with Bingham. Jack bowed to her better judgment. Calvin's response was to merely grunt that they could have given more notice.

As soon as Bingham arrived, Laurie and Jack went to his office. He regarded them curiously over the tops of his wire-rimmed glasses. He was clutching the morning mail, which he was in the process of going through.

"You want two weeks starting today?" he questioned with disbelief. "What's the rush? Is this some sort of an emergency?"

"We're planning on an adventure-type trip," Jack said. "We'd like to leave this evening."

Bingham's watery eyes went back and forth between Laurie and Jack. "You two aren't planning on getting married, are you?"

"Not that adventuresome," Jack said.

Laurie sputtered with laughter. "We're sorry not to have given more notice," she said. "The reason for the haste is because last night both of us were threatened over the Franconi case."

"Threatened?" Bingham questioned. "Does it have anything to do with that shiner you've got?"

"I'm afraid so," Laurie said. She'd tried to cover the bruise with makeup but had only been partially successful.

"Who was behind these threats?" Bingham asked.

"One of the New York crime families," Laurie said. "Lieutenant Louis Soldano offered to fill you in on it as well as talk to you about a possible mole for the crime family here in the medical examiner's office. We think we have figured out how Franconi's body was taken from here."

"I'm listening," Bingham said. He put the mail down and leaned back in his chair.

Laurie explained the story, emphasizing that the Spoletto Funeral Home had to have been given the accession number of the unidentified case.

"Did Detective Soldano think it wise for you two to leave town?" Bingham asked.

"Yes, he did," Laurie said.

"Fine," Bingham said. "Then you're out of

here. Am I supposed to call Soldano or is he calling me?"

"It was our understanding that he was going to call you," Laurie said.

"Good," Bingham said. Then he looked directly at Jack. "What about the liver issue?"

"That's up in the air," Jack said. "I'm still waiting on some more tests."

Bingham nodded and commented: "This case is a goddamned pain in the ass. Just make sure I'm informed of any breaking news while you're away. I don't want any surprises." He looked down at his desk and picked up the mail. "You people have a good trip and send me a postcard."

Laurie and Jack went out into the hall and smiled at each other.

"Well, it looks good," Jack said. "Bingham was the major potential stumbling block."

"I wonder if we should have told him we're going to Africa because of the liver issue?" Laurie asked.

"I don't think so," Jack said. "He might have changed his mind about letting us go. As far as he's concerned, he wishes this case would just disappear."

Retiring to their separate offices, Laurie phoned the Equatoguinean Embassy about the visas, while Jack called the airlines. She quickly learned that Esteban had been right about the ease of getting a visa and that it could be done that morning. Jack found Air

France happy to make all the arrangements, and he agreed to stop by their office that afternoon to pick up the tickets.

Laurie appeared in Jack's office. She was beaming. "I'm beginning to think this is really going to happen," she said excitedly. "How'd you do?"

"Fine," Jack said. "We leave tonight at seven-fifty."

"I can't believe this," Laurie said. "I feel like a teenager going on my first trip."

After making arrangements with the travel and immunization office at the Manhattan General Hospital, they called Warren. He agreed to get in touch with Natalie and meet them at the hospital.

The nurse practitioner gave each of them a battery of shots as well as prescriptions for antimalarial drugs. She also urged them to wait a full week before exposure. Jack explained that was impossible. The nurse's response was to say that she was glad they were going and not she.

In the hall outside the travel office, Warren asked Jack what the woman meant.

"It takes up to a week for these shots to take effect," Jack explained. "That is, except for the gamma globulin."

"Are we taking a risk, then?" Warren asked.

"Life's a risk," Jack quipped. "Seriously, there's some risk, but each day our immune systems will be better prepared. The main problem is the malaria, but I intend to take a hell of a lot of insect repellant."

"So you're not concerned?" Warren asked.

"Not enough to keep me home," Jack said.

After leaving the hospital, they all went to a passport photo place and had snapshots taken. With those in hand, Laurie, Warren, and Natalie left to visit the Equatoguinean Embassy.

Jack caught a taxi and directed it to the University Hospital. Once there, he went directly up to Dr. Peter Malovar's lab. As usual he found the aged pathologist bent over his microscope. Jack waited respectfully until the professor had finished studying his current slide.

"Ahhh, Dr. Stapleton," Dr. Malovar said, catching sight of Jack. "I'm glad you came. Now, where is that slide of yours?"

Dr. Malovar's lab was a dusty clutter of books, journals, and hundreds of slide trays. The wastebaskets were perennially overflowing. The professor steadfastly refused to allow anybody into his work space to clean lest they disturb his structured disorder.

With surprising speed, the professor located Jack's slide on top of a veterinary pathology book. His nimble fingers picked it up and slipped it under the microscope's objective.

"Dr. Osgood's suggestion to have this reviewed by Dr. Hammersmith was cracker-jack," Dr. Malovar said as he focused. When he was satisfied, he sat back, picked up the book, and opened it to the page indicated by a clean microscope slide. He handed the book to Jack.

Jack looked at the page Dr. Malovar indicated. It was a photomicrograph of a section of liver. There was a granuloma similar to the one on Jack's slide.

"It's the same," Dr. Malovar said. He motioned for Jack to compare by looking into the microscope.

Jack leaned forward and studied the slide. The images did seem identical.

"This is certainly one of the more interesting slides you have brought to me," Dr. Malovar said. He pushed a lock of his wild, gray hair out of his eyes. "As you can read from the book, the offending organism is called hepatocystis."

Jack straightened up from looking at his slide to glance back at the book. He'd never heard of hepatocystis.

"Is it rare?" Jack asked.

"In the New York City morgue I'd have to say yes," Dr. Malovar said. "Extremely rare! You see it is only found in primates. And not only that, but it is only found in Old World primates, meaning primates found in Africa and Southeast Asia. It's never been seen in the New World and never in humans."

"Never?" Jack questioned.

"Put it this way," Dr. Malovar said. "I've

never seen it, and I've seen a lot of liver parasites. More important, Dr. Osgood has never seen it, and he has seen more liver parasites than I. With that kind of combined experience, I'd have to say it does not exist in humans. Of course, in the endemic areas, it might be a different story, but even there it would have to be rare. Otherwise we'd have seen a case or two."

"I appreciate your help," Jack said distractedly. He was already wrestling with the implications of this surprising bit of information. It was a much stronger suggestion that Franconi had had a xenotransplant than the mere fact that he'd gone to Africa.

"This would be an interesting case to present at our grand rounds," Dr. Malovar said. "If you are interested, let me know."

"Of course," Jack said noncommittally. His mind was in a whirl.

Jack left the professor, took the hospital elevator down to the ground floor, and started toward the medical examiner's office. Finding an Old World primate parasite in a liver sample was very telling evidence. But then there were the confusing results that Ted Lynch had gotten on the DNA analysis to contend with. And on top of that was the fact there was no inflammation in the liver with no immunosuppressant drugs. The only thing that was certain was that it all didn't make sense.

Arriving back at the morgue, Jack went directly up to the DNA lab with the intention of grilling Ted in the hope that he could come up with some hypothesis to explain what was going on. The problem as Jack saw it was that Jack didn't know enough about current DNA science to come up with an idea on his own. The field was changing too rapidly.

"Jesus, Stapleton, where the hell have you been!" Ted snapped the moment he saw Jack. "I've been calling all over creation and nobody's seen you."

"I've been out," Jack said defensively. He thought for a second about explaining what was going on then changed his mind. Too much had happened in the previous twelve hours.

"Sit down!" Ted commanded.

Jack sat.

Ted searched around on his desktop until he located a particular sheet of developed film covered with hundreds of minute dark bands. He handed it to Jack.

"Ted, why do you do this to me?" Jack complained. "You know perfectly well I have no idea what I'm looking at with these things."

Ted ignored Jack, while he searched for another similar piece of celluloid. He found it under a laboratory budget he was working on. He handed the second one to Jack.

"Hold them up to the light," Ted said.

Jack did as he was told. He looked at the

two sheets. Even he could tell they were different.

Ted pointed to the first sheet of celluloid. "This is a study of the region of the DNA that codes for ribosomal protein of a human being. I just picked a case at random to show you what it looks like."

"It's gorgeous," Jack said.

"Let's not be sarcastic," Ted said.

"I'll try," Jack said.

"Now, this other one is a study of Franconi's liver sample," Ted said. "It's the same region using the same enzymes as the first study. Can you see how different it is?"

"That's the only thing I can see," Jack said.

Ted snatched away the human study and tossed it aside. Then he pointed at the film Jack was still holding. "As I told you yesterday this information is on CD-rom so I was able to let the computer make a match of the pattern. It came back that it was most consistent with a chimpanzee."

"Not definitely a chimpanzee?" Jack asked. Nothing seemed to be definite about this case.

"No, but close," Ted said. "Kind of like a cousin of a chimpanzee. Something like that."

"Do chimps have cousins?" Jack asked.

"You got me," Ted said with a shrug. "But I've been dying to give you this information. You have to admit it's rather impressive."

"So from your perspective it was a

xenograft," Jack said.

Ted shrugged again. "If you made me guess, I'd have to say yes. But taking the DQ alpha results into consideration, I don't know what to say. Also I've taken it upon myself to run the DNA for the ABO blood groups. So far that's coming up just like the DQ alpha. I think it's going to be a perfect match for Franconi, which only confuses things farther. It's a weird case."

"Tell me about it!" Jack said. He then related to Ted the discovery of an Old World primate parasite.

Ted made an expression of confusion. "I'm glad this is your case and not mine," he said.

Jack placed the sheet of celluloid on Ted's desk. "If I'm lucky, I might have some answers in the next few days," he said. "Tonight I'm off to Africa to visit the same country Franconi did."

"Is the office sending you?" Ted asked with surprise.

"Nope," Jack said. "I'm going on my own. Well, that's not quite true. I mean, I'm paying for it, but Laurie is going, too."

"My god, you are thorough," Ted said.

"Dogged is probably a better word," Jack said.

Jack got up to go. When he reached the door, Ted called out to him: "I did get the results of the mitochondrial DNA back. There was a match with Mrs. Franconi, so at least your identification was right."

"Finally something definitive," Jack said.

Jack was again about to leave when Ted called out again.

"I just had a crazy idea," Ted said. "The only way I could explain the results I've been getting is if the liver was transgenic."

"What the hell does that mean?" Jack asked.

"It means the liver contains DNA from two separate organisms," Ted said.

"Hmmmm," Jack said. "I'll have to think about that one."

COGO, EQUATORIAL GUINEA

Bertram looked at his watch. It was four o'clock in the afternoon. Raising his eyes to look out the window, he noticed that the sudden, violent tropical rainstorm which had totally darkened the sky only fifteen minutes earlier had already vanished. In its place was a steamy sunny African afternoon.

With sudden resolve Bertram reached for his phone and called up to the fertility center. The evening tech by the name of Shirley Cartwright answered.

"Have the two new breeding bonobo females got their hormone shots today?" Bertram asked.

"Not yet," Shirley said.

"I thought the protocol called for them to get the shots at two P.M.," Bertram said.

"That's the usual schedule," Shirley said hesitantly.

"Why the delay?" Bertram asked.

"Miss Becket hasn't arrived yet," Shirley explained reluctantly. The last thing she wanted to do was get her immediate boss in trouble, but she knew she couldn't lie.

"When was she due?" Bertram asked.

"No particular time," Shirley said. "She'd told the day staff she'd be busy all morning in her lab over at the hospital. I imagine she got tied up."

"She didn't leave instructions for the hormones to be given by someone else if she didn't arrive by two?" Bertram asked.

"Apparently not," Shirley said. "So I expect her at any minute."

"If she doesn't come in the next half hour, go ahead and give the scheduled doses," Bertram said. "Will that be a problem?"

"No problem whatsoever, Doctor," Shirley said.

Bertram disconnected and then dialed Melanie's lab in the hospital complex. He was less familiar with the staff and didn't know the person who answered. But the person knew Bertram and told him a disturbing story. Melanie hadn't been in that day because she'd been tied up at the animal center.

Bertram hung up and nervously tapped the top of the phone with the nail of his index finger. Despite Siegfried's assertions that he'd taken care of the potential problem with Kevin and his reputed girlfriends, Bertram was skeptical. Melanie was a conscientious worker. It certainly wasn't like her to miss a scheduled injection.

Snapping up the phone again, Bertram tried calling Kevin, but there was no answer.

With his suspicions rising, Bertram got up from his desk and informed Martha, his secretary, that he'd be back in an hour. Outside, he climbed into his Cherokee and headed for town.

As he drove Bertram became increasingly certain that Kevin and the women had managed to go to the island, and it angered him. He berated himself for allowing Siegfried to lull him into a false sense of security. Bertram had a growing premonition that Kevin's curiosity was going to cause major trouble.

At the point of transition from asphalt to cobblestones at the edge of town, Bertram had to brake abruptly. In his mounting vexation, he'd been unaware of his speed. The wet cobblestones from the recent downpour were as slick as ice, so Bertram's car skidded several yards before coming to a complete stop.

Bertram parked in the hospital parking lot. He climbed to the third floor of the lab and pounded on Kevin's door. There was no response. Bertram tried the door. It was locked.

Returning to his car, Bertram drove around the town square and parked behind the town hall. He nodded to the lazy group of soldiers lounging in broken rattan chairs in the shade of the arcade.

Taking the stairs by twos, Bertram presented himself to Aurielo and said he had to speak to Siegfried.

"He's with the chief of security at the moment," Aurielo said.

"Let him know I'm here," Bertram said, as he began to pace the outer office. His irritation was mounting.

Five minutes later, Cameron McIvers emerged from the inner office. He said hello to Bertram, but Bertram ignored him in his haste to get in to see Siegfried.

"We've got a problem," Bertram said. "Melanie Becket didn't show up for a scheduled injection this afternoon, and Kevin Marshall is not in his lab."

"I'm not surprised," Siegfried said calmly. He sat back and stretched with his good arm. "They were both seen leaving early this morning with the nurse. The ménage à trois seems to be blossoming. They even had a dinner party late into the night at Kevin's house, and then the women stayed over."

"Truly?" Bertram questioned. That the nerdy researcher could be involved in such a liaison seemed impossible.

"I should know," Siegfried said. "I live across the green from Kevin. Besides, I met the women earlier at the Chickee Bar. They were already tipsy and told me they were on their way to Kevin's."

"Where did they go this morning?" Bertram asked.

"I assume to Acalayong," Siegfried said. "They were seen leaving in a pirogue before dawn by a member of the janitorial staff."

"Then they have gone to the island by water," Bertram snapped.

"They were seen going west, not east," Siegfried said.

"It could have been a ruse," Bertram said.

"It could have," Siegfried agreed. "And I thought of the possibility. I even discussed it with Cameron. But both of us are of the opinion that the only way to visit the island by water is to land at the staging area. The rest of the island is surrounded by a virtual wall of mangroves and marsh."

Bertram's eyes rose up to stare at the huge rhino heads on the wall behind Siegfried. Their brainless carcasses reminded him of the site manager, yet Bertram had to admit in this instance he had a point. In fact, when the island was initially considered for the bonobo project its inaccessibility by water had been one of its attractions.

"And they couldn't have landed at the staging area," Siegfried continued, "because the soldiers are still out there itching to have an excuse to use their AK-47's." Siegfried laughed. "It tickles me every time I think of their shooting out Melanie's car windows."

"Maybe you're right," Bertram said grudgingly.

"Of course I'm right," Siegfried said.

"But I'm still concerned," Bertram said. "And suspicious. I want to get into Kevin's office."

"For what reason?" Siegfried asked.

"I was stupid enough to show him how to tap into the software we'd developed for locating the bonobos," Bertram said. "Unfortunately, he's been taking advantage of it. I know because he's accessed it on several occasions for long periods of time. I'd like to see if I can find out what he'd been up to."

"I'd say that sounds quite reasonable," Siegfried said. He called out to Aurielo to see to it that Bertram had an entrance card for the lab. Then he said to Bertram: "Let me know if you find anything interesting."

"Don't worry," Bertram said.

Armed with the magnetic pass card, Bertram returned to the lab and entered Kevin's space. Locking the door behind him, he first went through Kevin's desk. Finding nothing, he made a quick tour of the room. The first sign of trouble was a stack of computer paper next to the printer that Bertram recognized as printouts of the island graphic.

Bertram examined each page. He could tell that they represented varying scales. What he couldn't figure out was the meaning of all the surcharged geometric shapes.

Putting the pages aside, Bertram went to Kevin's computer and began to search through his directories. It wasn't long before he found what he was looking for: the source of the information on the printouts.

For the next half hour, Bertram was transfixed by what he found: Kevin had devised a way to follow individual animals in real time. After Bertram played with this capability for a while, he came across Kevin's stored information documenting the animals' movement over a period of several hours. From this information, Bertram was able to reproduce the geometric shapes.

"You are too clever for your own good," Bertram said out loud as he allowed the computer to run sequentially through the movements of each animal. By the time the program had run its course, Bertram had seen the problem with bonobo numbers sixty and sixty-seven.

With mounting anxiety, Bertram tried to get the indicators for the two animals to move. When he couldn't, he went back to real time and displayed the two animals' current position. They'd not changed one iota.

"Good lord!" Bertram moaned. All at once, the worry about Kevin vanished and was replaced with a more pressing problem. Turning off the computer, Bertram snapped up the printed island graphics, and ran out of the lab. Outside, he passed up his car to run directly across the square to the town hall. He knew it would take less time on foot.

He raced up the stairs. As he entered the outer office, Aurielo looked up. Bertram ignored him. He burst into Siegfried's office unannounced.

"I've got to talk with you immediately," Bertram sputtered to Siegfried. He was out of breath.

Siegfried was meeting with his food-service supervisor. Both appeared stunned by Bertram's arrival.

"It's an emergency," Bertram added.

The food-service supervisor stood up. "I can return later," he said and left.

"This better be important," Siegfried warned.

Bertram waved the computer printouts. "It's very bad news," he said. He took the chair vacated by the supervisor. "Kevin Marshall figured out a way to follow the bonobos over time."

"So what?" Siegfried said.

"At least two of the bonobos don't move," Bertram said. "Number sixty and number sixty-seven. And they haven't moved for more than twenty-four hours. There's only one explanation. They're dead!"

Siegfried raised his eyebrows. "Well, they're animals," he said. "Animals die. We have to expect some attrition."

"You don't understand," Bertram said with a tinge of disdain. "You made light of my concern that the animals had split into two groups. I told you that it was significant. This, unfortunately, is proof. As sure as I'm standing here, those animals are killing each other!"

"You think so?" Siegfried asked with alarm.

"There's no doubt in my mind," Bertram said. "I've been agonizing over why they split up into two groups. I decided it had to have been because we forgot to maintain the balance between males and females. There's no other explanation, and it means the males are fighting over the females. I'm sure of it."

"Oh my god!" Siegfried exclaimed, with a shake of his head. "That's terrible news."

"It's more than terrible," Bertram said. "It's intolerable. It will be the ruin of the whole program provided we don't act."

"What can we do?" Siegfried asked.

"First, we tell no one!" Bertram said. "If there is ever an order to harvest either sixty or sixty-seven, we'll deal with that particular problem then. Second, and more important, we must bring the animals in like I've been advocating. The bonobos won't be killing each other if they're in separate cages."

Siegfried had to accept the white-haired veterinarian's advice. Although he'd always favored the animals being off by themselves for logistical and security reasons, its time was past. The animals could not be allowed to kill each other. In a very real way, there was no choice.

"When should we retrieve them?" Siegfried asked.

"As soon as possible," Bertram said. "I can have a team of security-cleared animal handlers ready by dawn tomorrow. We'll begin by darting the splinter group. Once we have all the animals caged, which should take no more than two or three days, we'll move them at night to a section of the animal center that I will prepare."

"I suppose I'd better recall that contingent of soldiers out by the bridge," Siegfried said. "The last thing we need is for them to shoot the animal handlers."

"I didn't like having them out there in the first place," Bertram said. "I was afraid they might have shot one of the animals for sport or soup."

"When should we inform our respective bosses at GenSys?" Siegfried asked.

"Not until it is done," Bertram said. "Only then will we know how many animals have been killed. Maybe we'll also have a better idea of the best ultimate disposition. My guess is we'll have to build a separate, new facility."

"For that, we'd need authorization," Siegfried said.

"Obviously," Bertram said. He stood up. "All I can say is that it is a damn good thing

I had the foresight to move all those cages out there."

Raymond felt better than he had in days. Things seemed to have gone well from the moment he'd gotten up. Just after nine he'd called Dr. Waller Anderson, and not only was the doctor going to join, he already had two clients ready to plunk down their deposits and head out to the Bahamas for the bone marrow aspirations.

Then around noon Raymond had gotten a call from Dr. Alice Norwood, whose office was on Rodeo Drive in Beverly Hills. She'd called to say that she'd recruited three physicians with large private practices who were eager to come on board. One was in Century City, another in Brentwood, and the last was in Bel-Air. She was convinced that these doctors would soon provide a flood of clients because the market on the West Coast for the service Raymond was offering was nothing short of phenomenal.

But what had pleased Raymond the most during the day was whom he didn't hear from. There were no calls from either Vinnie Dominick or Dr. Daniel Levitz. Raymond took this silence to mean that the Franconi business had finally been put to bed.

At three-thirty, the door buzzer went off.

546

Darlene answered it and with a tearful voice told Raymond that his car was waiting.

Raymond took his girlfriend in his arms and patted her on the back. "Next time maybe you can go," Raymond said consolingly.

"Really?" she asked.

"I can't guarantee it," Raymond said. "But we'll try." Raymond had no control over the GenSys flights. Darlene had been able to go on only one of the trips to Cogo. On all the other occasions, the plane had been full on one of the segments. As standard procedure, the plane flew from the States to Europe and then on to Bata. On the return trip the same general itinerary was followed, although it was always a different European city.

After promising to call as soon as he arrived in Cogo, Raymond carried his bag downstairs. He climbed into the waiting sedan and luxuriously leaned back.

"Would you like the radio on, sir?" the driver asked.

"Sure, why not," Raymond said. He was already beginning to enjoy himself.

The drive across town was the most difficult part of the trip. Once they were on the West Side Highway, they were able to make good time. There was a lot of traffic, but since rush hour had not begun, the traffic moved fluidly. It was the same situation on the George Washington Bridge. In less than an hour Raymond was dropped off at Teterboro Airport.

The GenSys plane had not yet arrived, but Raymond was not concerned. He positioned himself in the lounge, where he had a view of the runway and ordered himself a scotch. Just as he was being served, the sleek GenSys jet swooped in low out of the clouds and touched down. It taxied over to a position directly in front of Raymond.

It was a beautiful aircraft painted white with a red stripe along its side. Its only markings were its call sign, N69SU, and a tiny American flag. Both were on the fin of the tail assembly.

As if in slow motion, a forward door opened and self-contained steps extended down toward the tarmac. An impeccably dressed steward in dark-blue livery appeared in the doorway, descended the stairs and entered the general aviation building. His name was Roger Perry. Raymond remembered him well. Along with another steward named Jasper Devereau, he'd been on the plane every trip Raymond had made.

Once inside the building, Roger scanned the lounge. The moment he spotted Raymond, he walked over and greeted him with a salute.

"Is this the extent of your luggage, sir?" Roger asked as he picked up Raymond's bag.

"That's it," Raymond said. "Are we leaving already? Isn't the plane going to refuel?" That had been the procedure on previous flights.

"We're all set," Roger said.

Raymond got to his feet and followed the steward out into the gray, raw March afternoon. As he approached the luxurious private jet, Raymond hoped there were people watching him. At times like this, he felt as if he were living the life that was meant for him. He even told himself that he was lucky he'd lost his medical license.

"Tell me, Roger," Raymond called out just before they reached the stairs. "Are we full on the flight to Europe?" On every flight Raymond had been on, there'd been other Gen-Sys executives.

"Only one other passenger," Roger said. He stepped to the side at the base of the stairs and gestured for Raymond to precede him.

Raymond smiled as he climbed. With only one other passenger and two stewards, the flight was going to be even more enjoyable than he'd anticipated. The troubles that he'd had over the previous few days seemed a small price to pay for such luxury.

Just inside the plane, he was met by Jasper. Jasper took his overcoat and jacket and asked if Raymond wanted a drink before takeoff.

"I'll wait," Raymond said gallantly.

Jasper pulled aside the drape that separated the galley from the cabin. Swelling with pride, Raymond passed into the main part of the plane. He was debating which of the deeply cushioned leather chairs to take when his eyes passed over the face of the other passenger. Raymond froze. At the same time, he felt a sinking feeling in his gut.

"Hello, Dr. Lyons. Welcome aboard."

"Taylor Cabot!" Raymond croaked. "I didn't expect to see you."

"I suppose not," Taylor said. "I'm surprised to see myself." He smiled and gestured toward the seat next to him.

Raymond quickly sat down. He berated himself for not taking the drink Jasper had offered. His throat had gone bone-dry.

"I'd been informed of the plane's flight plan," Taylor explained, "and since there was a window of opportunity in my schedule, I thought it wise for me to personally check on our Cogo operation. It was a last-minute decision. Of course, we'll be making a stop in Zurich for me to have a short meeting with some bankers. I hope you won't find that inconvenient."

Raymond shook his head. "No, not at all," he stammered.

"And how are things going with the bonobo project?" Taylor asked.

"Very well," Raymond managed. "We're expecting a number of new clients. In fact, we're having trouble keeping up with demand."

"And what about that regrettable episode with Carlo Franconi?" Taylor enquired. "I trust that has been successfully dealt with."

"Yes, of course," Raymond sputtered. He tried to smile.

"Part of the reason I'm making this trip is to be reassured that project is worth supporting," Taylor said. "My chief financial officer assures me that it is now turning a small profit. But my operations officer has reservations about jeopardizing our primate research business. So, I have to make a decision. I hope you will be willing to help me."

"Certainly," Raymond squeaked, as he heard the characteristic whine of the jet engines starting.

It was like a party at the bar in the international departure lounge at JFK airport. Even Lou was there having a beer and popping peanuts into his mouth. He was in a great mood and acted as if he were going on the trip.

Jack, Laurie, Warren, Natalie, and Esteban were sitting with Lou at a round table in the corner of the bar. Over their heads was a television tuned to a hockey game. The frantic voice of the announcer and the roar of the fans added to the general din.

"It's been a great day," Lou yelled to Jack and Laurie. "We picked up Vido Delbario, and he's singing to save his ass. I think we'll be making a major dent in the Vaccarro organization."

"What about Angelo Facciolo and Franco

Ponti?" Laurie asked.

"That's another story," Lou said with a laugh. "For once the judge sided with us and set bail at two million each. What did the trick was the police impersonation charge."

"How about Spoletto Funeral Home?" Laurie asked.

"That's going to be a gold mine," Lou said. "The owner is the brother of the wife of Vinnie Dominick. You remember him, don't you, Laurie?"

Laurie nodded. "How can I forget?"

"Who's Vinnie Dominick?" Jack asked.

"He played a surprising role in the Cerino affair," Laurie explained.

"He's with the competing Lucia organization," Lou said. "They've been having a field day after Cerino's fall. But my gut feeling tells me we're going to puncture their balloon."

"What about the mole in the medical examiner's office?" Laurie asked.

"Hey, first things first," Lou said. "We'll get to that. Don't worry."

"When you do, check out one of the techs by the name of Vinnie Amendola," Laurie said.

"Any particular reason?" Lou asked, as he wrote down the name in the small notebook he carried in the side pocket of his jacket.

"Just a suspicion," Laurie said.

"Consider it done," Lou said. "You know, this episode shows how fast things can change.

Yesterday I was in the dog house, whereas today I'm the golden boy. I even got a call from the captain about a possible commendation. Can you believe it?"

"You deserve it," Laurie said.

"Hey, if I get one, you guys should get one, too," Lou said.

Jack felt someone tap on his arm. It was the waitress. She asked if they wanted another round.

"Hey, everybody?" Jack called out above the babble of voices. "More beer?"

Jack looked first at Natalie who put her hand over her glass to indicate she was fine. She looked radiant in a dark purple jumpsuit. She was a third-grade teacher at a public school in Harlem, but didn't look like any teacher Jack could remember. From Jack's perspective her features were reminiscent of the Egyptian sculptures in the Metropolitan Museum that Laurie had dragged him in to see. Her eyes were almond-shaped and her lips were full and generous. Her hair was done up in the most elaborate corn-row style that Jack had ever seen. Natalie had said that it was her sister's forte.

When Jack looked at Warren to see whether he wanted more beer, he shook his head. Warren was sitting next to Natalie. He was wearing a sport jacket over a black T-shirt that somehow managed to hide his powerful physique. He looked happier than Jack had ever seen him. His mouth harbored a half smile instead of his normal expression of hard-lipped determination.

"I'm fine," Esteban called out. He, too, was smiling, even more broadly than Warren.

Jack looked at Laurie. "No more for me. I want to save some room for wine with dinner on the plane." Laurie had her auburn hair braided and was wearing a loose-fitting velour top with leggings. With her relaxed, ebullient demeanor and casual clothes Jack thought she looked like she was in college.

"Yeah, sure, I'll have another beer," Lou said.

"One beer," Jack told the waitress. "Then the check."

"How'd you guys make out today?" Lou asked Jack and Laurie.

"We're here," Jack said. "That was the goal. Laurie and the others got the visas, and I got the tickets." He patted his stomach. "I also got a bunch of French francs and a money belt. I was told that the French franc was the hard currency of choice for that part of Africa."

"What's going to happen when you arrive?" Lou asked.

Jack pointed over to Esteban. "Our expatriate traveling companion has taken care of the arrangements. His cousin's meeting us at the airport, and his wife's brother has a hotel."

"You should be fine," Lou said. "What's your plan?"

"Esteban's cousin has arranged for us to rent a van," Jack said. "So we'll drive to Cogo."

"And just drop in?" Lou asked.

"That's the idea," Jack said.

"Good luck," Lou said.

"Thanks," Jack said. "We'll probably need it."

A half hour later the group — minus Lou — merrily boarded the 747. They found their seats and stowed their carry-on baggage. No sooner had they gotten themselves situated than the huge plane lurched and was pulled from the gate.

Later when the engines began to scream and the plane began its dash down the runway to takeoff, Laurie felt Jack take her hand. He gripped it fiercely.

"Are you okay?" she asked.

Jack nodded. "I've just learned not to like air travel," he said.

Laurie understood.

"We're on our way," Warren exclaimed gleefully. "Africa, here we come!"

CHAPTER 19

"Are you asleep?" Candace whispered.

"Are you kidding?" Melanie whispered back. "How am I supposed to sleep on rock with just a few branches strewn over it?"

"I can't sleep either," Candace admitted. "Especially with all this snoring going on. What about Kevin?"

"I'm awake," Kevin said.

They were in a small side cave jutting off the main chamber just behind the main entrance. The darkness was almost absolute. The only light came from meager moonlight reflected from outside.

Kevin, Melanie, and Candace had been shuttled into this small cave immediately on their arrival. It measured about ten feet wide with a downward sloping ceiling that started at a maximum height roughly equivalent to Kevin's five feet ten inches. There was no back wall to this cave; the chamber simply narrowed to a tunnel. Earlier in the evening, Kevin had explored the tunnel with the help of the flashlight in hopes of finding another way out, but the tunnel abruptly ended after about thirty feet.

The bonobos had treated them well, even after the initially cold reception by the females. Apparently, the animals were mystified by the humans and intended to keep them alive and well. They'd provided them with muddy water in gourds and a variety of food. Unfortunately, the food was in the form of grubs, maggots, and other insects along with some kind of sedge from Lago Hippo.

Later in the afternoon, the animals had started a fire at the cave's entrance. Kevin was particularly interested in how they started it, but he'd been too far back to observe their method. A group of the bonobos had formed a tight circle, and then a half an hour later a fire was going.

"Well, that answers the question about the smoke," Kevin had said.

The animals had skewered the colobus monkeys and roasted them over the fire. The monkeys were then torn apart and distributed with great fanfare. Given all the hooting and vocalizations it had been obvious to the humans that this monkey meat was considered a great treat.

Bonobo number one had placed a few morsels of the feast on a large leaf and brought them back to the humans. Only Kevin had been willing to try it. He'd said it was the toughest thing he'd ever chewed. As far as taste was concerned, he'd told the women that it was strangely similar to the elephant he'd once sampled. The previous year, Siegfried had bagged a forest elephant on one of his hunting forays and after taking the tusks, he'd had some of the meat cooked up by the central kitchen.

The bonobos had not tried to imprison the humans and had not tried to inhibit Kevin and the women from untying the rope that bound them together. At the same time, the bonobos had made it clear that they were to stay in the small cave. At all times, at least two of the larger male bonobos remained in the immediate vicinity. Each time Kevin or one of the women tried to venture forth, these guards would screech and howl at the top of their lungs. Even more threatening, they would ferociously charge with bared teeth only to pull up short at the last minute. Thus they effectively kept the humans in their place.

"We're going to have to do something," Melanie said. "We can't stay here forever. And it's pretty apparent we'll have to do it while they are all sleeping, like now."

Every bonobo in the cave, including the supposed guards, were fast asleep on primitive pallets constructed of branches and leaves. Most were snoring.

"I don't think we should take the chance of angering them," Kevin said. "We're lucky they've treated us as well as they have."

"Being offered maggots to eat is not what I'd call being well treated," Melanie said. "Seriously, we have to do something. Besides, they might turn on us. There's no way to anticipate what they'll do."

"I prefer to wait," Kevin said. "We're a novelty now, but they'll lose interest in us. Besides, we're undoubtedly missed back in town. It won't take Siegfried or Bertram that long to figure out what we've done. Then they'll come for us."

"I'm not convinced," Melanie said. "Siegfried might take our disappearance as a godsend."

"Siegfried might, but Bertram won't," Kevin said. "He's basically a nice person."

"What do you think, Candace?" Melanie asked.

"I don't know what to think," Candace said. "This situation is so far beyond anything I'd ever thought I'd be involved in, that I don't know how to react. I'm numb."

"What are we going to do when we do get back?" Kevin said. "We haven't talked about that."

"*If* we get back," Melanie said.

"Don't talk that way," Candace said.

"We have to face facts," Melanie said. "That's why I think we should do something now while they're all asleep."

"We have no idea how soundly they sleep," Kevin said. "Trying to walk out of here will be like walking through a mine field."

"One thing is for sure," Candace said. "I'm

not going to be involved in any more harvests. I began to feel uncomfortable when I thought they were apes. Now that we know they're protohumans, I can't do it. I know that much about myself."

"That's a foregone conclusion," Kevin said. "I can't imagine any sensitive human being would feel differently. But that's not the issue. The issue is that this new race exists, and if they're not to be used for transplants, what's to be done with them?"

"Will they be able to reproduce?" Candace asked.

"Most assuredly," Melanie said. "Nothing was done to them to affect their fertility."

"Oh, my," Candace said. "This is a horror."

"Maybe they should be rendered infertile," Melanie said. "Then there'd only be a single generation to consider."

"I wish I'd thought of all this before I started this project," Kevin said. "The problem was that once I stumbled onto the ability to interchange chromosomal parts, the intellectual stimulation was so strong I never considered other consequences."

There was a sudden, bright flash of lightning momentarily illuminating the interior of the cave, followed by a loud clap of thunder. The concussion seemed to shake the entire mountain. The violent display was nature's way of announcing that one of the almost daily thunderstorms was about to inundate the island.

"Now, that's an argument in favor of my position," Melanie said, after the sound of the thunder died away.

"What are you talking about?" Kevin asked.

"That thunder was loud enough to wake the dead," Melanie explained. "And not one of the bonobos so much as blinked."

"It's true," Candace said.

"I think at least one of us should try to get out of here," Melanie said. "That way we could be sure that Bertram will be alerted as to what is happening out here. Bertram can also make arrangements for someone to come here and rescue the others."

"I guess I agree," Candace said.

"Of course you do," Melanie said.

There were a few moments of silence. Finally, Kevin broke it: "Wait a second. You guys are not suggesting that I go?"

"I couldn't get in the canoe much less paddle it," Melanie said.

"I could get in it, but I doubt I could paddle it in the dark," Candace said.

"And you two think I could?" Kevin asked.

"Certainly better than we could," Melanie said.

Kevin shivered. The idea of trying to get to the canoe in the dark knowing the hippos were out grazing was a scary thought. Even more scary was trying to paddle across the pond, knowing it was filled with crocodiles.

"Maybe you could hide in the canoe until it gets light," Melanie suggested. "The important thing is to get out of this cave and away from these creatures while they are sleeping."

The idea of waiting in the canoe was better than trying to cross the lake in the darkness, but it did not address the potential problem of running into the hippos in the marshy field.

"Remember it was your suggestion to come out here," Melanie reminded him.

Kevin started to strongly protest, but he stopped. In a way, it was true. He'd said that the only way to learn whether the bonobos were protohumans was to come to the island. But from then on, Melanie had been the one to call the shots.

"It was your suggestion," Candace said. "I remember it well. We were in your office. It was when you first raised the question about the smoke."

"But I only said . . ." Kevin began, but he stopped. From past experience, he knew he was ill-equipped to argue with Melanie, and especially when Candace supported her as she was now doing. Besides, from where Kevin was sitting, he could see a clear path of moonlight along the cave floor all the way to the entrance. Except for a few rocks and branches, there were no obstructions.

Kevin began to think maybe he could do it. Maybe it was best not to think of the hippos. Maybe it was true that the creatures' hospitality could not be counted upon, not because of the bonobo part of their heritage but because of the human part.

"All right," Kevin said with sudden resolve. "I'll try."

"Hooray," Melanie said.

Kevin pushed himself up onto his hands and knees. He was already trembling with the knowledge that there were fifty powerful and wild animals in the immediate environment that wanted him to stay where he was.

"If something goes wrong," Melanie said, "just get yourself back here in a hurry."

"You make it sound so easy," Kevin said.

"It will be," Melanie said. "Bonobos and chimps fall asleep as soon as it gets dark and sleep until dawn. You're not going to have any trouble."

"But what about the hippos?" Kevin said.

"What about them?" Melanie asked.

"Never mind," Kevin said. "I've got enough to worry about."

"Okay, good luck," Melanie whispered.

"Yeah, good luck," Candace echoed.

Kevin tried to stand up and start out, but he couldn't. He kept telling himself that he'd never been a hero, and this was no time to start.

"What's the matter?" Melanie asked.

"Nothing," Kevin said. Then suddenly from some place deep within himself, Kevin found the courage. He rose to a hunched-over position and began to pick his way along the path of moonlight toward the mouth of the cave.

As Kevin moved, he debated whether he would do better to move at a snail's pace or make an out-and-out dash for the canoe. It was an argument between caution and getting the ordeal over with. Caution won out. He moved with painstaking baby steps. Every time his foot made the slightest noise, he winced and froze in the darkness. All around him, he could hear the stertorous breathing of the sleeping creatures.

Twenty feet from the cave's entrance one of the bonobos moved so suddenly, the branches in his bed snapped. Again Kevin stopped in mid-stride, his heart pounding. But the bonobo had only stirred and was still breathing heavily, a sign of sleep. With additional light from the proximity of the cave entrance, Kevin could clearly see the bonobos sprawled about him. The sight of so many sleeping beasts was enough to stop him dead in his tracks. After a full minute of paralysis Kevin recommenced his progress toward freedom. He even began to feel the first wave of relief as the smell of the damp jungle replaced the feral scent of the bonobos. But that relief was short-lived.

Another clap of thunder followed by a sudden tropical downpour scared Kevin to the point that he almost lost his balance. It was only after frantic arm swinging that he managed to stay upright and in his planned path. He shuddered to think how close he'd come to stepping on one of the sleeping bonobos.

With another ten feet to go, Kevin could now see the black silhouette of the jungle below. The nocturnal sounds of the jungle were now audible over the bonobos' snores.

Kevin was close enough to begin worrying about how to make the steep descent to the ground when calamity struck. His heart leaped into his throat as he felt a hand on his leg! Something had grabbed him around the ankle with such force that instant tears formed in his eyes. Looking down in the half light, the first thing he saw was his watch. It was on the hairy wrist of the powerful bonobo number one.

"Tada," shouted the bonobo as he leaped to his feet, upending Kevin in the process. Luckily, the floor of that part of the cave was covered with refuse which broke Kevin's fall. Nevertheless, he landed on his left hip in a jarring fashion.

Bonobo number one's yell brought the other bonobos to their feet. For a moment, there was utter chaos until they all understood that there was no danger.

Bonobo number one let go of Kevin's ankle only to reach down and grasp him by his upper arms. In an amazing demonstration of strength, he picked Kevin up and held him off the ground at arm's length.

The bonobo gave a loud, long, angry vocalization. All Kevin could do was wince in pain at the animal's tight grip.

At the end of his tirade, bonobo number one marched into the depths of the cave and literally tossed Kevin into the smaller chamber. After a final angry word, he went back to his pallet.

Kevin managed to push himself up to a sitting position. He'd again landed on his hip, and it felt numb. He'd also sprained a wrist and scraped an elbow. But considering the fact that he'd been literally thrown through the air, he was better off than he'd anticipated.

More cries echoed inside of the cave, presumably from bonobo number one, but Kevin couldn't tell for certain in the darkness. He felt his right elbow. He knew that the sticky warmth had to be blood.

"Kevin?" Melanie whispered. "Are you okay?"

"As good as can be expected," Kevin said.

"Thank God," Melanie said. "What happened?"

"I don't know," Kevin said. "I'd thought I'd made it. I was right at the cave's entrance."

"Are you hurt?" Candace asked.

"A little," Kevin admitted. "But no broken bones. At least, I don't think so."

"We couldn't see what happened," Melanie said.

"My double scolded me," Kevin said. "At least that's what I think he was doing. Then he threw me back in here. I'm glad I didn't land on either of you."

"I'm so sorry I encouraged you to go," Melanie said. "I guess you were right."

"It's good of you to say," Kevin said. "Well, it almost worked. I was so close."

Candace switched on the flashlight with her hand shielding the front lens. She held it near Kevin's arm to check his elbow.

"I guess we're going to have to count on Bertram Edwards," Melanie said. She shuddered and then sighed. "It's hard to believe: we're prisoners of our own creations."

CHAPTER 20

Jack realized he'd been clenching his teeth. He was also holding Laurie's hand much harder than was reasonable. Consciously, he tried to relax. The problem had been the flight from Douala, Cameroon, to Bata. The airline was a fly-by-night outfit that used small, old commuter planes, just the kind of aircraft that plagued Jack's nightmares about his late family.

The flight had not been easy. The plane constantly dodged thunderstorms whose towering clouds varied in color from whipped-cream white to deep purple. Lightning had flashed constantly, and the turbulance was fierce.

The previous part of the trip had been a dream. The flight from New York to Paris had been smooth and blissfully uneventful. Everyone had slept at least a few hours.

Arrival in Paris had been ten minutes early, so they'd had ample time to make their connection with Cameroon Airlines. Everyone slept even more on the flight south to Douala. But that final leg to Bata was a hair-raiser.

"We're landing," Laurie said to Jack.

"I hope it is a controlled landing," Jack quipped.

He looked out the dirty window. As he'd expected, the landscape was a carpet of uninterrupted green. As the tops of the trees came closer and closer, he hoped there was a runway ahead.

Eventually, they touched down onto tarmac, and Jack and Warren breathed simultaneous sighs of relief.

As the weary travelers climbed out of the small, aged plane, Jack looked across the ill-maintained runway and saw a strange sight. It was a resplendent white jet sitting all by itself against the dark green of the jungle. At four points surrounding the plane were soldiers in camouflage fatigues and red berets. Although ostensibly standing upright, they'd all assumed varying postures of repose. Automatic rifles were casually slung over their shoulders.

"Whose plane?" Jack asked Esteban. With no markings it was apparent it was a private jet.

"I can't imagine," Esteban said.

Everyone except Esteban was unprepared for the chaos in the airport arrival area. All foreign arrivals had to go through customs. The group was taken along with their luggage to a side room. They were led to this unlikely spot by two men in dirty uniforms with automatic pistols holstered in their belts.

At first Esteban had been excluded from the room, but after a loud argument on his part in a local dialect, he was allowed in. The men opened all the bags and spread the contents onto a picnic-sized table.

Esteban told Jack the men expected bribes. At first Jack refused on principle. When it became apparent that the standoff was going to last for hours, Jack relented. Ten French francs solved the problem.

As they exited into the main part of the airport, Esteban apologized. "It's a problem here," he said. "All government people take bribes."

They were met by Esteban's cousin whose name was Arturo. He was a heavyset, enormously friendly individual with bright eyes and flashing teeth who shook hands enthusiastically with everyone. He was attired in native African costume: flowing robes in a colorful print and a pillbox hat.

They stepped out of the airport into the hot, humid air of equatorial Africa. The vistas in all directions seemed immense since the land was relatively flat. The late-afternoon sky was a faraway blue directly overhead, but enormous thunderheads were nestled all along the horizon.

"Man, I can't believe this," Warren said. He was gazing around like a kid in a toy store. "I've been thinking about coming here for years, but I never thought I'd make it." He looked at Jack. "Thanks, man. Give it here!" Warren stuck out his hand. He and Jack exchanged palm slaps as if they were back on the neighborhood basketball court.

Arturo had the rented van parked at curbside. He slipped a couple of bills into the palm of a policeman and gestured for everyone to climb in.

Esteban insisted that Jack ride in the front passenger seat. Too tired to argue, Jack climbed in. The vehicle was an old Toyota with two rows of benches behind the front bucket seats. Laurie and Natalie squeezed into the very back while Warren and Esteban took the middle.

As they exited the airport they had a view out over the ocean. The beach was broad and sandy. Gentle waves lapped the shore.

After a short distance, they passed a large unfinished cement structure that was weathered and crumbling. Rusted rebars stuck out of the top like the spines of sea urchins. Jack asked what it was.

"It was supposed to be a tourist hotel," Arturo said. "But there was no money and no tourists."

"That's a bad combination for business," Jack said.

While Esteban played tour guide and pointed out various sights, Jack asked Arturo if they had far to go.

"No, ten minutes," Arturo said.

"I understand you worked for GenSys," Jack said.

"For three years," Arturo said. "But no more. The manager is a bad person. I prefer to stay in Bata. I'm lucky to have work."

"We want to tour the GenSys facility," Jack said. "Do you think we'll have any trouble?"

"They don't expect you?" Arturo asked with bewilderment.

"Nope," Jack said. "It's a surprise visit."

"Then you may have trouble," Arturo said. "I don't think they like visitors. When they repaired the only road to Cogo, they built a gate. It's manned twenty-four hours a day by soldiers."

"Uh-oh!" Jack said. "That doesn't sound good." He'd not expected restricted access to the town and had counted on being able to drive in directly. Where he expected to have trouble was getting into the hospital or the labs.

"When Esteban called to say you were going to Cogo, I thought you'd been invited," Arturo said. "I didn't think to mention the gate."

"I understand," Jack said. "It's not your fault. Tell me, do you think the soldiers would take money to let us in?"

Arturo flashed a glance in Jack's direction. He shrugged. "I don't know. They're better paid than regular soldiers."

"How far is the gate from the town?" Jack

asked. "Could someone walk through the forest and just pass the gate?"

Arturo glanced at Jack again. The conversation had taken a turn in a direction he'd not expected.

"It is quite far," Arturo said evincing some unease. "Maybe five kilometers. And it is not easy to walk in the jungle. It can be dangerous."

"And there is only one road?" Jack asked.

"Only one road," Arturo agreed.

"I saw on a map that Cogo is on the water," Jack said. "What about arriving by boat?"

"I suppose," Arturo said.

"Where could someone find a boat?" Jack asked.

"In Acalayong," Arturo said. "There are many boats there. That's how to go to Gabon."

"And there would be boats to rent?" Jack asked.

"With enough money," Arturo said.

They were now passing through the center of Bata. It was composed of surprisingly broad tree-lined, litter-strewn streets. There were lots of people out and about but relatively few vehicles. The buildings were all low concrete structures.

On the south side of town, they turned off the main street and made their way along a rutted unpaved road. There were large puddles from a recent rain.

The hotel was an unimposing two-story concrete building with rusted rebars sticking out the top for potential future upward expansion. The façade had been painted blue but the color had faded to an indistinct pastel.

The moment they stopped, an army of congenial children and adults emerged from the front door. Everyone was introduced down to the youngest, shy child. It turned out that several multigenerational families lived on the first floor. The second floor was the hotel.

The rooms turned out to be tiny but clean. They were all situated on the outside of the U-shaped building. Access was by way of a veranda open to the courtyard. There was a toilet and a shower on each end of the "U."

After putting his bag in his room and appreciating the mosquito netting around the inordinately narrow bed, Jack went out onto the veranda. Laurie came out of her room. Together, they leaned on the balustrade and peered down into the courtyard. It was an interesting combination of banana trees, discarded tires, naked infants, and chickens.

"Not quite the Four Seasons," Jack said.

Laurie smiled. "It's charming. I'm happy. There's not a bug in my room. That had been my main worry."

The proprietors, Esteban's brother-in-law, Florenico, and his wife, Celestina, had prepared a huge feast. The main course was a local fish served with a turniplike plant called "malanga." For dessert there was a type of pudding along with exotic fruit. An ample supply of ice-cold Cameroonean beer helped wash it all down.

The combination of plentiful food and beer took a toll on the exhausted travelers. It wasn't long before all of them were fighting drooping eyelids. With some effort, they dragged themselves upstairs to their separate rooms, full of plans to rise early and head south in the morning.

Bertram climbed the stairs to Siegfried's office. He was exhausted. It was almost eight-thirty at night, and he'd been up since five-thirty that morning to accompany the animal handlers out to Isla Francesca to help get the mass retrieval under way. They'd worked all day and only returned to the animal center an hour earlier.

Aurielo had long since gone home, so Bertram walked directly into the manager's office. Siegfried was by the window facing the square with a glass in his hand. He was staring over at the hospital. The only light in the room was from the candle in the skull, just as it had been three nights before. Its flame flickered from the action of the overhead fan, sending shadows dancing across the stuffed animal trophies.

"Make yourself a drink," Siegfried said, without turning around. He knew it was Bertram, since they'd talked on the phone a half an hour earlier and made plans to meet.

Bertram was more of a wine drinker than an imbiber of hard alcohol, but under the circumstances he poured himself a double scotch. He sipped the fiery fluid as he joined Siegfried at the window. The lights of the hospital lab complex glowed warmly in the moist tropical night.

"Did you know Taylor Cabot was coming?" Bertram asked.

"I hadn't the faintest idea," Siegfried said.

"What did you do with him?" Bertram asked.

Siegfried gestured toward the hospital. "He's at the Inn. I had the chief surgeon move out of what we call the presidential suite. Of course, he was none too happy. You know how these egotistical doctors are. But what was I supposed to do? It's not like I'm running a hotel here."

"Do you know why Cabot came?" Bertram asked.

"Raymond said that he came specifically to evaluate the bonobo program," Siegfried said.

"I was afraid of that," Bertram said.

"It's just our luck," Siegfried complained. "The program has been running like a Swiss clock for years on end, and just when we have a problem, he shows up."

"What did you do with Raymond?" Bertram asked.

"He's over there, too," Siegfried said. "He's a pain in the ass. He wanted to be away from Cabot, but where was I supposed to put him: in my house? No thank you!"

"Has he asked about Kevin Marshall?" Bertram asked.

"Of course," Siegfried said. "As soon as he got me aside, it was his first question."

"What did you say?"

"I told the truth," Siegfried said. "I told him Kevin had gone off with the reproductive technologist and the intensive care nurse and that I had no idea where he was."

"What was his reaction?"

"He got red in the face," Siegfried said. "He wanted to know if Kevin had gone to the island. I told him that we didn't think so. Then he ordered me to find him. Can you imagine? I don't take orders from Raymond Lyons."

"So Kevin and the women have not reappeared?" Bertram asked.

"No, and not a word," Siegfried said.

"Have you made any effort to find them?" Bertram asked.

"I sent Cameron over to Acalayong to check out those cheap hotels along the waterfront, but he didn't have any luck. I'm thinking they might have gone over to Cocobeach in Gabon. That's what makes the most sense, but why they didn't tell anyone is beyond me."

"What a God-awful mess," Bertram commented.

"How did you do on the island?" Siegfried asked.

"We did well, considering how fast we had to put the operation together," Bertram said. "We got an all-terrain vehicle over there with a wagon. It was all we could think of to get that many animals back to the staging area."

"How many animals did you get?"

"Twenty-one," Bertram said. "Which is a tribute to my crew. It suggests we'll be able to finish up by tomorrow."

"So soon," Siegfried commented. "That's the first encouraging news all day."

"It's easier than we anticipated," Bertram said. "The animals seem enthralled by us. They are trusting enough to let us get close with the dart gun. It's like a turkey shoot."

"I'm glad something is going right," Siegfried said.

"The twenty-one animals we got today were all part of the splinter group living north of the Rio Diviso. It was interesting how they were living. They'd made crude huts on stilts with roofs of layered lobelia leaves."

"I don't give a damn how those animals were living," Siegfried snapped. "Don't tell me you're going soft, too."

"No, I'm not going soft," Bertram said. "But I still find it interesting. There was also evidence of campfires."

"So, it's good we're putting them in the cages," Siegfried said. "They won't be killing each other, and they won't be playing around with fire."

"That's one way to look at it," Bertram agreed.

"Any sign of Kevin and the women on the island?" Siegfried asked.

"Not in the slightest," Bertram said. "And I made it a point to look. But even in areas they would have left footprints, there was nothing. We spent part of today building a log bridge over the Rio Diviso, so tomorrow we'll start retrievals near the limestone cliffs. I'll keep my eyes open for signs they'd been there."

"I doubt you'll find anything, but until they are located we shouldn't rule out the possibility they went to the island. But I'll tell you, if they did go, and they come back here, I'll turn them over to the Equatoguinean minister of justice with the charge that they have severely compromised the GenSys operation. Of course, that means they'll be lined up out in the soccer field in front of a firing squad before they knew what hit them."

"Nothing like that could happen until Cabot and the others leave," Bertram said with alarm.

"Obviously," Siegfried said. "Besides, I mentioned the soccer field only figuratively. I'd tell the minister they'd have to be taken out of the Zone to be shot."

"Any idea when Cabot and the others will be taking the patient back to the States?"

"No one has said anything," Siegfried said. "I guess it's up to Cabot. I hope it will be tomorrow, or at the very latest, the following day."

CHAPTER 21

Jack awakened at four-thirty and was unable to get back to sleep. Ironically, the racket made by tree frogs and crickets in the courtyard banana trees was too much even for someone fully adjusted to the noisy sirens and general din of New York City.

Taking his towel and his soap, Jack stepped out on the veranda and started for the shower. Midway, he bumped into Laurie on her way back.

"What are you doing up?" Jack asked. It was still pitch dark outside.

"We went to bed around eight," Laurie said. "Eight hours: that's a reasonable night's sleep for me."

"You're right," Jack said. He'd forgotten how early it was when they'd all collapsed.

"I'll go down into the kitchen area and see if I can find any coffee," Laurie said.

"I'll be right down," Jack said.

By the time Jack got downstairs to the dining room, he was surprised to find the rest of his group already having breakfast. Jack got a cup of coffee and some bread and sat down between Warren and Esteban.

"Arturo mentioned to me that he thought you were crazy to go to Cogo without an invitation," Esteban said.

With his mouth full, all Jack could do was nod.

"He told me you won't get in," Esteban said.

"We'll see," Jack said after swallowing. "I've come this far, so I'm not going to turn back without making an effort."

"At least the road is good, thanks to Gen-Sys," Esteban said.

"Worst case, we've had an interesting drive," Jack said.

An hour later, everyone met again in the dining room. Jack reminded the others that going to Cogo wasn't a command performance, and that those people who preferred to stay in Bata should do so. He said that he'd been told it might take four hours each way.

"You think you can make out on your own?" Esteban asked.

"Absolutely," Jack said. "It's not as if we'll be getting lost. The map indicates only one main road heading south. Even I can handle that."

"Then I think I'll stay," Esteban said. "I have more family I'd like to see."

By the time they were on the road with Warren in the front passenger seat and the two women in the middle seat, the eastern sky was just beginning to show a faint glow of dawn. As they drove south they were shocked at how many people were walking along the road on their way into the city. There were mostly women and children and most of the women were carrying large bundles on their heads.

"They don't seem to have much, but they appear happy," Warren commented. Many of the children stopped to wave at the passing van. Warren waved back.

The outskirts of Bata dragged by. The cement buildings eventually changed to simple whitewashed mud brick structures with thatched roofs. Reed mats formed corrals for goats.

Once completely out of Bata, they began to see stretches of incredibly lush jungle.

Traffic was almost nonexistent save for occasional large trucks going in the opposite direction. As the trucks went by, the wind jostled the van.

"Man, those truckers move," Warren commented.

Fifteen miles south of Bata, Warren got out the map. There was one fork and one turn in the road that they had to navigate appropriately or lose considerable time. Signs were almost nonexistent.

When the sun came up, they all donned their sunglasses. The scenery became monotonous, uninterrupted jungle except for occasional tiny clusters of thatched huts. Almost two hours after they'd left Bata, they turned onto the road that led to Cogo.

"This is a much better road," Warren commented as Jack accelerated up to cruising speed.

"It looks new," Jack said. The previous road had been reasonably smooth, although its surface appeared like a patchwork quilt from all the separate repairs.

They were now heading southeast away from the coast and into considerably denser jungle. They also began to climb. In the distance they could see low, jungle-covered mountains.

Seemingly out of nowhere came a violent thunderstorm. Just prior to its arrival the sky became a swirling mass of dark clouds. Day turned to night in the space of several minutes. Once the rain started, it came down in sheets, and the van's old, ragged windshield wipers could not keep up with the downpour. Jack had to slow to less than twenty miles an hour.

Fifteen minutes later, the sun poked out between massive clouds, turning the road into a ribbon of rising steam. On a straight stretch, a group of baboons crossing the road looked as if they were walking on a cloud.

After passing through the mountains, the road turned back to the southeast. Warren consulted the map and told everyone they were within twenty miles of their destination.

Rounding another turn, they all saw what looked like a white building in the middle of the road.

"What the hell's this?" Warren said. "We're not there yet, no way."

"I think it's a gate," Jack said. "I was told about this only last night. Keep your fingers crossed. We might have to switch to plan B."

As they got closer, they could see that on either side of the central structure were enormous white, lattice-work fences. They were on a roller mechanism so they could be drawn out of the way to permit vehicles to pass.

Jack braked and brought the van to a stop about twenty feet from the fence. Out of the two-story gate house stepped three soldiers dressed similarly to those who'd been guarding the private jet at the airport. Like the soldiers at the airport, these men were carrying assault rifles, only these men were holding their guns waist high, aimed at the van.

"I don't like this," Warren said. "These guys look like kids."

"Stay cool," Jack said. He rolled his window down. "Hi, guys. Nice day, huh?"

The soldiers didn't move. Their blank expressions didn't change.

Jack was about to ask them kindly to open the gate, when a fourth man stepped out into the sunlight. To Jack's surprise, this man was pulling on a black suit jacket over a white shirt and tie. In the middle of the steaming jungle it was absurd. The other surprising thing was that the man wasn't black. He was Arab.

"Can I help you?" the Arab asked. His tone was not friendly.

"I hope so," Jack said. "We're here to visit Cogo."

The Arab glanced at the windshield of the vehicle, presumably looking for some identification. Not seeing it, he asked Jack if he had a pass.

"No pass," Jack admitted. "We're just a couple of doctors interested in the work that's going on here."

"What is your name?" the Arab asked.

"Dr. Jack Stapleton. I've come all the way from New York City."

"Just a minute," the Arab said before disappearing back into the gate house.

"This doesn't look good," Jack said to Warren out of the corner of his mouth. He smiled at the soldiers. "How much should I offer him? I'm not good at this bribing stuff."

"Money must mean a lot more here than it does in New York," Warren said. "Why don't you overwhelm him with a hundred dollars. I mean, if it's worth it to you."

Jack mentally converted a hundred dollars into French francs, then extracted the bills from his money belt. A few minutes later, the Arab returned.

"The manager says that he does not know

you and that you are not welcome," the Arab said.

"Shucks," Jack said. Then he extended his left hand with the French francs casually stuck between his index finger and his ring finger. "We sure do appreciate your help."

The Arab eyed the money for a moment before reaching out and taking it. It disappeared into his pocket in the blink of an eye.

Jack stared at him for a moment, but the man didn't move. Jack found it difficult to read his expression because the man's mustache obscured his mouth.

Jack turned to Warren. "Didn't I give him enough?"

Warren shook his head. "I don't think it's going to happen."

"You mean he just took my money and that's that?" Jack asked.

"Be my guess," Warren said.

Jack turned his attention back to the man in the black suit. Jack estimated he was about a hundred and fifty pounds, definitely on the thin side. For a moment Jack entertained the idea of getting out of the car and asking for his money back, but a glance at the soldiers made him think otherwise.

With a sigh of resignation Jack did a three-point turn and headed back the way they'd come.

"Phew!" Laurie said from the backseat. "I

did not like that one bit."

"You didn't like it?" Jack questioned. "Now I'm pissed."

"What's plan B?" Warren asked.

Jack explained about his idea of approaching Cogo by boat from Acalayong. He had Warren look at the map. Given how long it had taken them to get where they were, he asked Warren to estimate how long it would take to get to Acalayong.

"I'd say three hours," Warren said. "As long as the road stays good. The problem is we have to backtrack quite a way before heading south."

Jack glanced at his watch. It was almost nine a.m. "That means we'd get there about noon. I'd judged we could get from Acalayong to Cogo in an hour, even in the world's slowest boat. Say we stay in Cogo for a couple hours. I think we'd still get back at a reasonable hour. What do you guys say?"

"I'm cool," Warren said.

Jack looked in the rearview mirror. "I could take you ladies back to Bata and come back tomorrow."

"My only reservation about any of us going is those soldiers with the assault rifles," Laurie said.

"I don't think that's a problem," Jack said. "If they have soldiers at the gate then they don't need them in the town. Of course there's always the chance they patrol the waterfront, which would mean I'd be forced to use plan C."

"What's plan C?" Warren asked.

"I don't know," Jack said. "I haven't come up with it yet."

"What about you, Natalie?" Jack asked.

"I'm finding it all interesting," Natalie said. "I'll go along with the crowd."

It took almost an hour to get to the point where a decision had to be made. Jack pulled to the side of the road.

"What's it going to be, gang?" he asked. He wanted to be absolutely sure. "Back to Bata or on to Acalayong?"

"I think I'll be more worried if you go by yourself," Laurie said. "Count me in."

"Natalie?" Jack said. "Don't be influenced by these other crazies. What do you want to do?"

"I'll go," Natalie said.

"Okay," Jack said. He put the car in gear and turned left toward Acalayong.

Siegfried got up from his desk with his coffee mug in hand and walked to the window overlooking the square. He was mystified. The Cogo operation had been up and running for six years and never had they had someone come to the gate house and request entrance. Equatorial Guinea was not a place people visited casually.

Siegfried took a swig of his coffee and wondered if there could be any connection between this abnormal event and the arrival of Taylor Cabot, the CEO of GenSys. Both were unanticipated, and both were particularly unwelcome since they came just when there was a major problem with the bonobo project. Until that unfortunate situation was taken care of, Siegfried didn't want any stray people around, and he put the CEO in that category.

Aurielo poked his head in the door and said that Dr. Raymond Lyons was there and wished to see him.

Siegfried rolled his eyes. He didn't want Raymond around, either. "Send him in," Siegfried said reluctantly.

Raymond came into the room, looking as tanned and healthy as ever. Siegfried envied the man's aristocratic appearance, and the fact that he had two good arms.

"Have you located Kevin Marshall yet?" Raymond demanded.

"No, we haven't," Siegfried said. He took immediate offense at Raymond's tone.

"I understand it's been forty-eight hours since he's been seen," Raymond said. "I want him found!"

"Sit down, Doctor!" Siegfried said sharply.

Raymond hesitated. He didn't know whether to get angry or be intimidated by the manager's sudden aggressiveness.

"I said sit!" Siegfried said.

Raymond sat. The white hunter with his

horrid scar and limp arm could be imposing, particularly surrounded by evidence of his extensive kills.

"Let us clear up a point involving the chain of command," Siegfried said. "I do not take orders from you. In fact, when you are here as a guest, you take orders from me. Is that understood?"

Raymond opened his mouth to protest but thought better of it. He knew Siegfried was technically correct.

"And while we are talking so directly," Siegfried added, "where is my retrieval bonus? In the past, I've always gotten it when the patient left the Zone on his way back to the States."

"That's true," Raymond said tautly. "But there have been major expenses. Money is coming in shortly from new clients. You'll be paid as soon as it comes in."

"I don't want you to think you can give me the runaround," Siegfried warned.

"Of course not," Raymond blurted out.

"And one other thing," Siegfried said. "Isn't there some way you can hasten the CEO's departure? His presence here in Cogo is disrupting. Can't you use the patient's needs in some way?"

"I don't see how," Raymond said. "He's been informed the patient is capable of traveling. What more can I say?"

"Think of something," Siegfried said.

"I'll try," Raymond said. "Meanwhile,

please locate Kevin Marshall. His disappearance concerns me. I'm afraid he might do something rash."

"We believe he went to Cocobeach in Gabon," Siegfried said. He was gratified with the appropriate subservience in Raymond's voice.

"You're sure he didn't go to the island?" Raymond asked.

"We can't be totally sure," Siegfried admitted. "But we don't think so. Even if he did, he wouldn't be apt to stay there. He would have been back by now. It's been forty-eight hours."

Raymond stood up and sighed. "I wish he would turn up. Worrying about him is driving me up the wall, especially with Taylor Cabot here. It's just something else in a long string of problems going on in New York that have threatened the program and made my life miserable."

"We'll continue to search," Siegfried assured him. He tried to sound sympathetic, but in actuality, he was wondering how Raymond was going to respond when he heard the bonobos were being rounded up to be brought into the animal center. All other problems paled in the face of the animals killing each other.

"I'll try to think of something to say to Taylor Cabot," Raymond said as he started for the door. "If you could, I'd appreciate being informed the moment you hear about Kevin Marshall."

"Certainly," Siegfried said obligingly. He watched with satisfaction as the previously proud doctor beat a meek retreat. Just as Raymond disappeared from view, Siegfried remembered that Raymond was from New York.

Siegfried dashed to his door, catching Raymond on his way down the stairs.

"Doctor," Siegfried called out with false deference.

Raymond paused and looked back.

"Do you happen to know a doctor by the name of Jack Stapleton?"

The blood drained from Raymond's face.

This reaction was not lost on Siegfried. "I think you'd better come back into my office," the manager said.

Siegfried closed the door behind Raymond who immediately wanted to know how in the world the name "Jack Stapleton" had come up.

Siegfried walked around his desk and sat down. He gestured toward a chair for Raymond. Siegfried was not happy. He'd briefly thought of relating the unexpected request for a site visit by strange doctors to Taylor Cabot. He'd not thought of relating it to Raymond.

"Just before you arrived I got an unusual call from our gate house," Siegfried said. "The Moroccan guard told me that there was a van full of people who wanted to tour the facility. We've never had uninvited visitors before. The van was driven by Dr. Jack Stapleton of New York City."

Raymond wiped the perspiration that had appeared on his forehead. Then he ran both hands simultaneously through his hair. He kept telling himself that this couldn't be happening since Vinnie Dominick was supposed to have taken care of Jack Stapleton and Laurie Montgomery. Raymond hadn't called to find out what had happened to the two; he didn't really want to know the details. For twenty thousand dollars, details weren't something he should have to worry about — or so he thought. If pressed, he would have guessed that Stapleton and Montgomery were somewhere floating in the Atlantic Ocean about now.

"Your reaction to this is starting to concern me," Siegfried said.

"You didn't let Stapleton and his friends in?" Raymond asked.

"No, of course not," Siegfried said.

"Maybe you should have," Raymond said. "Then we could have dealt with them. Jack Stapleton is a very big danger to the program. I mean, is there a way here in the Zone to take care of such people?"

"There is," Siegfried said. "We just turn them over to the Equatoguinean minister of justice or the minister of defense along with a sizable bonus. Punishment is both discreet and very rapid. The government is eager to ensure that nothing threatens the goose that lays the golden egg. All we need to say is that they are seriously interfering with GenSys operations."

"Then if they come back, I think you should let them in," Raymond said.

"Perhaps you should tell me why," Siegfried said.

"Do you remember Carlo Franconi?" Raymond asked.

"Carlo Franconi the patient?" Siegfried asked.

Raymond nodded.

"Of course," Siegfried said.

"Well, it started with him," Raymond said as he began the complicated story.

"You think it is safe?" Laurie asked. She was looking at a huge hollowed-out log canoe with a thatched canopy that was pulled halfway up the beach. On the back was a sizable, beat-up outboard motor. It was leaking fuel as evidenced by an opalescent scum that ringed the stern.

"Reportedly it goes all the way to Gabon twice a day," Jack said. "That's farther than Cogo."

"How much rent did you have to pay?" Natalie asked. It had taken Jack a half hour of negotiations to get it.

"A bit more than I expected," Jack said. "Apparently, some people rented one a couple of days ago, and it hasn't been seen since. That episode has driven the rental price up, I'm afraid."

"More than a hundred or less?" Warren asked. He, too, wasn't impressed with the craft's apparent seaworthiness. "Because if it was more than a C note you got took."

"Well, let's not quibble," Jack said. "In fact, let's get the show on the road unless you guys want to back out."

There was a moment of silence while the group eyed each other.

"I'm not a great swimmer," Warren admitted.

"I can assure you that we are not planning on going into the water," Jack said.

"All right," Warren said. "Let's go."

"You ladies concur?" Jack asked.

Both Laurie and Natalie nodded without a lot of enthusiasm. At the moment, the noonday sun was enervating. Despite being on the shore of the estuary, there was not a breath of air.

With the women positioned in the stern to help lift the bow, Jack and Warren pushed the heavy pirogue off the shore and jumped in one after the other. Everyone helped paddle out about fifty feet. Jack attended to the motor, compressing the small hand pump on top of the red fuel tank. He'd had a boat as a child on a lake in the Midwest and had a lot of experience fussing with an outboard.

"This canoe is a lot more stable than it looks," Laurie said. Even with Jack moving around in the stern it was barely rocking.

"And no leaks," Natalie said. "That was my concern."

Warren stayed silent. He had a white knuckle grip on the gunwale.

To Jack's surprise, the engine started after only two pulls. A moment later, they were off, motoring almost due east. After the oppressive heat the breeze felt good.

The drive to Acalayong had been accomplished quicker than they'd anticipated, even though the road deteriorated in comparison to the road north of the Cogo turnoff. There was no traffic save for an occasional northward-bound van inconceivably packed with passengers. Even the luggage racks on the tops had two or three people holding on for dear life.

Acalayong had brought smiles to everyone's face. It was indicated as a city on the map but turned out to consist of no more than a handful of tawdry concrete shops, bars, and a few hotels. There was a cement-block police post with several men in dirty uniforms sprawled in rattan chairs in the shade of the porch. They'd eyed Jack and the others with soporific disdain as the van had passed by.

Although they had found the town comically honky-tonk and litter strewn, they'd been able to get something to eat and drink as well as procure the boat. With some unease, they'd parked the van in sight of the police station, hoping it would be there on their return.

"How long did you estimate it would take us?" Laurie shouted over the noise of the outboard. It was particularly loud because a portion of its cowling was missing.

"An hour," Jack yelled back. "But the boat owner told me it would be more like twenty minutes. It's apparently just around the headland directly ahead."

At that moment, they were crossing the two-mile-wide mouth of Rio Congue. The jungle-covered shorelines were hazy with mist. Thunderheads loomed above; two thunderstorms had hit while they'd been in the van.

"I hope we don't get caught out here in the rain," Natalie said. But Mother Nature ignored her wish. Less than five minutes later, it was pouring so hard that some of the huge drops splashed river water into the boat. Jack slowed the engine and allowed the boat to guide itself, while he joined the others under the thatched canopy. To everyone's pleasant surprise, they stayed completely dry.

As soon as they rounded the headland, they saw Cogo's pier. Constructed of heavy pressure-treated timber, it was a far cry from the rickety docks at Acalayong. As they got closer, they could see there was a floating portion off the tip.

The first view of Cogo impressed everyone. In contrast with the dilapidated and haphazardly constructed buildings with flat, corrugated metal roofs endemic to Bata and all of Acalayong, Cogo was comprised of attractive, tiled, whitewashed structures reflecting a rich colonial ambiance. To the left and almost hidden by the jungle was a modern power station. Its presence was obvious only because of its improbably tall smokestack.

Jack cut the engine way back as the town approached so they could hear each other speak. Tied along the dock were several pirogues similar to the one they were in, though these others were piled high with fish netting.

"I'm glad to see other boats," Jack said. "I was afraid our canoe would stand out like a sore thumb."

"Do you think that large, modern building is the hospital?" Laurie said while pointing.

Jack followed her line of sight. "Yup, at least according to Arturo, and he should know. He was part of the initial building crew out here."

"I suppose that's our destination," Laurie said.

"I'd guess," Jack said. "At least initially. Arturo said the animal complex is a few miles away in the jungle. We might try to figure out a way to get out there."

"The town is bigger than I expected," Warren said.

"I was told it was an abandoned Spanish colonial town," Jack explained. "Not all of it has been renovated, but from here it sure looks like it has."

"What did the Spanish do here?" Natalie asked. "It's nothing but jungle."

"They grew coffee and cocoa," Jack said. "At least that's my understanding. Of course, I don't have any idea where they grew it."

"Uh-oh, I see a soldier," Laurie said.

"I see him, too," Jack said. His eyes had been searching along the waterfront as they came closer.

The soldier was dressed in the same jungle camouflage fatigues and red beret as the ones at the gate. He was aimlessly pacing a cobblestone square immediately at the base of the pier with an assault rifle slung over his shoulder.

"Does that mean we switch to plan C?" Warren questioned teasingly.

"Not yet," Jack said. "Obviously, he's where he is to interdict people coming off the pier. But look at that Chickee Hut built on the beach. If we got in there, we'd be home free."

"We can't just run the canoe up onto the beach," Laurie said. "He'll see that as well."

"Look how high that pier is," Jack said. "What if we were to slip underneath, beach the canoe there and then walk to the Chickee

Hut? What do you think?"

"Sounds cool," Warren said. "But this boat is not going to fit under that pier, no way."

Jack stood up and made his way over to one of the poles that supported the thatched roof. It disappeared into a hole in the gunwale. Grasping it with both hands, he pulled it up. "How convenient!" he said. "This canoe is a convertible."

A few minutes later, they had all the poles out, and the thatched roof had been converted to a pile of sticks and dried leaves. They distributed it along both sides under the benches.

"The owner's not going to be happy about this," Natalie commented.

Jack angled the boat so that the pier shielded them as much as possible from the line of sight from the square. Jack cut the engine just at the moment they glided into the shade under the pier. Grasping the timbers they guided the boat toward shore, being careful to duck under crossbeams.

The boat scraped up the shady patch of shore and came to a stop.

"So far so good," Jack said. He encouraged the women and Warren to get out. Then, with Warren pulling and Jack paddling, they got the boat high on the beach.

Jack got out and pointed to a stone wall that ran perpendicular to the base of the pier before disappearing into the gently rising sand of the beach. "Let's hug the wall. When we clear it, head for the Chickee Bar."

A few minutes later, they were in the bar. The soldier had not paid them any heed. Either he didn't see them or he didn't care.

The bar was deserted except for a black man carefully cutting up lemons and limes. Jack motioned toward the stools and suggested a celebratory drink. Everyone was happy to comply. It had been hot in the canoe after the sun came out and especially after the canopy had come down.

The bartender came over immediately. His name tag identified him as Saturnino. In contradiction to his name, he was a jovial fellow. He was wearing a wild print shirt and a pillbox hat similar to the one Arturo had on when he picked them up at the airport the previous afternoon.

Following Natalie's lead, everyone had Coke with a slice of lemon.

"Not much business today," Jack commented to Saturnino.

"Not until after five," the bartender said. "Then we are very busy."

"We're new here," Jack said. "What money do we use?"

"You can sign," Saturnino.

Jack looked at Laurie for permission. Laurie shook her head. "We'd rather pay," he said. "Are dollars okay?"

"What you like," Saturnino said. "Dollars or CFA. It makes no difference."

"Where is the hospital?" Jack asked.

Saturnino pointed over his shoulder. "Up the street until you get to the main square. It is the big building on the left."

"What do they do there?" Jack asked.

Saturnino looked at Jack as if he were crazy. "They take care of people."

"Do people come from America just to go to the hospital?" Jack asked.

Saturnino shrugged. "I don't know about that," he said. He took the bills Jack had put on the bar and turned to the cash register.

"Nice try," Laurie whispered.

"It would have been too easy," Jack agreed.

Refreshed after their cold drinks, the group headed out into the sunlight. They passed within fifty feet of the soldier who continued to ignore them. After a short walk up a hot cobblestone street, they came to a small green surrounded by plantation-style homes.

"It reminds me of some of the Caribbean Islands," Laurie said.

Five minutes later, they entered the tree-lined town square. The group of soldiers lolling in front of the town hall diagonally across from where they were standing spoiled the otherwise idyllic tableau.

"Whoa," Jack said. "There's a whole battalion."

"I thought you said that if there were soldiers at the gate they wouldn't have to have any in the town," Laurie said.

"I've been proved wrong," Jack acknowledged. "But there's no need to go over and announce ourselves. This is the hospital lab complex in front of us."

From the corner of the square, the building appeared to take up most of a Cogo city block. There was an entrance facing the square, but there was also one down the side street to their left. To avoid remaining in view of the lounging soldiers, they went to the side entrance.

"What are you going to say if we're questioned?" Laurie asked with some concern. "And walking into a hospital, you know it's bound to happen."

"I'm going to improvise," Jack said. He yanked the door open and ushered his friends in with an exaggerated bow.

Laurie glanced at Natalie and Warren and rolled her eyes. At least Jack could still be charming even when he was most exasperating.

After entering the building, everyone shivered with delight. Never had air conditioning felt quite so good. The room they found themselves in appeared to be a lounge, complete with wall-to-wall carpeting, club chairs, and couches. A large bookcase lined one wall. Some of the shelving was on an angle to display an impressive collection of periodicals from *Time* to *National Geographic*. There were about a half dozen people sitting in the room, all of them reading.

In the back wall at desk height was an opening fronted with sliding glass panels. Behind the glass a black woman in a blue uniform dress was sitting at a desk. To the right of the opening was a hall with several elevators.

"Could all these people be patients?" Laurie asked.

"Good question," Jack said. "Somehow, I don't think so. They all look too healthy and too comfortable. Let's talk to the secretary or whoever she is."

Warren and Natalie were intimidated by the hospital environment. They silently followed after Jack and Laurie.

Jack rapped softly on the glass. The woman looked up from her work and slid the glass open.

"Sorry," she said. "I didn't see you arrive. Are you checking in?"

"No," Jack said. "All my bodily functions are working fine at the moment."

"Excuse me?" the woman questioned.

"We're here to see the hospital, not use its services," Jack said. "We're doctors."

"This isn't the hospital," the woman said. "This is the Inn. You can either go out and come in the front of the building or follow the hall to your right. The hospital is beyond the double doors."

"Thank you," Jack said.

"My pleasure," the woman said. She leaned

forward and watched as Jack and the others disappeared around the corner. Perplexed, the woman sat back and picked up her phone.

Jack led the others through the double doors. Immediately, the surroundings looked more familiar. The floors were vinyl and the walls were painted a soothing hospital green. A faint antiseptic smell was detectable.

"This is more like it," Jack said.

They entered a room whose windows fronted on the square. Between the windows were a large pair of doors leading to the outside. There were a few couches and chairs on area rugs forming distinct conversational groupings, but it was nothing like the lounge they'd initially entered. But like the lounge, this space had a glass-fronted information cubbyhole.

Jack again knocked on the glass. Another woman slid open the glass partition. She was equally as cordial.

"We have a question," Jack said. "We're doctors, and we'd like to know if there are currently any transplant patients in the hospital?"

"Yes, of course, there's one," the woman said with a confused look on her face. "Horace Winchester. He's in 302 and ready to be discharged."

"How convenient," Jack said. "What organ was transplanted?"

"His liver," the woman said. "Are you all

from the Pittsburgh group?"

"No, we're part of the New York group," Jack said.

"I see," the woman said, although her expression suggested she didn't see at all.

"Thank you," Jack said to the woman as he herded the group toward the elevators that could be seen to the right.

"Luck is finally going our way," Jack said excitedly. "This is going to make it easy. Maybe all we have to do is get a look at the chart."

"As if that's going to be easy," Laurie commented.

"True," Jack said after a moment's thought. "So maybe we should just drop in on Horace and get the lowdown from the horse's mouth."

"Hey, man," Warren said, pulling Jack to a stop. "Maybe Natalie and I should wait down here. We're not used to being in a hospital, you know what I'm saying?"

"I suppose," Jack said reluctantly. "But I kind of think its important for us to stick together in case we have to mosey down to the canoe sooner than we'd like. You know what I'm saying?"

Warren nodded and Jack pressed the elevator call button.

Cameron McIvers was accustomed to false alarms. After all, most of the time he or the

Office of Security was called, it was a false alarm. Accordingly, as he entered the front door of the Inn, he was not concerned. But it was his job or one of his deputies' to check out all potential problems.

As he crossed to the information desk, Cameron noted that the lounge was as subdued as usual. The calm scene bolstered his suspicions that this call would be like all the others.

Cameron tapped on the glass, and it was slid open.

"Miss Williams," Cameron said, while touching the brim of his hat in a form of salute. Cameron and the rest of the security force wore khaki uniforms with an Aussi hat when on duty. There was also a leather belt with shoulder strap. A holstered Beretta was attached to the belt on the right side and a hand-held two-way radio on the left side.

"They went that way," Corrina Williams said excitedly. She lifted herself out of her chair to point around the corner.

"Calm down," Cameron said gently. "Who exactly are you talking about?"

"They didn't give any names," Corrina said. "There were four of them. Only one spoke. He said he was a doctor."

"Hmmm," Cameron voiced. "And you've never seen them before?"

"Never," Corrina said anxiously. "They took me by surprise. I thought maybe they were to stay at the Inn since we had new arrivals yesterday. But they said they had come to see the hospital. When I told them how to get there, they left straightaway."

"Were they black or white?" Cameron asked. Maybe this wouldn't be a typical false alarm after all.

"Half and half," Corrina said. "Two blacks, two whites. But I could tell from the way they were dressed they were all American."

"I see," Cameron said, while he stroked his beard and pondered the unlikely possibility of any of the Zone's American workers coming into the Inn to say they wanted to see the hospital.

"The one who was talking also said something strange about his bodily functions working fine," Corrina said. "I didn't know how to respond."

"Hmmm," Cameron repeated. "Could I use your phone?"

"Of course," Corrina said. She pulled the phone over from the side of her desk and faced it out toward Cameron.

Cameron punched the manager's direct line. Siegfried answered immediately.

"I'm here at the Inn," Cameron explained. "I thought you should be apprised of a curious story. Four strange doctors presented themselves here to Miss Williams with the wish to see the hospital."

Siegfried's response was an angry tirade that

forced Cameron to hold the receiver away from his ear. Even Corrina cringed.

Cameron handed the phone back to the receptionist. He'd not heard every word of Siegfried's invective but the meaning was clear. Cameron was to get reinforcements over there immediately and detain the alien doctors.

Cameron unsnapped the straps over both his Beretta and the radio simultaneously. He pulled the radio free and made an emergency call to base while he started for the hospital.

Room 302 turned out to be in the front of the building with a fine view out over the square looking east. Jack and the others had found the room without difficulty. No one had challenged them. In fact, they hadn't seen a person as they'd made their way from the elevator to the room's open door.

Jack had knocked but it was obvious the room was momentarily empty although there'd been plenty of evidence the room was occupied. A television with a built-in VCR was on, and it was showing an old Paul Newman movie. The hospital bed was moderately disheveled. An open, half-packed suitcase was poised on a luggage stand.

The mystery was solved when Laurie noticed the sounds of a shower behind the closed bathroom door.

When the water stopped running, Jack had

knocked, but it wasn't until almost ten minutes later that Horace Winchester appeared.

The patient was in his mid-fifties and corpulent. But he looked happy and healthy. He cinched up the tie on his bathrobe and padded over to the club chair by the bed. He sat down with a satisfied sigh.

"What's the occasion?" he asked, smiling at his guests. "This is more company than I've had the whole time I've been here."

"How are you feeling?" Jack asked. He grabbed a straight-back chair and sat down directly in front of Horace. Warren and Natalie lurked just outside the door. They felt reluctant to enter the room. Laurie went to the window. After seeing the group of soldiers, she'd become progressively anxious. She was eager to make the visit short and get back to the boat.

"I'm feeling just great," Horace said. "It's a miracle. I came here at death's door and as yellow as a canary. Look at me now! I'm ready for thirty-six holes of golf at one of my resorts. Hey, any of you people are invited to any of my places for as long as you want to stay, and it will all be on the house. Do you like to ski?"

"I do," Jack said. "But I'd rather talk about your case. I understand you had a liver transplant here. I'd like to ask where the liver came from?"

A half smile puckered Horace's face as he regarded Jack out of the corner of his eye. "Is this some kind of test?" he asked. "Because if it is, it's not necessary. I'm not going to be telling anyone. I couldn't be more grateful. In fact, as soon as I can, I'm going to have another double made."

"Exactly what do you mean by a 'double'?" Jack asked.

"Are you people part of the Pittsburgh team?" Horace asked. He looked over at Laurie.

"No, we're part of the New York team," Jack said. "And we're fascinated by your case. We're glad you are doing so well, and we're here to learn." Jack smiled and spread his hands palm up. "We're all ears. Why don't you start from the beginning?"

"You mean how I got sick?" Horace asked. He was plainly confused.

"No, how you arranged to have your transplant here in Africa," Jack said. "And I'd like to know what you mean by a double. Did you by any chance get a liver taken from some kind of ape?"

Horace gave a little nervous laugh and shook his head. "What's going on here?" he questioned. He glanced again at Laurie and then at Natalie and Warren who were still standing in the doorway.

"Uh-oh!" Laurie suddenly voiced. She was staring out the window. "There's a bunch of soldiers running this way across the square."

Warren quickly crossed the room and

looked out. "Shit, man. They mean business!"

Jack stood up, reached out, and grasped Horace by the shoulders. He leaned his face close to the patient's. "You are really going to disappoint me if you don't answer my questions, and I do the strangest things when I'm disappointed. What kind of animal was it, a chimpanzee?"

"They're coming to the hospital," Warren yelled. "And they all have AK-47's."

"Come on!" Jack urged Horace while giving the man a little shake. "Talk to me. Was it a chimpanzee?" Jack tightened his hold on the man.

"It was a bonobo," Horace squeaked. He was terrified.

"Is that a type of ape?" Jack demanded.

"Yes," Horace managed.

"Come on, man!" Warren encouraged. He was back at the door. "We got to get our asses out of here."

"And what did you mean by a double?" Jack asked.

Laurie grabbed Jack's arm. "There's no time. Those soldiers will be up here in a minute."

Reluctantly, Jack let go of Horace and allowed himself to be dragged to the door. "Damn, I was so close," he complained.

Warren was waving frantically for them to follow him and Natalie down the central corridor toward the back of the building, when the elevator door opened. Out stepped Cameron with his Beretta clutched in his hand.

"Everyone halt!" Cameron shouted the moment he saw the strangers. He grabbed his gun in both hands and trained it on Warren and Natalie. Then he swept it around to aim at Jack and Laurie. For Cameron, the problem was that his adversaries were on either side of him. When he was looking at one group, he couldn't see the other.

"Hands on top of your heads," Cameron commanded. He motioned with the barrel of his gun.

Everyone complied, although every time Cameron swung the gun toward Jack and Laurie, Warren approached another step toward him.

"No one is going to get hurt," Cameron said as he brought the gun back toward Warren.

Warren had gotten within range of a kick, and with lightning speed his foot lashed out and connected with Cameron's hands. The gun bounced off the ceiling.

Before Cameron could react to his gun's sudden disappearance, Warren closed in on him and hit him twice, once in the lower abdomen and then on the tip of the nose. Cameron collapsed backwards in a heap on the floor.

"I'm glad you're on my team for this run," Jack said.

"We got to get ourselves back to that boat!" Warren blurted without humor.

"I'm open to suggestions," Jack said.

Cameron moaned and pushed himself over onto his stomach.

Warren looked both ways down the hall. A few minutes earlier, he'd thought of running down the main corridor toward the rear, but that was no longer a reasonable alternative. Halfway down the corridor he could see some nurses gathering and pointing in his direction.

Across from the elevators at eye-level was a sign in the form of an arrow that pointed down the hall beyond Horace's room. It said: OR

Knowing they had little time to debate, Warren motioned in the direction of the arrow. "That way!" he barked.

"The operating room?" Jack questioned. "Why?"

"Because they won't expect it," Warren said. He grabbed a stunned Natalie by the hand and propelled her into a jog.

Jack and Laurie followed. They passed Horace's room but the chubby man had locked himself in his bathroom.

The operating suite was set off from the rest of the hospital by the usual swinging doors. Warren hit them and went through with a straight arm like a football running back. Jack and Laurie were right behind.

There were no cases under way nor were

there any patients in the recovery room. There weren't even any lights on except for those in a supply room halfway down the hall. The supply room's door was ajar, emitting a faint glow.

Hearing the repetitive thumps on the operating room doors, a woman appeared from the supply room. She was dressed in a scrub suit with a disposable cap. She caught her breath as she saw the four figures hurtling in her direction.

"Hey, you can't come in here in street clothes," she yelled as soon as she'd recovered from her initial shock. But Warren and the others had already passed. Perplexed, she watched the intruders run all the way down the rest of the corridor to disappear through the doors leading to the lab.

Turning back into the supply room, she went for the wall phone.

Warren skidded to a stop where the corridor formed a "T." He looked in either direction. To the left at the far end was a red wall light indicating a fire alarm. Above it was an exit sign.

"Hold up!" Jack said, as Warren was preparing to dash down to what he imagined would be a stairwell.

"What's the matter, man?" Warren questioned anxiously.

"This looks like a laboratory," Jack said. He stepped over to a glazed door and looked inside. He was immediately impressed. Although they were in the middle of Africa, it was the most modern lab he'd ever seen. Every piece of equipment looked brand new.

"Come on!" Laurie snapped. "There's no time for curiosity. We've got to get out of here."

"It's true, man," Warren said. "Especially after hitting that security type back there, we've got to make tracks."

"You guys go," Jack said distractedly. "I'll meet you at the boat."

Warren, Laurie, and Natalie exchanged anxious glances.

Jack tried the door. It was unlocked. He opened it and walked inside.

"Oh, for crissake," Laurie complained. Jack could be so frustrating. It was one thing for him to have little concern for his own safety, but it was quite another thing for him to compromise others.

"This place is going to be crawling with security dudes and soldiers in nothing flat," Warren said.

"I know," Laurie said. "You guys go. I'll get him to come as soon as I can."

"I can't leave you," Warren said.

"Think of Natalie," Laurie said.

"Nonsense," Natalie said. "I'm no frail female. We're in this together."

"You ladies go in there and talk some sense into that man," Warren said. "I'm going to run down the hall and pull the fire alarm."

"What on earth for?" Laurie asked.

"It's an old trick I learned as a teenager," Warren said. "Whenever there's trouble cause as much chaos as you can. It gives you a chance to slip away."

"I'll take your word for it," Laurie said. She motioned for Natalie to follow and entered the lab.

They found Jack already engaged in pleasant conversation with a laboratory technician wearing a long white coat. She was a freckle-faced redhead with an amiable smile. Jack already had her laughing.

"Excuse me!" Laurie said, struggling to keep her voice down. "Jack, we have to go."

"Laurie, meet Rolanda Phieffer," Jack said. "She's originally from Heidelberg, Germany."

"Jack!" Laurie intoned through clenched teeth.

"Rolanda's been telling me something very interesting," Jack said. "She and her colleagues here are working on the genes for minor histocompatibility antigens. They're moving them from a specific chromosome in one cell and sticking them into the same location on the same chromosome in another cell."

Natalie, who'd walked over to a large picture window overlooking the square, hastily turned back into the room. "It's getting worse. An entire car load of those Arabs in black suits are arriving."

At that moment, the fire alarm in the building went off. It featured alternating sequences of three ear-splitting shrieks of a horn followed by a disembodied voice: "Fire in the laboratory! Please proceed immediately to stairwells for evacuation! Do not use the elevators!"

"Oh, my word!" Rolanda said. She looked around quickly to see what she should take with her.

Laurie grabbed Jack by both arms and shook him. "Jack, be reasonable! We have to get out of here."

"I've figured it out," Jack said with a wry smile.

"I don't give a good goddamn," Laurie spat. "Come on!"

They rushed out into the hall. Other people were appearing as well. Everyone seemed confused as they looked up and down the hall. Some were sniffing. There was animated conversation. Many people were carrying their lap-top computers.

Without rushing they moved en masse to the stairwell. Jack, Laurie, and Natalie met up with Warren who was holding the door. He'd also managed to find white coats which he distributed to the others. They all pulled them on over their clothes. Unfortunately, they were the only ones wearing shorts.

"They have created some kind of chimera with these apes called bonobos," Jack said

619

excitedly. "That's the explanation. No wonder the DNA tests were so screwy."

"What's he carrying on about now?" Warren asked with irritation.

"Don't ask," Laurie said. "It will only encourage him."

"Whose idea was it to pull the fire alarm?" Jack asked. "It was brilliant."

"Warren's," Laurie said. "At least one of us is thinking."

The stairwell opened up into a parking lot on the north side. People were milling about, looking back at the building, and talking in small groups. It was deathly hot since the sun was out and the parking lot was blacktop. A wailing fire siren could be heard coming from the northeast.

"What should we do?" Laurie asked. "I'm relieved we've gotten as far as we have. I didn't think it was going to be so easy to get out of the building."

"Let's walk over to the street and turn left," Jack said while pointing. "We can circle around the area to the west and get back to the waterfront."

"Where are all those soldiers?" Laurie asked.

"And the Arabs?" Natalie added.

"I'd guess they're looking for us in the hospital," Jack said.

"Let's go before all these lab people start going back into the building," Warren said.

They tried not to rush to avoid attracting any attention. As they neared the street they all glanced behind them for fear they were being watched, but no one was even looking in their direction. Everybody was captivated by the fire crew who'd arrived.

"So far so good," Jack said.

Warren was the first to reach the street. As he got a look to the west around the corner, he stopped abruptly and put his arms out to block the others. He backed up a step.

"We're not going that way," he said. "They've got a roadblock at the end of the street."

"Uh-oh," Laurie said. "Maybe they've sealed off the area."

"You remember that power station we saw?" Jack said.

Everyone nodded.

"That power has to get over here to the hospital," Jack said. "I'd bet there's a tunnel."

"Maybe," Warren said. "But the trouble is we don't know how to find it. Besides, I'm not thrilled about going back inside. Not with all those kids with AK-47's."

"Then let's try walking across the square," Jack said.

"Toward where we saw the soldiers?" Laurie questioned with dismay.

"Hey, if they're over here at the hospital, there should be no problem," Jack said.

"That's a point," Natalie agreed.

"Of course, we could always give ourselves up and say we're sorry," Jack said. "I mean, what can they do to us besides kick us the hell out. I think I've gotten what I came for, so it wouldn't bother me in the slightest."

"You're joking," Laurie said. "They're not going to accept a mere apology. Warren struck that man; we've done more than trespass."

"I'm joking to an extent," Jack agreed. "But the man was sticking a gun in our face. That's at least an explanation. Besides, we can leave a bunch of our French francs behind. Supposedly, that solves everything in this country."

"It didn't get us past the gate," Laurie reminded him.

"All right, everything but get us in here," Jack said. "But I'll be very surprised if it doesn't get us out."

"We've got to do something," Warren said. "The fire crew are already waving for the people to come back in the building. We're going to be standing out here in this god-awful heat by ourselves."

"So they are," Jack said, squinting against the sunlight. He found his sunglasses and put them on. "Let's try crossing the square before the soldiers return."

Once again, they tried to walk calmly as if they were strolling. They got almost to the grass, when they became aware of a commotion at the door into the building. They all turned to see a number of the black-suited Arabs push their way pass the lab techs who were entering.

The Arabs rushed out into the sundrenched parking lot with their neckties flapping and their eyes squinting. Each brandished an automatic pistol in his hand. Behind the Arabs came several soldiers. Out of breath, they stood in the hot sun, panting while scanning the neighborhood.

Warren froze, and the rest of the group did the same.

"I don't like this," Warren said. "The six of them have enough fire power to rob the Chase Manhattan Bank."

"They kind of remind me of the Keystone Cops," Jack said.

"I don't find anything about this comical at all," Laurie said.

"Strangely enough, I think we're going to have to walk back inside," Warren said. "With these lab coats on they're going to wonder why we're standing out here."

Before anyone could respond to Warren's suggestion Cameron came out the door accompanied by two other men. One was dressed like Cameron: clearly a member of the security force. The other was shorter with a limp right arm. He, too, was dressed in khaki but without any of the martial embellishments the other two sported.

"Uh-oh," Jack said. "I have a feeling we'll

be forced to use the apology approach after all."

Cameron was holding a blood-spotted handkerchief to his nose, but it didn't obstruct his vision. He spotted the group immediately and pointed. "That's them!" he yelled.

The Moroccans and the soldiers responded immediately by surrounding the trespassers. Every gun was pointed at the group, who raised their hands without being told.

"I wonder if they'll be impressed with my medical examiner badge?" Jack quipped.

"Don't do anything foolish!" Laurie warned.

Cameron and his companions walked over immediately. Silently, the ring around the Americans opened to allow them through. Siegfried stepped to the forefront.

"We'd like to apologize for any inconvenience," Jack began.

"Shut up!" Siegfried snapped. He walked around the group to eye them from all directions. When he got back to where he started, he asked Cameron if these were the people he'd encountered in the hospital.

"No doubt in my mind," Cameron said while glaring directly into Warren's face. "I hope you will indulge me, sir."

"Of course," Siegfried said with a slight wave of dismissal.

Without warning, Cameron punched Warren in the side of the face with a roundhouse blow. The sound was like a telephone directory falling to the floor. A plaintive whine escaped from Cameron's lips as he grabbed his hand and gritted his teeth. Warren did not move a muscle. He may not have blinked.

Cameron swore under his breath and stepped away.

"Search them," Siegfried commanded.

"We are sorry if we —" Jack began but Siegfried didn't let him finish. He slapped him with an open fist hard enough to turn Jack's head in the direction of the blow and raise a red welt on his cheek.

Cameron's deputy quickly relieved Jack and the others of their passports, wallets, money, and car keys. He gave them to Siegfried, who slowly went through them. After he looked at Jack's passport, he raised his eyes and glowered at him.

"I've been told you are a troublemaker," Siegfried said with disdain.

"I'd rather think of myself as a tenacious competitor," Jack said.

"Ah, arrogant as well," Siegfried snarled. "I hope your tenacity comes in handy once you are turned over to the Equatoguinean military."

"Perhaps we can call the American Embassy and resolve this," Jack said. "We are, after all, government employees."

Siegfried smiled, which actually only increased his scar-induced sneer. "American

Embassy?" he questioned with uncamouflaged scorn. "In Equatorial Guinea! What a joke! Unfortunately for you, it's out on the island of Bioko." He turned to Cameron. "Put them in the jail but separate the men and the women!"

Cameron snapped his fingers for his deputy. He wanted the four handcuffed first. While this was in progress he and Siegfried drew off to the side.

"Are you really going to hand them over to the Equatoguineans?" Cameron asked.

"Absolutely," Siegfried said. "Raymond told me all about Stapleton. They have to disappear."

"When?" Cameron asked.

"As soon as Taylor Cabot leaves," Siegfried said. "I want this whole episode kept quiet."

"I understand," Cameron said. He touched the brim of his hat and then went back to supervise the transfer of the prisoners to the jail in the basement of the town hall.

CHAPTER 22

"Something very strange is going on," Kevin said.

"But what?" Melanie said. "Should we get our hopes up?"

"Where could all the other animals be?" Candace questioned.

"I don't know whether to be encouraged or concerned," Kevin said. "What if they're having Armageddon with the other group, and the fighting spreads to here?"

"God almighty," Melanie commented. "I never thought of that."

Kevin and the women had been virtual prisoners for over two days. They had not been allowed to leave the small cave the entire time of their confinement, and it now smelled as bad or worse than the outer cave. To relieve themselves, they'd been forced to go back into the tunnel which reeked like a mini-cesspool.

They themselves didn't smell much better. They were filthy from wearing the same clothes and sleeping on the rock and dirt floor. Their hair was hopelessly matted. Kevin's face was covered with a two-day stubble. They were all weak from lack of exercise and food although each had eaten some of what was brought to them.

Around ten o'clock that morning, there'd been a sense that something abnormal was happening. The animals had become agitated. Some had rushed out only to return moments later, making loud cries. Early on, bonobo number one had gone out but had yet to return. That in itself was abnormal.

"Wait a second," Kevin said suddenly. He put up his hands to keep the women from making any noise. He strained to hear by turning his head slowly from side to side.

"What is it?" Melanie asked urgently.

"I thought I heard a voice," Kevin said.

"A human voice?" Candace questioned.

Kevin nodded.

"Wait, I just heard it!" Melanie said with excitement.

"I did, too," Candace said. "I'm sure it was a human voice. It sounded like someone yelling 'okay.' "

"Arthur heard it, too," Kevin said. They'd named the bonobo who most often stood guard at the lip of the small cave Arthur for no particular reason other than to have a way to refer to him. Over the long hours, they'd had what could have been called a dialogue. They'd even been able to guess at some of the meanings of the bonobo words and gestures.

The ones they were the most sure of included "arak," which meant "away" especially when accompanied by the spreading of fingers and a sweeping arm motion, the same gesture Candace had seen in the operating room. There was also "hana" for "quiet" and "zit" for "go." They were very sure of "food" and "water," which were "bumi" and "carak" respectively. A word they weren't too sure of was "sta" accompanied by holding up one's hands with palms out. They thought it might be the pronoun "you."

Arthur stood up and loudly vocalized to the few bonobos remaining in the cave. They listened and then immediately disappeared out the front.

The next thing Kevin and the others heard were several reports from a rifle: not an ordinary gun but rather an air gun. A few minutes later, two figures in animal-center coveralls appeared silhouetted against the hazy, late-afternoon sky at the cave's entrance. One was carrying a gun, the other a strong, battery-powered lamp.

"Help!" Melanie shouted. She averted her eyes from the strong beam of light but waved her hands frantically lest the men not see her.

There was a loud thump that echoed around the inside of the cave. Simultaneously, Arthur let out a whimper. With a confused expression on his flat face he looked down at a red-tailed dart that protruded from his chest. His hand came up to grasp it, but before he could, he began to wobble. As if in slow motion, he sagged to the floor and rolled over onto his side.

Kevin, Melanie, and Candace emerged from their doorless cell and tried to stand upright. It took a moment for them to stretch. By the time they did the men were kneeling at the side of the bonobo to give the animal an additional dose of tranquilizer.

"My god, are we glad to see you," Melanie said. She had to steady herself with a hand against the rock. For a moment, the cave had begun to spin.

The men stood up and shined the bright light on the women and then on Kevin. The former captives all had to shield their eyes.

"You people are a mess," the man with the light said.

"I'm Kevin Marshall and this is Melanie Becket and Candace Brickmann."

"I know who you are," the man said flatly. "Let's get out of this shithole."

Kevin and the women were happy to comply on rubbery legs. The two men followed. Once out of the cave, the three friends had to squint in the bright, hazy sunlight. Below the face of the cliff were a half dozen more animal handlers. They were busy rolling up tranquilized bonobos in reed mats and lifting them onto a trailer where they were carefully positioned side by side.

"There's one more up here in this cave,"

the man with the flashlight yelled down to the others.

"I know you two," Melanie said once she got a good view of the men who'd come into the cave. "You're Dave Turner and Daryl Christian."

The men ignored Melanie. Dave, the taller of the two, pulled a two-way radio out of a holder at his waist. Daryl started climbing down the giant steps.

"Turner to base," Dave said into the instrument.

"I hear you loud and clear," Bertram said on the other end.

"We got the last of the bonobos and we're loading up," Dave said.

"Excellent work," Bertram said.

"We found Kevin Marshall and the two women in a cave," Dave said.

"In what state?" Bertram asked.

"Filthy but otherwise apparently healthy," Dave said.

"Give me that thing!" Melanie said, reaching for Dave's radio. Suddenly, she didn't like being talked about disparagingly by an underling.

Dave fended her off. "What do you want me to do with them?"

Melanie put her hands on her hips. She was incensed. "What do you mean 'what to do with them'?"

"Bring them to the animal center," Bertram

said. "I'll inform Siegfried Spallek. I'm sure he'll want to talk with them."

"Ten-four," Dave said. He snapped off the radio.

"What's the meaning of this kind of treatment?" Melanie demanded. "We've been prisoners out here for more than two days."

Dave shrugged. "We just follow orders, ma'am. It seems as if you two have riled up the front office big time."

"What on earth is happening to the bonobos?" Kevin asked. When he'd first seen what the men were doing, he'd assumed it had all been for the purpose of their rescue. But the more he thought about it he couldn't understand why the animals were being loaded onto a trailer.

"The bonobos' good life on the island is a thing of the past," Dave said. "They've been warring out here and killing each other. We've found four corpses as evidence, all bashed with stone wedges. So we're caging them at the staging area in preparation for taking them all to the animal center. It'll be six-foot concrete cells from now on as far as I know."

Kevin's mouth slowly fell open. In spite of his hunger, exhaustion, and aches and pains, he felt a profound sadness for these unfortunate creatures who'd not asked to be created or born. Their lives had suddenly and arbitrarily been doomed to monotonous incarceration. Their human potential was not to be realized, and their striking accomplishments thus far would be lost.

Daryl and three other men were now on their way up with a litter.

Kevin turned to look back inside the cave. In the far shadows, he could see Arthur's profile near the lip of the chamber where Kevin and the women had been kept. A tear formed in the corner of Kevin's eye as he imagined how Arthur was going to feel when he awoke to find himself encased in steel.

"All right, you three," Dave said. "Let's start back. Are you strong enough to walk or you want to ride on the trailer?"

"How do you move the trailer?" Kevin asked.

"We've got an all-terrain vehicle on the island," Dave said.

"I'll walk, thank you," Melanie said icily.

Kevin and Candace nodded in agreement.

"We're awfully hungry, though," Kevin said. "The animals have only been offering us insects, worms, and marsh grass."

"We've got some candy bars and soft drinks in a locker on the front of the trailer," Dave said.

"That should be just fine," Kevin said.

The climb down the rock face was the hardest part of the trip. Once on the flat, the walking was easy, especially since the animal handlers had cleared the trail for the all-terrain vehicle.

Kevin was impressed with how much the workers had accomplished in so short a time. As he emerged into the marshy field south of Lago Hippo, he wondered if the canoe was still hidden in the reeds. He guessed it probably was. There was no reason it would have been found.

Candace was elated when she saw the earth-covered timber bridge and said as much. She'd been worrying how they were going to get across the Rio Diviso.

"You people have been busy," Kevin commented.

"We had no choice," Dave said. "We had to round up these animals in the quickest time possible."

Kevin, Melanie, and Candace began to get seriously fatigued on the last mile segment from the Rio Diviso bridge to the staging area. It was especially apparent when they had to step off the trail for the all-terrain vehicle to pass on its way back for the last trailer-load of bonobos. Stopping and standing just for a moment made their legs feel like lead.

Everybody breathed a sigh of relief when they emerged from the twilight of the jungle into the bustling staging area in the clearing. Another half dozen blue-coveralled workers were toiling under the hot sun. They were quickly unloading the bonobos from a second trailer and getting them into individual steel cages before the animals revived.

The cages were four-foot square steel boxes, making it impossible for all but the youngest animals to stand up. The only source of ventilation was through the bars in the doors. The doors were secured by an angled hasp that latched around the side beyond the animal's reach. Kevin was able to catch glimpses of terrified bonobos cowering within the cages' shadows.

Such small cages were supposed to be used only for transport, but a forklift was laboriously moving them into the shade of the north-facing wall of the jungle, suggesting they were staying on the island. One of the workers was manning a hose from a gasoline-powered pump and spraying the cages and the animals with river water.

"I thought you said the bonobos were going to the animal center?" Kevin asked.

"Not today," Dave said. "For the moment, there is no place to put them. It'll be tomorrow or the next day at the very latest."

There was no trouble getting over to the mainland because the telescoping bridge had been deployed. It was constructed of steel and had a hollow, drumlike sound as they treaded across. Parked alongside the bridge mechanism was Dave's pickup truck.

"Hop in," Dave said, while pointing into the truck's bed.

"Just one minute!" Melanie snapped. They were her first words since leaving the cave.

"We're not riding in the back of a truck."

"Then you'll walk," Dave said. "You're not riding in my cab."

"Come on, Melanie," Kevin urged. "It will be more pleasant back here in the open air." Kevin gave Candace a hand.

Dave went around and got in behind the wheel.

Melanie resisted for another minute. With her hands on her hips, her legs spread apart, and her lips pressed together, she looked like a young girl on the verge of a temper tantrum.

"Melanie, it's not that far," Candace said. She reached out her hand. Reluctantly, Melanie took it.

"I didn't expect a hero's welcome," Melanie complained. "But I didn't expect this kind of treatment."

After the damp oppressiveness of the cave and the moist hothouse of the jungle, the breezy ride in the back of the truck was unexpectedly pleasant. The bed was filled with reed mats that had been used to transport the animals, and they provided adequate cushion. The mats had a rather rank smell, but the group guessed they did, too.

They lay on their backs and watched patches of the late-afternoon sky appear between the branches of the overhead canopy of trees.

"What do you think they are going to do

to us?" Candace said. "I don't want to go back in that jail."

"Let's hope they just fire us on the spot," Melanie said. "I'm ready to pack my bag and say goodbye to the Zone, the project, and Equatorial Guinea. I've had it."

"I can only hope it will be that easy," Kevin said. "I'm also worried about the animals. They've been given life sentences."

"There's not much we can do," Candace said.

"I wonder," Kevin said. "I wonder what animal-rights groups would say about this situation."

"Now, don't say anything like that until we get the hell out of here," Melanie said. "That would drive everybody bananas."

They entered the eastern end of town, passing the soccer field and tennis center on their right. Both were in use, particularly the tennis center. Every court was taken.

"An experience like this makes you feel less important than you thought you were," Melanie commented while glancing at the players. "You're hidden away for two agonizing days and everything goes on just as it did before."

They all pondered Melanie's comment as they unconsciously braced for the sharp right-hand turn they knew was coming up to take them to the animal center. But instead, after the truck slowed, it stopped. Kevin sat up and looked ahead. He saw Bertram's Jeep Cherokee.

"Siegfried wants you to drive directly to Kevin's house," Bertram called to Dave.

"Okay!" Dave called back.

The truck lurched forward as Dave pulled out behind Bertram.

Kevin lay back down. "Well, that's a surprise. Maybe we're not going to be treated that badly after all."

"Maybe we can get them to drop Candace and me at our places," Melanie said. "They're more or less on the way." She looked down at herself. "The first thing I'm going to do is take a shower and change clothes. Only then am I going to eat."

Kevin got his legs under him and kneeled behind the truck's cab. He rapped on the rear window until he got Dave's attention. He then relayed Melanie's request. The response from Dave was a wave of dismissal.

Kevin repositioned himself on his back. "I guess you have to go to my house first," he said.

As soon as they hit the cobblestones, the ride was so jarring that they all sat up. Rounding the last turn, Kevin looked ahead expectantly. He was as eager to take a shower as Melanie. Unfortunately what he saw was not encouraging. Siegfried and Cameron were standing out in front of his house along with four heavily armed Equatoguinean soldiers.

One of the soldiers was an officer.

"Uh-oh," Kevin said. "This doesn't look promising after all."

The truck came to a halt. Dave hopped out and came around to put down the tailgate. Kevin was the first to climb out on stiff legs. Melanie and Candace followed.

Preparing himself for the inevitable, Kevin walked over to where Siegfried and Cameron were standing. He knew Melanie and Candace were right behind. Bertram, who'd parked in front of the pickup truck, joined them. No one looked particularly happy.

"We had hoped you'd taken an unannounced holiday," Siegfried said scornfully. "Instead, we find you have willfully disobeyed standing orders not to trespass on Isla Francesca. You're all to be confined to quarters here, in this house." He pointed over his shoulder at Kevin's.

Kevin was about to explain why they'd done what they had when Melanie pushed past him. She was exhausted and irate.

"I'm not staying here and that's final," she spat. "In fact, I quit. I'll be leaving the Zone just as soon as I can make arrangements."

Siegfried's upper lip hiked itself up to exaggerate his sneer. After a quick step forward, he backhanded Melanie viciously, knocking her down. Reflexively Candace dropped to one knee to aid her friend.

"Don't touch her," Siegfried shouted, as he drew his hand back as if to strike Candace.

Candace ignored him and helped Melanie up into a sitting position. Melanie's left eye was beginning to swell, and a trickle of blood slowly ran down her cheek.

Kevin winced and looked away, expecting to hear another blow. He admired Candace's courage and wished that he shared some. But he was terrified of Siegfried and afraid to move.

When another blow did not materialize, Kevin looked back. Candace had Melanie standing shakily on her feet.

"You'll be leaving the Zone soon enough," Siegfried snarled at Melanie. "But it will be in the company of the Equatoguinean authorities. You can try your insolence on them."

Kevin swallowed with difficulty. Being given to the Equatoguineans was what he'd feared most.

"I'm an American," Melanie sobbed.

"But you are in Equatorial Guinea," Siegfried snapped. "And you've violated Equatoguinean law."

Siegfried stepped back. "I've confiscated all of your passports. Just so you know, they will be given to the local authorities along with your persons. In the meantime, you are to stay here in this house. And I warn you that these soldiers and this officer have been ordered to shoot if you so much as take one step outside. Have I made myself clear?"

"I need some clothes," Melanie cried.

"I've had clothes for both of you women brought from your quarters and thrown into upstairs guest rooms," Siegfried said. "Believe me, we have thought of everything."

Siegfried turned to Cameron. "See that these people are taken care of."

"Of course, sir," Cameron said. He touched the tip of his hat before turning to Kevin and the women.

"Okay, you've heard the manager," he barked. "Upstairs you go and no trouble, please."

Kevin started forward but he detoured enough to go by Bertram. "They were using more than fire. They were making tools and even talking with each other."

Kevin walked on. He'd not seen any reaction in Bertram's face other than a slight movement of his perpetually elevated eyebrows. But Kevin was certain Bertram had heard him.

As Kevin wearily climbed to the second floor, he saw Cameron already organizing an area for the soldiers and the officer to occupy at the base of the stairs.

Up in the front hall Kevin, Melanie, and Candace eyed each other. Melanie was still sobbing intermittently.

Kevin breathed out. "This is not good news," he said.

"They can't do this to us," Melanie whimpered.

"The point is they are going to try," Kevin said. "And without our passports we'd have trouble leaving the country even if we were to walk out of here."

Melanie put her hands on either side of her face and squeezed. "I've got to get ahold of myself," she said.

"I feel numb again," Candace admitted. "We've gone from one form of captivity to another."

Kevin sighed. "At least they didn't put us in the jail."

Outside they heard multiple car engines start and vehicles pull away. Kevin went out onto the veranda and saw all the cars leaving except for Cameron's. Glancing up into the sky, he noted that twilight was deepening into night. A few stars were visible.

Turning back into the house, Kevin went directly to the phone. Picking it up, he heard what he'd expected to hear: nothing.

"Is there a dial tone?" Melanie asked from behind him.

Kevin replaced the receiver. He shook his head. "I'm afraid not."

"I didn't expect so," Melanie said.

"Let's take showers," Candace suggested.

"Good idea," Melanie said, making an effort to sound positive.

After agreeing to meet in a half hour, Kevin

walked back through the dining room and pushed open the kitchen door. As dirty as he was, he didn't want to enter. The smell of roast chicken teased his nose.

Esmeralda had leaped to her feet the moment the door opened.

"Hello, Esmeralda," Kevin said.

"Welcome, Mr. Marshall," Esmeralda said.

"You didn't come out to greet us like you always do," Kevin said.

"I was afraid the manager was still here," Esmeralda said. "He and the security man had come up earlier to say you were coming home and that you would not be able to leave the house."

"That's what they told me, too," Kevin said.

"I've made food for you," Esmeralda said. "Are you hungry?"

"Very much," Kevin said. "But there are two guests."

"I know," Esmeralda said. "The manager told me that as well."

"Can we eat in a half hour?" Kevin asked.

"Certainly."

Kevin nodded. He was lucky to have Esmeralda. He turned to leave, but Esmeralda called out to him. He hesitated, holding the door ajar.

"There are many bad things happening in the town," she said. "Not only for you and your friends, but also for strangers. I have a cousin who works at the hospital. She told me that four Americans came from New York and went into the hospital. They talked with the patient who got the liver from the bonobo."

"Oh?" Kevin questioned. Strangers coming from New York to talk to one of the transplant patients was a thoroughly unanticipated development.

"They just walked in," Esmeralda continued. "They were not supposed to be there. They said they were doctors. Security was called, and the army and the guards came to take them away. They are in the jail."

"My word," Kevin commented, while his mind veered off on a tangent. New York reminded him of the surprising call he'd gotten a week previously in the middle of the night from the GenSys CEO, Taylor Cabot. It had been about the patient Carlo Franconi, who'd been killed in New York. Taylor Cabot had asked if someone could figure out what had happened to Carlo from an autopsy.

"My cousin knows some of the soldiers who were there," Esmeralda continued. "They said that the Americans will be given to the Ministers. If they are, they will be killed. I thought you should know."

Kevin felt a chill descend his spine. He knew such a fate was what Siegfried had in mind for him, Melanie, and Candace. But who were these Americans? Had they been involved with the autopsy on Carlo Fanconi?

"It is all very serious," Esmeralda said. "And I am afraid for you. I know you went to the forbidden island."

"How do you know that?" Kevin questioned with amazement.

"In our town people talk," Esmeralda said. "When I said you were gone unexpectedly and that the manager was looking for you, Alphonse Kimba told my husband that you had gone to the island. He was sure."

"I appreciate your concern," Kevin said evasively and preoccupied with his thoughts. "Thank you for what you have told me."

Kevin went back to his own room. When he looked at himself in the mirror, he was surprised how exhausted and filthy he appeared. Running a hand over his beginning beard, he noticed something more disturbing. He was beginning to look a lot like his double!

After a shave, shower, and clean clothes, Kevin felt revived. The entire time, he mused about the Americans in the jail under the town hall. He was very curious and would have liked nothing better than to go and talk with them.

Kevin found the two women were equally refreshed. The shower had transformed Melanie into her irrepressible self, and she complained bitterly about the selection of clothes she'd been offered. "Nothing goes with anything," she complained.

They settled in the dining room, and Esmeralda began serving the meal. Melanie laughed, after looking around at the surroundings. "You know, I find it almost funny that a few hours ago we were living like Neanderthals. Then, presto, we're in the lap of luxury. It's like a time machine."

"If only we didn't have to worry about what tomorrow will bring," Candace said.

"Let's at least enjoy our last supper," Melanie said with her typical wry humor. "Besides, the more I think about it, the less likely I think it is that they can just foist us off on the Equatoguineans. I mean, they wouldn't be able to get away with it. This is almost the beginning of the third millennium. The world is too small."

"But I'm worried . . ." Candace began.

"Excuse me," Kevin interrupted. "Esmeralda told me something curious that I'd like to share with you." Kevin started by mentioning the phone call he got in the middle of the night from Taylor Cabot. Then he told the story about the arrival and subsequent incarceration of the New Yorkers in the town's jail.

"Well, this's just what I'm talking about," Melanie said. "A couple of smart people do an autopsy in New York, and they end up here in Cogo. And we thought we were so isolated. I tell you the world's getting smaller every day."

"So you think these Americans came here

following a trail that started with Franconi?" Kevin asked. His intuition was telling him the same thing, but he wanted reinforcement.

"What else could it be?" Melanie questioned. "There's no question in my mind."

"Candace, what do you think?" Kevin asked.

"I agree with Melanie," Candace said. "Otherwise, it's too much of a coincidence."

"Thank you, Candace!" Melanie said. While twirling her empty wineglass, she looked menacingly at Kevin. "I hate to interrupt this fascinating conversation, but where's some of that great wine of yours, bucko?"

"Gosh, I totally forgot," Kevin said. "Sorry!" He pushed back from the table and went into the butler's pantry that he'd filled with his mostly untouched wine allocation. As he was looking through the labels, which held little meaning for him, he was suddenly struck by how much wine he had. Counting the bottles in a small area and extrapolating it to allow for the entire room, he realized he had more than three hundred bottles.

"My word," Kevin said as a plan began to form in his head. He grabbed an armload of bottles and pushed through the swinging door into the kitchen.

Esmeralda got up from where she was sitting having her own dinner.

"I have a favor to ask," Kevin said. "Would you take these bottles of wine and a corkscrew down to the soldiers at the foot of the stairs?"

"So many?" she questioned.

"Yes, and I'd like you to take even more to the soldiers in the town hall. If they ask what the occasion is, tell them that I'm going away, and I wanted them to enjoy the wine, not the manager."

A smile spread across Esmeralda's face. She looked at Kevin. "I think I understand." From a cupboard she got the canvas bag that she used for shopping and loaded it with wine bottles. A moment later, she disappeared through the butler's pantry, heading for the front hall.

Kevin made several trips back and forth from his wine collection to the kitchen table. Soon he had several dozen bottles lined up, including a couple bottles of port.

"What's going on?" Melanie enquired after sticking her head into the kitchen. "We're waiting and where's the wine?"

Kevin handed her one of the bottles. He said he'd be a few minutes more and they should start eating without him. Melanie rolled the bottle over to look at the label.

"Oh, my, Château Latour!" she said. She flashed Kevin an appreciative grin, before ducking back into the dining room.

Esmeralda returned to say that the soldiers were very pleased. "But I thought I'd take them some bread," she added. "It will stimulate their thirst."

"Marvelous idea," Kevin said. He filled the canvas bag with wine and tested its weight. It was heavy, but he thought Esmeralda could handle it.

"Let me know how many soldiers are at the town hall," Kevin said as he handed her the bag. "We want to make sure there is plenty for everyone."

"There are usually four at night," Esmeralda said.

"Then ten bottles should be fine," Kevin said. "At least for starters." He smiled, and Esmeralda smiled back.

Taking a deep breath, Kevin pushed through the door into the dining room. He wanted to see what the women thought of his idea.

Kevin rolled over and looked at the clock. It was just before midnight, so he sat up and put his feet over the side of the bed. He turned off the alarm clock that had been set to go off at twelve P.M. sharp. Then he stretched.

During dinner, Kevin's proposed plan had sparked a lively discussion. In a cooperative effort, the idea had been refined and expanded. Ultimately, all three thought it was worth attempting.

After making what preparations they could, they all decided to try to get a little rest. But Kevin had been unable to sleep despite his exhaustion. He was too keyed up. There was also the problem of the gradually increasing noise from the soldiers. At first, it had just been animated chatter, but during the last half hour, loud, drunken singing had reverberated from below.

Esmeralda had visited both groups of soldiers twice during the evening. When she returned, she reported that the expensive French wine was a big hit. After her second visit, she told Kevin that the initial deliveries of bottles had been almost drained.

Kevin dressed quickly in the dark, then ventured out into the hall. He did not want to turn on any lights. Luckily, the moon was bright enough for him to see his way to the guest rooms. He knocked first on Melanie's door. He was startled when it was opened instantly.

"I've been waiting," Melanie whispered. "I couldn't sleep."

Together, they went to Candace's room. She, too, was ready.

In the living room they picked up the small canvas bags each had prepared and walked out onto the veranda. The vista was enticingly exotic. It had rained several hours earlier, but now the sky was filled with puffy, silver-blue clouds. A gibbous moon was high in the sky, and its light made the mist-filled town glow eerily. The jungle sounds were shockingly loud in the hot, moist air.

They had discussed this first stage in detail

so there was no need for talk now. At the far end of the veranda in the rear corner they secured the end of three sheets that had been tied together. The other end was dropped over the side to the ground.

Melanie had insisted on going first. She climbed nimbly over the balustrade, and lowered herself to the ground with inspiring ease. Candace was next, and her cheerleading experience stood her in good stead. She had no trouble making it down.

Kevin was the one who had difficulty. Trying to imitate Melanie, he pushed off with his feet. But then as he swung back toward the building he got twisted in the sheets so that he collided with the stucco, scraping his knuckles.

"Damn," he whispered, when he finally was standing on the cobblestones. He shook his hand and squeezed his fingers.

"Are you okay?" Melanie whispered.

"I think so," Kevin said.

The next stage of their escape was more worrisome. In single file, they inched along the back of the building within the shadow of the arcade. Each step took them closer to the central stairwell, where they could hear the soldiers. A cassette recorder playing African music at low volume had been added to the festivities.

They reached the stall where Kevin kept his Toyota LandCruiser and slipped in along the passenger side until they reached the front. According to previously made plans, Kevin eased around the car to the driver's-side door and quietly opened it. At that point, he was within fifteen to twenty feet from the inebriated soldiers who were on the opposite side of a reed mat suspended from the ceiling.

Kevin released the emergency brake and put the car in neutral. Returning to the women, he motioned to start pushing.

At first, the heavy vehicle resisted their efforts. Kevin lifted his foot to push against the house's foundation. That added amount of leverage made the difference; the car eased out of its parking slot.

At the lip of the arcade, the cobblestones of the street slanted downward in a gentle slope so rainwater would run away from the house. As soon as the rear wheels of the vehicle passed this point, the car gained momentum. All at once, Kevin realized that no additional force was needed.

"Uh-oh!" Kevin cried, as the car began to gain speed.

Kevin ran around the side of the car and tried to get the driver's-side door open. Given the car's increasing momentum, this wasn't easy. The car was now halfway across the alley and beginning to curve to the right down the hill toward the waterfront.

Finally Kevin succeeded in opening the door. In one swift move, he dove in behind the wheel. He got in position as quickly as possible, then jammed on the brakes. At the same time, he turned the steering wheel hard to the left so as to better align the vehicle with the street.

Fearful their efforts might have attracted the soldiers' attention, Kevin looked their way to check. The men were gathered around a small table supporting the cassette player and a half dozen empty wine bottles. The soldiers were happily clapping and stomping their feet, oblivious to Kevin's maneuverings with the car.

Kevin breathed a sigh of relief. The passenger-side door opened and Melanie climbed in. Candace got in the back.

"Don't close the door," Kevin whispered. He was still holding his ajar.

Kevin eased up on the brake. The car did not move at first, so he shifted his weight back and forth until he got the car rolling down the incline toward the waterfront. Kevin looked out the rear window, steering the vehicle as it began gathering speed.

They rolled for two blocks. At that point, the hill began to flatten out, and the car eventually came to a stop. Only then did Kevin slip the key into the ignition and start the engine. They all closed their doors.

They looked at each other in the half light of the car's interior. They were all keyed up and their pulses were racing. Everyone smiled.

"We did it!" Melanie asserted.

"So far so good," Kevin agreed.

Kevin put the car in gear. He turned right for several blocks to give his house a wide berth and headed for the motor pool.

"You're pretty sure no one will give us trouble at the garage," Melanie said.

"Well, there's no way to know for sure," Kevin said. "But I don't think so. The motor-pool people live a life of their own. Besides, Siegfried has probably kept the story of our disappearance and reappearance a secret. He'd have to if he were truly planning on handing us over to the Equatoguinean authorities."

"I hope you are right," Melanie said. She sighed. "I'm half wondering if we shouldn't just try to drive out of the Zone behind one of the trucks instead of bothering with four Americans we've never met."

"Those people got in here somehow," Kevin said. "I'm counting on their having had a plan to get out. Running the main gate should be considered our last-ditch option."

They pulled into the busy motor-pool facility. They had to squint under the glare of the mercury-vapor lights. They continued until they came to the repair section. Kevin parked behind a bay with the cab of a semi up on the hydraulic lift. Several greasy mechanics were standing under it, scratching their heads.

"Wait here," Kevin said, as he alighted from the Toyota.

He walked inside and greeted the men.

Melanie and Candace watched. Candace literally had her fingers crossed.

"Well, at least they didn't bolt for the telephone the moment they saw him," Melanie said.

The women watched as one of the mechanics sauntered off and disappeared through a door in the rear of the facility. He reappeared a moment later, carrying a lengthy hunk of heavy chain. He gave it to Kevin who staggered under its weight.

As his face turned a progressively brighter shade of red, Kevin stumbled back toward the LandCruiser. Sensing he was about to drop the chain, Melanie hopped out of the car to open the luggage area.

The vehicle lurched as Kevin dropped the chain onto the tailgate.

"I told them I wanted heavy chain," Kevin managed. "It didn't have to be this heavy."

"What did you say to those men?" Melanie asked.

"I said that your car got stuck in some mud," Kevin said. "They didn't bat an eyelash. Of course, they didn't offer to come and help, either."

Kevin and Melanie returned inside the Toyota, and they started back toward town.

"You're sure this is going to work?" Candace asked from the rear seat.

"No, but I can't think of anything else," Kevin said.

For the rest of the trip, no one spoke. They all knew this was the most difficult part of the whole plan. The tension mounted as they turned into the parking lot for the town hall and doused the headlights.

The room occupied by the army post was ablaze with light. As they got closer Kevin, Melanie, and Candace could hear the music. This group of soldiers also had a cassette player, only theirs was cranking out African music at full volume.

"That's the kind of party I was counting on," Kevin said. He made a wide turn and then backed toward the building. He could just make out the window wells for the subterranean jail within the shadows of the ground-floor arcade.

He stopped the car within five feet of the building and put on the emergency brake. All three gazed into the room occupied by the soldiers. They couldn't see much of the room and none of the soldiers because the line of sight was on an angle through an unglazed window. The window's shutter had been raised and hooked to the ceiling of the arcade. A number of empty wine bottles were on the sill.

"Well, it's now or never," Kevin said.

"Can we help?" Melanie asked.

"No, stay put," Kevin said.

Kevin climbed from the car and walked in under the nearest arch to stand within the shelter of the arcade. The sound of the music was deafening. Kevin's major concern was that if someone looked out the window, Kevin would be seen immediately. There was nothing to hide behind.

Looking down at the window well, Kevin could see the barred opening. Beyond the bars was utter darkness. There was not the faintest light within the cell.

Getting down on his hands and knees first, Kevin lay on the stone floor with his head over the lip of the window well. With his face close to the bars, he called out over the noise of the music: "Hello! Anybody in there?"

"Just us tourists," Jack said. "Are we invited to the party?"

"I understand you are Americans," Kevin said.

"Like apple pie and baseball," Jack said.

Kevin could suddenly hear other voices in the dark, but they were unintelligible.

"You people have to realize what a dangerous situation you've gotten yourselves into," Kevin said.

"Really," Jack said. "We thought this was how all visitors to Cogo were treated."

Kevin thought that whomever he was speaking with would certainly get along well with Melanie.

"I'm going to try to pull these bars out," Kevin said. "Are you all in the same cell?"

"No, we have two beautiful ladies in the cell to my left."

"Okay," Kevin said. "Let's see what I can do with these bars first."

Kevin got up and went back for the chain. Returning to the window well, he threaded one end through the bars into the abyss.

"Hook this around one of the bars a number of times," Kevin said.

"I like this," Jack said. "It reminds me of an old Western movie."

Back at the Toyota, Kevin secured the chain to the trailer hitch. When he got back to the window well he gently pulled on the chain. He could see it was tied securely around the central bar.

"Looks good," Kevin said. "Let's see what happens."

He climbed back into the vehicle and made sure it was in its lowest four-wheel drive gear. Looking out the back window, Kevin cautiously eased the car forward to take the slack out of the chain.

"All right, here we go," Kevin said to Melanie and Candace. He began to press on the accelerator. The heavy-duty Toyota engine strained, but Kevin couldn't hear it. The hum of the motor was drowned out by the frenzied beat of a popular Zairean rock group.

Suddenly, the vehicle lurched forward.

Hastily, Kevin braked. Behind them they heard a terrible clanging over the sound of the music like someone hitting a fire escape with a curbstone.

Kevin and the women winced. They looked back at the opening into the army post. To their relief, no one appeared to check out the awful sound.

Kevin jumped out of the Toyota with the intention of going back to see what had happened when he almost ran into an impressively muscled black man heading right for him.

"Good job, man! My name's Warren and this is Jack." Jack had come up alongside Warren.

"I'm Kevin."

"Cool," Warren said. "You back these wheels up, and we'll see what we can do with the other opening."

"How did you get out so quickly?" Kevin asked.

"Man, you pulled out the whole friggin' frame," Warren said.

Kevin climbed into the car and slowly backed up. He could see the two men had already detached the chain.

"It worked!" Melanie said. "Congratulations."

"I must admit it was better than I thought," Kevin said.

A moment later, someone thumped on the

back of the Toyota. When Kevin looked, he could see one of the men wave for him to go forward.

Kevin used the same driving technique he'd used the first episode. With approximately the same amount of power there was the same sudden release and unfortunately the same clanging noise. This time a soldier had appeared at the window.

Kevin didn't move, and he prayed the two men he'd just met did the same. The soldier proceeded to bring a wine bottle to his lips and in the process knocked several of the empties off the sill. They shattered on the stone pavement. Then he turned and disappeared back into the room.

Kevin got out of the vehicle in time to see two women being extracted from the second window well. As soon as they were free, all four rushed for the car. Kevin went around to detach the chain but found that Warren was already in the process of doing so.

They all climbed into the Toyota without discussion. Jack and Warren squeezed into the jump seats in the back while Laurie and Natalie joined Candace on the middle bench.

Kevin put the car in gear. After a final glance at the army post, he drove from the parking lot. He didn't switch on the lights until they were away from town hall.

The escape had been a heady experience for everyone: triumph for Kevin, Melanie, and

Candace; surprise and utter relief for the crew from New York. The seven exchanged terse introductions; then the questions started. At first, everyone spoke at the same time.

"Wait a second, everybody!" Jack shouted over the babble. "We need some order in this chaos. Only one person at a time."

"Well, damn!" Warren said. "I'm going first! I just want to thank you guys for coming when you did."

"I'll second that," Laurie said.

Having cleared the central part of town, Kevin pulled into the parking lot for the main supermarket. There were several other cars. He stopped and turned off the lights and the engine.

"Before we talk about anything else," Kevin said. "We've got to talk about getting out of this town. We don't have a lot of time. How did you people originally plan on leaving?"

"By the same boat we came in on," Jack said.

"Where's the boat?" Kevin asked.

"We assume it's where we left it," Jack said. "Pulled up on the beach under the pier."

"Is it big enough for all of us?" Kevin asked.

"With room to spare," Jack said.

"Perfect!" Kevin said with excitement. "I was hoping you'd come by boat. That way we can go directly to Gabon." He faced around quickly and restarted the engine. "Let's just pray it's not been found."

He drove out of the parking lot and began a circuitous route to the waterfront. He wanted to stay as far from the town hall and his own house as possible.

"We have a problem," Jack said. "We have no identification or money. Everything was taken from us."

"We're not much better off," Kevin said. "But we do have some money, both cash and travelers checks. Our passports were confiscated when we were put under house arrest this afternoon. We were destined for the same fate as you: to be turned over to the Equatoguinean authorities."

"Would that have been a problem?" Jack asked.

Kevin let out a little derisive laugh. In the back of his mind, he could see the skulls on Siegfried's desk. "It would have been more than a problem. It would have meant a hush-hush mock trial followed by a firing squad."

"No shit!" Warren said.

"In this country, it is a capital offense to interfere with GenSys operations," Kevin said. "And the manager is the one who decides whether someone is interfering or not."

"A firing squad?" Jack repeated with horror.

"I'm afraid so," Kevin said. "The army here is good at it. They've had a lot of practice over the years."

"Then we're even more in debt to you people than we thought," Jack said. "I'd no idea."

Laurie looked out the side window of the car and shuddered. It was just sinking in how seriously her life was on the line and that the threat was not yet over.

"How come you guys were in the soup?" Warren asked.

"It's a long story," Melanie said.

"So is ours," Laurie said.

"I have a question," Kevin said. "Did you people come here because of Carlo Franconi?"

"Whoa!" Jack said. "Such clairvoyance! I'm impressed, and intrigued. How did you guess? What exactly is your role here in Cogo?"

"Me, in particular?" Kevin asked.

"Well, all of you," Jack said.

Kevin, Melanie, and Candace looked at each other to see who wanted to speak first.

"We were all part of the same program," Candace said. "But I was just a minor player. I'm an intensive-care nurse for a surgical transplant team."

"I'm a reproductive technologist," Melanie said. "I provide the raw materials for Kevin to work his magic, and once he has, I see to it that his creations are brought to fruition."

"I'm a molecular biologist," Kevin explained with a sigh of regret. "Someone who overstepped his bounds and committed a Promethean blunder."

"Hold up," Jack said. "Don't go too literary on me. I know I've heard of Prometheus, but

I can't remember who he was."

"Prometheus was a Titan in Greek mythology," Laurie said. "He stole fire from Olympus and gave it to man."

"I inadvertently gave fire to some animals," Kevin said. "I stumbled on the way to move chromosome parts, particularly the short arm of chromosome six from one cell to another, from one species to another."

"So you took chromosome parts from humans and put them into an ape," Jack said.

"Into the fertilized egg of an ape," Kevin said. "A bonobo to be exact."

"And what you were really doing," Jack continued, "was custom-designing the perfect organ transplant source for a specific individual."

"Exactly," Kevin said. "It wasn't what I had in mind in the beginning. I was just a pure researcher. What I ended up doing was something I was lured into because of its economic potential."

"Wow!" Jack commented. "Ingenious and impressive, but also a little scary."

"It's more than scary," Kevin said. "It's a tragedy of sorts. The problem is I transferred too many human genes. I've accidently created a race of protohumans."

"You mean like Neanderthals?" Laurie asked.

"More primitive by millions of years," Kevin said. "More like Lucy. But they're intelligent enough to use fire, make tools, and even converse. I think they are the way we were four or five million years ago."

"Where are these creatures?" Laurie asked with alarm.

"They're on a nearby island," Kevin said, "where they have been living in comparative freedom. Unfortunately, that's all about to change."

"Why is that?" Laurie asked. In her mind's eye, she could see these protohumans. As a child she'd been fascinated by cavemen.

Kevin quickly told the story of the smoke eventually bringing him, Melanie, and Candace to the island. He related how they'd been captured and then rescued. He also told them about the creatures' fate of facing lifelong internment in tiny concrete cells purely because they were too human.

"That's awful," Laurie commented.

"It's a disaster!" Jack said with a shake of his head. "What a story!"

"This world isn't ready for a new race," Warren said. "We've got enough trouble with what we have already."

"We're coming up on the waterfront," Kevin announced. "The square at the base of the pier is around the next bend."

"Then stop here," Jack said. "There was a soldier there when we arrived."

Kevin pulled over to the side of the road and turned off the headlights. He kept the engine running for the air-conditioning. Jack and Warren got out the back and ran down to the corner. Carefully, they peeked around the bend.

"If our boat is not there, are there other boats around here?" Laurie asked.

"I'm afraid not," Kevin said.

"Is there another way out of town besides the main gate?" Laurie asked.

"That's it," Kevin said.

"Heaven help us," Laurie commented.

Jack and Warren came back quickly. Kevin lowered his window.

"There's a soldier," Jack said. "He's none too attentive. In fact, he might even be asleep. But we'll still have to deal with him. I think it best you all stay here."

"Fine by me," Kevin said. He was more than happy to leave such business up to others. If left to him, he wouldn't have had any idea what to do.

Jack and Warren returned to the corner and disappeared.

Kevin raised his window.

Laurie looked at Natalie and shook her head. "I'm sorry about all this. I suppose I should have known. Jack seems to have a penchant for finding trouble."

"No need to apologize," Natalie said. "It's certainly not your fault. Besides, things are looking a lot better than they did only fifteen or twenty minutes ago."

Jack and Warren reappeared in a surprisingly short time. Jack was holding a handgun, while Warren was carrying an assault rifle. They got into the back of the Toyota.

"Any problem?" Kevin asked.

"Nope," Jack said. "He was very accommodating. Of course, Warren can be very persuasive when he wants to be."

"Does the Chickee Hut Bar have a parking area?" Warren asked.

"It does," Kevin said.

"Drive there!" Warren said.

Kevin backed up, took a right and then the first left. At the end of the block he pulled into an expansive asphalt parking lot. The darkened Chickee Hut Bar was silhouetted ahead. Beyond the bar was the sparkling expanse of the broad estuary. Its surface shimmered in the moonlight.

Kevin drove directly up to the bar and stopped.

"You all wait here," Warren said. "I'll check on the boat." He climbed out with the assault rifle and quickly disappeared around the bar.

"He moves quickly," Melanie commented.

"You have no idea," Jack said.

"Is that Gabon on the other side of the water?" Laurie asked.

"It sure is," Melanie said.

"How far is it?" Jack asked.

"About four miles straight across," Kevin said. "But we should try to get to Cocobeach.

That's about ten miles away. From there we can contact the American Embassy in Libreville who will certainly be able to help us."

"How long will it take to get to Cocobeach?" Laurie asked.

"I'd estimate a little more than an hour," Kevin said. "Of course, it depends on the speed of the boat."

Warren reappeared and came to the car. Kevin lowered his window again.

"We're cool," Warren said. "The boat's there. No problem."

"Hooray," everybody replied in unison. They piled out of the car. Kevin, Melanie, and Candace brought their canvas bags.

"Is that your luggage?" Laurie teased.

"This is it," Candace said.

Warren led the group into the darkened bar and around to where there were steps to the beach.

"Let's move quickly until we get behind the retaining wall," Warren said. He motioned for the others to precede him.

It was dark beneath the pier, and everyone had to move slowly. Along with the sound of the small waves lapping against the shore was the noise of large crabs scampering into their sand burrows.

"We've got a couple of flashlights," Kevin said. "Should we use them?"

"Let's not take the chance," Jack said as he literally bumped into the boat. He made sure it was reasonably stable before telling everyone to climb in and move to the stern. As soon as everyone had done so, Jack could feel the bow become lighter. Leaning against the boat, he began to push it out.

"Watch out for the crossbeams," Jack said as he jumped aboard.

Everyone helped by reaching for the wood piles and pulling the boat silently along. It took them only a few minutes to travel to the end of the pier which was blocked by the floating dock. At that point they angled the boat out into moonlit open water.

There were only four paddles. Besides the men, Melanie insisted on paddling.

"I want to get about a hundred yards away from the shore before I start the motor," Jack explained. "There's no sense taking any chances."

Everyone looked back at peaceful-appearing Cogo whose whitewashed buildings shrouded in mist glimmered in the silver moonlight. The surrounding jungle limned the town with midnight blue. The walls of vegetation were like tidal waves about to break.

The night sounds of the jungle fell astern. The only noise became the gurgle of the paddles passing through the water or their scraping along the side of the boat. For a time, no one spoke. Racing hearts slowed, and breathing tended toward normal. There was time to think and even look around. The newcomers in particular were captivated by the arresting beauty of the nocturnal African landscape. Its sheer size was overwhelming. Everything seemed bigger in Africa, even the night sky.

For Kevin it was different. His relief of having escaped Cogo and having helped others to do so as well, only made his anguish about the fate of his chimeric bonobos that much more poignant. It had been a mistake to have created them, but abandoning them to a lifetime of captivity in a tiny cage compounded his guilt.

After a time, Jack picked up his oar and dropped it into the bottom of the boat. "Time to start the engine," he announced. He grasped the outboard and tilted it down into the water.

"Wait a second," Kevin said suddenly. "I have a request. Something I have no right to ask of you people, but it is important."

Jack straightened up from bending over the gas tank. "What's on your mind, sport?" he asked.

"See that island, the last one in the chain?" Kevin said while pointing toward Isla Francesca. "That's where all the bonobos are. They're in cages at the foot of a bridge to the mainland. I'd like nothing better than to go over there and release them."

"What would that accomplish?" Laurie asked.

"A lot if I could get them to cross the

bridge," Kevin said.

"Wouldn't your Cogo friends just round them up again?" Jack asked.

"They'd never find them," Kevin said, warming to his idea. "They'd vanish. From this part of Equatorial Guinea and stretching for a thousand miles inland is mostly virginal rain forest. It encompasses not only this country but vast regions of Gabon, Cameroon, Congo, and Central African Republic. It's got to be a million square miles, parts of which are still literally unexplored."

"Just let them go by themselves?" Candace asked.

"That's exactly the point," Kevin said. "They'd have a chance, and I think they'd make it! They're resourceful. Look at our ancestors. They had to live through the Pleistocene ice age. That was more of a challenge than living in a rain forest."

Laurie looked at Jack. "I like the idea."

Jack glanced at the island, then asked which direction was Cocobeach.

"We'd be going out of our way," Kevin admitted, "but it's not far. Twenty minutes tops."

"What if you let them out and they stay on the island?" Warren said.

"At least I could tell myself I tried," Kevin said. "I feel that I have to do something."

"Hey, why not?" Jack said. "I think I like the idea too. What does everybody else say?"

"To tell you the truth, I'd like to see one of these animals," Warren said.

"Let's go," Candace said enthusiastically.

"Okay by me," Natalie said.

"I couldn't think of a better idea," Melanie said. "Let's do it!"

Jack gave the engine cord a few pulls. The outboard roared to life. Pushing over the helm, Jack steered toward Isla Francesca.

CHAPTER 23

Siegfried had dreamed the dream a hundred times, and each time it had gotten a little worse. In it, he was approaching a female elephant with a young calf. He didn't like doing it, but a client couple demanded it. It was the wife who wanted to see the baby up close.

Siegfried had sent trackers out laterally to protect the flank while he and the couple neared the mother. But the trackers to the north became terrified when a huge bull elephant appeared. They ran, and to compound their cowardice, they failed to warn Siegfried of the danger.

The sound of the enormous elephant charging through the underbrush was like the thunder of an oncoming train. Its shrieks built to a crescendo, and just before impact Siegfried woke up bathed in sweat.

Panting, Siegfried rolled over and sat up. Reaching through the mosquito netting, he found a glass of water and took a drink. The problem with his dream was that it was too real. This was the incident through which he'd lost the use of his right arm and had the skin of his face flayed open.

Siegfried sat on the edge of his bed for a few moments before he realized the shrieking he'd thought was from his dream was coming from outside his window. A moment later, he realized the source: loud West African rock music emanating from a cheap cassette player.

Siegfried looked at the clock. Seeing that it was close to two A.M., he became instantly incensed. Who could be so insolent to make such noise at that time in the morning?

Sensing the noise was coming across the green in front of his house, he got out of bed and stepped onto the veranda. To his surprise and dismay the music was coming from Kevin Marshall's. In fact, Siegfried could see who was responsible: It was the soldiers guarding the house.

Anger coursed through Siegfried's body like a bolt of electricity. Ducking back inside his bedroom, he called Cameron and ordered the security director to meet him over at Kevin's. Siegfried slammed the phone down. He pulled on his clothes. As he left the house he grabbed one of his old hunting carbines.

Siegfried walked directly across the green. The closer he got to Kevin's, the louder the music became. The soldiers were in a puddle of light beneath a bare light bulb. Sprinkled across the ground at their feet were numerous empty bottles of wine. Two of the soldiers were singing along with the music while playing imaginary instruments. The other two appeared to have passed out.

By the time Siegfried got to the scene, Cameron's car had careened down the cobblestone street and screeched to a halt. Cameron jumped out. He was still buttoning his shirt as he approached Siegfried. He glanced at the inebriated soldiers and was clearly appalled.

Cameron started to apologize when Siegfried cut him off. "Forget about explanations and excuses," he said. "Get upstairs and make sure Mr. Marshall and his two friends are tucked in for the night."

Cameron touched the tip of hat in faint salute. He disappeared up the stairs. Siegfried could hear him pounding on the door. A moment later, several lights went on in the living quarters.

Siegfried fumed as he watched the soldiers. They hadn't even noticed his presence or Cameron's.

Cameron came back looking pale and shaking his head. "They're not there."

Siegfried tried to control his anger enough to think. The level of incompetence with which he had to work was astounding.

"What about his LandCruiser?" Siegfried snapped.

"I'll check," Cameron said. He ran back, literally pushing his way through the singing soldiers. He returned almost instantly. "It's gone."

"What a surprise!" Siegfried said sarcastically. Then he snapped his fingers and motioned toward Cameron's car.

Siegfried got in the front seat while Cameron climbed in behind the wheel.

"Call and alert your security force," Siegfried ordered. "I want Kevin's car found immediately. And call the gate. Make sure it hasn't left the Zone. Meanwhile, take me to town hall."

Cameron used his car phone as he maneuvered his vehicle around the block. Both numbers were stored in his phone's autodialer so it was a hands-free operation. Stomping on the accelerator, he headed north.

By the time they neared the town hall, the official search for Kevin's car had been initiated. It was readily determined that the vehicle had not tried to go through the gate. As they turned into the parking lot both heard the music.

"Uh-oh!" Cameron said.

Siegfried stayed silent. He was trying to prepare himself for what he now suspected.

Cameron pulled to a halt at the building. His headlights picked up the debris that had resulted when the bar frames had been yanked out of the wall. The pile of chain was visible.

"This is a disaster," Siegfried said with a tremulous voice. He stepped out of the car with the carbine. Although he had to hold the gun with one hand, he was an accomplished marksman. In quick succession he pulled off three rounds and three of the empty wine bottles on the windowsill of the army post burst into shards of glass. But the music did not falter.

Gripping the gun tightly in his good hand, Siegfried went over to the army-post window and looked in. The cassette player was on the desk with its volume pegged at max. The four soldiers were passed out either on the floor or slouched in the rickety furniture.

Siegfried raised the gun. He pulled the trigger and the cassette player flew off the desk. In an instant, the scene was thrust into a painful silence.

Siegfried went back to Cameron. "Call the colonel of the garrison. Tell him what has happened. Tell him I want these men court-martialed. Tell him to get a contingent of soldiers here immediately with a vehicle."

"Yes, sir!" Cameron intoned.

Siegfried stepped beneath the arcade and looked at the bars that had been pulled from the jail-cell windows. They were hand forged. Looking at the openings, he could tell why they'd come out so easily. The mortar between the bricks under the stucco had turned to sand.

To get himself under control, Siegfried walked all the way around the town hall. By the time he rounded the final corner, headlights were coming along the road. They turned into the parking lot. With screeching tires the security patrol car came to a halt next to Cameron's car, and the duty officer jumped out.

Siegfried cursed under his breath as he approached. With Kevin and the women plus the Americans missing, the bonobo project was in serious jeopardy. They had to be found.

"Mr. Spallek," Cameron said. "I have some information. Officer O'Leary thinks he saw Kevin Marshall's car ten minutes ago. Of course, we can quickly confirm it if it is still there."

"Where?" Siegfried asked.

"In the lot by the Chickee Hut Bar," O'Leary said. "I noticed it on my last tour."

"Did you see any people?"

"No, sir! Not a soul."

"There's supposed to be a guard down there," Siegfried said. "Did you see him?"

"Not really, sir," O'Leary said.

"What do you mean 'not really'?" Siegfried growled. He was fed up with incompetence.

"We don't make it a point to pay much attention to the soldiers," O'Leary said.

Siegfried looked off in the distance. In a further attempt to control his anger, he forced himself to notice how the moonlight reflected off the vegetation. The beauty calmed him to a degree, and he reluctantly admitted that he didn't pay much attention to the soldiers, either. Rather than serving any truly utilitarian purpose, they were just there; one of the costs of doing business with the Equatoguinean government. But why would Kevin's car be at the Chickee Hut Bar? Then it dawned on him.

"Cameron, was it determined how the Americans got into town?" Siegfried asked.

"I'm afraid not," Cameron said.

"Was a boat searched for?" Siegfried asked.

Cameron looked at O'Leary, who reluctantly replied. "I didn't know anything about looking for a boat."

"What about when you relieved Hansen at eleven?" Cameron asked. "When he briefed you, did he mention he'd looked for a boat?"

"Not a word, sir," O'Leary said.

Cameron swallowed. He turned to Siegfried. "I'll just have to follow up on this and get back to you later."

"In other words, no one looked for a goddamn boat!" Siegfried snapped. "This is a comedy around here, but I'm not laughing."

"I gave specific orders for a search for a boat," Cameron said.

"Obviously, orders are not enough, you lunkhead," Siegfried spat. "You are supposed to be in charge. You are responsible."

Siegfried closed his eyes and gritted his teeth. He'd lost both groups. All he could do at this point was have the colonel call the army post in Acalayong in the unlikely event the escapees might land there. But Siegfried was far from optimistic. He knew that if the tables were turned and he'd been the one fleeing, he'd go to Gabon.

All of a sudden, Siegfried's eyes popped open. Another thought occurred to him: a more worrisome thought.

"Is there a guard out at Isla Francesca?" he asked.

"No, sir. None was requested."

"What about at the bridge on the mainland?" Siegfried persisted.

"There was until you ordered it removed," Cameron said.

"Then, we're going right now," Siegfried said. He started for Cameron's car. As he did so, three vehicles sped down the street and turned into the parking lot. They were army jeeps. They swooped over to the two parked vehicles and stopped. All of them were filled with soldiers bristling with guns.

From the front jeep stepped Colonel Mongomo. In contrast to the slovenly soldiers, he was impeccably attired in his martial finery complete with medals. Despite the fact that it was night, he wore aviator sunglasses. He saluted Siegfried stiffly and said he was at his service.

"I'd be very appreciative if you took care of those drunk soldiers," Siegfried said in a controlled fashion, while pointing toward the post. "There's another group where Officer O'Leary can take you. And tell one of these jeeps full of soldiers to follow us. We may need their firepower."

Kevin motioned for Jack to slow down. Jack cut back on the throttle and the heavy pirogue quickly lost momentum. They had entered the narrow channel between Isla Francesca and the mainland. It was significantly darker than out in the open water because the trees on either side formed a canopy.

Kevin was worried about the rope for the feeding float and he'd positioned himself in the bow. He'd explained it to Jack so Jack was prepared.

"It's eerie in here," Laurie said.

"Listen to how loud the animals are," Natalie said.

"What you are hearing are mostly frogs," Melanie said. "Romantically inclined frogs."

"It's coming up just ahead," Kevin said.

Jack cut the engine then stood in order to tip the outboard out of the water.

There was a soft thud and a scraping noise as the boat passed over the rope.

"Let's paddle," Kevin said. "It's only a little way farther, and I wouldn't want to hit a log in the dark."

The dense jungle on the right fell away as they reached the staging area clearing. Once again they were in moonlight.

"Oh, no!" Kevin cried from the bow. "The bridge is not deployed. Damn!"

"That shouldn't be a problem," Melanie said. "I still have the key." She held it up, and it glinted in the low light. "I had a feeling it would come in handy someday."

"Oh, Melanie!" Kevin gushed. "You're wonderful. For a moment there, I thought all was lost."

"A deployable bridge that needs a key?" Jack questioned. "That's mighty sophisticated for out here in the jungle."

"There's a dock coming up on our right," Kevin said. "That's where we'll tie the boat up."

Jack was in the stern. He used his oar to back paddle so the bow turned toward the island. A few minutes later, they quietly bumped against wood planking.

"Okay, everybody," Kevin said. He took a breath. He was nervous. He knew he was out of character since he was about to to do something he'd never done before: be a hero of sorts. "Here's what I suggest. You all stay in the boat. At least for now. I really don't know how these animals are going to react to me. They're unbelievably strong, so there is a risk. I'm willing to take it for the reasons I've already talked about, but I don't want to put any of you in jeopardy. Is that reasonable?"

"It's reasonable, but I don't know if I agree," Jack said. "Seems to me you are going to need some help."

"Besides, with this AK-47 it's not as if we can't defend ourselves," Warren said.

"No shooting!" Kevin said. "Please. Particularly not for my benefit. That's why I want you all to stay here. If things go badly, just leave."

Melanie stood up. "I'm almost as responsible as you for these creatures' existence. I'm helping whether you like it or not, bucko."

Kevin made an expression of exasperation.

"No pouting," Melanie said. She climbed out of the boat onto the dock.

"Sounds like a party," Jack said. He stood up to follow Melanie's lead.

"You sit down!" Melanie said sternly. "At the moment, it's a private party."

Jack sat.

Kevin got out his flashlight and joined Melanie on the dock. "We'll work very quickly," he promised.

The first line of business was the bridge. Without it, the plan would fail no matter what the response was from the animals. Kevin put in the key. As he turned it on and pressed the green button, he held his breath. Almost immediately he heard the whine of a battery-driven electric motor from the mainland side. Then in slow motion the telescoping bridge extended across the dark river to make contact with the cement stanchion on the island.

Kevin climbed up on it to make sure it was solidly seated. He tried to shake it but it was rigidly in place. Satisfied, he got down, and he and Melanie hiked in the direction of the forest. They couldn't see the cages because of the darkness of the shadows, but they knew where they were.

"Do you have any plan or are we just going to let them all out en masse?" Melanie asked as they walked across the field. Kevin had the flashlight on so they could see where they were stepping.

"The only idea that came to my mind was to find my double, bonobo number one," Kevin said. "Unlike me, he's a leader. If I can make him understand, maybe he'll take the others." Kevin shrugged. "Can you think of a better idea?"

"Not at the moment," Melanie said.

The cages were all lined up in a long row. The smell was rank since some of the animals had been in their tiny prisons for more than twenty-four hours. As Kevin and Melanie walked along, Kevin shined the light in each enclosure. The animals awoke immediately. Some backed against the rear wall, trying to shield themselves from the glare. Others stood their ground obstinately, their eyes flashing red.

"How are you going to recognize him?" Melanie asked.

"I wish I could count on seeing my watch,"

Kevin said. "But the chances of that are slim. I suppose it's up to recognizing that awful scar he has."

"It's rather ironic that he and Siegfried have almost the same scar," Melanie said.

"Don't even mention that man's name," Kevin said. "My gosh, look!" The light illuminated bonobo number one's frightfully scarred face. He stared back defiantly.

"It's him," Melanie cried.

"Bada," Kevin said. He patted his chest as the bonobo females had done when he, Melanie, and Candace had first been brought to the cave.

Bonobo number one tilted his head and the skin between his eye furrowed.

"Bada," Kevin repeated.

Slowly, the bonobo raised his hand and patted his chest. Then he said "bada" as clearly as Kevin had.

Kevin looked at Melanie. They were both shocked. Although they had tentatively conversed with Arthur, it had been in such a different context, they'd never been entirely sure they were actually communicating. This was different.

"Atah," Kevin said. It was a word they'd heard frequently starting from the moment bonobo number one had yelled it when they'd first encountered him. They thought it meant "come."

Bonobo number one didn't respond.

Kevin repeated the word then looked at Melanie. "I don't know what else to say."

"Neither do I," Melanie said. "Let's go for it and open the door. Maybe he'll respond then. I mean it is hard for him to 'come' when he's locked up."

"Good point," Jack said. He stepped around Melanie to reach back along the right side of the cage. With trepidation, Kevin released the latch and opened the door.

Kevin and Melanie stepped back. Kevin directed the flashlight toward the ground rather than shine it in the animal's face. Bonobo number one emerged slowly and stood up to his full height. He looked to his left and then to his right before redirecting his attention at the two humans.

"Atah," Kevin said again while backing up. Melanie stayed in step.

Bonobo number one started forward, stretching as he walked like an athlete warming up.

Kevin turned his body around so he could walk easier. He repeated "atah" several more times. The animal's facial expression didn't change as he followed.

Kevin led to the bridge and climbed up on it. He again repeated "atah."

Bonobo number one hesitantly climbed onto the concrete stanchion. Kevin backed up until he was standing in the middle of the span. The bonobo came out onto the bridge warily. He glanced frequently from side to side.

Kevin then tried something they'd not tested on Arthur. Kevin strung bonobo words together. He used "sta," from the episode when bonobo number one tried to give the dead monkey to Candace. He used "zit," which bonobo number one had used to get them to go to the cave. And finally he used "arak," which they were quite sure meant "away."

"Sta zit arak," Kevin said. He opened his fingers and swept his hand away from his chest, the gesture that Candace had described in the operating room. Kevin hoped his amalgamated sentence said: "You go away."

After repeating the phrase once again, Kevin pointed to the northeast in the direction of the limitless rain forest.

Bonobo number one rose up on the balls of his feet and looked over Kevin's shoulder at the dark wall of mainland jungle. He then looked back in the direction of the cages. Spreading his arms he vocalized a series of sounds Kevin and Melanie had not heard, or at least not associated with any specific activity.

"What's he doing?" Kevin asked. At that point the animal was facing away from him.

"I could be wrong," Melanie said. "but I think he's making reference to his people."

"My god!" Kevin said. "I think he might

have understood my meaning. Let's let more of the animals out."

Kevin walked forward. The bonobo sensed his movement and turned to face him. Kevin hesitated. The bridge was about ten feet wide, and Kevin was concerned about coming too close. He remembered all too well how easy it had been for the bonobo to pick him up and throw him like a rag doll.

Kevin stared into the animal's face to try to see any emotion, but he couldn't. All he got was a repeat of the uncanny sensation that he was looking into an evolutionary mirror.

"What's the matter?" Melanie asked.

"He's scary," Kevin admitted. "I don't know whether to pass him or not."

"Please, not another Mexican standoff," Melanie said. "We don't have much time."

"Okay," Kevin said. He took a breath and inched around the animal while teetering on the edge. The bonobo watched him but didn't move.

"This is so nerve wracking!" Kevin complained when he climbed down from the bridge.

"Do we want him to stay here?" Melanie asked.

Kevin scratched his head. "I don't know. He might be a lure to get the others over here, but then again, maybe he should come back with us."

"Why don't we just start walking?" Melanie

said. "We'll let him decide."

Melanie and Kevin set out for the animal cages. They were pleased when bonobo number one immediately climbed from the bridge and followed.

They walked quickly, conscious that Candace and the other people were waiting. When they got to the cages they didn't hesitate. Kevin opened the door on the first cage while Melanie did the second.

The animals emerged quickly and immediately exchanged words with bonobo number one. Kevin and Melanie went to the next two cages.

Within only a few minutes, there was a dozen animals milling about, vocalizing and stretching.

"It's working," Kevin said. "I'm sure of it. If they were just going to run off in the forest here on the island, they would have already done so. I think they all know they have to leave."

"Maybe I should get Candace and our new friends," Melanie said. "They should witness this, and they can help speed things up."

"Good idea," Kevin said. He looked at the long row of cages. He knew there were over seventy.

Melanie ran off into the night while Kevin went to the next cage. He noticed that bonobo number one stayed nearby to greet each newly freed animal.

By the time Kevin had released a half dozen more animals, the humans arrived. At first, they were intimidated by the creatures and didn't know how to act. The animals ignored them except for Warren whom they gave a wide berth. Warren had brought the assault rifle, which Kevin guessed reminded the animals of the dart gun.

"They are so quiet," Laurie said. "It's spooky."

"They're depressed," Kevin said. "It could be from the tranquilizer or from having been imprisoned. But don't go too close. They might be quiet, but they are very strong."

"What can we do to help?" Candace asked.

"Just open the cage doors," Kevin said.

With seven people working, it took only a few minutes to get all the cages open. As soon as the last animal had emerged into the night, Kevin motioned for everyone to start toward the bridge.

Bonobo number one, who'd been shadowing Kevin, clapped his hands loudly just as he'd done when Kevin and the women had first come upon him in the cul-de-sac of the marshy field. Then he vocalized raucously before starting after the humans. Immediately the rest of the bonobos quietly followed.

The seven humans led the seventy-one transgenic bonobos in a procession across the clearing to the bridge of their freedom. Arriving at the span, the humans stepped aside.

Bonobo number one stopped at the cement stanchion.

"Sta zit arak," Kevin repeated as he spread his fingers and swept his hand away from his chest for the final time. Then he pointed toward the unexplored African interior.

Bonobo number one bowed his head momentarily before leaping up on top of the stanchion. Looking out over his people, he vocalized for a final time before turning his back on Isla Francesca and crossing the bridge to the mainland. The mass of the bonobos silently followed.

"It's like watching the Exodus," Jack quipped.

"Don't be blasphemous," Laurie teased. But, as with all teasing, there was an element of truth. She was truly awed by the spectacle.

As if by magic the animals melted into the dark jungle without a sound. One minute they were a restive crowd milling about the base of the bridge; the next minute they were gone like water soaking into a sponge.

The humans didn't move or talk for a moment. Finally, Kevin broke the silence. "They did it, and I'm pleased," he said. "Thank you all for helping. Maybe now I can come to terms with what I did in creating them." He stepped up to the bridge and pressed the red button. With a whine, the bridge retracted.

The group turned away from the stanchion

and began to trudge back to the pirogue.

"That was one of the strangest pageants I've ever seen," Jack said.

Halfway to the canoe, Melanie suddenly stopped and cried: "Oh, no! Look!"

Everyone's eyes darted across the river in the direction she was pointing. Headlight beams from several vehicles could be intermittently seen through the foliage. The vehicles were descending the track leading to the bridge mechanism.

"We can't get to the boat!" Warren blurted. "They'll see us."

"We can't stay here, either," Jack said.

"Back to the cages!" Kevin cried.

They all turned and ran toward the bulwark of the jungle. The moment they ducked behind the cages, the headlight beams swept across the clearing as the vehicles turned to the west. The vehicles stopped, but the headlights stayed on and the engines kept running.

"It's a group of Equatoguinean soldiers," Kevin said.

"And Siegfried," Melanie said. "I can recognize him anywhere. And that's Cameron McIvers's patrol car."

A searchlight snapped on. Its high-intensity light played along the row of cages then swept the bank of the river. It quickly found the canoe.

Even fifty yards away, they could hear excited voices responding to the discovery of the boat.

"This is not good," Jack said. "They know we're here."

A sudden and sustained burst of heavy gunfire shattered the tranquility of the night.

"What on earth are they shooting at?" Laurie asked.

"I'm afraid they're destroying our boat," Jack said. "I suppose that's bad news for my deposit."

"This is no time for humor," Laurie complained.

An explosion rocked the night air, and a fireball briefly illuminated the soldiers. "That must have been the gas tank," Kevin said. "So much for our transportation."

A few minutes later, the searchlight went out. Then the first vehicle made a U-turn and disappeared back up the track leading to Cogo.

"Does anybody have an idea what's happening?" Jack asked.

"My guess is Siegfried and Cameron are going back to town," Melanie said. "Knowing we're on the island, they probably feel pretty confident."

The headlights on the second vehicle suddenly went out, thrusting the entire area into darkness. Even the moonlight was meager since the moon had sunk low in the western sky.

"I preferred it when we had some idea where they were and what they were doing," Warren said.

"How big is this island?" Jack asked.

"About six miles long and two wide," Kevin said. "But . . ."

"They're making a fire," Warren said, interrupting Kevin.

A dot of golden light illuminated part of the bridge mechanism, then flared up into a campfire. The ghostly figures of the soldiers could be seen moving in the periphery of the light.

"Isn't that nice," Jack said. "Looks like they're making themselves at home."

"What are we going to do?" Laurie questioned despairingly.

"We don't have a lot of choice with them sitting at the base of the bridge," Warren said. "I count six of them."

"Let's hope they're not planning on coming over here," Jack said.

"They won't come until dawn," Kevin said. "There's no way they'd come over here in the dark. Besides, there's no need. They don't expect us to be going anywhere."

"What about swimming across that channel?" Jack said. "It's only about thirty or forty feet wide and there's no current to speak of."

"I'm not a good swimmer," Warren said nervously. "I told you that."

"This whole area is also infested with crocodiles," Kevin said.

"Oh, God!" Laurie said. "Now he tells us."

"But, listen! We don't have to swim," Kevin said. "At least, I don't think so. The boat that Melanie, Candace, and I used to get here is most likely where we left it, and it's big enough for all of us."

"Fantastic!" Jack said. "Where is it?"

"I'm afraid it's going to require a little hike," Kevin said. "It's a little more than a mile, but at least there's a freshly cleared trail."

"Sounds like a walk in the park," Jack said.

"What time is it?" Kevin asked.

"Three-twenty," Warren said.

"Then we only have approximately an hour and a half before daylight," Kevin said. "We'd better start now."

What Jack had facetiously labeled a walk in the park turned out to be one of the most harrowing experiences that any of them had ever had. Unwilling to use the flashlights for the first two to three hundred yards, they had proceeded by a process that could only be termed the blind leading the blind. The interior of the jungle had been entirely devoid of light. It was so utterly dark it had been difficult for anyone to even know whether their eyes were open or not.

Kevin had gone first to feel his way along the ground, making frequent wrong choices that required backtracking to find the trail. Knowing what kind of creatures inhabited the forest, Kevin held his breath each time he extended his hand or his foot into the blackness.

Behind Kevin, the others had aligned themselves in snakelike single file, each holding on to the unseen figure ahead. Jack had tried to make light of the situation, but after a time even his usually resourceful flippancy failed him. From then on, they were all victims of their own fears as the noctural creatures chattered, chirped, bellowed, twittered, and occasionally screamed around them.

When they finally deemed it safe to use the flashlights, they made better progress. At the same time, they shuddered when they saw the number of snakes and insects that they encountered, knowing that prior to the use of the flashlights they had been passing these same creatures unawares.

By the time they reached the marshy fields around Lago Hippo, the eastern horizon was faintly beginning to lighten. Leaving the darkness of the forest, they mistakenly believed the worst was behind them. But it wasn't the case. The hippopotami were all out of the water grazing. The animals looked enormous in the predawn twilight.

"They may not look it but they are very dangerous," Kevin warned. "More humans are killed by them than you'd think."

The group took a circuitous route to give the hippopotami wide berth. But as they neared the reeds where they hoped the small canoe was still hidden, they had to pass close by two particularly large hippos. The animals seemed to regard them sleepily until without warning they charged.

Luckily, they charged for the lake with a huge amount of commotion and crashing noise. Each multi-ton animal created a new wide trail through the reeds to the water. For a moment, everyone's heart fluttered in his chest.

It took a few minutes for everyone to recover before pushing on. The sky was now progressively brightening, and they knew they had no time to lose. The short hike had taken much more time than they had anticipated.

"Thank God it's still here," Kevin said when he separated the reeds and found the small canoe. Even the Styrofoam food chest was still in place.

But reaching the canoe posed another problem. It was quickly decided the boat was too small and too dangerous to carry seven people. After a difficult discussion, it was decided that Jack and Warren would stay in the reeds to wait for Kevin to bring the small canoe back.

Waiting was hell. Not only did the sky continue to get lighter and lighter, presaging imminent dawn and the possible appearance of the soldiers, but there was always the worry that the motorized canoe had disappeared. Jack and Warren nervously alternated between looking at each other and their watches, while fighting off clouds of insatiable insects. And on top of everything else, their exhaustion was total.

Just when they were thinking that something terrible had happened to the others, Kevin appeared at the edge of the reeds like a mirage and silently paddled in.

Warren scrambled into the canoe followed by Jack.

"The power boat's okay?" Jack asked anxiously.

"At least it was there," Kevin said. "I didn't try to start the engine."

They backed out of the reeds and started for the Rio Diviso. Unfortunately, there were lots of hippos and even a few crocodiles forcing them to paddle twice the usual distance just to keep clear.

Before they slipped into the foliage hiding the mouth of the jungle-lined river they caught a glimpse of some soldiers entering the clearing in the distance.

"Do you think they saw us?" Jack asked from his position in the bow.

"There's no way to know," Kevin said.

"We're getting out of here by the skin of our teeth," Jack said.

The waiting was as hard on the women as

it had been on Jack and Warren. When the small canoe pulled alongside, there were literal tears of relief.

The final worry was the outboard motor. Jack agreed to attend to it because of his experience with similar engines as a teenager. While he checked it over, the others paddled the heavy canoe out of the reeds into the open water.

Jack pumped the gas, then with a little prayer, pulled the cord.

The engine sputtered and caught. It was loud in the morning stillness. Jack looked at Laurie. She smiled and gave him the thumbs-up sign.

Jack put the motor in gear, gave it a full throttle, and steered directly south, where they could see Gabon as a line of green along the horizon.

EPILOGUE

Lou Soldano glanced at his watch as he flashed his police badge to get him into the Customs area of the international arrivals building at Kennedy Airport. He'd hit more traffic than he'd expected in the midtown tunnel, and hoped he was not too late to greet the returning world travelers.

Going up to one of the skycaps, he asked which carousel was Air France.

"Way down the end, brother," the skycap said with a wave of his hand.

Just my luck, thought Lou as he broke into a slow jog. After a short distance he slowed, and for the one millionth time vowed to stop smoking.

As he got closer, it was easy to see which carousel he was looking for. Air France in block letters showed on a monitor. Around it, the people were four deep.

Lou made a half circuit before seeing the group. Even though they were facing away, he could recognize Laurie's hair.

He insinuated himself between other passengers and gave Laurie's arm a squeeze. She turned around indignantly but quickly recognized him. Then she gave him a hug so fierce, his face turned red.

"Okay, okay, I give up," Lou managed. He laughed.

Laurie let him go so that he could give Jack and Warren a handshake. Lou gave Natalie a peck on the cheek.

"So, you guys have a good trip, or what?" Lou questioned. It was apparent he was all keyed up.

Jack shrugged and looked at Laurie. "It was okay," he said noncommittally.

"Yeah, it was okay," Laurie agreed. "The trouble was nothing happened."

"Really?" Lou said. "I'm surprised. You know, being Africa and all. I haven't been there, but I've heard."

"What have you heard, man?" Warren asked.

"Well, there's lots of animals," Lou said.

"Is that it?" Natalie asked.

Lou shrugged embarrassingly. "I guess. Animals and the Ebola virus. But like I said, I've never been there."

Jack laughed, and when he did, so did all the others.

"What's going on here?" Lou said. "Are you guys pulling my leg?"

"I'm afraid so," Laurie said. "We had a fabulous trip! The first part was a little harrowing, but we managed to survive that, and once we got to Gabon, we had a ball."

"Did you see any animals?" Lou asked.

"More than you could imagine," Laurie said.

"There, see, that's what everybody says," Lou remarked. "Maybe someday I'll go over there myself."

The luggage came, and they hoisted it onto their shoulders. They breezed through Customs and passed through the terminal. Lou's unmarked car was at the curb.

"One of the few perks," he explained.

They put the luggage in the trunk, and climbed in. Laurie sat next to Lou. Lou drove out of the airport, and they were immediately bogged down in traffic.

"How about you?" Laurie asked. "Have you been making any headway back here?"

"I was afraid you weren't going to ask," Lou said. "Things have been going down like you wouldn't believe. It was that Spoletto Funeral Home that was the gold mine. Right now, everybody is lining up to plea-bargain. I even got an indictment on Vinnie Dominick."

"That's fantastic," Laurie said. "What about that awful pig, Angelo Facciolo?"

"He's still in the slammer," Lou said. "We have him nailed on stealing Franconi's body. I know it's not much, but remember Al Capone was reeled in on tax evasion."

"What about the mole in the medical examiner's office?" Laurie said.

"Solved," Lou said. "In fact, that's how we have Angelo nailed. Vinnie Amendola has agreed to testify."

"So, it was Vinnie!" Laurie said with a mixture of vindication and regret.

"No wonder he's been acting so weird," Jack said from the backseat.

"There was one unexpected twist," Lou said. "There was someone else mixed up in all this who has taken us by surprise. He's apparently out of the country at the moment. When he comes back into the country, he's going to be arrested for murder of a teenager by the name of Cindy Carlson over in Jersey. We believe Franco Ponti and Angelo Facciolo did the actual killing, but it was at this guy's behest. His name is Dr. Raymond Lyons. Do either of you guys know him?"

"Never heard of him," Jack said.

"Nor I," Laurie said.

"Well, he had something to do with that organ transplant stuff you people were so interested in," Lou said. "But later for that. Right now I'd like to hear about the first part of your trip: the harrowing part."

"For that you'll have to buy us dinner," Laurie said. "It's kind of a long story."

GLOSSARY

BONOBO: An anthropoid ape classified as a species in 1933. Related to chimpanzees, they occasionally walk upright and are found only in a localized area of Zaire. The estimated population is less than twenty thousand.

CENTROMERE: A specialized portion of a chromosome that plays an important role in the reduplication of the chromosome during cellular division.

CHIMERA: A combination of a lion, a goat, and a serpent in Greek mythology. In literature, a chimera is a creation of the imagination: an impossible mixture. In biology, a chimera is an organism that contains genetically distinct cell types. In genetics, a chimera is an entity containing a mixture of DNA from different sources.

CHROMOSOME: An elongated structure in the nucleus of a cell that contains DNA. In humans and anthropoid apes, there are twenty-three pairs of chromosomes for a total of forty-six.

CICATRIX: A scar.

CROSSINGOVER: The exchange of parts of

chromosomes between chromosome pairs during meiosis.

DNA: The acronym for deoxyribonucleic acid, which encodes genetic information.

ENDOTHELIALIZATION: The healing of the inner surface of blood vessels by the cells that cover such surfaces.

FORENSIC PATHOLOGY: A branch of pathology that relates pathological science with civil and criminal law.

GENE: A functional unit of heredity that is composed of a sequence of DNA located at a specific locus or place on the chromosome.

GENOME: The complete complement of genes of an organism. In humans, the genome contains approximately one hundred thousand genes

GRANULOMA: A growth of a mixture of specialized cells as a result of chronic inflammation.

HISTOCOMPATIBILITY: A state when two or more organisms can share organs or tissue (e.g., identical twins).

HOMOLOGOUS CHROMOSOME: Chromosomes that are similar with respect to their genes and visible structure: e.g., each chromosome of a chromosome pair.

HOMOLOGOUS TRANSPOSITION: The exchange of corresponding portions of DNA between homologous chromosomes.

LYMPHOKINE: An immunologically active hormone produced by certain immune cells called lymphocytes.

MEIOSIS: A special type of cellular division that occurs during the creation of sex cells (eggs and sperm), resulting in each sex cell having half the usual number of chromosomes. In humans, each sex cell has twenty-three chromosomes.

MITOCHONDRIA: Self-replicating entities in cells that produce energy.

MITOCHONDRIAL DNA : DNA necessary for mitochondrial replication. It is inherited only through the maternal line.

MEROZOITE: A stage in the life cycle of some parasites that enables the organism to disperse and infect additional cells within the host.

PARASITE: An organism that lives on or in

another organism (or host). A parasite does not help the host; in fact, it typically harms the host.

PARASITOLOGY: A branch of biology dealing with parasites.

PATHOLOGY: A branch of medical science involving the cause, the process, the anatomic effects, and the consequence of disease.

RECOMBINANT DNA: A composite molecule of DNA that has been formed in the laboratory with DNA from separate sources.

RECOMBINANT DNA TECHNOLOGY: The applied science of separating, producing, and recombining segments of DNA or genes.

RIBOSOMAL PROTEINS: The proteins that form a ribosome. The DNA that codes for these proteins is species specific and is used to identify the species of tissue (e.g., to determine if blood is human blood or blood of a particular species of animal).

RIBOSOME: A cellular entity responsible for manufacturing all cellular protein.

TRANSGENE: An organism whose genome contains one or more genes from another species (e.g., pigs containing human genes to facilitate human reception of pig heart valves).

VACCINE: A substance given to an individual to produce resistance to disease or infection.

XENOGRAFT: An organ or tissue taken from one species and transplanted into another species. Generally, a xenograft refers to an animal organ or tissue that is transplanted into a human (e.g., a pig heart valve).